OUT OF THE DEPTHS OF DARKNESS

LAURA J. ELDRIDGE

OUT OF THE DEPTHS OF DARKNESS

*For my husband Steve, for pushing me out of my comfort zone
and making me sign up for the writing classes.*

CHAPTER ONE

Dakota Territory
October 1875

Angelica Barnes wrapped a blanket tightly around her slim shoulders, then dropped several pieces of wood into the well-used cast iron cooking stove as the kindling inside finally caught hold. Rubbing her frozen fingers, she closed the door and adjusted the damper.

Stepping to one of the windows, she scraped through the icy coating to look out at the stars, still visible in the dark sky. Dawn wasn't too far off.

Her father had built the two-room sod cabin with his own hands. Unlike other homesteads in the Dakota Territory, her cabin had real glass for the windows instead of murky, opaque oiled paper. It also boasted a small pantry and a fair-sized root cellar, small luxuries in such a desolate place.

The temperature had dropped fast last night, and it was going to take a while before the sun could chase away the frost that lay on the trampled grass outside. If she had read the signs correctly, snow would be falling come nightfall. It seemed that winter came faster every year, or maybe it just felt that way.

Pushing her long brown hair away from her face, Angelica shivered as she lit the kerosene lamp on the table. Back at the stove, she opened the side and added a few more sticks from the wood box to the small fire that crackled inside. The smell of the burning wood raised her spirits.

Purrsistence, a large calico, shuffled into the kitchen and gave a loud aggravated meow. Angelica smiled.

"You're too fat," Angelica told the cat fondly. "You should be out in the barn catching mice. That is your job, you know."

Purrsistence purred as she rubbed herself against her mistress's legs.

Angelica reached down and gave a quick pat to the feline before stepping to the door of the lean-to and grabbing the remains of the chicken pie that had been last night's dinner. She scooped out some of the meat and frozen gravy onto a plate, then set it on the iron cooktop.

Purrsistence protested loudly.

"You can wait a few minutes for it to warm up."

Breaking through the ice in the drinking bucket that she had filled the night before, Angelica ladled water into an old chipped, sapphire blue, enameled coffee pot. Next, she grabbed the coffee grinder from the shelf over the stove before sitting at the table and beginning the tedious task of grinding the coffee beans. As the rich aroma rose, it cleared the remaining cobwebs of sleep from her brain.

She could feel heat from the stove penetrate through her trousers as she placed the coffee pot on the hob. The pants, like the flannel shirt that she was wearing, had belonged to her father. Though he hadn't been a very large man, she'd had to take them in quite a bit to make them fit.

A quick glance at the stove revealed that the gravy had thawed. Using a piece of a flour sack to protect against the hot plate, Angelica checked to see that the meal wasn't too hot before setting the plate onto the floor.

"Breakfast is served," she told the cat. "Now if you don't need anything else, Your Highness, I need to get my own meal, and I have a long list of things to get done. I'm planning on finishing early so we can celebrate."

Purrsistence gave her a long stare before heading over to the dish.

Angelica was used to her companion's indifference, but she craved the sound of a human voice, even if it was only her own. "Don't tell me that you forgot that I turn twenty-three today?" she teased the cat, who paid her no attention at all.

Typical cat.

The coffee was ready, so Angelica threw in a handful of salt to settle the grounds and then, after a few minutes, poured herself a cup. Sitting at the small table, she wrapped her hands around the welcome warmth of the mug and stared into space.

It was worrisome that Jean Claude, her neighbor to the north, hadn't shown up with the firewood yet; it was unlike him to be late. He normally delivered it by the end of September when the weather was more predictable. Angelica had managed to find some small branches and tree trunks along with the occasional buffalo chip, but for all of that, her wood pile wasn't going to last very long. She had been surprised to find any of the large animal's dung, or *nik-nik* as the Sioux called it, since the animals had basically been hunted until only a few remained. Miners, soldiers, and settlers traveling through the plains had slaughtered the huge beast for their hides, leaving the carcasses to rot where they fell. There had been plenty of buffalo chips when Angelica had been a child. She and her mother would gather the dried fecal matter, a great source to use as fuel to help supplement the woodpile. Now, everything she had needed to be packed into the lean-to before it started snowing to keep it dry.

Angelica continued her one-sided conversation. "Feeding, milking, and cleaning stalls will take a little more than an hour. I'll work on the barn roof next, and then I'll stack the wood just before dark. If we're lucky, Jean Claude will be here today, and I can bank the stove so that it stays warm all night." She paused and furrowed her brow. "If he doesn't come soon, I'm not sure what we're going to do."

Done with her meal, Purrsistence moved closer to the stove and proceeded to wash her face.

"Fine. I can see that I'm boring you with my chore list. I'll stop talking now."

A glance out the window showed that the sky had lightened. She had time for another cup of coffee and something to eat.

Happy birthday to me, Angelica thought wryly. *A spinster by modern standards.* She sighed. It was hard to believe that she had been alone for three years now. Taking a sip, Angelica thought about her parents. Her father had been a land surveyor and her mother a teacher. She had been their only surviving child, the others placed in the tiny cemetery on the far corner of the property, their graves marked with several small crosses. Her mother named her Angelica, telling her it was because the Lord had finally blessed them with their own angel. It was a small farm, but her parents had thrived on it until they both caught pneumonia and died within days of each other.

Pity was not something Angelica had allowed herself over the years, but there were times, like today, she wished that she had someone besides the animals to talk to. Her nearest neighbor was over ten miles away, and the small town of Newcomb, where she bartered her cheese, canned goods, and cider, was twenty miles. That didn't give her a lot of opportunity to see anyone. She considered herself lucky that she owned her farm and did not have to rely on anyone else. She had overheard stories of women who hadn't any other choices but to marry strangers or become soiled doves at saloons.

"I have no intention of marrying a stranger, and I have no idea what a bird in a saloon has to do with a woman," she informed Purrsistence. "I'm going to eat the cake that I made last night and open the present I bought myself."

Even though she had cut the recipe in half, she had had to sell several jars of her preserves for a few spare cents to buy extra molasses and some raisins to be able to make the rare treat. In a surprising act of indulgence, she had also bought a dime novel that was wrapped up in the trunk at the end of her bed, ready to be unwrapped later. Tempted several times to open and read it, she was now glad that she had waited. It was something, the only thing, she had to look forward to.

• • •

Angelica snatched a hunk of cheese and a slice of bread from the small pantry shelf, then glanced out the window at the rapidly lightening sky. She stood in front of the stove's warmth as she ate before washing it down with the remains of her coffee. After rinsing out her cup and checking the stove's damper, she grabbed the clean milk bucket, shrugged into her father's wool jacket, blew out the lantern, and headed out to the barn.

The air was crisp, and the short grass around the house crunched under her shoes. Streaks of gold and pink colored the thin clouds, as if an artist had used them for a canvas, pushing back the remnants of night. Angelica's breath was visible as she pulled open the barn door and inhaled the familiar smell of cut hay and the distinct aroma of animals. Gracie, the cow, stuck her head over the stall door and gave a mournful moo, wanting to be milked as well as fed. The plow horse, Ranger, neighed and shook his head in greeting.

After giving both a small amount of oats, Angelica went back outside to the chicken coop. The birds ruffled their feathers as they stepped out of the warm coop, clucking their opinion of being confined.

"There you go, ladies." She scattered a small amount of feed onto the ground. While the chickens scratched in the dirt, Angelica gathered the eggs. Eight this morning. She still had more than she could possibly eat stored in the cellar. Tomorrow she'd pickle several batches to sell to the hotel in town. With that settled in her mind, she went back into the barn to milk Gracie.

• • •

Entering the kitchen half an hour later, Angelica noticed that it was much warmer than when she'd left it. She added another small piece of wood to the stove before she set about straining the milk. She would put some aside to make more cheese and butter, she decided. Several wheels of cheese in the cellar would be ready to sell next spring, when she went to town to replenish her supplies. Once the milk was strained, she poured it into jars which she then placed into the cold box in the lean-to.

Reluctantly leaving the warmth of the house, Angelica headed for the barn again. She let Gracie and Ranger out in the small pasture, mucked out their stalls and bedded them with fresh grass. The regular chores completed, Angelica made for the ladder on the side of the barn and climbed up to the roof.

●●●

The farm sat in a small depression on the prairie, which offered it shelter from the savage winds that often raced along the plains. There wasn't a cloud in the deep blue sky, but she could smell the snow coming. Angelica gripped the top rung of the ladder as she took in the view. It was a heady feeling being up there, looking at the Black Hills in the distance. They were wrapped in mystery, those faraway peaks, taunting and teasing her, just out of reach, a glimpse of something unattainable that created fleeting shadows. There were times that the loneliness of living alone on the prairie was so intense that she felt it smothering her like a blanket, trying to keep her tied down when her spirit wanted to soar and reach those distant monuments. She pushed the thought down. She was part of this land, and though she craved adventure, she knew that she was destined to stay rooted here. This was her home.

Surveying the roof, Angelica's heart sank. She knew that it was in bad shape, but it was worse than she thought. The whole thing would need to be replaced come spring. That's if there wasn't too much snow this winter and the roof held. Angelica hung her head for a moment. She didn't have the money to put a new roof on, and she had no idea how to do it herself. If she was extra frugal this winter, then she might be able to save enough money to pay for the lumber, then rely on the charity of her neighbors to help with the labor. Right now, she had to repair it as best as she could. There wasn't any other choice. Squaring her shoulders, she climbed back down the ladder. Her father had piled leftover wood shingles behind the barn, and she sorted through them. Most of the ones on the top were dried out and brittle, so she set those aside for kindling. Soon she had a fair-sized pile of shingles that she prayed was enough to cover the leaks until next year. Grabbing an armful, she went back up the ladder.

Her back was aching and her arms felt like lead weights from swinging the hammer all morning, but she was down to one section to patch when she stopped for lunch around midday. If she could finish it quickly, then she should have time to get the firewood cut and stacked before dark.

After nailing the last shingle down, Angelica inched her way backwards on her hands and knees, toward the ladder. Halfway to the edge, she felt the spongy wood start to bow before she heard a snap. Within seconds, the roof underneath her knees gave way, causing her legs to fall through the new hole. Instinctively, Angelica threw her arms outward and dug her fingers into the rough edges of the shingles to stop herself from falling further. She was caught up to her armpits, her breath coming in small gasps.

Angelica could feel the panic rising. There was no one around for miles. It was up to her to save herself, so she took a quick look around for anything that could help, but there was nothing within reach. Using her left arm, Angelica shifted her weight and moved her right hand to try to push herself upwards. There was a series of groans and snaps. Angelica froze. The sounds stopped. Carefully, she tried pushing herself up again, but without warning, the rotted wood surrounding her let go. There was no time to think as she fell through the air, her arms and legs flailing in a useless attempt to right herself. Her scream reverberated off of the walls of the old barn, scaring the livestock below. Angelica closed her eyes tight as the floor of the hay covered loft came rising up to meet her. There was a moment of searing pain, then everything went black.

•••

Angelica lay on the floor of the hayloft, the gaping hole in the roof above her. Sitting up, she gasped at the pain in her ribs and the shooting pain in her right arm. Cradling her arm to her chest, the memories of falling came back to her.

Tears sprang to her eyes. "Damn."

Living alone with winter approaching was daunting enough in good health. Having a broken arm and Lord knows how many broken ribs was just short of suicide.

If I can just get to the house.

Inch by excruciating inch, every move caused her waves of pain, she slid her body toward the ladder.

Finally, reaching the rungs, Angelica gulped in shallow gasps of air. The pain was making her dizzy and nauseous, and she wasn't sure that she had the strength needed to climb down. Yet, there was no other choice—she had to get to the house. Mentally straightening her backbone, she maneuvered around until she was sitting with her feet on the top rung. She wrapped her good arm around the rail and took a step down. Again, she inched her way down the ladder, sitting on each rung. Angelica had descended halfway when the dizziness overtook her. Her arm slipped and she fell the remaining way to the barn floor, the blackness rising up to meet her again.

•••

Luke stopped at the small stream to let his horse drink. Damn but it was cold this morning. It was going to snow soon, he could feel it, and he still had a ways to go to reach the nearest town. It wouldn't do to be caught out here with a storm on the way. A small snowstorm could turn into a blizzard in a matter of minutes, even this early in the season. People had frozen to death feet from their door, never mind out in the open prairie.

Squatting down, he filled his canteen with fresh water. Feeling eyes upon him, he turned quickly, his pistol already drawn. A white wolf stood on the embankment behind him, gold eyes watching his every move.

"Been wondering where you've been," he told the animal as he holstered his gun.

Walking over to his saddlebags, Luke withdrew several strips of beef jerky and held them out to the canine. It never blinked as it made its way down the embankment and took the food from his hand. Luke gave a rare smile and rubbed the animal's head. He had found the pup next to the dead body of its mother several years ago. While he was a firm believer that nature should take care of itself, something about the orphan had called to him.

It had been a good call.

Wolf had saved his hide on more than one occasion. Luke had raised the animal not to be dependent on him. He hadn't wanted a pet; he wanted the wolf to be free, and he expected him to leave at any time. He hadn't even bothered to give the pup a name, just referred to him as "Wolf." Several times the animal had disappeared, and he'd thought that would be it, but the wolf always came back. Luke didn't want to admit it to himself, but he enjoyed the company. He had been on a broken trail since the end of the Great Conflict between the states, unsure what it was that he was looking for. He figured that he would know it when he found it.

Luke climbed into the saddle and urged the horse up the embankment. It was beautiful country around here. A man could get lost in the solace the open prairie offered. As tempting as that thought was, Luke turned the gelding in the direction of Newcomb, the nearest town. He was on his way to pick up the mail and supplies before the snow started and made travel impossible. Looking at the sky, he figured that he would be getting to town just ahead of the snow. Setting his hat more firmly on his head and pulling his collar tighter, he nudged the horse into a gallop. Wolf trotted alongside.

•••

Luke had been riding for an hour when Wolf took off to his right. He paused to watch the animal race across the prairie.

Luke had ridden this route several times before and he knew that the animal was heading in the direction of a small ranch. According to the storekeeper in town, a woman had inherited the property several years back. Luke thought it was foolish for a woman to be out on this prairie alone, but he figured that was her business. He hoped that Wolf wasn't headed for her chicken coop. He shrugged; Wolf could take care of himself.

Luke was about a mile past the ranch when Wolf appeared again. The animal raced in from behind and nipped the back of one of the gelding's front legs. Luke had a hell of a time staying in the saddle as the horse sidestepped a second bite. It took all his experience to stay on the horse and not land on his ass. Swearing, he finally managed to calm the gelding and dismount. With narrowed eyes, he looked at the pup. Wolf was pacing, those gold eyes boring into his as if they could communicate the urgency of his message. Luke never hesitated. He swung back into the saddle and nodded his head. Wolf whirled around and ran back the way that he had just come.

A light plume of smoke swirled from the chimney of the sod house. Luke could see a cow and horse in the pasture. Wolf had torn down the hillside and had disappeared in the direction of the barn.

That ruled out Indians and outlaws, Luke decided. Wolf would have been more cautious if there was danger around, but he knew that the animal wouldn't have stopped him for something trivial.

Clicking his tongue, Luke urged the gelding down the worn road, past a small orchard that still had fruit clinging to branches, apples and peaches if he didn't miss his guess. Just the thought of apple pie brought to mind his mother. Best he didn't go down that path right now, he thought wryly. Last time he had talked to his mother, she had not been happy with him.

As he got closer to the house, Luke noticed that the wood pile consisted of a few logs, plus some branches and two small tree stumps. He shook his head. That wasn't enough wood to last a week.

He stopped the horse in front of a small wooden porch. He didn't like the fact that no one had come out to greet him. He figured visitors were rare out here.

Dismounting, Luke wrapped the reins loosely around the pommel of the saddle before turning to survey the barn. It was also built from sod but had a wood roof that had seen better days. Noticing the ladder leaning up against the side of the structure, his eyes were drawn upwards. That's when he saw the hole in the roof.

"Shit," he muttered as he headed for the barn door.

•••

Angelica felt her mother's arms, hugging her. She had been very cold and suddenly there was warmth. She heard her mother's voice, full of love and concern.

"Don't worry, my Angel," her mother said. "Everything will be fine. You still have so much to do, to see, to learn. You are strong, and we are very proud of you."

Angelica smiled. Her parents were alive, and she wasn't alone anymore. It had all been a dream, and she was finally waking up.

Lifting her head slightly, she opened her eyes. She was surprised to find herself lying on the cold, dirt floor of the barn. Something solid and warm was against her back, and as she moved, whatever it was shifted too. Turning her head slightly, Angelica met the unblinking gold eyes of a wolf, her face inches from its mouth. Panic welled up in her chest, and for a second, she couldn't comprehend what to do.

Then the adrenaline kicked in.

Rolling away from the animal, she gave a gasp of pain as her ribs protested. Crouching on her knees, never once taking her eyes from the animal, she pushed herself up to a half stance before cradling her right arm, which was throbbing. The wolf was still, yet watchful.

"Nice wolf," she crooned in a sing-song voice. "Stay right there. That's right, don't move."

Stepping slowly backwards toward the barn door, Angelica was feeling lightheaded and there were spots in front of her eyes.

"Don't faint, don't faint," she chanted in the same sing-song voice.

The wolf sat up and watched her intently, its gold eyes never blinking. Angelica had just reached the door when it gave a small yip and stood, causing Angelica to pause for a panicked moment. When the canine didn't move, she took another step backwards and bumped into something solid. Turning with a scream, Angelica found herself face to face with a large man. His expression was unreadable, and he had the bluest eyes she had ever seen.

Taking a few steps backward, Angelica realized that she was trapped between this man and the wolf. Which was safer? Her head was starting to throb, and the vertigo that she had been feeling before made her vision blurry.

"Are you all right, Miss?" the man asked, taking a step forward.

Angelica blinked a few times trying to focus back on his face. She was unable to form any words; it was taking all of her energy to stand upright.

Concern showed in his face. "Miss?"

He took another step forward and it startled her. Trying to step back, she became unbalanced. The man grasped her by the arms to steady her. She didn't have a chance to react as the pain in her right arm became so intense that she passed out.

CHAPTER TWO

Luke looked up at the gaping hole in the roof and then back down at the unconscious woman. Her long brown hair, some strands escaping from a bun, looked out of place against the man's trousers and jacket that she was wearing. She couldn't be more than eighteen by his estimation. The top of her head barely reached his chin. Blood dripped down the fingers of her right hand.

Didn't she have more sense than going up on a barn roof alone? He scooped her up and then strode toward the house.

Upon reaching the front door, he kicked at the latch, causing the door to pop open. Scanning the room, he headed for the bed against the back wall and gently laid her down. She was ice cold; he didn't need to add pneumonia to her list of injuries. Wolf had followed him to the porch.

"Come," he told the animal, tucking a quilt around the girl.

Wolf entered the cabin and lay down at the foot of the bed.

Luke hurried out to his horse to grab his saddle bags. He never went anywhere without his medical supplies. Old habits from his old life. Few people knew that he was a doctor who had been on the South side of the great conflict. Although he'd been honorably discharged, the experience still haunted him. He closed his eyes and bowed his head as memories of the overfilled makeshift army hospitals came flooding back, the faces of the boys who knew that they were dying, him unable to lie to them and tell them that they would see their loved ones again. He could still almost smell the stench of blood and death, see the bloody, broken shells that had once been his friends and comrades. It wasn't fair that with his medical knowledge, he couldn't save more lives.

Luke shook the memories away. He knew that they would creep back in when his guard was down but now was not the time to get lost in the past. With a deep, shaky breath, he returned to the cabin.

Wolf raised his head and watched as Luke entered the kitchen to grab some kindling and a few pieces of wood, which he took back into the larger room. He then set about building a fire in the stone fireplace. Once the kindling caught, he headed back into the kitchen. The reservoir in the stove was empty, so he poured some water from a bucket on the sideboard into the kettle and set it on the burner to heat before rummaging through cabinets, where he produced some rags and a bottle of whiskey. When the water was hot, he washed his hands with the lye soap and poured some more into a basin.

Setting the supplies beside the bed, he started his exam. Removing her jacket and shirt, he found a compound fracture of the humerus. The woman's eyes opened, and she stared at him without really seeing him, yet every time he moved her arm, she flinched.

He had seen every type of wound imaginable and unimaginable on the battlefield. Broken bones were some of the simplest injuries to treat. Yet if they weren't dealt with properly, they could turn into something much worse. Infection was always a risk, and if he didn't set her arm correctly, then she could be crippled for life. His mind went to his textbooks. The cabin faded away as Luke began to wash around the wound. Several years ago, he had read a paper by a Dr. Lister about the importance of sterilizing instruments, a fact which he wished he had known years before. Maybe he could have saved more soldiers. Not having any carbolic acid to use, he poured whiskey over them.

It was a nice clean break, not a lot of fragments. If he could get it aligned and keep it immobilized for several weeks, it should heal nicely. Her arm was so tiny in his hands, almost like that of a child.

Producing a clothed mask from his bag, he placed it over her nose and mouth before pouring several drops of chloroform on it. Then he waited several minutes. Her color stayed pink, her eyes closed, and her breathing deepened to that of someone sleeping. Adding a few more drops, he prodded at the protruding bone. There was no response. Convinced that she was anesthetized enough, he removed the mask from her face before gripping each end of her arm. It didn't take that much pulling to snap the bones back together. Satisfied that everything was in its proper place, he looked around and spied a sewing basket in the corner of the room. Rifling through the kit, he found a needle and thread. He dunked the needle into the whiskey, then began the process of stitching the gash closed.

More searching of the kitchen produced two wooden spoons that would act as splints to keep the bone from moving. He tied them in place with the rags that he had found. That accomplished, he started looking for wounds on her head. Her brown hair curled around his fingers as he felt her scalp. Finding nothing, he moved to her ribcage. Lifting her camisole enough to keep her modesty intact, he saw bruises that covered the right side of her torso. He felt each rib and was surprised that several were only cracked and not broken, like her arm. Still, unstable ribs were a dangerous thing; they tended to break loose and could cause internal damage well after the fact of injury. Using the remaining rags, he bound her ribs. She was amazingly light, so he was able to lift her with one hand. He finished his exam and was satisfied that nothing else was broken.

It was starting to get dark outside, and he could hear the cow calling for dinner and most likely needing to be milked.

He turned to Wolf. "Keep an eye on her."

Pulling on his jacket, he then grabbed the bucket from the counter and headed out to the barn.

•••

Angelica awoke to hear a dull, rhythmic thumping noise that sounded like someone was outside chopping wood. It took her a moment to realize that she was lying on her bed. The soft glow in the fireplace barely reached the corner where she lay. She tried to sit up but was unable to bend. Her right arm was heavy, and something was wrapped tightly around her chest, making it hard to move and breathe. Looking down, she was surprised to see that she wore only her camisole and pants under the blanket. What had happened to her shirt?

Taking small, calming breaths, she tried to gather her thoughts. She'd fallen through the barn roof and there had been a wolf with blue eyes that spoke like her mother. She shook her head. No, that wasn't right. She must have dreamed her mother's voice, and there'd been a man with blue eyes. Had there been a wolf? As she struggled to turn onto her left side, a movement on the floor, next to her bed, caught her attention and once again she looked into the eyes of a white wolf. Angelica's ribs protested as she gasped.

It took several painful tries to maneuver her legs over the side of the bed and to stand up. Grabbing one of her father's old shirts from a peg on the wall, she managed to maneuver her arm into the sleeve and button it closed with her left hand. Inching her way cautiously around the animal, who watched her with unblinking gold eyes and its head tilted to one side, Angelica headed for the kitchen. Obviously, the wolf belonged to whoever was outside chopping wood, as there would be no reason it would be in the house otherwise. It must be a pet. Considering that the stranger had bound her wounds and was doing chores, he couldn't be dangerous. *Could he*? She saw the outline of a man swinging an ax through the window as she grabbed her rifle. The wolf followed silently, watching her. Cradling the weapon in her left arm, she opened the door. A blast of cold wind and swirling snow made her take a step backwards. The wolf dashed past her and gave a small yip. The man finished the downward motion of the ax and split the wood cleanly.

With one hand, he swung the hatchet again and buried it into the large chopping stump. Picking up several pieces of wood, he walked toward her, his face shielded by his cowboy hat. She stepped aside to let him enter and closed the door as he dropped the wood into the box next to the stove.

Turning, he removed his hat, and Angelica got her first good look at him. His blond hair was long and in need of barbering, and his chin sported a day's growth of stubble. She guessed that he was in his early thirties. He towered over her five-foot-five frame, and as he shrugged out of his Mackintosh, she noticed that his shirt was store bought, and it stretched over his large shoulders. It was tucked neatly into the waistband of his corduroy pants. Suddenly, the small kitchen felt even smaller. She supposed that she should feel nervous being alone with a stranger, but she wasn't. His eyes mesmerized and reassured her. They conveyed that he had suffered great losses, and she felt a kinship with him on that score.

Angelica swayed slightly, breaking the spell that had befallen her. He seemed poised to catch her if need be, but he never moved.

Inclining his head toward the chair at the table, he said, "Might be better if you sat down, Miss."

His voice held the subtle hint of someone raised in the southern states. It reminded her of the time her grandmother had visited from Louisiana when Angelica was just a young girl, and she smiled at the memory. Her grandmother had stayed for a month and told wonderful stories of the plantations and colorful characters of the South. Angelica could picture everything so clearly. Beautiful magnolia trees draped with Spanish moss trailing into sparkling streams, riverboats that floated like elegant ducks up and down the river ways, bringing passengers and supplies. Imagining her grandmother and her friends sipping sweet, ice-cold lemonade on the veranda while suitors dropped by.

"Miss? Are you all right?"

His words snapped Angelica back to the present. He might have been discussing the weather or inquiring about her day for all the emotion that his voice held. She felt disappointed and that confused her. What did she expect him to say? Nodding her head, she moved to the table and sat down, cradling the rifle on her lap. Her mouth felt dry, and she swallowed visibly.

The man watched for a moment through narrowed eyes before turning to the stove and picking up the coffee pot. Taking it to the door, he threw the cold coffee out and headed for the water bucket. Filling the pot with water, he placed it back on the stove and set about feeding the fire. His movements were quick and sure, like a man who was used to doing for himself. Once the coffee was brewed, he brought her a cup then leaned back against the counter and waited.

Angelica took a gulp and looked at a spot just past his right ear. "I'm grateful that you happened to be passing by," she told him. "I'm not sure what I would have done on my own."

He shrugged. "Thank Wolf. He knew something was wrong. Made me turn my horse around."

"Well, I'm thankful to you both then." She wasn't sure how to continue. This man was beginning to unnerve her. What if he was a criminal or one of those sinister characters in her novels? She was at his mercy out here. He was so much bigger than she was. She fidgeted with her coffee cup. How did one ask if someone was of good moral character? She adjusted the rifle before taking another sip and sneaking a glance at him. He was watching her with narrowed eyes again. She could feel her cheekbones redden.

She was rarely alone in the company of a male, other than Jean Claude Baptiste, whom she made sure to meet out in the yard. Jean Claude was a French trapper who had settled thirty miles north of her farm. Years before, he had made a deal with her father: he bred his bull to Gracie every spring and, in exchange for the calves, cheese, and canned goods, he brought firewood every fall. The arrangement worked well for both of them, but Gracie was getting older, and Angelina would soon need to figure out how to replace her. She hoped to make a different bartering agreement that didn't involve the trapper, as Jean Claude made her very uncomfortable when he visited. In the last year, he was becoming more inappropriate in his dealings with her. He had started brushing up against her and making comments about how she was a grown woman now and he could give her sons. She didn't think he understood how much it was beginning to scare her.

Angelica shivered at the thought.

The thump of a mug on the counter brought Angelica back to reality, making her jump. The man had finished his coffee and had moved to kneel down in front of her. She gasped as he clasped her chin in his hand. It took her a moment to realize that the grip was firm, but it did not hurt.

"Relax," he said as he turned her head gently from side to side.

"What are you doing?" she squeaked, unnerved to have his face so close to hers.

"Looking for signs of head trauma," was his reply.

"Excuse me?"

He held up a finger in front of her nose. "Can you follow the path of my finger without moving your head?"

She stared stupidly at the digit, following its path for a moment.

This seemed to satisfy him as he rocked backwards on his heels and stood. "You had an accident. I wasn't sure if you hit your head, because you don't seem to be tracking too well."

No, she supposed she wasn't. Tracking well, that was. The morning had started out ordinarily enough. She'd done the chores and had tried to fix a barn roof. Before she could blink, she'd fallen and woken up face to face with a wolf, and now a strange man was fixing up her wounds. A most unusual day for her. Who wouldn't be thrown off balance?

"I'm sorry," she said, "I seem to have forgotten my manners. I'm Angelica Barnes." She held out her hand, trying to bring some semblance of normalcy to the situation. "I'm just a little confused. The last thing I remember was trying to get down the barn loft stairs and then waking up to your wolf. I am grateful for your help."

She thought for a moment that he wasn't going to take her hand, but his engulfed hers, and she felt a charge of electricity travel up her arm. He must have felt it too, because he released her hand quickly.

"Luke Wells," he replied.

Angelica felt the need to put some distance between them. "Mr. Wells, the least I can do for your kindness is to make you a home cooked meal." She started to rise slowly from her chair, but he took a step forward.

"You best sit there and take it easy. Let me know what you have on hand, and I'll cook."

She had never met a man that could cook, and he looked amused at her surprised reaction. His smile didn't quite reach his eyes, but it was there, nonetheless.

Her father had always referred to cooking as women's work, claiming that women could make a feast out of anything, while men only blackened things.

"All right," she murmured, settling gingerly back into the chair. "I was planning on heating up some chicken soup and making some dumplings. Everything's in the pantry."

Luke disappeared into the small, long room. Rows of shelves were filled with glass mason jars canned with the bounty of the past fall's crop. Stepping back into the kitchen, he shot her a questioning look. "Did you grow and can all of those jars yourself?"

"Yes," she replied, raising her chin.

"For just you, or is there a Mister Barnes that should be strolling in anytime?"

She could feel herself blushing. "No, it's just me."

"Seems like an awful lot of food for just one person."

It sounded like an accusation and for a moment she debated about answering. She didn't owe him or anyone for that matter an explanation. He didn't need to know that the root cellar, until that spring, had been filled with wheels of cheese, vinegar, canned goods, eggs, and apple cider, or that she bartered with the hotel and mercantile for the supplies that she required to get through the winter. She was proud of being independent and even had a small savings account at the local bank. Someday, when she had saved enough, she would see the world and all the sights that she had read about.

"I barter for goods in town," she finally answered.

He acknowledged her statement with a nod as he emptied the soup into a pot and placed it on the stove. Then he set about making the dumplings. His movements were confident, like someone that was used to doing for themselves. She was secretly impressed that he didn't ask for directions. As he spooned the mixture into the boiling soup, his gaze dropped to the wrapped book on the table. "I noticed there's a cake in the pantry. You celebrating a special occasion?"

Angelica wasn't sure why the question embarrassed her. *Was that censure she heard in his voice? Why shouldn't she make a birthday cake for herself or buy herself a present?* She met his gaze. "Today's my birthday."

"Is that so?"

She couldn't tell from the sound of his voice what his thoughts were. "Yes, that's so," she said haughtily. "I don't see anything wrong with indulging myself. I've worked hard all year, and I think that I deserve to celebrate."

Damn him, she thought. *This was her home, and she didn't need a stranger to come here and judge her, even if that stranger had helped her.*

Angelica jumped, causing her ribs to protest, when Luke stepped forward and put his hands on the table. He leaned in close.

"Ma'am, I'm the last person to judge someone. I was just trying to make polite conversation and make you more at ease. You're easier to read than a bear print on a muddy riverbed. You've been ready to bolt for the door since you woke up."

His intense gaze never changed, but his tone became hard. She felt the heat of mortification climbing into her cheeks. Before she could say anything, he continued.

"Everything that you've been thinking has been written right across your face. Two things you need to know: I am a gentleman in all ways that should concern you, and I'm also a medical doctor. You've never been safer. You might want to put that rifle away before you accidentally shoot me."

Angelica bristled at his words, but she stood and put the rifle back in its place behind the door. As she was returning to her chair, a sharp pain ran down her bandaged arm, causing her to wince. Closing her eyes, she willed the hurting to go away.

"I'm going to brew up some willow bark and echinacea tea for you," he said, straightening. He crossed the kitchen and grabbed saddle bags that she hadn't noticed from where they were propped next to the door. "The willow bark will relieve some of the aches and pains, and the echinacea will help fight off infection. Then when I'm sure that you didn't suffer some sort of head injury, I'll add a few more herbs for better pain control."

As Luke talked, he pulled a ladle of hot water from the stove's reservoir and poured it into a pan which he placed on the stove to boil. Collecting her coffee cup from the table, he rinsed it out and set it aside, then pulled out a small box from the saddlebags and placed it on the counter. Angelica couldn't see what was inside, but he removed two glass vials from it. Measuring out two teaspoons from one of the vials, he added it to the boiling water. From her advantage point, the vial's contents looked like dark pieces of twigs. Finding the canister of tea on the shelf above the stove, he spooned some ground leaves into her cup before adding herbs from the other vial. He let the mixture boil for a few minutes before taking the pan off the stove and pouring the contents over the tea leaves combination.

"Sugar or cream?" he asked. When she shook her head, he crossed the small kitchen and set the steaming concoction down in front of her. "It should have boiled longer, and most of the time it needs to steep for at least a half hour, but I think it will start helping anyways. Besides, I want to make sure that you aren't allergic to the salicin in the willow bark. It makes some people have awful stomach pain."

Angelica looked down at her cup doubtfully. Normally she would have put some of the hot water into her mother's teapot to warm it up. Then after pouring out the water, tea leaves would have been added with the boiling water poured over them. A proper cup of tea should seep for eight to ten minutes, according to her mother, before the leaves were strained and the tea was ready. This cup still had leaves and herbs floating in it. "Should we strain it before I drink it?"

Luke chuckled. "I wouldn't worry. Most of the people that get the stomach pains are ones that have more than four cups a day. You should be fine."

Raising the brew to her lips, she blew on it and took a small sip. It had an earthier flavor than her normal tea but otherwise it wasn't bad. Using her spoon, she fished out some of the larger pieces before taking another sip.

Luke gave her a nod of approval before turning around and checking on the chicken and dumplings. Satisfied that the dumplings were cooked, he spooned the hot mixture into two bowls, which he set on the table before taking the seat across from her. "As soon as this snow clears out, I'll take you to town."

She paused as she was about to pick up her spoon. The nerve of the man. "What do you mean, take me to town? I'm not going anywhere. I can't leave my livestock alone."

He took a spoonful of the delicious smelling soup and blew softly on it before looking at her again. "How are you going to take care of yourself, never mind any livestock? There's no firewood, and you'd never be able to swing an ax with cracked ribs and a broken arm, even if you had some. Your ax is basically useless the way it is. It should have been set into the chopping block when not in use to keep the blade from getting dull and rusted. I was barely able to chop the stumps out there." He shook his head. "No, I'm taking you into Newcomb, tomorrow, with the horse and cow. The chickens will have to fend for themselves."

Struggling to control her temper, Angelica tried another tactic. "Mr. Wells, I've been alone on this ranch for over three years and am quite capable of managing on my own. Jean Claude will deliver the firewood any day now. In fact, he should have been here last week. Also, the Indians are coming with the kindling in the next day or two for when they come to harvest the fruit. So, as you can see, there is no need to worry about me.

I'll be just fine."

She expected him to continue to argue, but he surprised her.

"How did you make a deal with the Indians?"

This was a safer topic than her going to town. She took a bite of dumpling and a sip of tea before she answered.

"Actually, it was my father who made the deal. He was a land surveyor, and he brought my mother here before land was available to claim. The government had told him that he could have his pick of land for himself. He found this place and planted fruit trees. After the first harvest, he had a lot of fruit left over."

Her mother had told her this story so many times that she felt as if she had actually been there.

"One day, while out surveying, he came across a small camp of Lakota Indians, mostly women and children. The guide he was with knew the language and he got talking with them. It seemed that since it was such a hot, dry summer, there wasn't a great harvest of the berries that they usually picked. They had sent the men ahead to hunt because they didn't have enough food to put away for the coming winter. My father told them that they could have what fruit we didn't harvest ourselves. He wasn't aware that you can't give an Indian a gift without getting something in return. They come to collect the fruit every year around this time, and they bring me kindling for my fire." She gave a small laugh at the memory of her father's face when the Indian woman had shown up with bundles of sticks for him.

Luke had finished his soup and he rose to put his bowl on the sideboard.

Angelica sat lost in reflection for a few minutes as she ate a few bites. The ache in her ribs had subsided and she was feeling relaxed. There had only been a few bright spots in the last three years to look forward to, and the Indians arriving was one of them. It was more than just the company. They were part of her family, and she was part of theirs.

A movement brought her back to the present. Luke had retrieved the cake and set it before her. "Seems a shame not to celebrate such a fine occasion," he said.

Searching his face for any sign of mockery, Angelica could find none. She was lonely, and the prospect of having another person to celebrate with was enticing.

Angelica flashed Luke a tentative smile. He would be gone soon, she realized, and even though she had just met him, she felt sad at the thought.

Luke took the smile as an affirmative, grabbing utensils and plates from their shelves. "How many candles should be on this cake?" he asked.

"Twenty-three," she replied.

He raised an eyebrow. "I would have bet that you weren't older than eighteen."

"You can't be too much older than I am."

"I was twelve when you were born," he informed her.

Not knowing what to say to that bit of information, she watched as he sat down and sliced each of them a piece of cake. What if it wasn't good? She'd cut the recipe in half, as she had thought it would just be her and Purrsistence eating the sugary dessert. She felt a little nervous as Luke took a forkful and put it into his mouth. For a few seconds, she had no idea if he liked it or not, but then he closed his eyes and nodded.

"Tastes as good as my mom used to make," he said. "My compliments to the baker."

Angelica could feel her face turning warm. "I've never baked for anyone before."

"Well, that's a shame. You seem to have a real knack for it."

This was all a new experience for Angelica. It had been a long time since she had sat down and had a meal with another person, never mind receiving a compliment. Later, when the walls were starting to close in, she would take out this memory and savor it, like the rereading of a well-loved novel.

The shadows had lengthened, and it was starting to get dark in the small room. Luke glanced at the window. "Most houses in this area don't have glass windows. Did you put them in?" he observed as he pulled the kerosene lamp from the center of the table, towards him and lifted the glass chimney. He turned up the wick before standing and crossing to the tin match box that was attached to the wall next to the stove. Striking a match, he cupped the flame as he returned to the lamp and lit it. Adjusting the flame, he set the chimney back in place.

Angelica blinked at the brightness. She was feeling tired, and it took a few seconds to realize that Luke was waiting for an answer to his question. "It was my father's way of showing my mother that even though they were living out in the wild prairie, she could still have a proper house, as she liked to call it."

She yawned. "I'm so sorry," she said, trying to suppress another yawn.

Luke stood. "Don't apologize. I'll go check on the animals and close them in for the night."

When he came in a half hour later, she was curled up on her bed, sound asleep.

CHAPTER THREE

Luke had a restless night and several times he'd gotten up to check on Angelica. Her breathing was normal, and she appeared to be sleeping peacefully. Now it was almost dawn. The snow had intensified in the early hours and was coming down at a fast pace. That meant he was stuck here for the next day or two. There was no way he could leave her out here alone, and she hadn't sounded too keen on the idea of going into town. She'd never be able to take care of the animals by herself, and he still wasn't sure that she hadn't suffered a concussion.

Luke turned onto his back and stared up at the ceiling. When he had heard that there was a woman living alone on a homestead, in the middle of Indian country, he assumed that she would be older, a widow perhaps. Not a woman barely out of girlhood, and a pretty one at that. He hated to admit it, but he admired her spunk. There were not too many men, never mind women, who could thrive out here. Life was unpredictable out on the prairie. Indian raids, fire, and accidents were just some of the dangers, but it was the sheer isolation that made people go mad. Most of the women and men, for that matter, that he knew would have sold out and moved to a safer location.

Getting up from his makeshift bed of blankets set on the kitchen floor, Luke stoked the stove's embers before adding some old wood shingles that he had found behind the barn. Then he grabbed the coffee pot. He didn't really want anything to drink but it gave him something to do. As the pot heated, he ladled more water out of the stove's reservoir that he'd filled the night before and washed his hands and face in the basin in front of the window. It was hard to believe that it was only October and there was at least six inches of snow covering the ground. No one with half a bit of sense would travel the prairie in a storm if they could help it. Damn, he hated being closed in. That's when the memories usually caught up with him. He should have headed south, to warmer weather, but he had had a debt to pay.

"The road to hell is paved with good intentions," he quoted wryly.

A movement outside caught Luke's attention, and he automatically reached for his pistol, which was never far from his side, before recognizing Wolf. Luke opened the door and the animal trotted in, snow covering the fur on its back. As soon as Wolf was inside, he shook, sending droplets of snow everywhere. Several drops landed on the stove and evaporated with a hiss.

Luke retrieved the crock containing leftover stew from the covered wooden box that was outside to the left of the door. It also contained the milk from yesterday's milking. It wasn't a surprise that everything was frozen solid. As he turned to shut the kitchen door, a large creature ran past him into the house, making him jump. The snow-covered animal shook, just as Wolf had, sending wet snow flying, and he'd be damned if it wasn't the biggest house cat Luke had ever seen. Calico, if he remembered his colorings right. The feline looked at him with large, round, green eyes and meowed.

Setting the frozen container on the stove, Luke set about making tea for when Angelica awoke. This time he intended for it to steep for the proper amount of time, so that she could get the most benefit out of the medicine.

When the stew had defrosted, he poured some into two bowls and set them on the floor. No surprise the cat had a good appetite.

"That's Purrsistence," Angelica's voice said from behind him, making him turn.

She wore a rose-colored dress that buttoned up the front. Absently, he noticed that the pattern had small flowers in it. She must have fastened the dress with her left hand, because he could see the splint, still in place, on the right. She'd cut the seam on the sleeve to fit the bandages' bulk. Her long brown hair was undone, and riotous curls flowed down her back. He stared at her for a moment. Now that she'd gotten some sleep, the color had returned to her cheeks, though her face still looked slightly pinched, revealing that she was still in pain. Even so, she was one of the most beautiful women that he'd ever seen. How was it that she was out here all alone?

"She has a bit of a cream problem," Angelica continued, breaking his train of thought.

Purrsistence had finished her breakfast and was looking up at him in adoration. Clearly, she wanted some more.

Angelica's comment was such an understatement that it bordered on ridiculous. Throwing his head back, Luke laughed. He hadn't done that since before the war. The sound was raw in his throat.

Purrsistence, unaware that she was being discussed, weaved her chubby body around his legs.

Gingerly, Angelica entered the room and sat down at the table.

"You hurting this morning?" Luke asked as he picked up Purrsistence's bowl and gave the feline a pat on the head.

Angelica nodded her head. "More so than yesterday," though the admission seemed reluctant.

"That's to be expected since the muscles have stiffened. There's more tea. It'll be ready in a few minutes."

He patted the feline again as he put down a second helping.

●●●

Angelica wasn't sure what to make of this man. It was in his favor that he liked animals, especially cats. Jean Claude had once found the feline sniffing at the hides that he had in his wagon. Cursing, he'd scruffed the cat and threatened to have her skinned. Purrsistence had turned into a wild animal, biting and gouging Jean Claude's hands. The trapper had thrown the cat as hard as he could. Fortunately, Purrsistence hadn't been hurt, but the two of them had been enemies ever since.

Angelica raised one eyebrow as the large cat rubbed up against the wolf. Clearly her cat didn't feel in any danger.

Satisfied that her beloved pet was in no peril, Angelica turned her attention back to Luke, who was setting a cup of tea down on the table before her.

She was not one to sit idle and be waited on, and as she wrapped her hand around the mug, her gaze fell on the milk bucket that was set on the counter, next to the door. "I was going to make some cheese yesterday before I fell. There should be plenty of milk to make an extra batch or even two. I'll need some help, but I insist that you take some with you when you go." She paused, and her eyes got big. "Of course I should also pay you for your doctoring. I don't keep any money here, but I could send a note with you to the bank in Newcomb. Just let me know what your fee is."

●●●

Luke felt insulted. He hadn't thought about payment. Helping her had been the right thing to do. His mother had raised him and his siblings up to always lend a hand and to be charitable. *Neighbors helped neighbors,* she constantly said. Elizabeth Wells made sure that everyone shared in the bounty of harvest and butchering season. Shoes and necessities invariably found their way to the ones that needed them the most, and it was typically done in a way to maintain the dignity of the receiver.

Luke could understand Angelica's not wanting to be beholden to him. Himself, he hated being indebted to anyone. In fact, he should have been in Texas or Mexico right now, but there had been a debt he had owed to one of the ranchers, one of his friends. It was the last of the obligations that he had acquired during the war, then he would be free to disappear.

"You don't owe me anything Angelica. It was just damn lucky that Wolf and I were passing by when we did." Picking up the bowls, he set them on the sideboard before heading toward the door. "Drink your tea and I'll make some breakfast after I finish the chores. Then if you feel up to it, I'll help you."

His coat was on the peg by the back door. Shrugging into it, he grabbed the milk bucket from the counter and without another word, he and Wolf went out into the snow.

•••

Angelica sat at the small table, sipping her tea, wondering if she had just offended Luke or not with her offer to pay him. Isn't that what doctors did, help sick and injured people and get paid for their services? So why did she get the impression that he was annoyed with her? The medicine in the tea was starting to work on the ache in her ribs, yet it hadn't touched the throbbing in her right arm.

What would have happened to her if he hadn't come along? Would she have died out there, in the barn, all alone? Nobody to mourn her death until her friend, Meda and her tribe or Jean Claude happened to stop by? It seemed like such a lonely existence.

It took several painful tries to get out of the chair. After spooning out some hot water from the stove, she washed her face and hands. Peering into the wavy glass above the sink, she was somewhat surprised to see that her reflection had remained the same; the changes seemed to be all on the inside. With long practiced movements, Angelica prepared for turning milk into cheese.

•••

There was no sign of Wolf when Luke returned from the barn and gave

Angelica a stern look as he surveyed the kitchen. She'd washed the dishes, swept, and scrubbed down the counter and table before gathering her cheese-making utensils.

"How is it that you became a doctor?" she asked to distract him from the lecture that she felt was coming.

His expression told her that he wasn't fooled by her question. "My father was a doctor, as was my grandfather." He set the steaming milk bucket on the sideboard and took off his coat, hanging it on a peg. "It only seemed natural to follow in their footsteps. I had been going on calls with them since I was seven years old."

Angelica had already brought in the crocks of milk from the outside box earlier. It had been difficult to scoop them up with one arm since they were heavy, but she had managed it. Lifting the lid of one, she peered inside. The milk was still semi-frozen. "My grandmother was from Louisiana, and she said her accent was a southern one. Are you from Louisiana too?"

Luke shook his head. "No ma'am. I'm from a small town in South Carolina. At least I was before the war." He made a lot of noise moving pans around.

"I've read that South Carolina was the first state to secede from the Union. I just can't understand why men would keep slaves and then go to war to kill other men. I heard a few cowboys in town say that the Confederates got what they deserved." Her brow furrowed. "I think that there's enough milk here to make some butter too. Let me get the churn and molds."

She didn't notice that he kept his back to her as she disappeared into the pantry to find the butter implements. When she reemerged, he was washing his hands in the dishpan and looking out the window. There was something about his stance that made her pause.

"What's wrong?" she asked, stopping at the pantry doorway.

Letting out a heavy sigh, he straightened and picked up a dish towel to wipe his hands before turning to look at her. His eyes had a look in them that she didn't understand.

"Talk of home and the war brings up memories I'd just as soon forget." With that being said, he changed the subject. "You're going to have to show me what to do, as I have no idea how to make cheese or butter for that matter."

Angelica felt as if she had upset him somehow, but she pasted on a smile. "These just need to be washed and then we start with the butter. It's easy, you just have to keep turning the churn till butter forms and then remove the lumps and pat them into molds."

"Sounds like just the job for me. Where's the milk churn?" he asked.

She handed him a fair-sized glass jar which had a metal top and watched as he turned it around in his hands with a confused expression on his face. Most likely he had expected a wood churn with a hole in the lid, like most frontier houses had. This churn had a crank on the top that spun several metal paddles which fit into the jar. When the handle was turned, the paddles mixed the milk, separating and creating butter.

Angelica watched as he turned the crank a few times before unscrewing the cap and plunging the contraption into the dishwater.

•••

He'd made a mistake staying on at this ranch, with this woman, Luke decided. He was turning the lever on the milk churn as she was preparing the molds to receive the butter that was starting to show through the glass. He should have packed her and the animals and hustled them into town as soon as she had awoken this morning, snow or no snow. Now he was responsible for her and stuck.

The clean scent of the soap that she had used to wash her hands tickled his nose as she stood near him to check on his progress. It smelled like flowers and not the harsh smell of the lye soap he used at Landon's.

"I've never seen a churn like this one before," he said as he watched the butter form.

Angelica smiled wistfully. "My father liked to spoil my mother. I think he felt somewhat guilty about bringing her out here, so far from town." Her eyes took on a faraway look. "He insisted on the glass for the windows, and every time he came home from town, he would bring us both a present."

She held up a butter mold. "This was one of the last things that he brought. He had them shipped from back East for her." Showing Luke the inside, he could see that there was a pattern cut into the wood. Angelica rubbed her finger along the grain. "Her favorite flower was the forget-me–not. So, he had someone carve them into the butter molds. My mother loved them."

Before Luke could find something to say, she instructed him to unscrew the cap and fish the chunks of butter out of the cream. Placing the pieces into a bowl, she gently washed the cream from them and patted them dry.

Luke busied himself with pressing the newly made butter into the molds, while she emptied out the remaining liquid into a jar, then she quickly rinsed the entire contraption before refilling the churn with more milk.

Turning the crank once again, he wondered if Landon was getting worried about him. Luke had been on an errand to get some supplies for his friend when Wolf had sent him here. Landon's wife, Mary was eight

| 32 |

months pregnant and having lost his first wife and child in childbirth, Landon had called in a favor, asking Luke to be around for this birth in case of any complications. Once mother and child were found to be healthy, Luke was free to get on his horse and try to keep ahead of the ghosts and memories that were constantly following him.

By late afternoon, they had made multiple batches of butter and two wheels of cheese. It had been a slow process as Angelica had to rely on Luke for most of the work. Luke had brought the butter to the creek where a wooden box, lined with tin, was submerged. Living alone, Angelica didn't have a large icehouse like Landon did. There were several small, salted hams and roasts in the box, along with some slabs of bacon.

Locking the top and setting it back down into the water, Luke then returned to the house to find Angelica trying to roll out dough to make biscuits. Without a word, he took the rolling pin from her hand and pointed at a chair. Surprisingly, she didn't argue with him and sat down.

"Why won't you let me take you to town?" he asked. "At least for the winter, until you've healed fully."

She shook her head. "This is my home," she stated simply. "What would I do in town? It would cost money to stay in the hotel there. How would I pay them?" She looked around the kitchen. "I know that it isn't much, but someday I hope to build myself a bedroom off the back. With light yellow walls and white curtains." Her voice was filled with longing. "I'll fix my grandmother's rocker that's in the barn and sit in it to rock my babies to sleep someday. There would also be a small room where the wash tub would be so that I don't have to bathe in the kitchen anymore." She looked embarrassed at speaking her dream out loud.

Grabbing a glass, Luke pressed it into the dough. Pulling the circular biscuit out, he placed them into the cast iron pan. "That sounds like a fine plan, but it still doesn't explain why you can't go to town and heal."

He put the biscuits in the oven. When he turned, she was wiping a tear away. "My parents loved this land. I love this land, and I won't leave it." She looked out the window. "They are buried here, and I can't bear the thought of them out here alone." Her voice cracked at the end.

Luke decided to change the subject. "It'll be nice to have some homemade biscuits instead of hardtack." He shrugged into his jacket and grabbed the milk bucket. "I'll go milk the cow. I'm assuming that you want to make some more cheese tomorrow since there is plenty of milk left?"

"If you don't mind," she answered. "That way I can send some with you to bring to your friend, for your kindness."

She was worried that he would get upset again, talking about payment, but he just nodded and left the house. He had told her that he was staying with his friend Landon, but he didn't say too much beyond that.

No matter what, he wasn't meant to stay.

•••

Angelica got gingerly out of bed. She hurt all over. There was no sign of Luke when she entered the kitchen, but the room was warm. A mug was set aside on the counter with the teapot next to it. Angelica lifted the lid to find the contents still steaming. She poured herself a cup and sat down at the table. Taking a few sips, she wondered about Luke.

He hadn't said much about himself other than he was a doctor and that he grew up in South Carolina. She surmised that he had been in the civil war by the way he had reacted to her comment about the South. It only made sense that he would have been recruited to help the wounded.

She heard his footsteps as he brought the morning's milk in from the barn. A blast of cold air preceded him as he opened the door and stepped into the kitchen. There was no sign of Wolf or Purrsistence.

Luke set the bucket on the draining board and shook himself out of his jacket. Draping the garment over the back of the chair, he gave her an assessing look.

"How are you feeling today?"

How was she feeling today? "I'm still very sore and tired." It was hard to admit, as she had never been sick a day in her life.

He nodded. "I'm not surprised. I think you overdid it yesterday."

She watched as he turned and strained the milk into a clean pail before covering it. Opening the door, he set the bucket into the box in the lean to, then set about gathering eggs and setting a skillet onto the stove. She watched as he took a couple of potatoes and sliced them.

The room seemed smaller with him in it. It was a new experience, being waited on, and Angelica was at a loss of what to do or say.

Luke spooned some lard into the skillet before adding the potato slices to one side and cracked eggs to the other.

"We could water glass eggs or make some more cheese," she suggested.

He stopped for a moment to turn and look at her. "Water glass eggs?"

"Yes," Angelica replied. "The hens lay many more eggs than I could possibly eat, so I put them in mason jars with pickling lime and water." She took a gulp of tea. "The eggs stay good for at least eighteen months. I sell a lot to the hotel in Newcombe, and no one can tell that they have been preserved."

He looked impressed, so she continued. "I sent all my jars into town in August and the hens aren't laying too many right now, but I still have more than I need at the moment. I should have picked up more of the sodium silicate, but I think I still have enough to do several more large jars." She felt as if she was babbling.

Luke nodded his head in approval. "I'm impressed," he said as he cooked. "I had heard about a woman living out on the prairie alone and I have to admit, I thought that it was a foolish thing for a woman to do."

Using a flour sack, Luke lifted the skillet off the stove and scraped the contents onto two plates. He sprinkled both with some salt and pepper. Bringing the plates to the table, he placed one in front of her before sitting on the other side of the table. He handed her a fork.

"Of course, I figured the person living here was a widow and older than the Black Hills," he continued.

She narrowed her eyes at him, which he ignored. "I admire your resourcefulness, but I still believe that I should take you into town for the winter. There is no way you can run this ranch alone with a broken arm, no wood, and bad weather on the way."

Angelica had lost her appetite and pushed the plate away. "I'm not leaving my ranch."

Luke pushed her plate back at her and continued to eat his breakfast. "Why do you want to stay here so badly?" he asked. "It must be terribly lonely, especially in the winter, and I would think a young woman such as yourself would rather go to dances or the theater than muck out a stall."

Her stomach growled, so she took a bite of eggs. They were actually very good. "I love this ranch," she said between bites. "My whole history is here. Everywhere I look, I remember my parents or some special memory. Where else could I go, and what would I do?" She gestured to the room. "Everything you see around you is mine. I'm not beholden to anyone."

She put her fork down and sat back in the chair. "I hope to someday meet a man that falls in love with me and wants to settle here with me. Raise children. I can't think of a prettier place to stay."

Luke sat back as well. "I hope that for you as well," he said.

Why did that sentence make her suddenly want to cry?

He continued, "I've been all over this country, and while the Dakotas have some pretty places, they can't compare to some other places I've seen."

Angelica was intrigued and welcomed the change of subject. "Tell me about your favorite place."

Luke crossed his arms and thought for a moment. "Well, every place has its own beauty, but I've never seen anything as impressive as the ocean. I've seen both the Atlantic and Pacific oceans, and I don't have the words to describe them. The water and waves change daily. Some days the waves are calm and make a rhythmical sound that lulls you, and the next day they can be huge and crash so loud that you can hear them from a mile away." Luke got up from the table and placed the dishes on the sideboard.

Angelica had never seen the ocean, but she had been to several of the nearby lakes and rivers. She remembered the gentle lapping of waves, but she couldn't envision those waves being large and loud as they crashed to the shore. Someday, she promised herself, she would go see the ocean for herself.

"Why is that your favorite place?" she asked.

He was gathering water to wash the dishes with his back to her. She watched as he looked up and out the window. "I guess the way that it had a rhythm and rhyme to it and how small I felt looking out from the beach," he finally answered. "The sunrises are stunning on the Atlantic, and the Pacific has the sunsets to match, and the waves continue to the shore no matter the weather. It gives a body hope…" He didn't finish the thought.

Angelica wanted to ask him hope for what, but she had a feeling that he wouldn't answer if she did. There was a sadness to Luke that she didn't understand.

"I feel well enough to water glass the eggs, and I'd love to hear about more places if you have more stories," she said softly.

He'd finished with the dishes and was wiping out the skillet before hanging it back on its hook. "I might be persuaded to tell you about the Clifton waterfalls that span Canada and New York, or the exploring expedition I did with Joseph Ives of a grand canyon on the Colorado river in 1858 when I was eighteen."

She narrowed her eyes at him again. "Persuaded how?"

He smiled. "By you promising to rest today and to consider the possibility of me taking you to town."

"I will take it easy today," she promised, "but I still won't consider going to Newcomb."

Luke shook his head, but he had a slight smile. "Fair enough, but I guess I won't tell you about the hot springs in Arkansas where you can relax in water that is warmer than your bath water and stays hot. Nope, I won't tell you about the healing properties that it is said to contain either."

Angelica felt her eyes widen and her mouth dropped open. Warmer than bathwater and she didn't have to keep reheating it to keep it warm? That would be a dream come true.

"I'm still not going to town," she said, standing up, "but I sure would like to hear about all the places you've been to."

Luke gave a small laugh as she disappeared into the pantry to gather her supplies.

•••

The clock was chiming three when Angelica glanced out the window. It had been four days since she had fallen through the barn roof, and she and Luke had finished making more cheese and were in the process of cleaning up the kitchen. Movement in the orchard told Angelica that her Sioux friends had arrived. Smiling, she grabbed her father's coat, wrapped it around her, and went to the door. Pulling it open, she almost ran into an Indian woman, about her own age.

"Meda, oh I'm so happy to see you." Angelica grabbed her friend's hands with her left. "Come in and tell me where you've been. I've been so worried."

Meda smiled as she was pulled into the kitchen. She was tall and held herself proudly, until she caught sight of Luke. Quickly she lowered her eyes to the floor.

"It's okay, this is Mr. Luke Wells, and he is a friend. You have nothing to fear from him, I promise." Angelica gave Luke a look full of meaning. She hoped that he could figure out what that meaning meant. Indians were treated horribly by most white people, so they had learned to be as invisible as possible. The few times that they had to cross paths with the white settlers had taught them to be wary and to keep their gaze downward. Any gesture or look could be misconstrued. They trusted Angelica; she had honored her father's treaty with them.

Luke was still drying his hands after washing the dishes.

"I'm pleased to meet you, ma'am," he said. Moving slowly, he pulled back two chairs from the table. "Why don't the two of you sit down and chat. I have some more chores to do."

Meda's face didn't register her surprise at his gesture. Glancing up at Luke, she gave a slight smile and a small nod.

Angelica filled the coffeepot with water and set it on the stove. Cups were placed on the table along with her mother's teapot, which she spooned in tea leaves. It had been ages since she had sat down with another woman for some tea. It was one of the many things that each of them looked forward to every year.

"Ma'am?" Meda questioned as soon as the door had closed behind Luke.

Angelica took a minute to look over her old friend. Meda's long black hair hung down her back in a braid that was intertwined with a beaded leather string. Her feet were encased in buffalo lined moccasins and her robe was a brown antelope hide, lined with rabbit fur. Meda shrugged out of the robe, revealing her cow skin shirt and leggings adorned with colored beads and dyed porcupine quills, arranged into colorful patterns. A bone necklace lay pale against her sun darkened skin.

"I knew that he would treat you respectfully. He has been such a gentleman." Angelica brought the coffee pot over to the table and poured the boiling water into the teapot before slowly lowering herself into a chair.

Meda tilted her head as she studied Angelica. "I can see that I was right to be worried. We traveled as fast as we could to get here because I was afraid for you. Tell me how you were hurt."

Angelica poured the tea and told her friend about falling through the roof and waking up to find Luke and the wolf in her barn.

After Angelica was done, Meda's gaze moved to the door. "It's interesting that Luke has shown up at this time."

Angelica didn't know what to say to that. Meda's given name was Nahimana, which meant *mystic* in Lakota, because she had started having premonitions and dreams when she was a young girl. Her grandmother had nicknamed her Meda, meaning *prophetess*, and that was the name she had gone by for as long as Angelica had known her.

Meda continued, "The wolf spirit came to my fire several weeks ago, on the eve of the full moon. It spoke of this man with great healing power and how the wolf would guide him to you." Pausing, she glanced out the window to where Luke could be seen sorting and stacking the kindling that the Indians had brought. From the expression on her face, she seemed to be making up her mind about something. Having decided, she turned and looked Angelica in the eye.

"There is something coming. I got the impression that it is evil. The spirit would say no more, except that this was a lesson not just for you but also for the man with the broken soul."

A chill ran through the Angelica. It was what her mother termed the feeling of someone walking on your grave. Meda had shared stories of her visions before, but none had ever included her. Standing, Angelica began to pace. How should she react? Should she panic? Was Luke the man with the broken soul, and what did that even mean? If he left, would whatever bad thing that was coming follow him and leave her alone? Could she live with herself knowing that he might be in danger, and she'd sent him away to fight it on his own?

Questions kept swirling through her mind. Angelica voiced some of them out loud. "What type of evil? Will I know what it is when it arrives? Is it something that Luke brought here?" A thought occurred to her. "Or is it already here?" Her voice rose with panic.

It was all very confusing. Why couldn't this wolf spirit just tell them what was coming so that they were ready for it?

Angelica grew up knowing that there was danger all around her. She just had to take a walk to the small cemetery where her family was buried to know that life was fleeting. She'd never been afraid to live out on the prairie because her faith had always carried her through.

A small band of soldiers had stopped by several months before. The Lieutenant had tried to persuade her to leave the area, but she'd refused and sent them on their way. She'd forgotten about their visit.

With Custer's troops finding gold in the Black Hills, miners and gold diggers flocked to the area in search of striking it rich, violating the treaty giving the area to the Indians. The Black Hills, or He Sapa as the Lakota called the area, were sacred to their culture. They believed it to be the site where the first Indian arrived in this world. It was known as *wakama ognaka y cante*—the heart of everything that is.

Now, soldiers were everywhere, trying to force the Indians to the reservations. The white settlers were hunting on the Indian's hunting ground, causing the Indians to starve. Burial mounds were being desecrated and looted. Tempers were flaring and there were rumors that a war was brewing between the plains Indians and the army. Renegade Indians roamed the plains, causing trouble in desperate attempts to drive the white man away. Meda had said that Sitting Bull, a Hunkpapa Lakota Sioux holy man, was having premonitions of a great battle against the army. Sitting Bull was Meda's distant cousin, and she always spoke about him with great respect.

Now Meda reached across the table and took Angelica's hand. "Do not be afraid. The spirit told me so that we could prepare. I am here and will help fight this evil. You are not alone."

Angelica felt better. It was not surprising that Meda would know how she was feeling. They had grown up together, sharing a bond like sisters. When her parents were alive, they let her stay in Meda's tepee and live among Indians while the tribe harvested the fruit. Angelica learned their customs and language, and Meda learned hers.

Two days after Angelica's parents' deaths, Meda had arrived at her doorstep. She said that the wind had whispered Angelica's name to her. The eighteen-year-old had thought nothing of heading across the plains, alone, to help her friend. Angelica always admired Meda's freedom and bravery and never doubted her friend's ability to know things when others did not. Taking a deep breath, Angelica decided that she would try to be as brave. Knowing that Meda would face the challenge and never doubt that they could defeat it made her feel calmer. Well, she could do that too. Squaring her shoulders, Angelica changed the subject as they finished their tea.

• • •

Meda closed the kitchen door tight behind her as the sharp wind tried to push her back. Pulling up her hood, she climbed over the snow drift that had been deposited against the house. Her tribe would have set up camp in the clearing behind the barn, so that was the direction that she walked. Angelica had offered for her to stay in the house, but Meda wouldn't be able to sleep in such a confined space. She needed the open air and stars. White men tried to fight Mother Earth, while the Indians embraced her.

Meda shook her head. She was worried. Somehow the balance was off, and this snowstorm was just the beginning. There had been plenty of signs along the way. The muskrat's den had several layers, and the buffalo's fur was the thickest that even her great-grandfather had ever seen. Streams had dried up, and there had been no rain to replenish the grass that would be needed in the spring. The worst had been that several times the ground had shaken beneath her feet. The elders offered sacrifices to the Great Spirit and performed the Sun dance, but still the signs continued.

Meda reached the barn, which offered some shelter from the whipping wind, and leaned against the rough boards for a moment. She'd told Angelica that an evil was coming that they could fight; however, she didn't tell her friend that she had no idea what to do or that she was scared.

• • •

Luke was still worried about the lack of firewood, even though Meda's tribe had brought a half a cord of kindling. They seemed to understand that she couldn't survive out here without the wood, so they'd brought as much as they could carry. The wind and snow hampered his ability to go very far, but with the help of several of the braves, they'd managed to get a respectable pile of logs together. It should hold her for a couple of weeks if she banked the stove early. Angelica kept insisting that someone was coming with several cords any day now. Luke hoped so, because she wouldn't make it through the winter without it. Since Meda could take care of the animals, he planned on leaving for town the following morning. He'd get the supplies for Landon's ranch that he had originally set out for, then he'd stop and check on Angelica on his way back.

•••

Luke began moving the hay to the other side of the loft. Most of it was salvageable, barring any more holes in the roof, and there should be enough to last the livestock till spring, which was one worry off his mind. As he worked, he ignored the gaping hole that Angelica had fallen through. She could easily have been crippled or killed. It was a surprise that the whole roof hadn't let go, as badly rotted as it was. No patch was going to fix it. The entire thing needed to be replaced before the heavy snow of winter arrived. He sighed. From what he knew of Angelica, she would be right back on this roof as soon as he was out of sight, ready to take on a task that was definitely beyond her capabilities.

Living in such close quarters, Luke found Angelica to be an extraordinary woman. Growing up in the South, women were expected to be genteel and helpless, though he knew that that was just an act. His mother was one of the strongest people that he knew. When she wanted something done, there wasn't anything that could stop her. Angelica was a lot like her. It just didn't occur to her that she couldn't do it herself and damn it if she wasn't out here in the middle of nowhere, making it work.

Taking a seat on the edge of the loft, Luke wiped the sweat from his forehead. He didn't want to admit it, but he was going to miss Angelica. He would have expected her to be uneducated, living out here in the middle of nowhere, but she was quite smart. Sitting at her kitchen table and talking with her made him forget about his past for a while. It made him wish for things that he had no damn business wishing for, and that scared him like nothing had before. It was time for him to leave.

Standing up, he continued moving the hay while he mentally made plans.

The sky was just brightening when Luke walked out of the barn with his horse already saddled. The Indians were stirring over at their camp; he could smell something cooking in the light morning breeze. Tightening the cinch, he tried not to remember the hurt that he had seen in Angelica's eyes when he'd made his goodbye the night before. She recovered quickly before smiling, but the pain had been there, nonetheless. It tore at him. They'd known each other for less than a week, but on some level, it was as if he had always known her. They came from two different worlds, he reminded himself; the faster he got back to his, the better.

Luke was about to mount when he saw her in the doorway. Her light colored, makeshift sling was in stark contrast to the dark dress that she wore. Regret washed over him. He wanted to promise her the world, but it would be an empty promise.

She warned him last night about some evil coming into his life, but he knew that the warning was too late. Evil and he were already well acquainted. Nothing could compare to what he had seen and lived through. On some level, he would actually welcome something, anything, that he could fight, instead of the memories that he couldn't change. At least fighting would give the pretense of being alive, because he had felt nothing for so long.

Luke acknowledged her by tugging at the brim of his hat before he pulled it down over his eyes. Swinging into the saddle, he rode off without a backward glance.

CHAPTER FOUR

Luke stopped his horse in front of a fair-sized whitewashed building. The sign in front proclaimed it to be the Newcomb Hotel. Outside, in front of the large glass window, was a boy about ten years old, sitting on a bench. The youngster's pants and shirt were a size too small, and they'd been mended quite a few times. But he was clean, and his hair was combed.

"Is there a livery in this town?" Luke asked as he dismounted.

"Yes sir," the boy replied, squinting up at him. "It's at the end of Main Street." He pointed to his left without taking his eyes off Luke.

With the sun out, the temperature was rising, causing the snow to melt and leaving mud in its wake.

"You interested in earning five cents?" Luke asked.

"Depends on what I have to do."

Luke bit back a chuckle. "My horse needs a good rubdown and some real sweet hay. Is that something you can handle?"

The grin was purely lightning. "Sure thing, mister."

The kid caught the coin and proceeded down the street with his horse. Luke stepped onto the wooden sidewalk and walked toward the mercantile. Glancing around, he noticed that Newcomb was a decent size for a town in the middle of nowhere. Business owners were washing windows or sweeping off the boardwalk in front of their shops. Several streets branched off from the main one, leading to neat rows of houses. There were the ever-present saloons, invariably found in most frontier towns, and even a church with a steeple. Most likely it doubled as a school.

Reaching the mercantile, Luke grabbed onto the door handle and looked over his shoulder. Maybe he could talk Angelica into moving closer to town. That way she would be safer.

A balding, stout man was behind the counter on the far end of the store, helping two women as they decided on fabric for linens. The sleeves of his shirt were rolled up as he pulled bolts of fabric down from shelves. He placed them on the table and unrolled one for inspection. His once-white apron was dingy with stains, and he looked slightly harassed. Luke assumed that the women were mother and daughter, as they had the same pinched face and high-pitched voice. They kept touching the fabric and shaking their heads.

Perusing the shelves while he waited, Luke noticed a selection of books. It made him think of the present that Angelica had bought for herself. Touching the leather bindings, he pulled one out. Skimming through it revealed that it was a story about princesses, knights, and dragons. Not dwelling too deeply into his reasoning, he headed back to the counter, book in hand. The women had finalized their purchases and with side glances at him, they left the store.

Luke placed the book on the counter and pulled out the list of supplies that Landon had given him. The clerk looked over the list and promised to have it ready in several hours.

Holding up the book, he said, "I'll pay for this separately."

The man beamed when Luke plunked down a coin.

Shoving the tome into the pocket of his jacket, Luke left the store and headed in the direction of the livery. He was going to need a buckboard to get all the supplies back to the ranch. Landon usually kept one in town for such cases.

Luke was passing the stagecoach station just as a large wagon was pulling away. A matronly looking woman was herding a small group of children, who clung to each other, to the far end of the boardwalk. Luke counted seven youngsters, and each of them had a piece of paper pinned on their shirt or dress.

Luke's stomach lurched. He knew that these kids were most likely orphans that came out of the already overcrowded orphanages. They were sent by train to the west in hope that they would have a brighter future. Since the tracks didn't run this far north into the Territories, they must have been brought up by a freight wagon. Luke knew that some people took these children and raised them as their own, but others treated them no better than slaves. Working from sunup to sundown, never lawfully adopted, those children had nothing to show for themselves when they became of legal age.

The woman was lining the children up according to size and gender. Two boys were having none of it. The older boy looked to be about twelve years old, while the other was about nine, and the little girl that they had put between them couldn't have been older than four. They were obvious siblings, their resemblance unmistakable.

Even though it was none of his business, Luke stopped on the opposite boardwalk.

"We are not getting separated," the older boy was telling the woman, his words clipped.

From the expression on her face, this was not a new argument. She sighed heavily as if the weight of the world was on her shoulders. "I know that's what you want, William, but you all have a better chance of getting homes if you split up. I'll try to keep the three of you in the same territory so you have a possibility of seeing each other, but that's about all I can promise."

William shook his head in disagreement. "I'll run away the first chance I get. I'll find them and take them with me."

The boy caught Luke's gaze and locked on. Luke couldn't miss the despair and desperation that he saw in the boy's eyes. There was also an unspoken plea in that look.

Reluctantly, Luke shook his head. William's eyes hardened and he turned back to the matron.

Luke continued on his way to the livery. There was nothing that he could do. He had no home, and he sure as hell didn't need to be saddled down with three kids. Besides, he didn't think that he would make good father material. A father was someone that was always around.

After arranging that the buckboard be sent to the mercantile, Luke completed a few more errands. There didn't seem to be a threat of snow in the air, so barring any delays, he should make good time back to Angelica's ranch, reaching it just before sundown. That left just enough time to have a meal at the hotel.

The dinner hour was almost gone when Luke made his way into the dining room of the hotel and took a seat next to the window that afforded a view of Main Street. The place was deserted except for an older couple sitting several tables away.

They both appeared to be in their early sixties. The man was balding, and his eyes kept darting around the room. The woman's graying hair had been yanked back in such a tight bun that it pulled the skin around her eyes back, giving her a somewhat surprised look. Both were extremely thin, and their clothes had seen better days.

A waitress came out of a door with a single plate of fried chicken and set it in the middle of the couple's table before heading over to Luke. With a quick smile, she took his order and disappeared through the same door again.

Alone, Luke stared out the window and tried unsuccessfully to get the image of the three children out of his mind. It took a while before the hushed conversation at the other table began to penetrate his brain.

"I ain't taking more than one," the woman was saying, her haggard face showing her displeasure. "We'll be lucky if we can feed one more. I'd take the smaller boy 'cause he probably don't eat much, but he won't be able to do the chores like that older boy."

"You need that girl to help in the garden and we can hire out the younger boy. He could do odd jobs and such. Make us some extra money." The man licked his lips. His voice had a whining quality to it. "That older boy will be trouble we don't need. He got a wild look in his eyes."

The woman lowered her voice and Luke, who was trying not to eavesdrop, had to listen really hard to hear her.

"I ain't taking the girl," she repeated. "I know what went on in the barn with Rachel instead of you working the fields. That girl was only twelve when she gone run off. We still had six years of work we should have gotten out of her. I won't have any more shenanigans like that." She sat up straight and pulled her shawl up around her shoulders. Her posture was one of pure righteous indignation.

Where was that indignation when poor Rachel needed it?

"That older boy will come around to our way of thinking with some swipes of your belt or a few missed meals." She licked the chicken grease from her fingers.

The man mumbled something under his breath.

The waitress came back just then and placed Luke's meal before him. He just stared at it.

That couple most likely was talking about the orphans at the stagecoach station. Picturing that little girl, never mind any child, in the clutches of the couple at the next table made his stomach turn. They had talked about beatings and starving kids like it was an everyday thing. He reached for his drink and took a sip. It was apple cider, Angelica's apple cider. She had told him that she supplied the hotel with cider, cheese, and canned goods.

Angelica.

A plan began to form in Luke's mind. Angelica had room for three orphans; she wouldn't be alone. Grabbing a bandana from his back pocket, he used it to wrap up the fried chicken. Throwing a silver dollar on the table, he turned and headed for the station. The couple at the other table paid no attention to his departure.

Reaching the depot, he found the platform deserted. The door was locked, so he pounded on the glass of the ticket window. The shade was down, but it moved slightly as someone peeked around it.

"We're closed," said a muffled voice.

"I'm looking for the woman with the orphans," Luke called into the window.

The shade went flying up, then a small man, no taller than Luke's mother, stood in the void. The man's large handlebar mustache quivered with excitement.

"Did you find the missing children?" the clerk asked.

Luke knew before he even asked that the missing children were William and his siblings. He also knew why they had run away. They wanted to stay together. He would have done the same thing in their place, foolish as it was. A prickle of fear took root in his stomach. Winter was coming early to the Dakotas, and three kids out on the prairie alone didn't stand a chance.

He turned and strode off the platform.

"Wait," the clerk called after him. "What about the children?"

Luke never broke his stride. His mind was going over the layout of the town.

If I was twelve years old, where would I hide?

The saloons were out. Children weren't allowed in them, and they would be conspicuous. The several stores that lined Main Street would be too public. They would be found in a matter of minutes.

Standing in the middle of the street, he found himself staring at the church. Walking toward it, he thought he saw a flash of movement in the belfry. He wasn't ready to examine the relief he felt. Slowing his pace to a leisurely one, he entered the church. Sitting down in one of the pews, he could hear the sounds of children trying to be quiet.

The afternoon sun poured through the windows on the left side, illuminating the white walls and the simple altar. He looked at the carved cross behind the pulpit and felt nothing. It had been a long time since he had been in a church. His parents had been God-fearing people, and he and his siblings had spent a good portion of their youth reading and reciting from the Bible. The world made sense when one believed in a heaven. Then the War Between the States showed him what Hell really was. Where was his loving and merciful God then? He had prayed for those boys, and his prayers had been lost in the smoke of the cannons and cries of the wounded. His faith had been shattered like the calm of a lake after a pebble is skipped along its surface, the ripples reaching out wide until they hit the shore, then are lost.

Like me, he thought.

He'd been wandering with no direction, never staying in one place very long, trying to keep the memories at bay. He couldn't afford to feel the pain of caring again. He made a quick stop at his family's farm after the war. His mother had begged him to stay. They had all pleaded with him, saying that he should just move past the horrors that he had seen. If only he could. He'd left the house at first light, while everyone was still sleeping. It had seemed easier that way. He'd been wandering ever since. Now here he was sitting in a church in the middle of the Dakota Territory looking for some orphans.

He listened for a moment. The boys were trying to be quiet, but their sister was having none of it. Every time they shushed her, she would ask a question in a loud voice. Luke grinned.

"Might as well come on down," he called to the ceiling.

The boards stopped creaking and for a moment all was silent.

"Look, I know that you're up there. Come on down. We need to talk."

It took several minutes of deliberation between the brothers. Finally, the trap door in the back of the room opened and the oldest brother climbed down the ladder. He walked up the side of the pews and sat down across the aisle, at a safe distance.

The woman had called him William. The boy's brown hair was cropped short, and Luke remembered hearing somewhere that orphanages shaved the children's hair to keep lice from becoming a problem. William's clothes were clean, but they'd seen a lot of wear. Most likely he would grow out of them by next spring. His shoes looked as if his toes were about to break through at any moment.

Luke watched William's face. The kid looked proud but also nervous and ready to bolt at any minute. There was something about William that bothered Luke. It was his eyes, he decided. They had seen so much for a boy of his age. That look reminded him of the young soldiers back on the battlefield. It was their eyes that haunted his sleep. Well, he didn't want to add this boy's eyes to the menagerie that obsessed his dreams.

Luke cleared his throat. He was taking a chance offering these kids a place to live with Angelica when he hadn't even talked with her yet. Yet he knew that if Angelica said no, then he would take them back to Landon's ranch and see if a place could be made there for them. Hell, he might just send them to his mother. She would love to have three children around. She kept complaining that she had yet to be a grandmother.

"I'm not able to take you myself," Luke stated.

The boy's face that had held wariness changed in an instant. Jumping to his feet, he looked angry and disappointed.

"I knew you were up to something," William said. "Why'd you track us down? I'll take care of my brother and sister, mister. You just go back to where you came from and forget about us."

He made a move to run to the back of the church. Luke held up his hand.

"Hear me out. I know this woman who lives on a farm about twenty miles from town. She lives alone. I haven't had a chance to talk to her yet, but I'd like to take you three and see if she would agree to be your guardian. If she can't, then I'll take you to a ranch that I'm staying at and see if they have a place for the three of you there."

The boy studied him for a moment.

"We won't be split up. I'm almost fourteen years old and I can take care of the three of us." The boy stood straighter as he talked.

"I'm sure that you will do the best that you can. This woman, Angelica, is recovering from a fall and could use some help." He paused for a moment. "I'll make you a deal. If she agrees but you and your siblings don't like it there, then in the spring I'll come get you and take you somewhere else."

Now where did that promise come from? He hadn't wanted to get emotionally involved. He'd just wanted to get both these kids and the thought of Angelica out on the prairie by herself off his conscience.

"You don't live there?"

"No, I travel a lot. Do we have a deal?"

While they had been talking, the younger boy and sister had made their way down the ladder and were standing at the back of the church. The boys exchanged looks.

"It would be better than that old mean couple," the younger boy said. "They were only interested in how much work we could do, and the man kept trying to touch Carol Anne."

Luke's stomach clenched. The thought of Carol Anne alone with the couple from the hotel dining room brought out a feeling of rage that he hadn't experienced in years. He needed to get these kids to Angelica's and fast. Once he knew that everyone was settled and safe, he could move on. Lowering his eyes, he remembered the chicken wrapped up in the bandana.

"You kids hungry?" he asked.

Carol Anne was the first to move. With the directness of a child, she ran up to him and stared at the food.

"May I have a piece, please?" she asked.

This time it wasn't his stomach that clenched but his heart. She had just stamped a little piece of it for herself. "Sure, sweetheart, sit down right here and help yourself."

It took the boys a few minutes before they too came forward and asked for a piece. Luke learned that the younger boy's name was Matthew and that they had lost their parents in a tenement fire three years before. After the fire, ten-year-old William hid them in abandoned apartments throughout New York. He worked odd jobs to get enough money for food while Matthew stayed out of sight with Carol Anne. They were brought to the orphanage when, not having any means of heating the apartment, William went to a neighbor for help. Carol Anne had gotten a bad cold, there were no jobs to be found, and food became scarce. Thinking that it was in the children's best interest, the neighbor reported them to the authorities.

"I never stole nothing," William told him. "There were plenty of beggars and thieves, but I worked like my daddy did. I earned it."

Luke placed his hand on the boy's shoulder. "I know that your daddy would have been proud to have such brave children. Let's go find the orphanage woman and see about getting you to Angelica's."

●●●

They found Mrs. Bishop at the hotel, pacing back and forth in front of the large dining room window that Luke had been looking out not too long before. A cup of tea sat forgotten on a table nearby. The older couple Luke had seen earlier was nowhere in sight; the room was empty except for Mrs. Bishop.

Twirling at the sound of their footsteps, the elderly woman placed a hand to her black, bombazine-covered ample bosom and gasped. Taking a few unsteady steps forward, she pulled out a chair and slumped into it. Luke was afraid that she was going to faint, her face was so white, but she rallied and sat up straight again.

"You children have given me a fright!" she told them sternly, as they stood uncertain in the doorway. Focusing on Luke, she said, "I am very grateful to you, sir, for finding them and returning them."

Luke decided that he liked Mrs. Bishop. She showed genuine concern about the children. People liked to talk about helping, but in his experience, not too many of them were willing to leave their homes and family to actually follow through. Mrs. Bishop spoke with the cultured accent of someone from the Northeast, yet here she was in the wilds of the Dakota Territory, caring for orphans.

Taking off his hat, he approached her table. "Name's Luke Wells, ma'am, and I'd like to talk to you about these children."

"Please, Mr. Wells, have a seat." She gestured to the chair opposite her. Turning and pinning the children with a look, she pointed to a bench that was against a wall. "Children, sit over there and try to stay out of trouble."

• • •

Mrs. Lucinda Bishop was in her early sixties. Her record of adopting out orphans had been spotless, so she was immensely relieved that the children had been found safe. In the five years that she had been taking these trips, these three had been the hardest of all to place. Several people would have taken them separately, but William was adamant about keeping his brother and sister with him. Once he found out that a prospective adopter only wanted one of them, he threatened to run away and kidnap his siblings back unless they were adopted together. People just shook their heads and picked another child.

Secretly, Lucinda admired William for his resolve, but they had come farther into the Dakotas because of it, and she was tired and more than ready to head back to New York. Her husband most likely didn't even notice she was gone, but she missed socializing with her friends and seeing her grandchildren. Producing a white handkerchief from inside her sleeve, she dabbed at her eyes. It would be good to be home.

Lucinda hadn't liked the last couple that had shown interest in William. The man kept trying to touch little Carol Anne, and the woman had looked at William as if he was a servant ready to work. They totally ignored Matthew. The couple began to argue at the depot about just getting William. Lucinda intervened, and when she'd turned around, the children were gone. The couple had been furious and left empty handed since homes had already been found for the other children. Unfortunately, she was running out of options for keeping them together. Now she looked at Luke. He seemed like a nice man, though he could use a haircut. Hopefully there was a wife at home and enough room for all three.

"Well, Mr. Wells, how can I help you?"

Luke leaned in a little. "I have a possible home for all three children. I've been staying with Miss Angelica Barnes, who owns a farm outside of town. She lives alone and has plenty of room. I just have to ask her, but I'm confident that she would say yes."

Lucinda couldn't believe her ears. Did this man just offer his harlot as a proper guardian for the children? Were standards so lacking in the West that this was considered proper? Words failed her for several moments. Sitting up straight, she gave him a cold look.

"Mr. Wells, are you suggesting that I send these precious children to a woman of questionable character? Never in all my years of charity work have I received such a request. I should report you to the authorities immediately!"

Mr. Wells' mouth fell open and then, to her surprise, he threw his head back and laughed. Why, the man was a lunatic! The faster she and the children left this town, the better. She started to rise when he touched her arm. Fearful, she drew back from him.

"I'm sorry, Mrs. Bishop but you must have misunderstood me. Miss Barnes is an acquaintance of mine and she is a respectable lady. She had an accident several days ago, and since I am a doctor, I've been helping her out. She would have a wonderful home for them."

Lucinda wanted to believe him, but she hesitated. Turning, she looked over at the children. Hope was evident in the boys' eyes, though they tried not to show it. Carol Anne sat between them and kept smiling at Mr. Wells. One thing Lucinda had learned a long time ago was that children had a sixth sense about people. This situation seemed too good to be true, but if it was, then it solved all their problems. Lucinda bit her bottom lip. It was a habit that she had developed in childhood. The pain helped her focus on the problem.

Looking skeptically at Luke, Lucinda sat back. A lot rode on this man telling the truth. Sending these children out into the prairie without accurately assessing the situation could be disastrous. The newspapers back home were filled with stories of the dangers of the West. Indians, gunslingers, and outlaws were rampant out here. Why, there were rumors of possible train robberies on every one of the trains they took coming out here. What she wouldn't give to be on one of those trains right now, heading home, back to civilization.

Mr. Wells smiled. It was one of those smiles that didn't quite reach the eyes. It was intriguing. This man seemed so sure of himself, yet there was something emanating from him that spoke of a deep sadness, a vulnerability of sorts. Her instincts told her to trust him, but her head needed to be sure. She took a sip of her tea, stalling for time.

He spoke before she could. "I was planning on heading back to Miss

Barnes's farm tonight, but now it's too late to start. If you and the children would come with me tomorrow, you could meet Miss Barnes and see if she was agreeable to the arrangement. If so, then you can be back in town in time to catch the afternoon stagecoach. I'll be in front of the hotel at seven tomorrow morning." He stood. "Miss Barnes supplies this hotel with cider, cheese, and other canned goods. I'm sure that the management will give you a character reference. Now if you'll excuse me, I have some things to see to."

With his hat in his hands, Mr. Wells nodded at the children and strode out of the dining room. Lucinda watched the children look after him longingly. He had certainly painted a rosy picture of a wonderful future for them. She just hoped that it was true, or she would be forced to shoot Mr. Wells herself.

CHAPTER FIVE

It was too quiet. Except for the ticking of the clock and Purrsistence's purring echoing in the small room, there were no other noises to mask the passing of time.

This is ridiculous, Angelica thought, plunking down her coffee mug and glaring at the door. Luke had only been gone for one day. She remembered feeling this way when her parents had died, but then she had thrown herself into surviving that winter. There had been too many things to keep her busy. After a while, she had grown accustomed to the silence. Luke's presence had changed all that.

She needed something to do, but her choices were limited, being trussed up like a steer at branding time. The snow outside was melting, leaving slippery mud. Angelica was afraid that she would fall and re-injure herself. Thankfully, Meda and some of the other women were taking care of the animals, so they didn't need her help. All the canning had been done weeks ago, and the house was already spotless.

Angelica sighed. Fingering her mug, she stared off into space. The truth was she hadn't expected to miss Luke so much. He had woven his way into her life, and now his absence was leaving a large void. Well, she wasn't one to sit around and mope. Surely there were things that she could do. Maybe she could finish that quilt that she had started but never seemed to have enough time to work on. Only her right arm was in a sling and there was no way she could use a needle and thread. Then Angelica remembered the book that she had bought herself for her birthday. Her birthday. Was that only a week ago? Somehow, her world had been forever changed that day.

Up till then, her home had been the most important thing to her. This was where all her memories were, where she belonged and where her parents were buried. She felt that her very existence depended on this land.

Now she wasn't so sure.

Luke had inadvertently shown her what she was missing out on. He talked of places that she had only dreamed about. Places where giant crevices had been made in the earth by a river and it took a full day to climb down to the bottom. Trees that grew so tall that they blocked out the sun and of the ocean, where the land ended at the water, creating huge waves. She sighed again. Things were confusing. Being alone and self-sufficient had been enough for the past three years. Then Luke had come along and shattered her peaceful world.

Squaring her shoulders, Angelica took a deep breath. She didn't intend to sit around, waiting for him to get back. Spring wasn't that far away. It was about time that she did some things that she wanted to do. Follow her dreams. The land would always be here. Once she'd seen what was out there, maybe she would find someone that wanted to share the ranch, settle down, and have some children. For a moment, she wondered if Luke could be that someone, but she knew that he wasn't. Demons were chasing him, and he thought he could outrun them. He had told her a little about the war, but it's what he didn't tell her that was more revealing.

"He's lost his path with God," her mother would have said. "Sometimes you have to walk with the devil awhile before you can see the path that will take you out of the depths of darkness. No one can make you see the light until you are ready."

Well, Luke wasn't ready to see the light yet. That was obvious. Maybe he never would. It hurt a little to think that he had just ridden off this morning without looking back once. She'd watched from the kitchen window until he disappeared from sight.

No sense dwelling on something she had no control over. Having made that decision, she got up to find her book. It was going to be a long day.

•••

William was the first one out the hotel door the next morning and found Luke leaning against a buckboard that was full of cut lumber and brown wrapped packages. A black carriage, with two brown Morgan horses, was tied up a few feet away.

"Mrs. Bishop says she'll be joining you in five minutes," William told Luke.

"That's good."

Licking his lips, William watched Luke for a moment out of the corner of his eye. He was good at sizing people up. Living on the streets had taught him some harsh lessons. One of his first lessons was to never take people at face value. Some of the city's well-to-do were often seen prowling in the shadows at night looking for victims. Yet he had seen a beggar woman save a litter of kittens that someone had tied into a bag and thrown into the river from a bridge. No, it was all about their actions. Sort of like playing cards.

William used to watch several of the men in his building play poker. He needed to learn to read the other players they told him. Each player had certain movements or actions that showed if they were bluffing or had the cards that could win. Some were better at hiding them than others.

William studied Luke as the older man checked the harness on one of the horses, stroked their noses, and spoke quietly to them. This man was hard to read. One minute he was saying that he couldn't take them in, but he had a place for them to go. Then in the next breath he'd promised that if they didn't like Miss Barnes, he would come to get them. William was inclined to think that Luke was lying, but he had no way of knowing. Well, if they didn't like Miss Barnes, then he would just find a way to get them back to a place where they could blend into and survive.

"You'll like Miss Angelica's place," Luke said.

The voice brought William back from his thoughts. How did he know what William had been thinking? Had William said them out loud? "That so?"

Luke grinned. "Yeah, that's so. Plenty of work to keep you busy, but you'll have enough time to be a kid too."

Pretty words, but William wasn't buying them. His world for the last four years had been about staying alive. Life on the streets had taken away his childhood and thrust him into a man's role. Nothing else mattered other than keeping the three of them together and surviving. This man had no idea the things that he had seen and done. Now he was talking about doing things that kids do. Well, too late for that.

He turned and looked Luke in the eye. "Carol Anne will probably do just that, and maybe Matthew will too. I'll be busy earning our keep."

Luke's eyes narrowed, and he looked as if he wanted to say something, but just then Matthew, Carol Anne, and Mrs. Bishop stepped out of the hotel. Luke shifted his attention to the others. Grinning, he knelt down to talk to Carol Anne, and a tiny stab of jealousy tugged at William's heart as Carol Anne smiled at Luke. Things had been hard on all three of them, but the boys tried to keep things positive for the small girl. The orphanage had been tough enough on the boys, but they had had each other. Carol Anne was put into the girls' dormitory and suffered from the estrangement. The nights had been the worst for her. The other girls told William that Carol Anne had had nightmares every night, calling out for her parents or her brothers. The headmistress, Mrs. Nixon, wanted to adopt them quickly, as she felt that they were disrupting the balance of the orphanage. She also wanted them to be adopted separately, as she felt that would be the easiest, but William was adamant about the three of them staying together. Mrs. Nixon and William argued many times, and somehow William managed to keep them together, for now. In a last-ditch effort, the headmistress sent them on the last train of the season heading west. The prairies were unpredictable for weather after October, and soon only the supply trains would be making the trek. Mrs. Bishop seemed sympathetic to Williams's plight, but he could tell that she was tired and wanted to go home. That she was even considering Mr. Well's offer, sight unseen, said a lot. William knew that one way or another, they would not be taking the train back to the city.

"The women will ride in the carriage, and the boys can ride in the buckboard with me," Luke was saying. He pointed at a boy not much older than William who was approaching the group. "Ned will drive you back to town, Mrs. Bishop, in time for the two o'clock stage if everything is satisfactory."

William could see that Mrs. Bishop was impressed. It seemed that Mr. Wells was betting on Miss Barnes taking them in.

Matthew stopped next to William. Matthew was the sensitive one in the family, their mother used to say. He was scared of everything. He spent most of his time with his nose stuck in a book. It used to bother William until he found out that Matthew was pretty smart.

Unfortunately, having all that information hadn't helped him to be any braver. William looked at his younger brother. Matthew was staring at the horses, his eyes wide. They hadn't really been around animals in years. William was about to say something to his brother, but Luke beat him to it.

"Have you had any experiences with horses?" he addressed the younger boy.

Matthew shook his head, yet he never took his eyes off the team.

"Nothing to be nervous about," Luke replied. "Just need to make sure that you never surprise a horse. They spook easily. Make friends with them and they'll follow you around like a puppy dog. One or two sugar cubes should do the trick."

William watched as Luke steered Matthew to the buckboard and had him pat the gelding tethered to the back. Luke kept talking, and William could see Matthew relax under the constant flow of words.

Ned helped Mrs. Bishop and Carol Anne into the carriage. Luke watched Matthew climb into the buckboard and then turned to look at William. There was a question in that look, but William barely saw it. It was time to go meet Miss Barnes and see if their luck had changed. Taking a deep breath, he stepped to the wagon and hoisted himself up.

•••

The landscape was blinding in spots where the snow hadn't melted. William squinted and covered his eyes, trying to make out things in the distance. The outline of the black hills kept getting lost in the glare.

"Having a hard time seeing?" Luke asked conversationally. "You'll need a good hat out here that helps stop some of the snow blindness. The rest you just get used to."

William didn't reply. How did one get used to this desolate place? They were from the city, where he could flit from shadow to shadow without being seen, even though he was surrounded by people. They had survived with people tossing him a penny or two to help them do something they were too lazy to do themselves.

There was no sound except the clopping of the horses as they went further into the vastness. The farther they got from town, the more William could feel the panic starting to well up in his stomach. He hadn't realized that the ranch would be in the middle of nowhere. How was he to get his brother and sister away if this place turned out to be worse than the orphanage?

"You'll want to keep looking at the landscape behind you," Luke told them, breaking into William's thoughts. "When you head for town, the view will be different. Most city slickers get lost because they don't look for reference points. The prairie changes constantly, but the horizon pretty much stays the same."

William and Matthew both turned to look back. There wasn't much to see but some wisps of smoke on the horizon as the town disappeared from sight.

"How can you be sure that a storm won't catch us out here?"

Matthew was constantly worrying. Not that the thought hadn't crossed William's mind since they'd started out.

Luke gave the question some thought. "Well, I can't be sure, but I've been in these parts long enough to have a feeling about the weather. The animals are always a good indication if the weather is going to change. See those black dots over there? Those are buffalo. If the weather was going to turn, then they would be closer together and not so spread out. That way they can huddle and stay warmer. Keeps them from wandering away from the others too."

Matthew peered at the buffalo as if they could communicate with their mind. William turned and checked the horizon again.

"How far is this ranch?" William asked.

"About two hours out of town for a horse and rider, three or so for a full wagon. I'm pushing the horses a little faster than normal so that Mrs. Bishop can make it back in time for the stagecoach."

William chewed on that information for a moment. "What happens if Mrs. Bishop doesn't like this place, or if your friend doesn't want to keep us?" He hadn't wanted to ask the question, but he needed a plan before he got there.

Luke glanced over at him. "I told you in the church. If Miss Barnes can't take you, then I'll bring you to the ranch that I'm staying at, and we'll work something out."

"Mrs. Bishop might not let you take us on just a promise. She'll want this woman to sign adoption papers, and that gives her all the legal rights to us. Not you."

Luke kept his eyes locked on the horizon and took a deep breath. "I don't have all the answers, William. All I know is that Miss Barnes is a good person and has plenty of room for all of you. If I had more time, I would have gone back and asked her so you would know for sure. Then she'd have come to town to meet with Mrs. Bishop. You'll just have to trust that this is all going to work out somehow."

William didn't meet Luke's gaze. Instead, he looked out at the wasteland that was about to become their new home. One thing he was proud of was his ability to adapt. He would watch and wait. If things weren't working out, then he would be prepared to flee. He just had no idea where to yet.

•••

They were almost to the ranch when Wolf met them. Sitting on a small rise, the canine assessed the small procession like a king surveying his kingdom. With a joyful yip, he bounded down the slope and broke into a trot next to the carriage. Mrs. Bishop gave a squeal of fright. Carol Anne, wanting to pat the "doggy," tried leaning over the side of the carriage and it was all Ned could do to keep her in the moving vehicle.

Luke was always amazed that the animal knew just the right place to be.

He turned to say something to the boys when he noticed Matthew's face. Damn, but he forgot that this boy was afraid of everything.

"What's the matter, Matthew?" he asked nonchalantly. "Never seen a white wolf before?"

Matthew shook his head. William was looking at Luke with narrow eyes. Smart kid, that one. Would probably grow up to be a lawyer or a con man. Or was that the same thing?

"You must not be worried about the wolf, or you would have shot at it," William said.

Luke gave him a grin before reaching out and putting a hand on Matthew's shoulder. "Good observation. Wolf has been with me since he was a pup. He's free to come and go as he pleases, but he's still a wild animal. Lately, he pleases to stay with me or Miss Barnes." Gently he addressed Matthew. "Trust your instincts. Next time, assess the situation before you become afraid. You're a bright kid. If you let fear take over, then you're going to have a rough time out here, because things are constantly changing. A man needs to think on his feet."

Matthew looked at Luke hesitantly. "I'm better at reading books and learning that way," he said in a small voice.

Luke squeezed his shoulder. "Nothing wrong with book learning, but those books can't replace experience, and you can't get experience until you get out there and try things. Understand?"

Matthew looked thoughtful and nodded.

•••

Angelica heard a wagon and hurried to the window. Subconsciously, she smoothed her hair before she looked out. She frowned when she saw the boys. Luke hadn't mentioned anything about picking up children to take back to the ranch where he worked, not that he had told her much about anything. They seemed quite young to be ranch hands. Maybe they were one of the workers' children and they had come in on the stage.

Grabbing her shawl, she stepped out onto the porch. Luke was pulling the buckboard up to the barn door, and to Angelica's surprise, a carriage stopped in front of where she was standing.

Angelica recognized Ned from town and gave him a smile. There was an older woman in the carriage who gave her an appraising look. Angelica felt as if she was a side of beef put up on the auction block.

Shaking off the feeling, she stepped and waited as Ned helped the visitor down from the carriage, then said, "Hello, I'm Angelica Barnes."

"Mrs. Lucinda Bishop," came the clipped yet not unkind reply.

"Well, Mrs. Bishop, please come in and I'll make you a cup of tea. You must be frozen traveling in this weather." Angelica wasn't sure why, but there was something unsettling in Mrs. Bishop's arrival.

A small girl was sitting on the carriage seat, and she hadn't moved or stopped staring at Angelica since the carriage had arrived.

"Hello there," Angelica said to her. "What's your name?"

"Carol Anne," the little girl breathed.

"Would you like to come in for a little milk tea and some cookies?"

Carol Anne's eyes got as big as dinner plates. "You have cookies?" There was awe in her voice.

"Why I sure do. I made them just this morning." Her book hadn't held her attention, so she had decided to bake instead. Not only did she have cookies, but two fresh loaves of bread. She had regretted making so much food, but now she was thankful that she had something to offer the visitors.

Carol Anne scampered down from the carriage. Mrs. Bishop put a hand on the young girl's shoulder to keep her from running off. "Be on your best behavior," the older woman warned her.

Before she could ask what business, Mrs. Bishop was on, Luke and the two boys joined them. Luke looked like a man that was going to have to drag a cat into a bathtub.

"I see that you ladies have met. Uh…Angelica, may I speak to you alone, in the barn, before you head inside with Mrs. Bishop?"

Angelica gave him a quizzical look, but she smiled and nodded her head. "Why don't you, Carol Anne, and the boys go on in and get warm," she told Mrs. Bishop. "There are apple cookies cooling on the sideboard. Help yourselves. I'll be inside in a few minutes."

Luke put his hand behind Angelica's elbow and steered her toward the relative privacy of the barn. Ned was unharnessing the team and gave them a nod as they passed.

●●●

Now that he was here, Luke saw several flaws in his plan. What if Angelica didn't like children? What if something bad happened to them all out here while he was miles away? It already bothered him that she was out here all alone, but now was he going to have to worry about all of them out here on the open prairie? Why hadn't he thought this through last night when he had been tossing and turning?

He watched as she walked over to check on the horse and cow.

"Those children came out West on the orphan train," he started. "Mrs. Bishop is from the orphanage, and I was hoping that you would take in all three." The words just seemed to form in midair, because he didn't remember fashioning them into a sentence, but he was relieved when they were said.

Angelica turned slowly to look at him, surprise evident in her face. "You want me to take in three orphans? Why? Why would you want them to come live out here in the middle of nowhere? Those children need to be in a town with a school, with other children to play with."

Luke put up a hand to stop her flow of words. "Hear me out," he started to say, but it seemed as if Angelica was building up a head of steam.

"It's to ease your conscience, isn't it? So, you can ride out and not feel guilty for leaving me here because I'm a woman. Let me tell you something, Luke Wells, I've been alone on this ranch for three years, and I'm perfectly capable of taking care of myself!"

He started to protest, but the realization hit him that she was right. Guilty as charged. Bringing those kids out here meant that he could stop worrying about them. Angelica wouldn't be alone, the kids would be together, and he was free to move on. It had been a total selfish act on his part, yet he didn't really regret it.

Without thinking, he stepped forward and gently took hold of her shoulders. "I think that you are one of the most capable women that I've ever met," he said, looking into her startled eyes. "Those kids were going to be split up. There was another couple there. The wife only wanted William and talked about starving or beating him to make him obey. The husband wanted Matthew and Carol Anne, and it wasn't for the chores that she could do." He ignored her intake of breath. "I brought them here to ask for your help. They need you, and I think you need them too, but if you say no, I'll take them with me to Landon's and find them a place there. The decision is up to you."

Maybe it was the close proximity or maybe it was because she trusted the sincerity in his voice, but she seemed to relax a little. It came at a personal cost to admit that he needed her. He became aware that he was still gripping her shoulders. Another place or time, and he would have pulled her toward him and taken the path offered, but this was here and now. Mrs. Bishop and the children were inside the house waiting for them. He wasn't meant to stay, but the children were.

He let go of her and stepped back both mentally and physically. He couldn't read her face as she stared at him for a minute before turning away.

"Let's go meet your guests," she said.

Was that a good thing or a bad thing? He couldn't tell. Hell, the woman had one of the best poker faces that he had ever seen. There was no choice but to follow her to the house and see what she had decided.

•••

Angelica was seething as she made her way toward the house. She wasn't sure if she was angrier with Luke or about the couple in town. If the story was true, then she really couldn't fault Luke for intervening and offering them a better life. She just couldn't shake the feeling that he did it out of guilt, so that he could go back to his friend's ranch and not have to worry about her being out here alone.

I've been doing just fine, she thought to herself, *without a man!*

Stopping on the porch, Angelica straightened her skirt and smoothed back her hair. Then acting as if she had unexpected guests all the time, she opened the door and entered the house.

Mrs. Bishop and the two smaller children were seated in the kitchen at the table. The larger boy was leaning against the wall, next to the door, looking like he wanted to bolt through it. Pasting a smile on her face Angelica fairly marched into the room, Luke several paces behind. A quick glance to the sideboard showed Angelica that none of the cookies had been touched. For some unknown reason, she felt a stab of irritation at that. "I'm sorry for the delay. Let me get you some tea and please. Help yourself to the cookies."

"Do you usually have sweets for breakfast?" Mrs. Bishop wanted to know.

"Of course not." She plunked the plate of cookies into the center of the table. "I only bake them for special occasions. I must have known somehow that you were coming."

The children exchanged looks. Angelica could tell that they wanted to snatch a cookie off the plate, but that they were afraid of what Mrs. Bishop would say. What was it like going without? Needing permission to eat a cookie before lunch? Her mother had always been baking cookies, pies, and such. As children, Angelica and Meda would hang around to sample the goodies as soon as they came out of the oven.

Mrs. Bishop bit her lip as if she wanted to say something but had thought better of it. Then she rearranged herself on her chair before saying, "Miss Barnes, we have several matters to discuss. I trust that Mr. Wells has explained the situation and as to why we are here?"

Luke had already begun the task of making tea, ladling water into the kettle and placing it on the stove to heat. Pulling several mugs from shelves, he placed them on the counter before grabbing the tea pot and spooning in tea leaves. There was nothing left for Angelica to do but stand and face the older woman. Her mother had always taught her to just speak her mind. She wasn't good at pretense.

"Mr. Wells has informed me that these children came in on the stagecoach and you are looking for a home for them. I have to admit, I was surprised that he thought of me to take them." That was an understatement.

Mrs. Bishop looked at Luke. "I was surprised as well."

Sitting down in the open chair, Angelica took a deep breath. "I'm not sure what you need to know. I've lived on this ranch my whole life. I am twenty-three years old."

Mrs. Bishop's back was ramrod straight. "Mr. Wells told me that you live here alone. I have to tell you that that concerns me." She eyed Angelica's sling. "What will you do if the children get sick or hurt?"

It was a fair question, and Angelica took a moment to think about it. "No one can make any promises regarding something like that. We'd deal with what comes along, I imagine."

Mrs. Bishop didn't look pleased with the answer, but she didn't pursue it. It seemed as if something else was on her mind. "If I'm not mistaken, we saw tepees set up behind your barn." She left her unspoken question hanging between them.

The water had boiled, and Luke filled the teapot before setting it and the cups in front of Angelica.

For a moment, anger overcame Angelica, but she tapped it down. Of course, this woman would be afraid of Indians. She was from back East and probably heard stories of all the terrible things Indians did to white settlers. How could she know that they were basically gentle people that were just fighting to keep their way of life?

Grateful for the small distraction, Angelica poured tea for herself and Mrs. Bishop. Placing a small amount in another teacup, she instructed Luke to grab the milk from the outside box, which she used to fill the rest of the cup before adding a small spoonful of brown sugar.

Carol Anne looked surprised when it was placed before her. "I've never had tea before," she said softly, her eyes wide.

Angelica smiled somewhat sadly. She had started drinking milk tea when she was a small girl, with her mother. It was one of her favorite memories.

The boys shook their heads at her silent offer to join. No doubt they thought tea was a women's drink.

"Yes, those are tepees behind my barn," she finally addressed Mrs. Bishop's question. "They've come to harvest the rest of the fruit in the orchard like they have been doing since I was a child. It's mostly Lakota women and children, with a few braves, and I consider them my friends."

The older woman picked up her tea and took a delicate sip before she spoke. "I admit that I have reservations about offering the children to you, but frankly I am running out of time and choices. There is no possibility of them going back East with me and staying together. The headmistress of the orphanage, Mrs. Nixon, will be forced to separate them." She glanced at William before looking back at Angelica. "You seem to be doing well for yourself out here. I spoke with the owner of the hotel, and he sang your praises about all the food you supply them with." She took another sip and sat up straighter, if that was even possible, and then the words came out in a rush. "Are you considering adopting them, or are they going back with me?"

Angelica came around to liking Mrs. Bishop. The woman had a genuine affection for her charges, though she tried not to show it. Glancing at each of the kids, Angelica could see the hooded hope in their eyes. What would have happened to her if her parents had died when she was still a child? Would she have been put in an orphanage if there wasn't any family to take her in? While she had become accustomed to being alone, there were times that it was so quiet she thought she'd go mad for wanting to hear the sound of another human's voice.

She could feel Luke's presence behind her, waiting for her answer. If she said no, he would take them with him when he left, and then she would be all alone again. Could she bear that?

Without any more thought, she turned to address William. "I don't know much about raising children. I was an only child and am used to being by myself. I'm sure I'll make some mistakes and we'll disagree about some things, but you'll have a home together if you want to stay here with me."

The only sound was the ticking of the clock. It was William that spoke first.

"We'd be willing, Miss Barnes. I'll be fourteen in three months. I'm a hard worker and Matthew can help out too. Carol Anne's only four, but she can gather eggs and do some house chores. We'll earn our keep."

His words broke Angelica's heart.

"That's just it," she told him. "You don't need to earn your keep, and for heaven's sake, call me Angelica. Take your cookies, then why don't you go introduce yourselves to Gracie. She's the cow. The horse's name is Ranger."

The children didn't need to be told twice. Grabbing cookies, they were gone within a second.

Angelica turned to Mrs. Bishop.

"Let's figure out the details, shall we?"

CHAPTER SIX

William couldn't sleep. Crawling out of the bed that he'd shared with Matthew, careful not to wake his sleeping brother, he draped a blanket around his shoulders and sat on the edge of the loft, looking down on the darkened room below. His heart was racing. It was a heady feeling knowing that someone in this big world actually wanted the three of them to be part of their family. It was also terrifying. What if this Miss Barnes was like the headmistress of the orphanage? Mrs. Nixon had made his life a living hell. Since he was older, she'd put him to work the first day they'd arrived. His job was to clean the drafty, rundown place from top to bottom, and when he was finished, he had to start cleaning it over again. He scrubbed walls and floors until his fingers were raw and bleeding. Once Matthew tried to help him but had been caught. Mrs. Nixon sent Matthew to another orphanage as punishment. Carol Anne screamed for three days. Nothing could stop her screaming until they had returned Matthew.

William grinned to himself. His sister was only four, but she was smart. She could turn the tears on in a second. She learned quickly how to play the game to survive the orphanage. Once, bullies were trying to steal some of the few possessions that they'd bought with them, Carol Anne maneuvered one of the house mothers into her room, and the thieves had been caught red-handed.

This place was about as different from the orphanage as they could get. Miss Barnes was much prettier than Mrs. Nixon, and much younger. She also could bake. His stomach rumbled at the thought of her cookies. Also, they were the only kids for miles. They didn't have to stand in a long line for the privy or to get their meals. Last night was the first night that the three of them hadn't gone to bed hungry.

William couldn't see the bed in the corner of the room where Miss Barn—Angelica, he corrected himself—and his sister were still sleeping. He figured that Angelica was going to wake up pretty sore. Sleeping with Carol Anne was like sleeping with a champion prize fighter. She was constantly squirming, and her knees and elbows always found their mark. He and Matthew used to roll up blankets to place between them and Carol Anne, but they still always woke up bruised.

He thought that he and Matthew would be sleeping out in the barn, but Angelica had been appalled at that idea. So Mr. Wells had climbed into the small loft, under the low eaves, and brought down a mattress, which Angelica and Carol Anne filled with new hay. Matthew swept out the small space, and William put fresh covers on the bed. This is where she had slept, Angelica told them. She promised to stitch up another mattress as soon as she could so that they each would have their own. He and Matthew slipped in between soft linens that smelled clean, like when their mother was alive. The orphanage bedding had been rough and smelled of the heavy lye soap that they used to wash them once a month.

It was chilly in the small house as William slipped on his shoes and silently made his way down the ladder. Gray light filtered into the kitchen through the windows, creating outlines of the table and chairs. William lit the kerosene lantern in the middle of the table, causing the soft glow to chase away the shadows. He didn't like the dark. Too many things liked to hide in its folds, and those things weren't usually good. He nearly jumped out of his skin when the fat cat he had seen the night before came out from behind the stove and rubbed up against his leg. Its purring echoed in the small room.

The fire had been banked last night, so he stirred the coals before adding some old shingles to feed it. He'd noticed the lack of a woodpile yesterday when he had been out exploring the farm. There was a fair amount of kindling stacked, but he hoped that there was a pile of fire logs that he didn't see somewhere on the property. In the city, the abandoned apartment's walls that they used for shelter were uninsulated, and the windows drafty. It had been difficult to find coal, wood, or anything that they could burn to keep warm. Though this house's sods walls were sturdy and the glass windows intact, William never wanted to feel that cold again.

There was a soft knock on the kitchen door. Before William could open it, Luke stepped inside with an armful of odd-shaped wood. A mild breeze followed his entrance. The cat bolted out the open door.

"It's going to be a warm day," Luke said, dropping the load in the wood box. "Most of the snow has melted off the barn roof and it should dry out quickly. You up for helping me fix it today? I could use a strong back."

William stood a little straighter. He wasn't used to being asked to help. Most grownups just told kids what to do. That Luke had treated him like a man and not a boy filled him with a pride that he hadn't felt in a long time. Not since his parents had been alive.

"I've never done any carpentry before," he told Luke, afraid that that made a difference, "but I'm a fast learner. You just tell me what to do and I'll do it."

Luke gave him a grin. "Go finish getting dressed. Then wake your brother. We'll do the chores, have some breakfast, and then start on that roof."

William nodded and ran back to the loft.

•••

Somehow Carol Anne had managed to turn herself around in the middle of the night, and Angelica awoke to remove the child's foot from her right ear. She'd placed as many rolled-up blankets that she could find in between herself and the little girl, but every move had sent a wave of pain down her arm and through her torso. Angelica finally retreated to get a restless sleep upright in the farthest corner of the bed. Rubbing her protesting ribs, Angelica managed to scoot forward and sit on the side of the bed without waking the girl.

There was a trundle bed somewhere. She'd have to have Luke find it and set it up for Carol Anne, or else she'd have bruises on top of the ones she already had. Slipping her work dress on, Angelica headed for the kitchen. It was warm in the house, and she could smell the coffee brewing. Sitting in a chair, she put on her shoes before throwing her father's jacket around her shoulders and heading outside. Water dripped from the roof as the rising sun's rays began to warm the ground. There were more areas of bare, muddy earth showing than snow.

A flurry of activity behind the barn drew her attention. Tepees were being broken down and packed up. Meda had told her briefly last night that there was a small break of good weather coming and this was when the tribe would travel south to their winter grounds. Meda would stay for another week or so and then meet up with her family.

Angelica was touched that her friend would stay to help her out. She had to admit that the thought of being left alone with three children was a scary proposition. What if they didn't like her and wouldn't do anything she said? William was just as tall as she was and probably a lot stronger, being a boy. What if they decided to run away? She had been an only child and hadn't even considered not listening to her parents. Living out here alone, she was pretty much set in her ways and used to doing things that she wanted to do. Now everything was about to change.

You will do fine, she heard her mother's voice in her head. *Listen to what your head tells you to do and follow it with your heart.*

She pulled her jacket tighter around her.

What if Luke wanted to stay? A voice nagged in the back of her head.

"I wouldn't let him," she said out loud.

Liar, taunted the voice. *If Luke wanted to stay, then you would have the family that you have always wanted. You wouldn't be alone anymore.*

"I'm fine being alone," she said haughtily, but she knew it for the lie that it was.

She had been fine until Luke and his wolf had ridden into her life. They had shown her that she was lonely. The Indians were leaving, and then Luke would leave, followed by Meda. She would be all alone with the children. She'd miss Luke terribly, but he hadn't made her any promises.

Taking a deep breath, she squared her shoulders. She'd never failed at anything she had tried. She wouldn't fail now. Those children needed her. Luke had promised them a home and that was what she would provide.

Feeling better, she turned and made for the back of the house.

●●●

The ridge beam of the barn was solid, Luke saw, as were most of the rafters. Yet, years of storms had ripped off shingles, exposing the sheathing to the weather, causing the wood to soak up water and rot. Luke wondered briefly as to why Angelica's father hadn't built the barn out of sod, but it didn't really matter at this point. The man must have had his reasons. Luke had spent yesterday stripping the shingles, replacing rotted rafters and shoring up some of the others. It had been a safe place to hide while Angelica talked with Mrs. Bishop and for long after the older woman had left. He didn't figure himself to be a coward, but there was something daunting about facing a woman that was angry, especially when that anger was directed towards him. Why was Angelica so mad anyway? He thought she'd be happy to have children around for company. So maybe he hadn't given any of them much of a choice, but he knew that these children belonged here. Deep down, he was pretty sure that Angelica knew it too.

Luke began to remove more shingles and tossed them down to where William and Matthew were waiting. William removed the nails, and

Matthew piled the wood over with the rest of the kindling. With the shingles removed, Luke assessed the full extent of damage. The whole west side needed the sheathing to be replaced. It's about what he figured. Standing on the ladder, he removed the first two sections of boards. William handed up new boards to him. After replacing several courses, he had William join him.

He watched as the young man climbed the ladder and stepped onto the roof. There was something about William that tugged at him. Losing his parents at such a young age must have been devastating, yet the boy had used his brains and kept his family united. Even when they had been sent to the orphanage, the boy had fought to keep his siblings together. That took a lot of character. Unfortunately, without direction and guidance, these kids could have ended up in places that Luke didn't even want to think about. He had done the right thing to bring them here.

Taking a deep breath of clean air, he looked around at the view. This farm sat on some of the best real estate in the Dakota Territories. Angelica's father had known what he was doing when he had settled here. Plenty of water, rich soil, and the depression was just low enough to escape some of the worst winds. It wasn't surprising that Angelica had clung to the ranch.

"Where are the Indians going?" William wanted to know.

Turning, Luke looked down at the small tribe that was loading their horses and carts. Years of conflict and fighting for their way of life had left a shadow over them, yet they maintained a quiet dignity.

"They're heading for their wintering grounds. Angelica lets them take the leftover fruit in the orchard. They dry it and it helps them survive the winter. In return, they bring her kindling."

"Why would she trade with Indians? Everybody knows that Indians can't be trusted. They're just dirty savages."

Luke pinned him with a look. "Meda hears you say that, and she'll box your ears. Indians are just fighting to keep their way of life. They've been kicked off their land and put on reservations. The government has lied to them so many times that they don't trust any of us. There are renegades out there, but mostly they are proud, honest, and decent people."

Grabbing a board, he started to hammer it in place. "I treat every man as my equal until they prove otherwise. You'd do best to remember that you're in Indian Territory, and making friends with the Indians is in your best interest."

William looked at the tribe again. Luke could see the wheels going around in his head as he digested that advice. Damn, he'd like to be around when this kid was old enough to go out into the world. The world wouldn't be ready for him. Kinda reminded him of himself in lots of ways. But he wouldn't be around. He needed to get back to Landon's, then as far away from people as he could possibly get. Somehow that seemed like a bleak future. Unfortunately, it seemed to be his.

"Come on," he said to the boy. "Let's get this roof tight before supper."

●●●

Angelica knew that Luke was working on the barn roof; she could hear the pounding of hammers. She had been surprised that he had bought wood, tar paper, and shingles without discussing it with her first and had confronted him about it last night. In typical Luke fashion, he had told her not to worry about the expense.

"Of course I'm going to worry about the expense!" She had said, hand on her hip. "I planned on replacing it in the spring, after I sold this year's canning and cider."

"It wouldn't have lasted that long," he told her flatly. "I'm not leaving here wondering if you are going to be foolish and head up there again, or worse, have the whole thing fall in while someone is in there. Take the money that you were going to spend and put it towards things that you need for you and the kids."

He'd turned and walked away without giving her a chance to respond. She had stood a long time in the darkened yard, looking up at the stars.

Now, peering out the window, Angelica had been appalled to see William standing on the peak of the barn. It took all of her self-control not to run out there and order him down. The boy was almost fourteen, just shy of a man, she reminded herself. Lakota boys had already started their journey toward manhood around that age. Luke was a smart man; she had to trust that he knew what he was doing, but he could have at least consulted her and asked her permission, since she was now the children's legal guardian.

Slamming a few pots and pans made her feel better, but the noise woke Carol Anne. Angelica looked up to see the small girl trying to carry Purrsistence. Her tiny arms were wrapped around the fat calico's chest, and the feline's back legs were practically dragging on the ground. It appeared that the cat was content, as Angelica could hear purring rumbling into the kitchen. Carol Anne had slept in one of Angelica's mother's old shirts. It was obvious by the meager clothes that the children had brought and their worn condition that something had to be done about replacing them. Sooner than later. Their wardrobe was made for city living, where the buildings were close together and they spent most of their time indoors.

Out here on the prairie, in the winter, they required heavier clothes because of the fierce winds and dropping temperatures.

She was mentally going over all the fabric that she had stashed away for quilts and such when Matthew walked through the door, struggling with several oversized bundles wrapped in brown paper and tied with string.

"What's all this?" she asked, taking a package from him and placing it on the table.

Luke had adjusted the sling so that her arm was at a more comfortable angle, and he'd loosened the bindings on her ribs. It was a blessing to be able to move more freely.

"Luke told me to bring them in. Said to tell you that if you needed anything else, to write it down and he'd see what he could do."

With that cryptic message, Matthew disappeared out the door.

"Can I open one?" Carol Anne asked shyly.

Angelica smiled down at her. The little girl's hair was tangled from her wild movements in the night, and she was dwarfed by the shirt.

"Sure, you can sweetheart. Just be careful, because I don't know if there is anything breakable in there."

Carol Anne nodded solemnly. Dropping the cat, she approached the table and climbed up onto a chair. Very slowly, she unwrapped one of the bigger bundles. A multitude of fabric spilled onto the table, and on closer inspection, they turned out to be ready-made clothes. Picking a dress from the pile, Angelica could tell it was several sizes too big for Carol Anne, but if she took it in, then it would last the little girl several years. Trust Luke to offer the solution to her being limited in her ability to sew. He must have noticed the state of the children's clothes too. There were two nightgowns, stockings, a jacket, several more dresses, and a pair of shoes for Carol Anne. Each of the boys had several pairs of shirts, pants, socks, shoes, and a jacket. There were even hats for the boys. Other bundles contained yards of fabrics that would make anything else that they might need: cottons, linens, homespun, and even a few yards of wool. Thread, yarn, and other sewing items completed the package.

Angelica was overwhelmed. Luke had brought in sacks of flour, sugar, beans, and potatoes, along with spices and other provisions last night. Added to the wealth of goods on the table, the amount was staggering. It seemed as if he'd thought of everything that they might need. There would be plenty of fabric left over to make quilts for each of the boys and for Carol Anne to make one for her hope chest. Angelica's mother taught her to sew when she was just about Carol Anne's age. Now it would be her turn to pass down the tradition. She'd planned to teach any children she was fortunate to have, everything her parents had taught her. Now it seemed as if she would be teaching things sooner than expected. Which reminded her—she needed to find her old school primers. Matthew told her last night that he loved to read, but she would have to find out about their schooling history and set up lesson plans accordingly. Suddenly there seemed to be hundreds of things to do.

"Come on, Carol Anne. Let's put this stuff away and get you some breakfast and a bath. Then I'll measure one of these dresses to take in for you."

Carol Anne looked at the clothes on the table in wonder. "I've never had a new dress before. What if I get it dirty?" There was a hint of panic in the girl's voice.

Angelica sat down and pulled her to her. "These clothes are for you to wear and play in. If they get dirty, then we'll wash them. They are a gift." She wiped the hair out of Carol Anne's face. The girl didn't look convinced.

Angelica sighed. "Let's cook some breakfast. We have a lot of things to do today."

At Carol Anne's nod, Angelica turned back to the kitchen. It didn't take her long to get eggs and potatoes frying in the cast iron skillet. Standing at the stove, her thoughts began to take over. It was sad that a four-year-old was worried about getting dirty. There wasn't anything that she could say that would convince them that this was now their home and that it was okay to be children. They would just have to learn that over time. The boys had looked relieved when she'd told them that they would be sleeping in the loft. Angelica overheard William telling Matthew that he expected to sleep in the barn. Angelica couldn't imagine what the three of them had been through. As much as she wanted to throttle the man, she could understand why Luke was drawn to them.

Placing the food in front of Carol Anne, Angelica went into the pantry for the copper tub. The boys had filled the reservoir in the stove last night, so there was plenty of hot water.

Thankfully it wasn't a heavy tub, and Angelica managed to lift it off its peg on the wall. Rolling it into the kitchen, she set it under the spigot on the stove and filled it a quarter of the way full with the hot water before adding water from the bucket on the sideboard. Testing the temperature, she kept adding cool water until she felt it was just right. Grabbing a bar of soap and a flour sack, Angelica helped Carol Anne into the tub. It was soon obvious that the young girl had no idea how to wash herself.

"Didn't you take baths at the orphanage?" she asked the girl as she washed Carol Anne's short blond hair.

Carol Anne shook her head, sending bubbles and water over the kitchen and Angelica. "I'd stand in a tub and get a bucket poured over me. Then one of the house mothers would wipe me down with soap before another bucket. This is much more fun."

Angelica decided that she would stop asking questions, since she didn't like the answers. It was better that she not know. One of these days, she'd send a blistering letter to tell the orphanage what she thought of their parenting skills. For now, she'd just have to close her mind to the thought that there were other children in their care.

"Angelica?" Carol Anne's voice broke into her thoughts.

"Yes, sweetheart?"

"Are you mad at me? You look mad."

Angelica reached for the flour sack and pulled the girl from the tub. Oh, she was mad all right. "No sweetie, I'm not angry at you. I was just thinking of something sad. But you being clean makes me very happy."

Carol Anne giggled as Angelica rubbed her hair until it stood on end.

"Let's try on those dresses. I think I can manage to take one in so you can start wearing it. Would you like that?"

As Carol Anne squealed with delight, Angelica decided that maybe she wasn't as annoyed with Luke as much as she thought. He was fixing her barn roof, had saved the children from a horrible situation, and bought them more clothes then they had probably had in all of their short lives. Maybe she'd make something special for dinner. Just as a thank you, of course.

Liar, said that nagging voice.

"Oh, shut up," she muttered, turning to follow Carol Anne.

CHAPTER SEVEN

The sun was setting as Luke hammered the last nail in place. It had taken a lot of work, but he was happy with the outcome. This roof had bothered him since the first day he saw it. The hole was a constant reminder of just how dangerous living out here could be. He didn't want to think how different things could have turned out if Wolf hadn't made him turn around. Maybe, if infection didn't set in or her ribs didn't move, Angelica might have been okay. Most likely she would have become a cripple, the way her arm had been broken. Meda had arrived not too long after he did, but that was no guarantee that Angelica would have been fine.

His thoughts shifted to the kids. Without the delay of attending to Angelica, he would have finished his errands and been back at Landon's ranch by the time they'd arrived. Where would they have ended up? Fate was a funny thing.

William was inside the barn starting the evening chores, and Matthew was nowhere in sight. Luke, left alone on the roof, watched the sun set, and it filled him with a sudden sense of loss. It was the end of one day and the beginning of the night. It seemed to signify that it was time to leave this place. The longer he stayed here, the harder it was thinking about going. He had responsibilities. The debt he owed Landon wasn't repaid yet. He'd accepted that the horrors of war would never let him settle down and forget. So why was that bothering him now? The answer was clear. He could be happy here if he let himself. Angelica was everything he was looking for in a wife—a partner. The kids were ready-made for them, though he would like a child or two of his own. Unfortunately, he knew that it was never going to happen. All of them deserved better than the shadow of a man he'd become.

Glancing at the house, he could see smoke rising lazily from the stove pipe, and a soft glow of light lit the windows. Everything he ever wanted was within reach, and the thought made him break out into a cold sweat. Running a hand over his face, he made a mental note to finish up anything left tomorrow and get back on the road to Landon's ranch as fast as he could. They'd forget about him in a couple of weeks. Maybe someday, he'll stop in and see how they'd grown up. Maybe not.

With one last look at the horizon where the sun had disappeared, taking its warming rays with it, he climbed down the ladder. His brain was already starting to distance himself from the occupants of the hours; sadly, it would take his heart much longer.

•••

William could tell that there was something different about Luke. Up on the barn roof, Luke had been relaxed and talked to him like he was a man, an equal. He'd felt important, as if his opinions and effort meant something. Now the older man was quiet and reserved.

Entering the house, they found Angelica in the act of pulling a small roast from the oven. In the pan, potatoes, carrots, and onions swam in the juice from the meat. It smelled like heaven to William. Carol Anne looked almost unrecognizable in a store-bought dress; her clean hair held back with bows. She twirled and laughed, showing off her new clothes.

"There are things for you and Matthew too!" she told him, dragging them both over to a chair. "Luke got them in town." The little girl clapped her hands together as she laughed.

Luke was solemn when William thanked him, but William didn't think that that was what was bothering him.

Now, sitting at the kitchen table, William watched the way Luke avoided looking at Angelica. So that was it. William let out his breath and relaxed his shoulders. If Luke was sweet on Angelica, then maybe he would stick around. He'd told them that he had to go back to some ranch, but maybe now Luke would go and do what he needed to and come back. Then they could be a family. That thought made William feel guilty. He had a mother and father. They'd been a family. He wasn't looking for someone to replace them. He just needed someplace to be safe with his brother and sister until he was older and could take care of them. It was best if he didn't get too comfortable here. Best if he kept to his original plan of working off any debts that they accrued. Of course, he knew that Carol Anne wouldn't want to leave Angelica. Angelica was a kind person; it was hard not to like her. Carol Anne would just have to understand that when it came time to go, she would have to say goodbye.

He felt better as he dug into his dinner. After all, he had worked up an appetite today. That should have paid off some of the debt of those clothes.

•••

"I'll be leaving the day after tomorrow." Luke hadn't meant to say it bluntly like that, but there it was; he couldn't take back the words now. He wasn't sure if it was relief or dread that he felt.

Angelica had been in the process of putting her fork to her mouth but placed it back on her plate. "I see," she said.

I see? What the hell did that mean? Is she happy or upset that he was leaving? And what difference does it make? You've made up your mind to leave. It doesn't matter what she thinks.

But it did matter. If Angelica begged him to stay, there with her; would he? Was he strong enough to open his heart and care for her and the children?

You can't fear losing something that's not there to lose.

Luke couldn't bear the thought of her or the children contracting cholera, measles, diphtheria, or any of the other diseases that could wipe them all out in the blink of an eye. He knew that he was being selfish, yet he had watched too many once-healthy boys die. Not just from the wounds of a senseless war, but by infections and diseases that he had no defense against. All of his so-called medical knowledge hadn't helped them; instead, it had just prolonged their suffering and agony. There was no way he could go through that hell again. It was best if he got on his horse, finished his business at Landon's, and moved on, putting this place as far behind him as he could. Physically anyway.

Now, looking around the table at the five pairs of eyes staring at him, he felt like a coward. Meda was the only one looking at him with understanding. It seemed that she knew that he was running away but wasn't going to hate him for it. Carol Anne didn't understand the implications of what he had said, but she could obviously feel the tension in the room. Luke couldn't bear the confusion in the little girl's eyes.

"Did we do something wrong?" Matthew asked.

Luke gave a half-hearted grin. "No, you didn't do anything wrong. It's just I was on an errand for someone, and they were expecting me back a few days ago. I finished the barn roof sooner than expected because I had a great crew. There's a few things that I need to finish up tomorrow, and then

I have to leave." The words tore at him.

He focused on a spot above Angelica's head.

"When will you be back?" Matthew wanted to know.

When would he be back? How did he tell them that it would be a long time, if ever? He glanced at Meda for help.

She seemed to ponder the plea that was in his eyes before responding. "It is dangerous to be out on the plains in the winter. Most likely we would not see him before spring."

That seemed to appease Matthew and Carol Anne. Luke was relieved. It was such a simple answer. The plains were unpredictable any time of year, as many settlers had lost their lives in unexpected blizzards. Even the trains shut down from October to April so as to not be stranded.

William was looking intently at him, and by the look on his face, he wasn't fooled by the simple explanation. Neither was Angelica. Luke knew that they would never understand why he couldn't stay. He wasn't ready to share the horrors that he had seen and suffered. Maybe he never would be. Men had put shotgun barrels in their mouths and pulled the triggers to escape the memories that he was trying to forget. While he had never attempted suicide, he had courted with death. It dulled the memories and pain to know that he was just inches away from being free.

Somehow, Luke made it through the rest of the meal without having to make any more explanations or any promises.

●●●

The children insisted on washing the dishes, so Angelica took the opportunity to go out to the barn and check on the animals. The familiar smells and sounds soothed her. Ranger came out for the carrot that she had brought him, and as she stroked his head, she had an overwhelming urge to cry. Luke hadn't made her any promises, and she had known from the beginning that he wasn't there to stay. So why did it seem so wrong that he was leaving?

●●●

Luke was putting the last stitch in the incision on what was left of a young soldier's leg when the cannonball tore through the tent, shattering one of the support beams. Splinters showered the men that lay below on the surrounding cots, causing them to scream in pain as they were impaled by the shards.

The force of the blast threw Luke backwards, knocking the breath out of him as he hit the hard dirt. Sitting up, he cradled his head for a moment as his ears rang from the explosion. There was no other sound.

How did a cannonball make it from the battlefield to the hospital tent? The army hospital where he was located, just outside the battle at Shenandoah Valley in Virginia, was set up to be far enough away, several miles in fact, to be relatively safe but close enough to get the wounded back quickly.

Luke's chest felt like it was on fire, and he could feel the splinters working themselves deeper as he moved. Feeling dazed, he looked at the blood that still covered his hands from the amputation that he had just finished and was surprised to see fresh spots dripping onto them. Slowly feeling at his face, he could feel a wound on his right cheek that began to drip faster after he brushed at it.

Other noises began to penetrate the ringing in his ears, and he barely had time to gain his feet when Union soldiers stormed into the tent. Luke was paralyzed in disbelief as the Union soldiers began to shoot, stab, and slice the throats of the wounded as they lay in their cots. This was out and out murder. These casualties had been no threat. Some of the wounded were first-year cadets, barely fifteen years old. Code of conduct should have made them prisoners of war.

Smoke from gunpowder filled the tent and Luke's lungs. He stumbled forward, unable to see five feet in front of him. His foot caught on something, and he looked down into the face of the boy he'd just finished surgery on. Blood trickled from the boy's mouth. Half of his chest had been blown away.

Anger and rage seared through Luke's veins. Without thinking, he rushed forward. Grabbing a Union soldier that had trained his rifle on another patient, Luke spun him around and smashed his elbow into the man's nose. Then grabbing the rifle as the man fell to the floor, he used it as a club, taking four more soldiers down before they realized that he was there. Reason had disappeared. This was a fight for survival. Later, he would berate himself for going against the Hippocratic Oath of doing no harm, but for now, he was fighting for those boy's lives.

Pandemonium filled the small area. It was hard to separate the wounded from the enemy. Rifle shots rang out everywhere and men were screaming. Bodies littered the floor as the tent began to collapse around them.

Luke felt the blade of a bayonet slip into his back. The pain was searing. Slipping on the blood-soaked dirt, he managed to turn and pull his attacker to him, breaking the man's neck. As his victim fell, he was stunned to see that the boy couldn't have been more than sixteen.

A blast went off near Luke's head. He could feel himself falling, yet he felt no pain. Bodies cushioned his fall, and as the blood seeped into his clothes, he lost consciousness.

•••

Luke bolted from his pallet and crouched, ready to flee, every nerve ending on alert. Sweat rolled down his back and his breath came in painful gasps. He could still feel the blade as it sliced through his skin and hit his rib.

Would this memory ever stop haunting him?

It had been months since it had been that vivid. He could still smell the gunpowder smoke, feel the bullet that had grazed his scalp, and see the lifeless bodies of those boys. They had thought that he was dead. By the time his troop had shown up, there was nothing but carnage. He had been the only survivor. The Army had shipped him out as soon as it was safe, gave him an honorable discharge, and called him a hero. The problem was he didn't feel like a hero; he felt like a murderer.

The Union Army had been in retreat when it had come across the makeshift hospital, he had found out later.

Luke sat back on the pallet and willed his breathing to slow. Reaching into his saddlebag, he pulled out a fresh shirt. He was yanking it over his head when he noticed movement from the doorway. He had slept on the kitchen floor in case Angelica or one of the children had needed him. Concern filled him when he saw Angelica.

"What's wrong?" he asked, standing up.

Her long brown hair had been braided, and it hung over her shoulder. She had grabbed her shawl and had draped it over her nightgown.

"I heard you yell out," she said.

Pulling the shawl tighter around her, she stepped into the room and sat down at the kitchen table.

"Talk to me, Luke. I know that you've been running from some horrible memories from the war, but the war has been over for ten years. Isn't it time to let those memories go? Find some peace?"

She would never understand, and he knew that he wouldn't be able to handle the look of loathing and disgust on her face if she ever found out the truth about him. This place, with her and the children, was what was right with the world. How could he put those images into her head and take away the innocence? He couldn't. The memories were eating at him, and the guilt was like a lead weight around his neck.

When he didn't respond, she continued. "We had travelers who had fled from the war. They told of all sorts of awful things. I can't imagine living with those memories, but I know that God doesn't give you more…"

He cut her off. "God? What do you know about what God does? You've lived a sheltered life, Angelica. How many men's blood stains your hands? Did you ever wonder why you survived while the God you know so well let your brothers, sisters, and parents die?" Raking his fingers through his hair, he could feel the anger taking over. "I watched innocent boys cut down before they even had a chance to grow a beard. I held their lives in *my* hands, not God's."

The words came out harshly in the darkened room, and she flinched. He began to pace the small kitchen. How did he explain the horrors that he had seen, that he had done? How god-fearing men could shoot each other in fields and leave the wounded to die slow, agonizing deaths? For what, money? The bondage of another human being for profit? Where was her God when those boys were getting their throats slit as they lay helpless? Luke knew. God had abandoned them and had let the devil dictate.

The room was becoming unbearably hot, and the walls felt as if they were starting to move in on him. It had been foolish to stay here, with her. That's why he had to ride out and never come back. It was better this way. She could never understand the demons that followed him, that clawed at his soul and pulled him to a place that sometimes he feared that he would never come back from.

Turning back to face her was one of the hardest things he'd ever done, but he owed her some honesty. "People seem to think that I should get over the war, but the memories haunt me. They are a part of me, of who I am. I can't explain it to you, and I'm not going to try." He began to pace again. "I'll be going, and I'm not planning on coming back. I know that it's a rotten thing to bring you three children and then take off, but those children need you. You might not admit it now, but you need them too."

He paused, but she remained motionless.

"I'll set up a bank account in town for you. That way if you or the children need anything, you'll have some money."

That statement did get a rise out of her. Eyes flashing, she stood. "Keep your money. I've got plenty of my own. I'm asking you to stay with me. Not because of the children, but because you want to. I thought that we'd built something between us these last two weeks, and I was hoping that you felt it too."

Her eyes bored into his. He was the first to look away. The hope in her face tore at him like nothing else could, and he couldn't bear to face it.

She seemed to understand that it was over and turned toward the door.

She stopped in the doorway, with her back to him. "I feel sorry for you, Luke. You are a kind, generous man, but for some reason, you don't think that you deserve to have anything good in your life. Forgive yourself. War makes men do horrible things, usually because they have no other choice." Her voice became a whisper. "I hope you figure out that you're human, just like the rest of us. Come back and visit if you ever find peace." With that, she left him alone.

He felt like a jackass, though not nearly as useful.

•••

Angelica didn't sleep at all. Mortification rose up within her. She had asked Luke to stay, and he hadn't said a word. How was she going to face him today? What must he think of her boldness?

Carol Anne moved in her sleep and threw an arm over Angelica. The child had been tucked into the trundle bed, but sometime during the early hours, she'd crawled into bed with her. They would have to break that habit if Angelica ever hoped to get a good night's sleep again.

Angelica heard Luke depart the house minutes after she had exited the kitchen last night but hadn't heard him return. Had he left for good? What would the children think if he hadn't said goodbye to them?

He told her that he wasn't ever coming back, then in the next sentence, he'd offered her money like she was some hired governess. His words had left a bitter echo in her ears, and Angelica squeezed her eyes closed at the memory of them. She felt like the doomed heroine who was fated to fall for the wrong man in a love story that didn't have a happy ending.

Oh, for heaven's sake, she imagined her mother's voice saying. *You have three children to think about now. Stop feeling sorry for yourself and get up and face the day.*

Angelica missed her mother's no-nonsense approach to life. Lillian had been a schoolteacher back East when she had met Robert Barnes. They'd met at a lecture at one of the universities.

"Your father was a scoundrel in those days," her mother used to say, laughing. "I wouldn't have anything to do with him, but he finally grew on me."

Her father would wink and reply, "Your mother liked scoundrels. She just wanted me to earn her hand."

Their marriage had seemed so effortless. Hardly a cross word would pass between them.

Luke was right; she had lived a sheltered life, but that didn't mean that she was naïve to the evils out there. It just meant that she was content with

| 86 |

the blessings that she'd been given.

Carol Anne turned over again and almost pushed Angelica from the bed. Might as well get up and start breakfast, she thought, before she landed on the floor. Her body was recovering, but she was still sore in some places, and Carol Anne wasn't helping the healing process with her wild sleeping habits. Being careful not to wake the slumbering child, Angelica got out of bed and dressed quickly.

As Angelica stoked the fire to life, her eyes fell to the blankets of Luke's makeshift bed. He would be leaving tomorrow morning, if he hadn't already. She had certainly hit a raw nerve with him last night, and the depth of his suffering surprised her. It would seem that war was not just fought physically on the battlefield but also mentally reached deep into the soul. She'd seen a very different man than the one that she had come to know over the last two weeks. He'd talked of holding men's lives in his hands; his grief had almost been palpable. There was no doubt that he was tormented with guilt and regret.

Angelica stepped to the window, yet all she could see was her reflection in the dim light of the lantern's reflection on the glass, as it was still dark outside. Well, Luke might not believe in God, but she did. She would have to have faith that he would find forgiveness and peace. Taking a moment before the children awoke, she bowed her head and said a prayer.

•••

Jean Claude's hip joint popped as he heaved himself from the pile of furs and blankets on the floor that he used as bedding. With his breath visible in the cold air, he moved to the small stove and stirred the ashes. Throwing in some kindling, Jean Claude turned and surveyed the room. The small area was crowded, with furs and hides covering most of the available surfaces. He'd won the shack from an old prospector in a poker game over twenty years ago. Of course, the old miner had sworn that it was a cabin in great condition, not a rotting shack that tilted to one side and was one breezy gust from collapsing. Trading a rifle for an Indian tepee, he'd used the buffalo hide to replace the front and most of the side walls. It served its purpose.

The kindling was crackling, so he opened the stove again and threw in some buffalo chips. Ignoring the strong, foul odor, Jean Claude made his way to the tent opening and stood just outside to relieve himself. Adjusting his pants, he turned back inside to grab some dried jerky before shrugging into his coat and heading out to the pasture.

Frost crunched under Jean Claude's boots as he walked. He hated to admit it, but he was feeling all of his fifty-four years.

His muscles ached from loading the wagons this week with the wood for Angelica. He'd lived his entire life outdoors trapping, fishing, and living off the land, not cutting and hauling logs.

Tearing off a piece of the jerky with his teeth, he wondered why he made the journey every year.

Reaching the pasture gate, which consisted of two old iron bars and a spring mattress tied across them, Jean Claude swore as it swung back and forth in the light breeze. A quick glance around didn't reveal any oxen, or his horse for that matter, and there were no tracks in the frosty grass, so the animals must have gotten out last night. They could be anywhere. Jean Claude swore louder. He'd have to wait for Nate to arrive and send the boy out to look for them.

●●●

Nate was late. Jean Claude had specifically told him that he wanted to leave about an hour before dawn, and now here it was practically noon. Jean Claude hadn't listened to the boy's whining excuse but had blistered the younger man's ears with his rage before sending him out to find the missing oxen. Thankfully, they hadn't gone too far and were brought back fairly quickly and hitched to the wagons.

Jean Claude was just climbing up onto the wagon seat when Jeb, the owner of the trading post where Jean Claude sold his furs, arrived on his horse. Setting the handbrake on the wagon, Jean Claude waited, no emotion showing on his face. He knew why Jeb was there, and he silently cursed. Had Nate been on time, they would have been gone hours ago, and Jeb would have had to wait to talk to him until he'd gotten back.

Last winter had been tough for trapping. With soldiers and miners coming into the territory, game was getting scarce, causing Jean Claude to travel further north to set his traps. Oftentimes, it was over a week or even two before he could get back and check on them. Several times, he'd found that predators had eaten what was in his trap before he could get back. This winter seemed even less promising. It was the same with the firewood.

Jean Claude spat on the ground next to the wagon. The army was cutting down trees to build forts everywhere, and the miners were taking the rest to build shacks on their claims. Now here he was, over two weeks late in loading and delivering the wood for Angelica, and now he had to deal with Jeb.

●●●

Jeb reined his horse so that he was facing Jean Claude yet far enough away from the wide horns of the oxen. Even from that distance, Jeb could smell the stench coming off the trapper, and his nose twitched. He took in Jean Claude's greasy, unkempt dark hair and his untrimmed beard that looked like pieces of food were hanging from it. Jeb also noticed that the buffalo coat that he had once admired was dull and spotted with stains. Pursing his lips, he could feel Jean Claude's beady eyes on him. Best that he say what he came here to say and get back to his store. "I've come to see if you have the furs that you owe me," he said, his voice slightly too loud.

Jean Claude spat again, causing Jeb's horse to take a step back. The movement caused another wave of odor to head his way. Jeb waited a moment, and when it was clear that Jean Claude wasn't going to answer, the storekeeper felt his face flush. "I need those furs by next week, or I'll be looking for someone else that can deliver."

Barely waiting for Jean Claude's nod of response, Jeb turned his horse around and without a backwards glance, he headed back to town.

•••

Seething, Jean Claude released the wagon's brake and snapped the reins to get the oxen moving. Settling his buffalo robe around him, he led the way out of the barnyard.

Halfway to Angelica's, one of the wagon wheels came off, then Jean Claude was up to his ass in axle grease. By the time he had fixed the wheel and set out again, the sun was halfway across the sky.

It was thirty miles to Angelica's, and the best that the ox could do with such a heavy load was about eighteen miles a day. He'd hoped to get an early start and be there by lunchtime tomorrow, but it looked as if this trip was going to take an extra day. If only Angelica wasn't so stubborn and would just come live with him. Times were definitely changing. Once he could have had his pick of women. Back about ten years ago, he was living with a Chippewa squaw, and the old widow Anderson was practically begging him to come live with her. If it hadn't been for her nosey nephew, he would have been living on easy street right about now. Her husband had been wealthy and had left her well off.

The oxen plodded dutifully forward. He had sent Nate ahead. Once it started to turn dark, the boy would make camp, and Jean Claude would catch up to him there. That was, if he didn't have any more problems with wheels and such.

Not having much else to do, his mind began to wander. Looking back at the past, it seemed like his good luck had changed to bad after meeting Lillian Barnes. He could see her in his mind, clear as day. Angelica's mother had been a real beauty. Of course, Angelica was attractive, but she didn't seem to glow the way Lillian had. Lillian was full of fire, just how Jean Claude liked his woman. Unfortunately, that fire was directed at her husband. She had seen how Jean Claude had looked at her, and she had told him in no uncertain terms to stay away from her and her family. But they had needed each other. The sale of the calves helped bring in enough money that he could keep trapping, while the Barnes needed the milk and wood that he could supply them to survive. Then Lillian and her husband had died. Jean Claude had thought Angelica would turn to him in need, but she had been too damn self-sufficient. He had shown up, but she had kept him to the original bargain. It was crucial that he get Angelica to agree to let him take control of the ranch. His funds were running low, and with Jeb breathing down his neck, there weren't too many options left. Besides, since Lillian was gone, Angelica would be the closest thing to her that he could possess.

It was dark now, and he could see the glow of the fire up ahead. Slapping the whip across the oxen's back, he turned them towards it.

•••

The ranch had been neglected without a man around to do the heavier work. With William and Matthew's help, Luke had plowed the field and put in winter rye, which would be tilled under in the spring to replace the nutrients the new garden would need. The chicken coop was cleaned out, Ranger's bridle stitched and oiled, and a new hole dug for the privy to be moved. Luke had noticed the night before that the buckboard had a damaged wheel. Finding some old tools from the barn, he showed the boys how to fix it. Then he taught them how to grease and oil the wheels and tools to keep them in good repair. William and Matthew had caught on to the work quickly, eager to help and learn.

At sunset, Luke had sent the boys inside to eat while he began gathering more tools. They had protested, but he had stopped them with a look. He needed to start separating himself from them and Angelica. Problem was that his heart ached even though he knew that this was for the best.

•••

Meda found Luke in the far pasture, putting in the last post. The fence had rotted, and it was a surprise that the horse and cow hadn't wandered off.

He hadn't heard her approach; she just seemed to materialize next to him. Luckily his rifle was some distance away or he might have shot her before realizing who she was. A lantern cast a small pool of light onto his work area, and Meda's face was lost in the shadows.

"You are leaving at daybreak." It was a statement, not a question.

"Yep."

She studied him for a moment. "The wolf spirit came to me again last night. It spoke of you. It told of a great battle that had wounded your soul."

Luke flinched. Meda must have overheard him talking with Angelica about the war.

She continued, "The spirit has guided you here for a reason. There is something bad coming. You must stay."

A strong gust of wind came from nowhere as if to give emphasis to her statement. The lantern flickered wildly, and he could have sworn for a second her face was that of a wolf. Then the flame stabilized, and the illusion disappeared.

Shoving the post into the ground, he turned away from her dark eyes. "I have no special powers, Meda. I'm just a man haunted by ghosts."

Luke's body was tired, but his mind was racing. It wasn't that he didn't believe in visions and such. Several times he had come across a person that claimed they could see the future, and damn if they weren't right on a few predictions. It was just that they spoke in riddles. Their supposed vision wasn't exactly what they foretold. Some old woman had stopped him in the street several months back and had told him that he would find all the riches life had to offer, but he needed to beware of the two predators. He was still trying to figure that one out.

Shoveling the dirt back into the hole around the post gave him something to do. "I can't stay, Meda. I'm not good for them, and most likely I'm the evil that you speak of. I'll only cause them pain."

Meda snorted. "I only see pain when you leave. She and the children have no defenses against this. You must stay, or their fates will haunt your soul too."

He felt that statement slam into his gut. Bending forward against the pain, he grimaced. His guilt knew no bounds, but his soul's dance card was full. Turning his head, he glared at her. "That was unfair. I brought those children here, to her, to be safe. Don't tell me that I brought them into danger because some spirit told you that. You know nothing about what haunts my soul. I have no power. Go back to your spirits and tell them to go foretell someone else's fortune, because I'm not interested." His voice was low and savage.

Meda met his stare unblinkingly. Then she nodded and turned, disappearing as silently as she had arrived.

Luke spiked the shovel into the ground and ran his hands through his hair. He should have left this morning, but there had been too many things that needed to be fixed and finished. Also, he had to make sure that the boys could handle some of the responsibilities of running the ranch. Now he had the weight of some spirits warning to carry around with him.

Looking up at the stars, he suddenly felt older than his thirty-five years. It seemed that he had lived twice that long. Gathering up the tools, he headed back toward the barn.

CHAPTER EIGHT

Luke was hitching the horses to the wagon that he had packed the night before when the sun's first rays appeared. As the soft pinkish, gold light reflected off the windows, Luke couldn't help but remember last night. It had been past midnight when he'd gone into the kitchen and found the plate of food that Angelica had kept warm for him. That surprised him. His experience was when women were upset, they generally didn't do nice things for the person they were upset with. He'd eaten even though he hadn't been hungry. Going through the motions, his mother would have said. Thankfully, she wasn't here, because she likely would have had much more to say.

As much as he didn't want to leave, Luke was worried about getting back to Landon and Landon's second wife, Mary, who was pregnant and due within the month. Landon was a childhood friend, and they had been put into the same regiment when the war started. Landon hadn't owned slaves, not believing in the practice even though he was a farmer. He had told Luke that he fought because he figured it was his duty as a Southerner. They'd looked out for each other through those four long years, like brothers. Luke had taken several bullets out of Landon, while it had been Landon who'd searched for him that day in the hospital tent and found a doctor to save him.

Like himself, Landon hadn't been able to go back to South Carolina. Landon's family farm had been burnt to the ground and the Reconstruction had taken over, leaving him nothing.

Luke had a chance encounter with an old neighbor several years before and learned that Landon was settled in the Dakota's running a cattle ranch. He'd also learned that Landon's wife and son had died in childbirth and that Landon was crazy with grief. Luke had been unable to face his friend, so he sent a telegram voicing his condolences and moved on to the next town.

Several years later, Luke was surprised when a Pinkerton detective had tracked him down to deliver a telegram from Landon informing him that he'd remarried and was asking for a promise for Luke to be there for the birth of his unborn child. That had been seven months ago. He'd agreed without hesitation.

Luke hadn't been sure if his surviving had been a miracle or a curse, but he would honor the debt that he owed his friend and make sure that Landon's baby was delivered safely.

•••

William was the first to emerge from the house. He carried a milk bucket and a determined look on his face. Luke mentally prepared for the conversation that he knew was coming.

"I want a promise from you," William began, surprising him.

"I don't make promises."

William was not to be derailed. "Well, you need to make this one. You said that you'd be back in the spring to check up on us and would take us somewhere if we didn't like it here."

Luke nodded. It had seemed an easy way to convince the children to come with him at the time. Now he had regrets. Promises weren't something he gave out lightly. Unfortunately, he hadn't thought that one through. It was going to be painful to come back and see Angelica. What if she had found a husband while he was gone? He'd rather not know. However, he had made the promise and would follow through with it, no matter what.

"Yes, I made that deal, and I will keep it. As soon as the danger of snow is over, then I'll come and see how you're doing."

William held out his hand and they shook on it.

•••

They had all come out to say goodbye to him, except Angelica. Everything in Luke's being was urging him to get started, but yet he tarried. Something elemental inside him needed to see her one last time. He was deciding whether he should go and find her or just ride out when she appeared at the kitchen door. Her image was already burned into the fabric of his being, yet he still caught his breath at the sight of her.

Her brown hair was pulled back, and a riot of curls ran down her back.

She wore a blue dress that had a collar of white lace. The color of the dress made her brown eyes more vivid—or was that just his imagination?

She stepped back and let him into the kitchen. Now that the time had come to leave, he wasn't sure what to say. It was Angelica that broke the silence. "I'll be forever grateful that you were passing by when you did and for finding the children and bringing them here." Her voice was soft. "I packed you some things to take back with you. There's some of the cheese that you helped me make. You'll need to let it age. Also, there's some apple cider and apple vinegar." She indicated some bundles on the kitchen table. "The small package is for your breakfast. I figured you'd be hungry in a while."

He had spent most of last night practicing what he was going to say at this moment, but he realized that there were no words that would make her understand. They, her and the children, were better off without him.

Purrsistence ambled into the kitchen just then and rubbed up against his leg. Damn, he was even going to miss the cat. Reaching down, he scratched her head. Purring, she looked up at him with trusting eyes.

"I have to go," Luke said, straightening up. "I promised William that I would stop back in the spring and check on you. I'll keep that promise, but if you need me, I'll be wintering at my friend's ranch. It's about a day's ride to the north."

This was harder than he thought it would be. Angelica didn't say anything, just nodded and began to gather the bundles of food. He had expected her to tell him that he was being a coward or rail at him about leaving her alone with three children. That he could have handled, not this polite, impersonal conversation.

They had reached the buckboard, and Luke stowed the packages in the back. Without thinking, he reached out and cupped her cheek before pulling her forward and kissing her forehead, not daring to kiss her lips. Stepping back, he fiddled with his hat. "Someday you'll realize that I did you a favor by not staying. I wish you the best." Then he placed the hat on his head and climbed into the buckboard.

Without a backwards glance, he flicked the reins, and the wagon lurched forward.

•••

It took every last ounce of Angelica's self-control not to chase after him. If only he would glance back, at least once, to see her standing there—but he never did. Her hair whipped her face, but she paid it no mind. Somehow, she knew that things would never be the same again. This man had changed everything. There were reminders of him everywhere she looked; it was going to be hard to forget him. But she didn't want to forget him. She wanted him here, to stay with her and the children, not be just a memory. Unfortunately, he didn't feel the same.

A small hand touched hers, breaking her vigil. Looking down, she saw Carol Anne staring up at her. The little girl's eyes were round, and she was frowning. "Will he ever come back?" the small girl asked.

Angelica glanced at the now deserted road before tucking the small hand into hers and forcing a smile. "I don't know, sweetie. I hope so."

Silently, she said goodbye to him and sent it on the wind toward the direction that he had disappeared. Then turning, she headed back to the house, still holding Carol Anne's hand. They entered the kitchen, and Carol Anne ran ahead into the other room. It was then that Angelica saw the book lying on the table. It looked expensive, with its leather cover and gold embossed lettering. She reached for it gingerly, afraid that it was just an illusion, but her fingers touched its smooth surface. He had left her a gift. That was surprising, since the man wanted to disappear from their lives without a trace. Her hand caressed the cover slowly; savoring the moment then opened it to the first page. There, in Luke's bold handwriting, he had written her a note.

For Miss Angelica Barnes, for the occasion of her 23rd birthday. Fondly, Luke Wells MD

He had put the date under his name.

She stared at the word "fondly." Was that all he thought of her? Tears came to her eyes, and she had an overwhelming urge to fling the book across the room. Instead, she hugged it to her chest. The only gifts she'd ever received had been from her parents or relatives. That he had taken the time and money to buy it filled her with a bittersweet sadness. This was one of those gifts that she would treasure into her old age. Maybe someday she could look back and say that she remembered him fondly as well, but right now, there were too many emotions to pick just one. Anger, resentment, and disappointment fought with hurt, sorrow, and grief over his leaving. They could have been happy together if he had just taken the chance, she was certain of that. A tear slipped down her cheek.

Hearing footsteps outside, she made a quick swipe at her cheek and turned toward the stove.

William and Matthew came in with the milk and eggs from the morning chores. The few minutes that it took to strain the milk gave her some time to regain her composure. She slipped the book onto the shelf with her mother's cookbook.

The boys paid no attention to her as they helped themselves to the plate of fried eggs and toast that was in the warming oven. It was amazing how much growing boys ate, Angelica silently marveled. She made a mental note to hatch some chicks to keep up with the obvious demand. Maybe she should get another cow as well.

Calling for Carol Anne, she filled a plate for the child. It was somewhat comforting to watch the children sit down and eat.

"Aren't you gonna have breakfast?" William asked.

Angelica had no appetite, so she shook her head. "I'll have something later."

He gave her that assessing look that she was beginning to recognize.

"I promise," she said.

He didn't look quite convinced, but he let the subject drop. She knew that he was going to watch her, though, to make sure that she wouldn't pine away. It was kind of sweet, knowing that he was looking out for her.

Since the boys had already done the morning chores, Angelica began to make a mental list of what needed to be done. Today seemed like a good day to see where the children stood in their studies, since she had found her old school primers. It was going to be a long winter, and the sooner that they settled into a comfortable routine, the better.

●●●

Luke was halfway to Landon's when he realized that Wolf wasn't with him. That wasn't surprising. Wolf came and went as he pleased. It was just that he was feeling lonely on this ride, and he would have welcomed the company. He knew that he was doing the right thing, yet every fiber in his body was shouting for him to stop and turn around. To head back to Angelica's.

Pulling up on the reins, he looked out at the barren landscape. The early snow had flattened the prairie grass, turning it brown. Clouds blocked out the sun, making the countryside even more depressing—or maybe it was just reflecting his mood. There was nothing as far as the eye could see. Empty. A vast wasteland that only allowed visitors to pass through, never allowing them to grab hold and flourish, or at least it seemed that way to Luke.

Setting the wagon's brake, he climbed down and paced in front of the horses. He'd spent the last ten years drifting from one location to the other, and it had been enough for him. Why was Angelica so different? There'd been places before this that he'd never had a problem leaving. He'd known several women that he could have been happy with, but in the end, he always moved on. They cried and pleaded, but it hadn't affected him. He'd made them no promises. Yet Angelica hadn't cried or pleaded; she just wished him well, even making him lunch. So why couldn't he get the image of her watching him leave out of his mind? He hadn't needed to turn around to know that she was standing there; he had felt it in every cell of his body. He'd felt her disappointment and pain as if it were his own.

Climbing back into the wagon and turning it toward the northern trail took all of Luke's willpower. He flicked the reins angrily, startling the horses. They bolted forward, and he was nearly thrown backwards. Swearing out loud, he slowed the horses back to a trot. Several miles later, he pulled them to a stop again. There were two trails that wove their way in front of him. One led west, while the other led due north, toward Landon's.

Luke put the reins in his left hand and rubbed his eyes with his right. There was no going back; he had made the decision, and he would stick with it. Torturing himself like this was going to get him nowhere. Mary was due in several weeks. After he safely delivered her baby and mother and child were doing well, then he could lay low for the winter. Once spring arrived, he would honor his promise to William and then head for Texas or Mexico, where he'd heard from someone that a man could ride for weeks and not see another soul. Which suited him just fine.

Looking behind him at the open prairie, just for a second, Luke couldn't help wishing that things could have turned out different.

CHAPTER NINE

Meda awoke at first light and began to take the tepee down. The wind was blowing out of the north and there was a heaviness to it, like it was saying time had run out and evil was on its way. Meda ignored it as much as she could. There was no sense in trying to interpret the vision that she had been given until she saw what they faced. There was always a lesson to be learned; it was important to remember that things were not always what they appeared to be, yet some things were exactly what they seemed. The wise ones knew what they could change and what they could not.

This vision worried Meda. It seemed that whatever was coming now was just a part of the evil that would eventually arrive. Meda didn't think that this was a lesson for her, but that she was here only to observe and teach. That was something new for her.

Moving her tepee gave her the advantage of being able to see most of the property, lowering the chances that anything could sneak up on her. With long practiced movements, she wasted no time. It never hurt to prepare.

●●●

It was past midday by the time that Jean Claude's wagon crested the small rise and started down the trail toward Angelica's ranch. He frowned as he took in the new barn roof. Last time he was here, he could have sworn the thing was one storm from collapsing. Shingles had been missing, and he had noted the smell of moldy hay, an indicator that it had been leaking. Certainly, she hadn't done it herself? Pulling the wagon to the side of the house, he stopped in front of the lean-to. Nate pulled his wagon up behind him.

Son of a bitch but he was getting old. This trip seemed to take more out of him each year. He'd have to find his flask of whiskey and take a few swigs to help loosen the muscles that had stiffened on the ride. Rolling his shoulders, Jean Claude heard the kitchen door open behind him. Smiling wasn't something that he did a lot of, but he was game to give one a try as he turned. The smile, more of a grimace, froze on his face as he looked down into the eyes of a small girl. She was young, but he got the impression that she was sizing him up.

"Who are you and what are you doing here?" he asked, in his heavy French-Canadian accent.

The child didn't flinch at the rough tone of his voice. "I'm Carol Anne, and I live here now."

That statement threw him. Angelica had sold the farm and moved? It had taken him months to get all of this wood together, three days to haul it here, and it had been for nothing? He could have been out on his trap lines, making some money for himself, getting Jeb off of his back. Anger built up in him. How could Angelica have done this to him? She had no right to sell the ranch without consulting him. She owed him. Hadn't he kept his end of the bargain all these years to help her out?

Some of the anger must have shown on his face, causing Carol Anne to turn and run back into the house. Jean Claude had no choice but to climb down out of the wagon and wait for Carol Anne's father to come out. Hopefully they could make a deal on the firewood, and he wouldn't have wasted a trip. It would cost him a lot of money to have hauled this wood for nothing. He had hired Nate to drive the second wagon. Angelica usually loaded the boy up with cheese, cider, and preserves. Nate came from a large family, and the food would have been payment enough. Now he, Jean Claude, would have to come up with the money himself. This whole trip seemed to have been fraught with bad omens from the start.

Where the hell was that whiskey? Jean Claude was rummaging under the seat when he heard the kitchen door open again. Trying another semblance of a smile, he straightened and turned. For a moment he couldn't comprehend that it was Angelica, not Lillian who stood in the doorway. The vision had Lilian's eyes, her thick brown hair and curvy figure; just how he remembered them.

"Jean Claude, Nate, I was beginning to worry about you."

The voice was what brought him back to the present. Disappointment slammed into his gut like a ramrod. This wasn't his beautiful Lillian. This was the child that she had had with that imbecile husband of hers, the child that should have been his. Of course, she was a woman and not the son that he would have hoped for. Still, women had their uses. Now that Angelica was all grown up, she would serve his purpose very nicely. Unless she had gone and gotten herself married to a widower. Then he would have to revise his plans.

"Mon cheri, Jean Claude always comes through." He placed a hand to his chest, trying his best to look hurt. Nate, standing next to him, gave a small cough, which earned him a glare from Jean Claude.

Angelica smiled. "I'm sorry, I didn't mean to imply that you weren't coming. Just with the snow arriving early this year, I was afraid that you wouldn't be able to get through for a while."

He was insulted by her words, but he didn't let it show. Stupid girl. His father had been a trapper, and Jean Claude had grown up in the wilderness. A little bit of snow was not anything to him. He had survived blizzards, cyclones, and anything else Mother Nature had thrown his way. Nothing kept him from getting to where he wanted to go.

He was forming a reply when two young boys came around the front of the house and stood next to Angelica. She turned and smiled at them, then turned back to him.

"Jean Claude, I'd like you to meet my children. This is William and Matthew. You met Carol Anne when you came in. The boys can help you unload the wagons while I start supper. You and Nate feel free to put your things in the barn."

She turned and made her way back into the house along with the girl. *Dismissing him like he was the hired help.* Once again, the anger surged up. Someday soon, he would be the one in control of this house and Lillian's brat. Turning, he spit. The two boys were looking at him, and one of them was wrinkling his nose.

"What's the matter with you?" he barked at the smaller boy.

It was the older boy that answered. "Nothing. He's fine."

Jean Claude didn't like the way the older boy was looking at him. This kid was going to be a problem. Angelica hadn't mentioned a husband, but that didn't mean that there wasn't one. He'd just have to bide his time and see what was going on here. He motioned to Nate; it was time to unload this infernal wood.

•••

Angelica closed the door and leaned back against it before taking a deep breath. She had forgotten how bad Jean Claude smelled. He hadn't changed much since she last saw him. Wearing the same buckskin pants, fleeced shirt, rabbit lined boots, and that buffalo coat that had seen better days. Brown greasy hair still fell past his shoulders, and his beard appeared to have dried things stuck in it. He had explained to her once that he didn't bathe very often because smelling like animals made it easier to live among them. Unfortunately, it didn't make it easy for people to live with him. Usually, he slept in the barn when he was here.

She had a moment of sympathy for Gracie and Ranger.

Carol Anne had gone back to her seat at the table and resumed working on her letters, using the slate Angelica had used as a child. "Is that scary man gone?" she asked.

Angelica smiled. Jean Claude was very rough around the edges, and no doubt he would frighten a young child. "He'll be here for a day or two. Don't worry, he's really not so bad. He just lives alone and isn't used to little girls."

Turning to the stove, she missed the look Carol Anne gave her.

•••

William didn't like the look of this stranger. The city had been crawling with cruel men and women. They were easy enough to spot. There was something in their manner and eyes, a malevolence that lurked below their façade of humanity. They were always looking for an easy victim. They enjoyed feeding off the suffering of others, waiting for the perfect opportunity to pounce. William would bet his next meal that Jean Claude was one of those people.

William loaded his arms with wood from the wagon and headed for the rapidly growing pile. It hadn't taken the four of them long to unload the first wagon and start on the second. Jean Claude had moved slower and slower until it was the younger boys that were doing all the work. Jean Claude also asked a lot of questions. He wanted to know if Angelica had married their father, and when he heard about Luke, he wasn't pleased. William implied that Luke was gone temporarily and would be back soon.

Jean Claude drove the first wagon away and hadn't returned yet. That was fine with William. The old geezer stunk worse than some of the slaughterhouses that he'd find odd jobs at. The sooner they emptied the wagons; the sooner Jean Claude would be on his way home. Unfortunately, according to Nate, this was only half of the wood. That meant Jean Claude would be making another trip.

William cursed Luke for leaving. It was obvious that Angelica didn't understand the threat Jean Claude posed, and William doubted that Angelica knew that the smelly French-Canadian was attracted to her, and not in a good way either. Not like Luke had been. It just proved what William had already figured out. Even though she was ten years older than he was, Angelica was very naïve.

There had been definite lust in the trapper's eyes, but there had also been something akin to hatred. William could understand the lust. Angelica was beautiful. There weren't many women out here in the middle of nowhere, and one with Angelica's looks and intelligence were rare. It was the hatred that William didn't understand. How could anyone hate Angelica?

William felt older than Angelica in a lot of ways. Her only tragedy was the loss of her parents, and she was mostly all grown when that had happened. Angelica hadn't had to fend for a brother or a sister. She'd been making apple pies while he, William, brought home scraps for the three of them to survive on. As sad as it was, William figured that Carol Anne had more survival skills then Angelica.

The last of the wood was stacked, and Nate drove the second wagon to the barn.

•••

The weather was mild, yet there was a definite bite to the air, along with the threat of a storm. Angelica didn't want Jean Claude in the house; his smell was bad enough outside, and inside it would be unbearable, so with help from the boys, they set the table and chairs out onto the front porch. It was downright uncharitable of her, she thought. Jean Claude had traveled out of his way to bring her firewood, and she should be treating him like a guest, not like some, well, like a smelly trapper. However, this arrangement would work just fine for now.

Her thoughts automatically went to Luke. It was hard not to compare the two men. Luke lived alone too, but he smelled of the outdoors. Like the scent of the pine trees that grew on the distant mountains: crisp, clean, male. Jean Claude smelled like he lived among the animals.

Luke had talked to her like she was smart and that her opinion mattered to him. He made her feel important. Jean Claude treated her like she was still a child. He laughed at her ideas. However, he'd been a friend of her parents, so she had known him all her life. He was like an uncle to her in many ways. Hadn't he always come through with the wood and checked on her regularly? Angelica was grateful, and some day she vowed to make it up to him.

Still, she silently wished that it was Luke that she was setting the place at the table for.

•••

Jean Claude inserted himself at the head of the table. The six of them ate in relative silence even though Angelica had tried to get a conversation going, but she was met with short, clipped responses. Angelica had looked for Meda to join them but couldn't find her. It was obvious that the children didn't like Jean Claude. William kept glaring at him from the end of the table, and Matthew avoided looking anywhere but his plate. Carol Anne didn't eat much and asked to be excused early. Nate ate silently, keeping his head down and only answered when spoken to directly. Jean Claude for his part shoveled food into his mouth like he hadn't eaten in months. Living on his own for years hadn't really taught him manners in polite society. He ate with his mouth open, and it was the sight and smell of the blackened teeth that made Angelica lose her appetite. She kept her eyes averted. When she had to speak to him, she focused on a spot above his right shoulder. It was a relief when the meal was finally over. Matthew bolted for the house, and Nate retreated to the barn, leaving Angelica and William to entertain Jean Claude.

The trapper pushed his chair back and belched loudly. To Angelica's disgust and amazement, he pulled out a hunting knife and proceeded to flick bits of food out of his teeth. Some pieces flew through the air, while others added to the menagerie of particles on his chin. Angelica was quick to move the bowls of leftover food out of range.

"Saw some buffalo tracks several miles back. I'll head out early and see if I can't get a hide or two."

Angelica disliked the thought of him shooting a buffalo, but she knew that there was no talking him out of going. The buffalo had been the main means of survival for the Lakota people for hundreds of years. They utilized every part of the animal. The hides became tepees and clothing, the bones used for weapons, and the horns used to make spoons and cups. The huge animals had once been plentiful on the plains, but since the miners, settlers, and soldiers started the trek west, the herds had been decimated, leaving the Lakota and other tribes to starve and no recourse other than the reservations that the government banished them to. Trains would stop if there was one of the animals in range to let passengers off to shoot it, just for the fun of it. The worst part being that they would only take the hide and let the carcass rot where it fell. Good thing Meda wasn't here to hear this.

"You'll be heading home soon?" William wanted to know.

Jean Claude's knife stopped its flicking motion. Pulling it away from his mouth, Jean Claude twirled it in his hand as he stared at the boy. "I'll be here for several days," he said, his eyes narrowing. "There's need for a man around here."

Angelica could see William bristle. "I'm man enough to run this ranch," William told him hotly.

It was all she could do not to roll her eyes. She was getting tired of hearing how she needed a man around. William was thirteen and hadn't even lived on a ranch, yet he thought that he could do better just because he was a male. She had run this ranch just fine by herself, so she told both of them that.

William looked embarrassed and a little hurt. Jean Claude, on the other hand, ignored her statement as usual. "You think that you've done a good job, but there are things only a man can take care of. I heard of this Luke helping, but I'm sure that there are things that still need to be," his glance slid to Angelica, "attended to."

A small trickle of revulsion ran down Angelica's spine, but she tamped it down. Of course, she shouldn't read too much into Jean Claude's words; he was only talking about the ranch.

With a sudden movement, Jean Claude flicked his knife into the table, making Angelica and William jump.

Smirking, he stood and faced Angelica before pulling the blade from the table. "Lillian wanted me to take care of you. I plan to do just that." He slipped the knife back into his boot. Without another word, he turned and headed to the barn.

Drat! Angelica thought. If Jean Claude thought that she was incapable of being on her own, then she had the feeling that he would become a nuisance, fast. The man was the most thick-headed man she knew. It was just her luck that the man she wanted to stay had run as fast as he could, while the one she needed to leave suddenly had feet of lead.

Jean Claude had to go home sometime. Didn't he?

CHAPTER TEN

The snow started after sunset, driven horizontal by the howling wind as if trying to scour the landscape bare. Meda sat in her tepee, staring into the fire burning in the middle of the small space. Her mother had had the gift of sight, of foretelling the future. It had been passed down from mother to daughter for generations. The men looked for visions during the sweat lodge ceremony, or while performing the Sun Dance. Meda didn't need the ceremonies to help her see. The wolf spirit had been visiting her for as long as she could remember, and occasionally he would bring the owl spirit with him.

To the Lakota, the owl symbolized intuition and clairvoyance. Known as the messengers of secrets and omens, the large bird was believed to have a link to the world beyond, since it could see into the darkness. Some considered them an omen of death.

Meda's owl spirit had bestowed her with the gift of hearing the departed, but she knew that her ancestors weren't dead. They had simply moved on to the next place, beyond the light, where they could watch over their loved ones and send messages back. One just had to listen.

Closing her eyes, Meda heard a sound outside her doorway, different from that of the howling wind. Grabbing her hunting knife, she moved to the opening and slowly untied the rawhide binding that kept the flap from flailing in the wind. Standing back, she waited to see who would come through the door. As the flap whipped open, a white blur of snow entered the tepee and shook. Meda relaxed with a small laugh. Lowering the knife, she grabbed the waving material before retying the rawhide bindings and turned to face Wolf.

Wolf surveyed his surroundings before plopping down on the other side of the fire with his head on his paws, his golden eyes reflecting the light from the flames.

Meda knelt back down on her mat and drew her woolen blanket loosely around her. Next, she grabbed a wooden bowl and spooned some stew into it before setting it in front of the large canine.

"Are you listening to the ancestors too? They are restless tonight." Pulling the blanket up around her shoulders, she concentrated for a moment. "I can only hear some words. Greed. Lies. Need for…something." She shook her head, her long black braid falling over her shoulder. "It doesn't make sense."

Wolf lifted his head and regarded her. His eyes narrowed slightly.

"Don't look at me that way. I'm doing my best, but the wind is making the voices mix together. I know Jean Claude is a threat, but he's been coming here for years. Why are the spirits warning me now? What has changed?"

Wolf began eating the stew as she talked.

"Luke should have stayed."

The wind increased its intensity, causing the fire to pop and the flames to leap higher.

Meda shook her head. So many voices. They blended so as to be unrecognizable. It worried her that the wind was teeming with warnings, yet she felt pride that her ancestors were watching over her. She was sure they knew that she had adhered to the old ways even though the Long Knives were driving the Lakota to reservations. Many Sioux and other tribes' children had been sent off to Eastern schools, forcing them to give up the Lakota way of life. Cutting their hair and making them pray to a different spirit. As a small child, she'd heard many stories of children being whipped, beaten, and locked in closets to get them to adhere to the white man's ways. Meda knew that Sitting Bull was very worried about the way the Lakota and other tribes were being pushed out by the white settlers. The soldiers, who were called Long Knives for the long swords that they carried, were everywhere.

Meda closed her eyes. Angelica and her family were the only whites that had kept their promises to the Lakota. Year after year, Meda and her family took the extra fruit off the trees and dried it. It helped to keep them from starving in the winter months. Angelica had become a blood sister to her during Meda's fourteenth winter.

Opening her eyes, Meda knew that whatever danger Angelica was in, she would fight to the death to save her.

Wolf finished his stew and was now watching her. Not for the first time, she wished that he could talk. She was sure that he knew what danger was coming and could better prepare her. Closing her eyes again, she once again concentrated on the wind.

At first, Meda couldn't make out any words. Her ears hurt from the straining, but then a whisper caught her attention. Excitement raced along her veins. She leaned closer to the fire.

"Do you hear that?" she asked Wolf. "It sounds like my grandmother. She has been gone for five winters."

If her grandmother was trying to tell her something, then Meda knew that it was important. Woman of the Sage had been powerful in the tribe. She was said to have magical healing powers, and her visions almost always came true. Meda had spent many hours learning about plants and medicines and listening to stories from her grandmother. Nothing was written down; everything was passed to the next generation through verbal accounts. Someday, Meda knew, she too would pass the history and teachings of the Sioux down to her daughters and sons.

"Danger…little one…need medicine man…make whole…" the voice said.

Meda repeated the words out loud. Wolf sat up and locked gazes with her. Meda let out the breath with a frustrating whoosh.

"I don't understand," she snapped at Wolf. "Does little one mean Carol Anne? What is she in danger from? Our medicine man is a good four-day ride away and four days back! I've tried to call on the wolf spirit for another vision, but it won't come."

Wolf growled at her.

"What? What am I missing?" Throwing her hands into the air, she glared at the wolf. As she watched, he began sniffing at the grass and started to dig. Several times, he looked up at her as he was digging.

Meda's mind was working. What was he trying to tell her? What did digging have to do with Carol Anne being in danger? Digging. The ground. Earth. The white man had flocked to the Black Hills because of gold buried in the earth. Once there, they broke their word and took over the land that belonged to the Lakota. Was there gold or something as valuable on Angelica's land? A lone woman and children would be no match for them. They could take what they wanted, and that included Angelica and the children.

"Does the land have something to do with this coming danger?"

Wolf stopped digging and gave a small yip.

"I'll take that as a yes," Meda said as she began to pace back and forth.

She'd been blinded by the arrival of Jean Claude. Everything had pointed to him as the danger. Now there were the Long Knives to consider. They were much more of a threat than Jean Claude.

"I had not thought about the land. Are Long Knives coming to take Angelica's land? Will they hurt her or the children?"

Wolf growled.

That didn't make her feel any better. Getting Angelica to leave the ranch would be next to impossible. Meda knew that Angelica would stay and try to reason with the white men, but what if it wasn't the Long Knives but some other type of white man?

Sitting back down to the fire, she looked over at Wolf.

"We need to plan. I will call on the spirits again for another vision. You need to stick close. Don't let any of them out of your sight."

Wolf sat up and met her eyes.

Meda got the impression that he already knew what needed to be done; he was just waiting for her to catch up.

•••

Angelica couldn't sleep. Nights like this always made her restless, and it didn't help that the wind was so strong that it caused the chimney to make a high-pitched whistle. Not wanting any downdrafts to cause hot ashes to be blown onto the wood floors, she had doused the fire in the fireplace and had just left the stove burning. Unfortunately, smoke was pushed back down the stove pipe and into the house, making the air sooty and dry.

The children were asleep, and Angelica could hear one of the boys coughing from the living room. It had been too smoky in the loft, so she had insisted that they sleep on the ground floor for the night.

Tossing and turning for a few more minutes, she finally threw back the covers and got out of bed. Careful not to wake Carol Anne, Angelica wrapped herself in a quilt as the cold air of the room made her shiver. As the heat from the stove didn't reach back into the area, the floor was ice cold. Angelica grabbed her mother's slippers and hopped back and forth on the balls of her feet as she put them on.

Lighting a candle, she made her way to the kitchen after checking that the boys were covered with enough blankets to keep them warm.

Deciding to have a cup of tea, she filled the coffee pot with water and nearly jumped out of her skin as a shadow detached itself from the blackness and jumped down from the far corner of the counter.

"Darnation Purrsistence, you nearly made my heart stop!"

The calico's green eyes never blinked as she walked across the floor to rub herself against Angelica's legs, her purring adding to the sound of the ticking clock and the whistling, howling wind.

There was a comfort to sitting at the kitchen table and cupping the hot mug between her hands. It'd been an interesting day, Angelica thought to herself. Thankfully, Jean Claude had finally shown up with half the wood. It had been her greatest worry. Without the right supplies out here in the winter, it meant the difference between life and death. If only the snow held off for a few more days, then Jean Claude and Nate would soon be well on their way home.

It surprised her when Jean Claude proclaimed it his duty to take care of her. When had he promised her mother such a thing? As far as Angelica could remember, every time he had shown up, her mother would decide that it was time for the two of them, she and Angelica, to do some chores on the other side of the property. Of course, her mother would always be back in time to cook supper and feed the men. It just seemed that Jean Claude hadn't stayed so long in those days.

There didn't seem like she could do much about Jean Claude except wait for him to leave. It bothered her that the children had obviously disliked him from the start. The trapper was definitely rough around the edges, but he always managed to come through for her. She supposed that it was normal for them to be wary of strangers. They had only shared some of their experiences with her, and what they'd left out, she could only guess at.

Purrsistence jumped onto her lap and Angelica absentmindedly stroked the purring cat. Before the children arrived, she had plenty of solitude. It wasn't that she didn't like the company now; it was just nice to have a few minutes for herself.

Purrsistence startled her by jumping up on the table, a low growl replacing her purring. Angelica had only seen her pet act this way once before, and that was when Jean Claude had found her in his wagon. The minute she'd seen the trapper, she had let out a deep guttural sound. Jean Claude had scruffed the hissing feline and flung her as hard as he could. Fortunately, Purrsistence hadn't been hurt in the scuffle. Now the large cat sat crouched, the hair standing up along her back as she stared at the kitchen window. All Angelica could see was her and Purrsistence's reflection in the weak light. Whatever the feline sensed, she was not happy about it. Angelica moved to the window, but there was nothing but swirling snow.

"It's all right," she told the agitated cat. "It's just the wind or a coyote.

Come on, let's go back to bed."

Picking up the candle, she shooed the cat off the table and went back into the other room.

•••

Jean Claude stepped to the side, out of sight, as Angelica peered through the windowpane. His dark coat blended into the shadows, and he doubted she could see far with the snow swirling in the howling wind. He'd spotted the faint candlelight as he passed the house on his way back to the barn. Peering in, he'd seen Angelica sitting at the kitchen table. Her long hair had been loose, making her look so much like his Lillian. He had actually taken a few steps toward the door, ready to take what he had fantasized about all these years. Then the cat had somehow known that he was there, and its movement was what had brought him back to reality. This wasn't Lillian; it was Angelica, and there were three brats in the house and Nate in the barn. The oldest one would certainly put up a fight.

The light disappeared from the window.

She was going back to bed, a bed that he intended to share, and soon. He couldn't just force her to turn the ranch over to him, and he wasn't planning on taking a wife. Besides, there was now the problem of the three children. He needed to get rid of them so they couldn't come back and ruin everything.

An idea swirled in the back of his brain. He wondered why it hadn't occurred to him sooner. He decided that he would head back north at daybreak to make some arrangements.

Smiling, he made his way back to the barn.

CHAPTER ELEVEN

Luke pulled the collar of his jacket tighter as snowflakes like tiny shards of ice hit the exposed skin of his face. The wind, sounding like a speeding train, drowned out the cows' bawling as they were being herded to the lower pastures. To quote his father, it was colder than a well digger's ass. Though his father hadn't ever worked as a well digger, so Luke wasn't sure, and certainly wasn't about to ask, how the elder man would know such a thing.

He had been back at Landon's for over two weeks now. Mary was doing fine, and Luke figured that it would be at least another week or two before the baby decided to present itself. In the meantime, he kept busy by helping the ranch hands move the cattle. Since the herd was so big, they decided to move it in several trips. This was the last of them. The weather was making the cattle restless. They wanted to turn back and seek the shelter of trees that they had just left. Unfortunately, there wouldn't be enough water and grass to sustain them for the winter there. Moving them closer to the ranch meant that they could bring the animals hay when the weather became too dangerous to travel far.

Luke whirled his horse around and went after a cow that had broken away from the group. Getting ahead of the racing animal, he managed to turn it back. The ground was so frozen that the large group hardly made a dent in it as it passed over.

Luke reined his horse and trailed the herd. Though he couldn't see very far in front of him, he knew that Landon owned the land for as far as the eye could see on a clear day. It made him think of Angelica's property and what it would be like to own a piece of land that made you want to put down roots and hold on. How did a man let the past catch up to him, face it, and plan for a future?

It was good to see Landon again. To talk to someone who knew where he came from and who had also experienced the same horrors. Landon understood the darkness that festered in his mind, though he didn't agree with Luke's self-imposed seclusion. Landon fought his own demons, and Luke envied him that he seemed to have conquered them. The first day he'd arrived, they'd sat up talking and reminiscing past midnight.

The wind died down for a few minutes, and Luke made out the lights of the ranch house through the falling snow. The soft glow in the windows was a welcoming sight. It promised warmth and protection. Off to the right, a thousand heads of cattle clustered together in the lower pasture in stands of trees, causing the rest of the herd to break into a run. It seemed as if they were ready to get out of the biting wind and huddle together for warmth.

After the gate was shut behind the last cow, Luke turned his horse and headed for the barn. The warmth was almost smothering after the cold, and his ears still rang with the fury of the wind. He rubbed the gelding down, gave it a handful of grain, tossed in some hay, and filled the water bucket before heading across the yard toward the house.

The tantalizing smell of something roasting in the oven greeted him as he came in from the back porch and into the kitchen. His mouth began to water, and his stomach gave a low rumble. The large room was heated by a massive stove on one end, where a small colored woman stood stirring something in a pot. Her black hair was just starting to show streaks of gray. Turning, she watched as he shrugged off his coat and hung it on a peg by the door.

"Lordy, Luke, you are going to catch your death out there. You best come sit at the table and I'll fix you right up with something warm."

Old Kate had been with Landon's family from before he was born, though she wasn't a slave but a free woman. Landon's father, Gabriel, had been passing a neighboring farm when he had seen a young slave girl, who couldn't have been older than ten years old, being tied to a whipping post. A small crowd had gathered, and a woman was screaming. The elder man spurred his horse across the lawn as fast as he could, but the overseer was already plying his whip by the time he reached them. Without waiting for his horse to stop, Gabriel jumped from the saddle and wrenched the lash out of the surprised man's hand. Neither he nor Old Kate ever spoke of what happened next, but Gabriel had arrived back at his farm, the young girl riding in the saddle in front of him. She had suffered several lashes of the whip and was understandably terrified and in pain. Freedom papers were written for her the same day, yet Gabriel had waited until she had healed before presenting them to her. He had asked her to stay on as a nanny for his children and he would pay her a governess wage. Old Kate had readily agreed, since there had been no other place for her to go, her parents having been sold at the public market two years before. She'd learned to read and write, and her speech was that of a southern lady, until she got mad or excited, usually by something Landon or Luke had done.

Luke had found out, years later, that her crime had been rebuffing the advances of the plantation owner's son. Every time he saw the scar on the side of her neck, it caused a small burst of anger deep in the pit of his stomach.

It had been a pleasant surprise to see her here at Landon's. She was part of some of the best memories of his childhood.

Old Kate flitted around the kitchen with well-practiced movements. Setting a cup of hot coffee in front of him, she continued to talk. "Don't know why you are out there like some hired hand. You are a doctor, not some cowpoke. You should be resting up, waiting for that young un to be born!" She went back to the stove. "Goodness, it'll be nice to have a little one around again. Been too long."

Luke smiled into his cup. It seemed that Old Kate was happiest when there were lots of children around. He and Landon had called her Old Kate for as long as he could remember, but he didn't imagine that she was more than fifteen years older than himself.

Old Kate poured herself a cup and sat down across the table from him. Her eyes were sharp as she took a sip and studied him. "There's something different about you." This time she squinted at him as if she was concentrating hard to read his mind. "You were gone quite a while, and I'm guessing there's some woman looking down the road for you." That assessing gaze again. "I raised you boys to be respecting women. I'm hoping you aren't dallying with some lonely widow, because I'll be right upset."

Luke held up his hand in mock surrender. If Old Kate knew the true story, that he had left Angelica on the plain with three children, well, she'd probably dunk his head into the dishwater for sure. He was saved from answering by a huge man entering the kitchen.

Landon stood over six foot three in his stocking feet, sporting broad shoulders and a barrel chest that tapered down to a trim waist. He told Luke that he had built the ranch with extra wide doorways to fit his large frame. Ink black hair was brushed back from his face and just touched his shoulders. Rugged features framed startling blue eyes. He was dressed in a homespun brown shirt and lighter colored pants, and he was carrying a worn pair of boots. "Damn cat scratched up my boots again," he complained.

Dropping them next to the stove, he grabbed himself some coffee before leaning against the counter and looking back and forth between the two of them. "Did I interrupt something?"

"Old Kate's just letting me know that I shouldn't be out rounding up cows when there's a baby waiting to be born." Luke ignored the look she gave him.

Landon seemed to turn a shade paler at the mention of his unborn child. Luke knew that his friend was terrified about the impending birth. Who could blame him? He had lost his first wife and child during childbirth. It was supposed to have been a joyous occasion. Instead, Landon had dug two graves. Now with this child's due date approaching fast, Landon was showing signs of stress. Luke knew that Landon blamed himself. His first wife had been a tiny woman, and from what Luke had gathered from Old Kate, who'd attended the birth, the baby had been very large and presented breech. The labor had lasted too long. In the end, neither could be saved. For the thousandth time, he wished he had been there. He knew that he could have saved them both. The filthy field hospital was a long time ago, and he'd learned a lot since then.

"Relax, buddy," Luke told him. "I'll be right there the whole time."

Landon was still holding his mug, and Luke was afraid that it was going to shatter in his grip. Pushing back his chair, Luke went and stood next to his friend. Placing a hand on the bigger man's shoulder, he said, "Trust me, Landon, by this time next month, you'll be dangling a baby on your knee and planning for the next."

A voice from behind them said, "You might at least consult me before you go making plans for the next one."

A very pregnant Mary entered the kitchen and smiled at the three of them. Luke watched as she waddled toward the table, and he felt his neck grow warm. "I'm just saying that by this time next month, this will all be just a memory to tell your grandchildren."

Crossing over to the table, Landon moved and pulled out a chair for his wife. Mary lowered herself into the chair and leaned back. Her dishwater blonde hair was in a neat braid, and her large stomach strained at the cloth of her service calico. Luke watched the baby move from left to right. Movement was good. That's what the baby was supposed to do. He made a mental note that the baby hadn't dropped.

Just for a moment, he wondered what Angelica would look like carrying his child. The pain at that thought caught him by surprise. It was something visceral, something that his soul seemed to ache for that he had been unaware of.

"Luke?"

Snapping back to the present, he realized that Landon had been talking to him. "Sorry, I was thinking of something."

He refused to meet Old Kate's assessing eyes. It never failed to amaze him how she saw everything.

"I was saying that now that the cattle are closer to the house, I'm sure that the boys can handle them. Give us a chance to continue that game of chess we never got to finish and catch up on some more old times."

Luke walked to the other side of the kitchen and looked out at the wind-driven snow. Landon had moved back to leaning against the counter. He gave off the appearance of a man that was calm and relaxed, but Luke wasn't fooled. Landon wanted him to be closer to the house and Mary. One thing that Luke knew about babies was that they came when they damn well wanted to, and it usually wasn't when he was sitting around waiting for them.

"You can't keep him a prisoner in the house until the baby is born," Mary told her husband, as if reading Luke's mind.

Luke turned and looked at her. Obviously, she wasn't fooled either. Rubbing her stomach, she gave him an apologetic smile.

"I know that you most likely have somewhere else to be, and we're obliged that you're here, but don't let my lunkhead of a husband scare you. I've been cooped up in this house for the last month, and I would give anything to be able to get out and go somewhere, anywhere." She held her hand up to still the protest from her husband, who had pushed himself away from the counter. "No, I have no plans on leaving the house. It will just be nice when I can."

It seemed that they tensed up when she had made her first statement, and they relaxed at the second, though Luke had his doubts that she would have gotten very far considering the size of her belly.

Good thing Landon had made the doorways extra wide, he thought. *This kid appeared to be at least a ten pounder. With luck, any girls would take after their mother.*

Old Kate rose from her chair. "Well, you best go and start that game of yours then," she told the men. "Supper will be ready soon." Turning to Mary, her voice became quieter. "You, Missy, need to go lie down to rest. Lord knows once that baby comes, no one is going to get any sleep. All this talk of running about is just nonsense."

With the precision of a general, she shooed them out of the kitchen.

•••

Even though Landon laid off most of the ranch hands for the winter, the remaining cowboys were kept busy with repairing equipment and hanging out in the bunkhouse, leaving Luke alone with his thoughts. With so much time to think, he had to face that his nightmares were becoming more frequent. They always started the same way—the screams, the confusion, the sounds of death, the smoke from the cannons. Recently, however, they had changed. The soldiers in the beds had been replaced with William, Matthew, and Carol Anne.

In his dreams, the children lay helpless as Union soldiers sliced their throats. Luke fights to reach them, but he is constantly slipping backwards as the ground becomes thick with their blood, and he falls to his knees. Then he sees Angelica as she is being carried away by the enemy. Her voice is pleading with him to save her, to save the children and bring them all home. He tries to get to his feet on the slippery ground, but he can't get a footing. He can hear Angelica's cries as she disappears from view. It's then that he realizes that he has failed her, has failed them all. He awakens, gasping for air, drenched in sweat, his hand outstretched.

•••

Luke was going stir crazy. Not that the house was small. Landon came from old money in the South, and he could see the conflict that had been coming and prepared himself well. The ranch covered over thirty thousand acres and three thousand heads of cattle, double that in the spring. The bunkhouse could sleep thirty ranch hands, and there were a handful of other buildings, several that some of the cowboys and their families lived in. There was even talk about building a schoolhouse for all the children that were running around.

After awakening from another nightmare, Luke made his way to Landon's study. Stirring the ashes, he got a small blaze going in the massive fireplace and was in the process of pulling a leather chair closer to the hearth when there was a sound at the doorway. It was still several hours before the household would awaken and start another day, but there stood Landon.

"Thought I heard someone up and roaming around," Landon said as he too pulled a chair up to the warmth of the fire. "Never known you to be a night owl before, but it seems you spend more time awake then you do sleeping."

Luke glared at him, causing Landon to laugh. "You know as well as I do that there are no secrets on a ranch. Hell, cowboys gossip worse than women, and there's plenty of talk going on about you. Have to admit, I'm curious myself." The big man leaned back in his chair and crossed his right leg over his knee.

Luke stared into the flames.

"You know me well enough to know that I'm not going to pry, but you're like a brother to me, Luke. There is something bothering you, we can all see it." He paused and then cleared his throat. "If you're in trouble with the law…"

It was Luke's turn to laugh. "You're a good friend, Landon, but no, I'm not in trouble with the law."

Landon was right though; they were like brothers. Yet, Luke wasn't ready to share what he felt about Angelica. In fact, he wasn't sure he could put into words what he felt for her. The war had shown him how fast everything that he had loved and believed in could be taken away. He didn't think that he could care about something or someone again. Yet, Landon had done it, twice. Luke wasn't sure that he would have taken that second chance, never mind the first.

"How do you learn to trust in something again?" He wasn't aware that he asked the question until he heard his own voice.

Landon took a few seconds to think it over. "It's a leap of faith," he finally answered. "I thought after the South was defeated that nothing was ever going to be normal again. How could it be? The plantation was gone, my family was scattered. I married and was about to have a child. Then it was all taken away from me. I honestly didn't care if I lived or died, came real close to ending it a couple of times too. Then I met Mary. She's taught me that things happen for a reason and that God is still worth praying to. She loves to say that faith is believing in things, even if it's against all odds." He sighed. "The war has been over for a long time, Luke. It's time to put those memories where they belong, in the past. Life is unpredictable. There will be plenty of disappointments and loss but think of what there is to gain."

Luke let the words sink in. God, he wished that it was that simple, but the remnants of the nightmare still clung to him. Suddenly, he wanted to tell his friend about Angelica, to hear someone tell him that he had done the right thing. He had told Landon that he had helped out a neighbor, but he had never gone into specifics.

Outside, the sky was beginning to lighten, and they could hear the howl of a far-off wolf. Inside, the fire crackled and the warmth swirled around them. Luke wondered if it was the heat from the fire or the lonely cry that suddenly was making him sweat. Taking a deep breath, he began. "You know that ranch that's down in the hollow halfway to town?" he asked.

At Landon's nod, he continued.

"Well, I found the woman hurt. She'd fallen through the barn roof and somehow Wolf knew and led me there. I stitched her up and took care of her for a couple of days. Her name is Angelica, and she lives out there all alone, and damn it if she doesn't run that ranch better than any man. I tried to get her to go to town, but she wouldn't budge. I hated leaving her out there, but a tribe of Lakota that are her friends showed up, and I finally made it into town. I don't know what possessed me, but there were three orphans who had just arrived on the orphan wagon, and I offered them a home with Angelica. William is the oldest, then Matthew, then Carol Anne, who's four."

Landon's eyebrows shot up. "You brought this injured woman three orphans to take care of and then you left? You are either the bravest man I know or the stupidest!"

Luke squirmed in his seat. He knew how it sounded, but it had seemed like the solution to the problem at the time. "I told them if they didn't like it at Angelica's, that I would be back in the spring and find them somewhere else to live."

"What did this Angelica have to say about that?" Landon wanted to know.

"I don't think she knew about that conversation," he finally said. "I told her that I would check on them in the spring."

Again, Landon's eyebrows shot up.

"What?" Luke wasn't sure he wanted to know.

"Well, it seems that you painted yourself into a corner here. She's raising these children, and by spring she'll probably be quite attached to them. I don't see how you can just go in there and take them away."

"I'm hoping that that's the case," Luke replied honestly. "It bothered me to leave her out there all alone. It seemed like fate that the children showed up when they did. There was a couple that wanted Carol Anne, but those children were what Angelica needed." He proceeded to describe the conversation that he had overheard in the dining room. "So, you can understand how I couldn't let them take Carol Anne."

Landon clenched and unclenched his massive fists as if imagining finding the man from town and beating him senseless. Luke thought about that couple's conversation and wondered where poor Rachel had gotten off to. Hopefully, she had found a better place.

"So, this spinster is taking care of these children out in the middle of Indian Territory, alone? What's to stop renegade Indians, or soldiers for that matter, from taking advantage of them?" Landon asked.

The light in the windows had turned gold as the sun sent tentacles of sunshine across the frozen ground. Sounds of the stove being stoked to life came from the kitchen as Old Kate began her morning routine. Yet Luke felt cold inside at Landon's question.

Had he inadvertently put the children in danger? Meda and the Lakota kept an eye on Angelica, but they wouldn't be a match for any soldiers. As it was, things were heating up between the Indians and American soldiers. Since gold was found in the Black Hills, treaties were being broken, and the government wanted the Indians to be confined to the reservations or moved to schools where they were to learn the white man ways.

Angelica wasn't the spinster that Landon obviously was picturing. She was young, beautiful, and intelligent. Luke shook off the images that came so readily to his mind; they were too reminiscent of his nightmare.

Avoiding his friend's eyes, Luke replied, "Angelica's smart, and she knows what the risks are out there, and besides, there is a trapper that watches out for her too. Maybe he'll be able to get her to move to town or something."

Luke stood. He needed something to take his mind off this conversation. "Guess I'll go see if Old Kate needs me to bring in some wood for the stove."

Without a backward glance he headed out of the room.

•••

Landon sat for a moment, staring into the fire. He had met Robert Barnes and his wife, Lillian, years ago when he had first arrived in the Territory. In fact, Robert had surveyed this ranch for him. The Barnes had been a young couple, a few years older than himself with a young daughter. The girl had been pretty, but he remembered thinking at the time that she was going to be a beautiful woman if she grew up to look like her mother. Going over the conversation with Luke, he began to fill in the holes in his friend's story. Landon had never seen Luke so worked up about a woman. He had described the children with affection, but there had been something in his voice when he had talked about this Angelica. Unless he missed his guess, his friend cared about this woman, and it scared the hell out of him.

A grin hovered on Landon's lips as he rose from his chair. Obviously, this Angelica had grown up to be as beautiful as her mother. Whistling to himself, Landon headed for the stairs. He was looking forward to spring.

CHAPTER TWELVE

Angelica glanced up from her sewing as Carol Anne came in with the morning's eggs. It was hard to believe that it had been weeks since both Luke and Jean Claude had left, and over a month since the children had been brought to her, no more than strangers, scared, confused, and lost. Now, knowing them better, she couldn't imagine her life without them.

William was a boy on the brink of manhood, treating her as if she was fragile and might break. It amused and annoyed her that he didn't think she was capable of doing any of the work he deemed a man's job. She was constantly pointing out that she had run this ranch by herself for years, but it didn't change his view. He worked hard from sunup to sundown, giving her a glimpse of the man that he would become. His parents had been raising him right before their untimely deaths.

Matthew was a quiet boy who excelled at his lessons and constantly had a book in his hands. In the beginning, he had only replied if spoken to, but lately he had been telling her stories from the books he had read when he had managed to sneak into the city library. He was fascinated with astrology and inventions and swore someday that man would somehow make it to the moon. Angelica had smiled at that statement. It was good for boys to have their dreams.

Carol Anne was very smart, reading at a second-grade level. Though she was only four, she had a remarkable ability to manipulate both her brothers into doing what she wanted. The best part was neither brother had figured out that they had been pawns used by a master chess player. It was hard to say no to such an innocent looking face.

As Angelica watched, Carol Anne carefully put away the eggs. Then the young girl began to hop up and down as she waited impatiently for her brothers to come in with the morning's milk. The little girl was excited that Angelica would be showing them how to make butter. It amazed Angelica how much growing children, especially boys, could eat, and it had taken her a little while to realize that someone was sneaking food after they had all gone to bed. She had watched carefully and had been surprised to find that it had been Carol Anne sneaking into the kitchen at night. She hadn't confronted her about it, knowing that the only reassurance that would change her fears would be time.

Angelia set the dress that she had been working on aside and rubbed her arm. Although it was well over a month with the cast, she had been afraid to remove it. Luke had told her that it would take six to eight weeks to heal, and she wasn't taking any chances by taking the offending dressing off early. Unfortunately, the darn thing was making her arm itch like crazy. Taking one of her knitting needles, she ran it under the bandages and pulled back and forth. It was pure bliss to itch the skin that she hadn't been able to reach.

William and Matthew arrived with the milk.

Since it was the four of them now, they would be making larger batches than the one she and Luke had made, and it would take most of the morning, as they had been saving the cream from the milk all week. Angelica had found her mother's large wooden butter churn the night before, and it was washed and ready. She was thankful for that, as she wasn't sure she could use the glass churn without breaking into tears.

After placing the milk buckets into a basin of cold water, Angelica waited until the thermometer reached fifty-five degrees before pouring milk into the wooden churn. A long-handled plunger had been fitted through the lid, and the boys took turns pulling the plunger up and down, as it was too tall and heavy for Carol Anne. Angelica remembered how much her arms used to ache when she and her mother had taken turns at the task.

Ten minutes later, small grainy particles could be seen in the liquid that came up through the plunger's hole in the lid. Angelica waited for the particles to get bigger before she removed the cover. Lumps of butter floated in the buttermilk, some of them bigger than her fist. Taking a long-handled spoon, she fished them out and placed them into a large bowl. Once all the lumps were collected, she handed Carol Anne the spoon and showed the four-year-old how to scrape the lid and plunger to dislodge the butter that clung to them.

"Matthew," Angelica instructed, "use the crock over there and pour the buttermilk into it, please. Good. Can you bring it down to the spring and put it inside the cooling bin?"

As the younger boy poured out the liquid, she turned to William. "We need to fill the churn with cold water and clean all the milk out. It's going to take several buckets."

"Why?" William wanted to know, pouring in the water. "We're just putting more milk in."

"If one batch is bad, you won't ruin the next batch."

After he agitated the plunger for two to three minutes, the water was changed and the process repeated until there was no trace of milk left. Meanwhile, the butter was placed on the sideboard, where Angelica washed it, added salt, and wrapped it into a damp cheesecloth before placing a skillet on top to press all the moisture from it. Grooves in the wood allowed the liquid to run along them and into the sink. Later, the batch would be set aside to dry a little before being formed into balls or pressed into the molds.

•••

"I was thinking that we should get some pigs come spring," Angelica stated a little while later. "We're going to need another cow, too. The way you kids are eating, I'll need to double the number of chicks to be able to have enough eggs for the hotel. I'll have to ask Jean Claude what he'll want for a calf."

William shot a look at Matthew and then back to Angelica. "We can skip lunch and just have some bread and cheese for dinner, and I don't need no breakfast neither."

Angelica put aside the thermometer that she was using to see if the next batch of cream was ready to be churned and looked up at him. His expression was worried.

"I wasn't complaining that we didn't have enough food," she said carefully. "It's only that I never had time enough to tend pigs, and there were always more than enough eggs and chickens for just me. Now that you are here to help me, it just makes sense to expand."

All three of the children had stopped what they were doing but turned back to their chores at her words. William poured more milk into the churn.

"The orchard needs to be pruned, mulched, and tended. I let a lot of the trees go because I just didn't have the time. With all of us working here, come spring, we can get every tree in the orchard to produce and have plenty for ourselves, the Indians, and the hotel."

There was a brief silence as each weighed her words. It was Matthew who broke it. "Why do you give the Indians the extra fruit? Seems like you could have sold more to the hotel."

Angelica smiled. "My father made a bargain with the Indians years ago. He had come across Meda's tribe, and they had been starving. It didn't seem right to him to have extra fruit when they had nothing. They are proud people, and they would never have accepted charity. A bargain was the only way to help them."

Carol Anne brought butter over to her and she began to fill the molds.

"Most of my best childhood memories are when Meda and her tribe were here for the harvest. It would have been a very lonely childhood without her. She's my best friend, and I will always honor the pact that my father made."

"What about Jean Claude?" William wanted to know. "We know that he brings you firewood for a cow or two…" He paused. "But there should be someone in town that sells wood. I'm sure that they would trade for goods too."

Angelica sighed. She had known that the children didn't like Jean Claude, and heaven knew that Jean Claude hadn't made any secret that he didn't like them either. Turning and leaning back against the counter, she looked at all three of them. "I know that Jean Claude is hard to like, but he has always come through for me. Firewood is nonexistent out here, and Newcomb isn't like the city, where things are readily available. This is what works for me living out here. This ranch is where I was born and raised. It's home, and most likely I'll live here till I die."

Till she died. That thought brought an overwhelming sense of sadness. There were so many places that she had heard about and wanted to experience. Now it seemed that she was destined to stay on her land until she perished. Before her accident and meeting Luke, that might have been enough for her, but now, well, it was downright depressing. Unfortunately, Luke had shown her just how lonely she'd been. While the children were a comforting presence, she knew that someday they would leave and find lives of their own. Then once again, she would be left alone. It would be an adequate life but one that would leave her wanting. Was she selfish to want more?

"…next time we go to town." William had continued talking.

"I'm sorry, I missed that."

He gave her a quizzical look. "I said, with the extra fruit and vegetables that we can grow, I'm sure that we can find someone to make a deal on firewood the next time we go to town."

She leveled a look at him. "You need to trust me." She looked around at all of them. "I know the best way to run this ranch. I do not want to hear any more about Jean Claude. You will be polite to him when he returns with the rest of the wood, and that's the end of that. Let's finish the churning, and I'll make a big batch of buttermilk biscuits for dinner."

William looked ready to argue, but in the end, he must have thought better of it. Nodding, he turned back to the churn and took over for Matthew.

Angelica went back to filling the molds. She hadn't missed the look the boys had shared. She sighed inwardly. If she knew anything about men, it was that this conversation was far from over.

•••

Carol Anne was picking up the last of the small branches that William had pruned from the trees and bringing them over the kindling pile when she had the feeling of being watched. She glanced around. William was putting away the ladder he had been using, Matthew was behind the barn filling the wheelbarrow with compost, and Angelica was on the far side of the house, hanging up the washing. There was no sign of Meda. The tingling sensation at the back of her neck persisted. When they lived in the orphanage, there were always hidden eyes watching her every movement. The advantage of being four was that grownups didn't watch you very long. They seemed to think that she couldn't cause very much trouble.

Dropping the branches into the pile, she walked over to the water pump. She was too small to pull the handle up and down, but there was a bucket half filled with water, and a cup hung on the edge. Dipping the cup into the water, she glanced around as she drank. It was a trick she had learned. If she appeared to be doing something mundane, the observer usually took the time to scan around the area and did not notice that she was glancing around too. There weren't too many places to hide, but her attention was caught by a movement in the underbrush bordering the far side of the orchard. Hanging the cup back onto the bucket, she swiped her arm across her face and made for the barn. Entering the dark space, she let her eyes adjust and then raced through to the back. Slipping out the back door, she moved to the edge of the barn and fell to her knees. Peering around the corner, she looked at the place where she had seen movement.

"What are you doing?"

The voice behind her almost made her scream out loud. Turning her head, she looked up at Matthew. Grabbing his hand, she pulled him down beside her.

"Someone is in that underbrush over there. I could feel them watching me," she whispered to him.

Matthew peered in the direction she pointed. "This is the prairie, Carol Anne, not the orphanage. There ain't nobody sneaking around the bushes watching you. It's probably a wild animal."

Carol Anne shook her head. "It ain't any wild animal. I know when I'm being watched, Matthew. There's someone in those bushes."

She could tell that he didn't believe her, but that wasn't anything new. Her brothers often dismissed things that she told them. She hated being four. Well, almost five, since her birthday was less than three months away.

"C'mon," Matthew said, standing, "I'll prove that there isn't anybody there."

With that, he walked around the side of the barn and called to William, who was crossing the yard.

"What's going on?" William wanted to know.

Matthew kept walking as he filled him in. Carol Anne hung back. The underbrush was heavy and thick, yet there was some space close to the ground. It would offer a good cover for anyone wanting to go unnoticed. She had used it several times while Jean Claude had been around.

"I'm gonna show her that there isn't anyone in there watching us," Matthew told his brother as knelt to look under the foliage.

They all jumped as a rabbit, frightened by their sudden presence, skittered away out of the back of the underbrush with surprising speed and noise. Carol Anne squealed and covered her eyes. Matthew fell backwards and William stepped back several feet.

"Damnation, that startled me!" Matthew stood up and laughed. "Told you that there wasn't anyone in the bushes, just some old jack rabbit."

Carol Anne crossed her arms. "I know when I'm being watched, and it wasn't by some dumb old rabbit either!" Sticking her tongue out at him, she ran back towards the house.

Matthew looked at his older brother. William had been unusually quiet. "What do you think?"

William looked around. "Carol Anne doesn't usually make up stories," he said thoughtfully. "We're out in the middle of nowhere. Who would be sneaking in the bushes wanting to watch us? Angelica's friends with all the Indians, and besides, Luke said that they've moved back to the reservations for the winter." He turned, walking back to the barn, Matthew falling in step with him.

"Maybe she's looking for our attention." Their voices grew faint as they entered the barn.

•••

Not ten feet from where the boys had stood, a beetle toddled through the sand and leaves under the dense overgrowth. The insect moved at a steady pace and was out of sight when the sand, in the spot that the jack rabbit had bolted, began to shift. Two dark eyes opened and scanned the barnyard. The Indian had covered his head and upper body with white clay, making it so he blended with the light sand. His black hair had been braided and covered with sticks and leaves. Long rawhide pants and tall moccasins were the only things that he wore. He began to slither backwards, and he might as well have been the sunlight that filtered through the thickness for all the disturbance he created. He had been there for hours. Patience was something that he had learned as the years passed. There was a time for everything.

Reaching the clearing behind the bushes, he worked his way to the small creek that ran past the far side of the valley. Using the edge of the bank for cover, he made his way to where his horse waited. Vaulting onto the painted back, the Indian was miles away before he slowed down. Taking a chunk of buffalo jerky from a small pouch, he let the paint set the pace. He had been careful to watch the women and boys, but he hadn't really paid attention to the girl. Since she would be no match for him, he had dismissed her. That she'd felt his presence was a surprise. He'd watched grown men for weeks and they never knew that he was even there. He felt a tiny stab of respect for the child, even if she was the spawn of the white man. Of course, he still had a job to do. That hadn't changed.

He knew about the white woman who had befriended the Lakota. It meant nothing to him. He'd been banished from his tribe as a young warrior by Sitting Bull. He had vowed to rid the plains of the white man. It sickened him that Sitting Bull and the other chiefs had resigned themselves to the ways of the Long Knives.

Finishing his jerky, he turned the horse to the north.

CHAPTER THIRTEEN

Jean Claude tossed the last piece of wood into the wagon with more force than necessary, making the horses jump. Winter was coming fast and early, and the pelts of the animals he was catching in his traps were some of the best that he had seen in years. It pissed him off that he was about to deliver wood, like some servant, instead of working his traps. He could get Jeb off his back with just a couple of good pelts.

Scratching his beard, he made for his cabin. Grabbing a sack of food and his rifle, he headed back to the wagon and climbed up onto the seat. Releasing the brake, he flicked the reins, and the horses bolted forward as if eager to be on the move. He made sure that several people saw him and his full wagon as he rolled through town. That way they can say that he had kept his bargain to Angelica. His story would be that he managed to save Angelica but not the children or Meda. Eventually, she would accept him.

Not long into the ride, his thoughts turned to the Indian whom he had met nearly ten years before. Jean Claude had never been able to pronounce all those god-awful Indian names with their crazy sounds, and the Indian had laughed at him and said that he was known by the white man as Ghost. He could sneak into a village and steal someone from their bed without being seen or heard, like an apparition. They feared him as they did the dead. It went without saying that he considered himself the ghost of death. That he was a renegade without a tribe, just a castoff, made Jean Claude careful of his dealings with him. Over the years, they had scratched each other's back, so to speak. When Ghost needed weapons or such, it had been Jean Claude that had helped. Now that Jean Claude wanted Angelica and her ranch, he had immediately called on Ghost to make the children disappear. He had thrown Meda in as a bonus, knowing that capturing and selling the cousin of Sitting Bull would entice Ghost to help him like nothing else.

Jean Claude was taking a risk, being out on the open prairie in November. The weather had already been unpredictable, and blizzards were common. Not that he was worried about getting lost; he thrived on the elements. It's just that he wanted to wait till the spring thaw. That way he could have continued his trapping, but Ghost had visited him two days earlier.

Jean Claude spat as he remembered. He'd been out all day working the trap line, and he was tired and hungry. The son of a bitch just stepped out of thin air. Jean Claude had nearly knifed the bastard before he realized who he was. The smug look on the Indians face almost changed his mind.

"I want dark haired woman."

So, he had already been to Angelica's. Wordlessly, Jean Claude walked around him and went into his cabin. He knew that Ghost would follow. He took his time taking off his jacket, throwing it in a pile of furs next to the door. While his back was to the savage, he took the small pistol out of his pocket and palmed it. The coffee pot was still on the stove where he had left it two days ago. Pouring himself a cup of the dark liquid, he sat down at the whiskey barrel that served as a table.

Taking a sip of the cold brew, he looked at Ghost over the rim of his cup. "The deal was the brats and Sitting Bull's cousin. The woman is mine."

Damn but he hated savages. Couldn't trust the sneaky sons of bitches. Someday soon, the army was just going to have to kill them all or keep them to the reservation. Then he wouldn't have to compete for the furs from them. It was bad enough that other fur traders were pouring into the territory. The bloody government was putting up outposts all over the Dakotas, and game was getting scarce. When the gold panned out in the Black Hills, most of the white settlers would be moving on. The unforgiving nature of the prairie would see to that. His mind skittered over the fact that Angelica's ranch was thriving in the middle of the area he considered to be nothing but wasteland.

Ghost's expression didn't change. His stance seemed relaxed, but Jean Claude knew that if he made a wrong move, the Indian would be across the room in a heartbeat with a knife to his gut. It seemed that the Indian didn't trust him anymore than he trusted the Indian. That knowledge made him pleased. That meant that Ghost wasn't sure about him. Good. It was always an advantage to keep your enemies guessing. While he needed Ghost to get rid of the children and Meda, he didn't like dealing with someone that could slice his throat and disappear into the shadows before his body hit the ground.

It had taken a while, but they had come to an understanding. Angelica was Jean Claude's, but Ghost wanted to grab the snot-nosed brats and Meda while there was no moon. That meant that he had had to pack up the wood and leave his traps. Now here he was out in the middle of the prairie again on his way to Angelica's.

The wagon hit a gopher hole and jerked Jean Claude back to the present.

Reaching beneath the seat, he brought out a flask of corn mash liquor. Damn but it was getting cold out here, and the dampness was starting to creep into his bones. Taking several swigs from the flask helped him to forget about the aches and pains. The horses plodded on as Jean Claude continued to drink.

●●●

It was almost dark when Jean Claude decided to stop and build a camp for the night. Climbing down from the wagon, he was surprised that he felt a little unsteady. Unscrewing the top of the flask, he went to take another swig but found that it was empty. Making his way around the horses by holding onto their bridles, he managed to unhitch them and lead them to the stream for a drink. Bringing them back to his makeshift camp, he set stakes so that they could feast on the long grass. Grabbing some jerky and another full jug, Jean Claude arranged his bedroll on the ground under the wagon. Settling himself for the night took a little bit of doing. Somehow his hands weren't cooperating with him. Taking some large swigs from the jug helped to steady him.

Lying back, he realized that his dream was finally coming true. Lillian would be his at last.

●●●

Meda was at the stream fishing when the vision came. The wolf spirit was only a mist on the far bank that shimmered and glowed. Taking the shape of the wolf, its eyes seemed to pulsate as they looked at her.

"The paths are about to cross. Beware of the seventh that has no soul." The voice came from inside her head. "You will need the strength of all, including the white man that walks with wolves, to fight this evil."

"But Luke is gone," she replied.

"His healing power is great. Without it, you will fail."

The glow started to fade, and the mist began to disperse. Meda wanted to cry out for it to tell her more, but she knew that the spirit would only tell her what it wanted her to know. Well, the time was almost here. She had known, of course, that it had been coming, but she felt unprepared. If her grandmother had been alive, she would have known how to deal with whatever was coming.

Gathering up the fish that she had caught that morning, Meda offered thanks for the food and turned toward the house. Climbing the bank, she noticed a footprint in the soft soil. It was too big to be hers, and it was made by someone wearing moccasins. She was the only one around that wore moccasins, and the size was that of a man's. From the look of the print, it had been there several days. The impression showed that it was moving away from Angelica's. Had it been someone from her tribe, they would have certainly stopped in to see her. So why hadn't this one?

Because this one didn't want to be seen.

Following the prints backwards, she lost them in the short grass near a briar patch. There were several places where a body could hide and watch them undetected. But why? Angelica was a friend to the Lakota. The other plain Indians knew that she was under their protection. A chill ran up Meda's spine.

Meda headed toward the house. Should she tell Angelica? She decided against it. Angelica had been afraid when she heard about the original vision. Meda didn't want to leave to go find Luke, but the vision said that they could not win without him. Her options were limited. She would have sent the white wolf, but she hadn't seen him in almost a week. William and Matthew were too new to the plains; they wouldn't know how to survive.

The weather had been clear and sunny for the last couple of days, but Meda knew that that could change at any time. What worried her the most was that there would be a new moon at the end of three sunsets. It would be a perfect time for something or someone to make its move, for there would be no shadows to give away its presence. Leaving the gutted fish on a peg outside the kitchen door, she headed for her tepee. There were lots of preparations to do.

●●●

Jean Claude's rip-roaring hangover wasn't helped by all the prairie dog and gopher holes that the wagon wheels hit. Feeling like there was a marching band beating on his skull, he put his head in his hands. Maybe he had a little too much to drink last night, but it had never bothered him before. He'd wanted to take a swig to help calm the pounding in his head, but he'd finished the jug before he had fallen asleep. What he wouldn't do for a cup of strong coffee right at the moment. His mind and stomach skittered away from the thought of food.

Last night, dreams of Lillian seemed so real. He could smell her scent and feel the silky smoothness of her hair. She smiled coyly at him, laughing when he tried to pull her towards him, somehow always staying just out of reach. Well, it didn't matter now. He was on his way to collect what should have been his years ago. Angelica would learn to obey him. He could make her his Lillian.

The wagon hit another hole, and it almost unseated him. Looking at the position of the sun, he figured that he would be at Angelica's in another two hours. Then he could have the brats unload the wood and he could settle in.

Coming to a small stream, Jean Claude stopped the horses and let them drink. It was turning into one of those crisp fall days. The sky was pale blue, and thick fluffy clouds skittered across the sun, creating shadows that raced across the plain. Hauling himself off the wagon bench, Jean Claude limped around for a moment, letting his cramped muscles stretch. Crouching down to scoop up a handful of water, he noticed the print on the bank. Judging by the size of the print, it was made by a large wolf, and it was only a few hours old. Standing back up, Jean Claude scanned the area. A flash of white in the distance caught his attention. There, out of shotgun range, was a white wolf staring at him. It was one of the biggest Jean Claude had ever seen, and he had never seen a pure white one before. The pelt alone would be worth a small fortune. Excitement that he hadn't felt in years shot like lightning through his body. Licking his lips, he edged toward the wagon and his rifle. As his fingers wrapped around the cold metal, he remembered that he had a wagon full of wood and Ghost was expecting him. There was no time to track and hunt the massive animal. Spitting, Jean Claude watched as the animal trotted away, in the opposite direction of Angelica's, moving like it didn't have a care in the world.

"Go and run, you bastard," he muttered as the prize disappeared from sight. "I'll be coming for you next."

He climbed back up onto the wagon bench and grabbed the reins. Clicking to the horses, he started once again towards Angelica's, but his mind was on the wolf.

● ● ●

Angelica hung the last of the laundry on the line and then rubbed the back of her aching neck. Wash day had certainly been easier when it had just been her clothes. Looking up at the sun, she figured that the children would be coming in from their chores in a few minutes. She would just have enough time to change out of her wet clothes and brush her hair before the three of them came charging through the door, famished. The thought brought a smile to her face. It seemed so long ago that she had dreaded the thought of being cooped up in the house alone for the winter.

Turning toward the house, a flash of white in the orchard caught her attention. Raising her hand to shield her eyes, she could see that Wolf was on the far side. Even from this distance, she could see that the fur on his back was raised. His stance was one of wariness, and he was still as a statue as he seemed to be staring at something in the briars. Angelica watched as he sniffed the ground and took a step closer. He nosed under the bushes for a moment, then he seemed to follow the scent as he headed down out of sight to the creek.

Shaking her head, Angelica headed to the house. The weather had been usually mild after the initial snowstorm, and she'd taken the opportunity to do the wash and air out the bedding. Meda had been predicting another storm coming for later in the week, and from the way she talked, they were going to be buried with snow. After lunch, she'd have the boys bring in the bedding while she and Carol Anne cut up vegetables for the dinner stew. Hopefully, by morning the laundry would be dry and she could spend tomorrow pressing it.

In her bedroom, behind a blanket that she had hung up for privacy, Angelica was pulling one of her service calicos over her head when she heard a wagon pulling to a stop outside. Her right hand was clumsy as she tried to hook the row of small buttons on the bodice of her dress. She had done half of them when she heard Carol Anne come bursting through the front door, breathlessly calling her name. Some of her lace camisole with a small amount of cleavage was still showing as Angelica rounded the blanket to address the girl.

"Carol Anne, can you help with the rest of these buttons, please?"

There was a moment of silence that caused her to look up. William stood beside his sister. His mouth was slightly agape, and his eyes were locked on to her bosom. He gulped audibly. Behind them, just in the doorway, stood Jean Claude, and there was no mistaking the look of lust in his eyes. Angelica could feel the blush creeping across her face. She clutched the rest of the bodice together.

"I'm so sorry, I didn't realize that you were here, Jean Claude. We weren't expecting you today. You must have brought the rest of the wood…that was so kind of you. If you'll excuse me for a moment, I'll be right out. Carol Anne, if you could just help me."

She knew that she was babbling, but she couldn't help it. Ducking back around the blanket, she sat down on the bed and put her head into her hands. Carol Anne stood in front of her and didn't say a word. There were sounds of footsteps retreating, and then they heard the front door close.

"Why are you sad?" Carol Anne wanted to know.

Angelica took a deep breath and attempted a smile. "I'm not sad, sweetie. I'm embarrassed."

"Why?"

She pulled the little girl onto her lap and rested her chin on the top of Carol Anne's head. "Well, I didn't realize that William had come in with you, or that Jean Claude was standing in the doorway. A lady never shows her under things to a man that is not her husband."

"But William and Matthew see me in my nightgown all the time."

Angelica smiled. Life was so simple for children. They hadn't been expecting Jean Claude, and she had been blind to the fact that William wasn't a child anymore but a young man on the brink of adulthood. He had grown up fast on the streets, had shouldered adult responsibilities. She should have realized.

Squeezing the little girl tight, Angelica knew that she couldn't stay behind this curtain forever. Besides, the sooner they unloaded the wood from the wagon, the sooner they could send Jean Claude on his way.

Standing the little girl up, she said, "It's okay while you're little to let your brothers see you in your nightgown. When you get older, we'll talk more about it."

Carol Anne seemed content with that and began to help her button her bodice.

•••

While the boys were emptying the wagon, Jean Claude headed to the creek, his mind still full of the whiteness of Angelica's skin. Anger bubbled in his veins. He had always treated her like a lady, but she was nothing but a whore, flaunting herself in front of the boy and himself. She was nothing like his Lillian. It was her father's blood that corroded Lillian's.

Running his hand through his beard, he looked out at the shallow water. The heat of his body cooled as he thought of the plan that he and Ghost had devised. Two days. That was all he had to wait. Two days and the brats would be gone, sold to Indians farther west as slaves, never to be heard from again, along with Sitting Bull's cousin. Then he was free to take Angelica, sell the ranch, and exercise his husbandly rights anytime he wanted.

His body responded to that thought well ahead of the event.

CHAPTER FOURTEEN

Luke braced himself against the bed frame and pulled with all his might. A resounding snap echoed in the large room. The cowboy, lying prone on the bed, didn't move. Rotating the arm that he held, Luke felt the shoulder joint. Sure enough, it had popped back into the socket. Taking the bandage that Old Kate had provided, he bound the arm to the man's chest. The cowboy snored, still under the influence of the chloroform that Luke had administered earlier.

Luke had been out on the range, enjoying the warm respite, when a rider caught up with him. One of the boys had been thrown from his horse, and they thought his arm was broken. On exam, Luke found a deep six-inch gash in the skin of the upper arm and then had determined that the shoulder had just been dislocated. Most likely it had gotten in the way of the horse's hoof. Once his patient was anesthetized, it didn't take Luke long to repair the wound and bandage it. With a couple of weeks' worth of rest, the cowboy would be able to resume his duties.

Luke washed his hands in the basin of hot water that Old Kate had brought him earlier before sitting next to the bed to monitor his patient. Chloroform was a fickle anesthetic. Too little meant that his patients felt everything, and too much could lead to death.

They had brought the cowboy to the bunkhouse. The boy couldn't have been more than eighteen, and his smooth face reminded Luke of William. Usually, Luke tried to stay too busy to think of Angelica and the children, but there were times, like now, when they crept into his thoughts, and it gnawed at him. He had hoped that by getting them settled, it would have been enough to stop worrying about them, but lately they haunted his dreams. Last night, he had a dream that Wolf showed up to Landon's and tried to drag him back to the ranch to fight off some invisible demon.

The cowboy shifted and groaned, indicating the chloroform was wearing off and he would be awake soon.

Luke felt the walls closing in on him. He wished that Mary would hurry up and have her baby and that spring would come faster so that he could check on Angelica and the children and move on.

Glancing at the sleeping form to make sure that the boy was still breathing, Luke stood and walked over to the stove. A fire was blazing inside to help keep the chill at bay. Grabbing a mug from the shelf above, he poured a cup of coffee and crossed to the window. Being a doctor, he was used to biding his time to see if a wound would turn septic or if the head injured would come out of the coma and be able to recognize anyone. Most times the body would heal; it was the soul that was sometimes irreparably scarred. Time could be a blessing or the wounded's worst enemy.

Leaning his forehead against the cold glass, Luke took a deep breath. It seemed that time had become his nemesis since he'd left Angelica. It mocked him, taunted him, and stretched his nerves and patience to the breaking point.

Another, louder groan from the bed brought his head around. The cowboy's eyes were open, and he was trying to sit up. Setting the mug on the table, Luke crossed to his patient.

"Hold on there, cowboy," Luke told the man, a boy really, as he pushed him back down onto the mattress. "Give yourself a minute before you try to sit up."

The cowboy took a few seconds to try to focus on him before he managed it. "Hey Doc, somebody sick?"

"No, you got thrown from your horse, dislocated your shoulder, and gashed up your arm. I gave you some chloroform. You remember?"

The cowboy furrowed his brow with concentration. "I was rounding up some strays down by the riverbed when the bank collapsed, and I got thrown. I thought I broke my arm."

His speech was slow and his voice slightly thickened, but those things were to be expected after coming out of anesthesia. So far so good.

"Let me help you." Luke grabbed the boy by his good arm and gently pulled him forward. Positioning a pillow behind the cowboy's back, Luke slowly lowered him so that he was leaning against the pillow and the wall. Perching on the edge of a chair, ready in case the cowboy passed out, he watched his patient.

"You didn't break anything." Luke told him belatedly. "I popped your shoulder back in and put some stitches in your arm. You'll have to keep the sling and bandage on for about a week, but other than that, I think you'll be fine."

The cowboy looked relieved at his words. A knock on the door interrupted any further conversation. Luke opened it to find several cowboys standing outside. One of them stepped forward, hat in his hand, and asked if their friend was okay. Luke smiled and assured them that he was before stepping aside to let them in. By the time that he headed out to the main house, his patient was telling his audience about his "near brush with death." Of course, he was also taking a whole bunch of ribbing about being thrown.

Reaching the kitchen door, Luke looked back at the bunkhouse. The cowboy was going to be fine, and the boy would probably tell the story into his old age. By then the story would have grown to mythical proportions. A ghost of a smile hovered on Luke's lips. He envied the boy his future, one that hadn't been blemished with more than a fall from a horse and a dislocated shoulder and a few stitches. A future that didn't contain a lifetime of nightmares or loneliness.

If only spring would hurry up and arrive.

• • •

The days took on a sort of predictable routine. Luke spent them helping out with any of the hundreds of tasks that came daily with a large ranch. Occasionally, he attended to a wound here or there.

Landon's wife Mary showed no sign of getting ready to go into labor, and that concerned Luke. Her due date was still two weeks away, but the baby should have turned and started to prepare going into the birth canal. That it hadn't gave him a bad feeling. It was a breech birth that had taken the life of Landon's first wife and child.

Luke had previously sent a letter to his old university asking about options for delivering a breech baby, and he had been disappointed with the results. Cesarean surgery was only successful in saving the baby, usually after the mother was deceased. While the procedure didn't seem too difficult to perform, doctors couldn't agree on how to post treat the mother if she survived the surgery. Some surgeons left the abdomen open to drain, while others packed the womb with herbs and bandages before sewing it closed. Either way, the mother usually became ill and died within a week. The other problem was that anesthesia was not good for the baby, and many had been lost to its unpredictable effects. Luke showed nothing of his misgivings to anyone, but he saw that same worry in Old Kate's eyes when she looked at Mary's bulging abdomen.

●●●

Old Kate gave voice to her thoughts when he arrived early to the kitchen for breakfast. It was still dark outside, and the kerosene lantern didn't do much to chase away the shadows. One of them fell across Old Kate's face as she served him some eggs.

"You thinking that this babe is going to try to come hind end first like the other one?"

Luke pushed his eggs around the plate, his appetite gone. There was no use lying to her, and besides, he figured that she had helped birth as many babies as he had. If this was going to be a breech presentation, then he was going to need all the help he could get.

"Yes, I'm thinking that's why the baby hasn't dropped yet, but there's still some time. I've been looking through my medical books, and there's a few things that we can have Mary do to try to turn it naturally. Exercises and such. They're new methods, but they're worth a try." He rubbed his hand across his face. "I just don't know how to approach it so that I don't worry her or Landon."

"Then you just tell the mother and don't bother the husband," a female voice said from behind them.

They both turned to see Mary standing in the doorway, still in her nightgown with Landon's coat wrapped around her. Luke got to his feet. She shuffled into the kitchen, motioned to Luke to sit back down, and then sat heavily into a chair.

"Now what are you doing listening to people's private conversations?" Old Kate asked her, hands on her hips.

Mary smiled serenely at her, apparently undaunted. "Since the conversation concerned me, I thought I would join in." Turning to Luke, she grew serious. "Now what are these exercises that you read about?"

Luke had to admire the way that she looked him in the eye when it was obvious that she was scared. It was that courage and determination that it took out here in the West. It took a certain kind of woman to live out in the middle of nowhere and face the unknown. That thought made him think of Angelica. He figured that she would like Mary.

He realized that Mary was patiently waiting for an answer. "If we can turn the baby before you go into labor, that would be the safest for both you and the baby. I've never seen these moves used, so I'm not sure if they work, but I think it's our best bet right now. Though we have to prepare in case they don't."

The thought of telling Landon that his child was another potential breech baby was a daunting one. His friend had already seen the worst possible outcome of such a presentation, and it would take a lot of faith and strength to prepare for another. Landon was like a brother to him and had saved his life that day at Shenandoah Valley. Luke couldn't afford to fail now, and if this child meant to enter this world ass first, well, he was damn well going to be prepared to make it happen. It was the constant waiting that was starting to wear on his nerves. However, a doctor's life always seemed to be a waiting game, as the outcome always relied on the particular circumstances and patient.

"Don't worry about Landon. You just leave him to me," Mary said, straightening her back and wrapping the coat more firmly around her shoulders. "I have faith that the Good Lord has a plan and will bless us with a fine, healthy baby. That's why he sent you here to us, Luke."

Her words sent a wave of apprehension down his back. He wasn't God, and for all his training, there were plenty of times that he had lost a patient even though he had done everything that he could. It was a burden on his soul to have such blind faith placed into his hands, knowing that the fates could snatch it away in the blink of an eye. It was good that she had such faith, though; Luke had seen how the mind could heal when there was hope. He had also seen despair bring down a healthy man or woman in days.

Old Kate must have been thinking along the same vein, for she placed a hand on his shoulder and squeezed. "Everything is going to be fine. I'm going to fix you a good breakfast," she said, eyeing Mary. "And then you are going straight back to bed and rest."

They all knew better to argue with Old Kate when she got something in her mind, so Mary just nodded demurely, and Luke went back to finishing his breakfast.

•••

It was after dinner when Luke made his way out onto the front porch. He studied the waning moon and pulled his coat's collar up against the chill that was in the air. It was just a sliver in the dark sky and gave off only a glimmer of light. It was hard to believe that he had been gone from

Angelica's for over a month now. November could hit the plains hard, and even if he wanted to go see her and the children, it was foolhardy to think about it this time of year. Storms came up fast and without warning. The wind could blow from any direction, making snow impossible to see through, and when the temperature dropped, a man could wander in circles until he froze to death. Oftentimes, people strung a rope between outbuildings to be able to find their way back. Without the rope, Luke had heard of people walking within inches of a structure and heading out into the open prairie because they hadn't known the building was there.

He knew it was his imagination, but the moon seemed to mock him. In a few days it would be a new moon, and then it would begin the buildup to being full. Most babies made their appearances during a full moon, which meant he was running out of time for this baby to turn and present normally.

Luke rubbed a hand over his face. God, he was tired. They had tried all the exercises from his books and a few that he had learned in some Indian villages, but so far, the baby hadn't budged an inch. Mentally, he had begun the process of preparing for having to put Mary under anesthesia, though it was his last option.

He'd gone over the procedure in his head again and again until he was sure that he could perform it in his sleep. In fact, there were some mornings when he wasn't so sure that he hadn't done it already.

Winter hadn't even started, and he already had that closed in feeling. Since the war, he hadn't stayed in one place for longer than a month. This constant closeness, first at Angelica's and now here, was causing him to become anxious and edgy. Seeing the obvious love between Landon and Mary wasn't helping either. Luke was happy for his friend, there wasn't anyone else more deserving of it, but it was something that he knew he could never have for himself, and it was eating at him.

His nightmares were becoming more frequent, and the ghosts of his past seemed to be catching up. God, he wished this baby would turn and decide to come out early. Then he could make a break for the south, maybe Texas or New Mexico, somewhere where he could just keep riding.

The front door opened behind him, yet he didn't need to turn around to know that it was Landon who had followed him. He'd have known those footsteps anywhere.

Landon leaned up against the nearest post and looked up at the moon too. "I know that you're practically jumping out of your skin by being cooped up, but I appreciate you being here, Luke."

Landon wasn't one to waste words. Luke let out a chuckle. He never could fool his friend, but on the other hand, Landon could never fool him either. Landon had more to say, and Luke was sure that he wasn't going to like it.

"Before you give me some lecture, Landon, let me tell you right now. I'll see that your child is born into this word safe and sound, and you have my word that I will do my best to keep Mary safe too. But I'll be high tailing it south as soon as I can, snow or no snow. I'm not cut out to forget the past, and I can't blindly put my faith in a God I don't believe in."

Landon was silent for a bit, letting the words hang in the air between them before he said, "I guess you aren't the man I thought you were. You seem to think that you can outrun the truth. It was a war. Men and boys died, and there is no way you could have changed that or saved them all. You want to punish yourself for things beyond your control. Stop being a damn martyr."

Luke felt like he had been suckered punched in the gut. Landon was like a brother to him, and his opinion mattered to Luke. To hear those words, words that revealed his deepest fear and shame, well, they cut deep. He said, "I thought you of all people would understand. I should have saved more, but instead, I took lives that weren't mine to take. They were just kids, for Christ's sake. I went against everything I believed in. Who am I to have anything while those boys are dead?"

Landon said, "Don't try to bullshit me, Luke. I've known you my whole life, and I never saw you back away from anything, but since the war, it seems that you're so scared to believe in something or someone that you'll go to the depths of hell to avoid them. It takes courage to stand and fight for something or someone that you care about, even if the odds are stacked against you."

Landon paused and turned to look directly at Luke.

"You didn't lose your faith in God back there in the battlefields; you lost faith in yourself. We had to make some hard choices, and it's tearing you up inside. I know you, Luke. You won't forgive yourself, and you don't think that you deserve to be happy, never mind loved." He let out a deep sigh. "We all did things that we aren't proud of, but I'll be damned if I'll set myself up in purgatory for the rest of my life. God punished me with the loss of my first child and wife, and I consider my dues paid."

Taking a step forward, he leaned in to look Luke in the eye. "You can lie to yourself all you want, but you'll never be able to outrun the memories. Face them head on and forgive them, forgive yourself, or they'll end up destroying you and any chance of happiness that you could possibly have."

His speech done, Landon went back inside, letting the door slam behind him.

Luke looked back at the moon. Coming from Landon, that had been a virtual sermon. Of course, his friend could never understand. He had sworn an oath that he would cause no harm, that he would only help and heal. He had failed that promise. The lives of the men that he had killed weighed like anchors on his soul, and God had been the one that had tied the ropes around his neck. No passage of time was ever going to change that. No amount of forgiveness either.

The wind was picking up, and a cold shiver went through him. Landon's words echoed in his head. What would be his dues? If he forgave himself and faced his demons, then what? If he made a life with Angelica and the children and something happened to them, he would never forgive himself. Besides, there was always the fear that he could take that rage inside him and use it again. If he was going to be honest with himself, that was his biggest fear. What if he turned that rage against someone that he loved? He'd never be able to live with himself. No, it was best if he just kept riding and stayed away from everyone.

A lone wolf howled in the distance. The sound was an echo of what he felt inside.

CHAPTER FIFTEEN

William walked away from the house feeling strange. He entered the barn and climbed the ladder to the loft, where he had arranged walls of hay to create a small room, in the back far corner, away from everyone. Come spring, he was going to see if Angelica would let him sleep there. Sharing a constant space with Matthew was wearing on his nerves. The house was too small for four people; they were frequently tripping over each other. Now that he didn't have to constantly babysit his siblings, he felt that he could indulge in the need for some privacy.

Sitting down on an old milk stool that he'd found, William stared at the back wall. He couldn't get the image of Angelica with her bodice undone out of his mind. It wasn't like he hadn't seen plenty of women in lesser stages of undress before. When they'd lived on the streets, there had been plenty of "ladies of the evening," as the lady next door liked to call them, in the neighborhood. Their blouses had been cut low, and occasionally he had even seen an ankle or knee, yet they hadn't made him feel like he did right now. Not for the first time, he wished that his dad or Luke were around to talk to. Lately, his body and thoughts had been foreign to him, usually when Angelica was near.

He wasn't stupid. He knew that he was sweet on Angelica, and he also knew that she thought of him as a little boy. She was in love with Luke. William had heard her ask Luke to stay that night that Luke's nightmare had awakened her. It had woken him too. Creeping to the edge of the loft, he had listened as Luke had proclaimed that he wasn't coming back. That he had only brought them there to ease his conscience about leaving

Angelica alone.

He had been relieved and angry when Luke had left. Yet he'd made Luke promise to come back in the spring so that William could show him how well he could run the ranch. Run it like a man, not the boy they all seemed to think he was. Stepping up after his parents were killed and keeping his siblings together until the neighbor had turned them in had been hard, but he had managed it. Maybe fate had stepped in, because if she hadn't turned them in, they wouldn't have been on the orphan train and met Luke or Angelica. Whether that was a good or bad thing remained to be seen.

Slight rustling noises from below made him turn and listen. Inching his way to the edge of the loft, he peered over. William could see Carol Anne crouched down behind the small wagon that Angelica used to carry the fruit from the orchard once it was harvested. He was about to call down to her, but before he could, Carol Anne whirled and ducked out the back door of the barn. Less than three seconds later, Jean Claude came through the front door of the barn. Several traps dangled from his hands, and he was muttering to himself.

William watched as Jean Claude stopped at the work bench and set the traps down. Looking around, Jean Claude spotted a small pail. William grimaced as the older man reached into the pail and scooped out what appeared to be axle grease. Using his fingers, he smeared it on to the rusty metal. When he was satisfied that they were covered with the greasy concoction, he wiped his hands on the front of his jacket and gathered the traps up.

"There," he said, "Let that white son of a bitch escape these." With that, Jean Claude headed out the same door, Carol Anne had disappeared out of moments before.

"Tarnation," William muttered as he headed for the stairs.

He assumed that Jean Claude must have seen Wolf. Somehow, he needed to stop Jean Claude from setting those traps. Reaching the barn floor, he ran to the back door. Carol Anne and Jean Claude were nowhere in sight. Should he try to stop the old trapper, or should he warn Angelica and let her try to reason with him? Both ideas seemed impossible. Jean Claude wasn't going to listen to either one of them.

"What's wrong?"

William whirled to find Meda behind him. "Jean Claude is setting out wolf traps, and I think Carol Anne is trying to stop him."

Meda closed her eyes, and her face seemed to relax, and she swayed slightly. William wasn't sure if she was going to faint. He stood there hesitantly for a moment, torn between catching her if necessary and running after his sister. Meda was a stranger to him and an Indian at that, but she was also Angelica's friend. Luke had said that if he was going to live in Indian country, then he needed to make friends with them. Meda had been nothing but kind to him and his siblings, so he figured that he should make sure that she was all right. Besides, Carol Anne could avoid Jean Claude for days; he would never even know that she was watching him.

As he reached out to take her arm, Meda startled him by opening her eyes. Grabbing William by the shoulders, she pushed him toward the front of the barn. "Gather your brother, and I will get your sister. Find a place and be prepared to hide. Don't come out until you know that it is safe. If they can't find you, then they can't take you away."

"Who the heck are they?" he wanted to know, digging in his heels.

Meda looked exasperated but she stopped pushing him.

"I believe that Jean Claude wants Angelica and this ranch, and he will stop at nothing to get them. I feel that he is not alone. I know that you think you are a man, but this is something that can't be won by strength. You must trust me; all of our lives depend on it. Now go and do as I say."

With that, she turned and was gone. William wasn't sure what she was talking about, and he was torn between following her or going to find Matthew. Deciding that he should find Matthew first before he followed anyone, just in case she was right, he headed toward the house. Last time he had seen Matthew, his brother had been up on his bed with his nose in a book.

•••

Carol Anne sprung the trap with a piece of firewood. Its lethal steel jaws took chunks out of the wood, sending chips flying into the air. It was the last of the traps that she had watched Jean Claude set out earlier. He had hidden them along several paths around the house, and this one had been placed down by the creek, in a patch of reeds. It was on the route where animals, Wolf included, liked to come and quench their thirst.

Grabbing the trap by the chain, Carol Anne dragged it into the slow-moving water and let it sink out of sight. Splashing back to shore, she headed up the path and ran into Meda.

"You play a dangerous game, little one," Meda told her. "Jean Claude will be angry that his traps have yielded nothing but firewood."

"I don't care," Carol Anne retorted, her face set in defiance. "He's not going to hurt Wolf or any other animal around here."

Meda kneeled so she was on Carol Anne's level. "I do not want any animals hurt either, but we must be careful."

"Why?"

Meda decided. It would do the child no good to lie. If they were to get out of whatever was coming alive, then, she decided, they all had to know what they were to face. Watching the children for the last month, she knew that Carol Anne was smarter than any of them gave her credit for. "Jean Claude wants to take Angelica away and knows that we will try to stop him. I feel that he has not come here alone. We need to be ready for anything. Angering him will only cause him to react faster and meaner."

Rising, she took Carol Anne by the hand, and they began walking up the path, back toward the house. The day had started out sunny yet cool, but now dark storm clouds were coming in from the north, blocking out the sun. The wind had picked up, bringing the promise of snow on its blustery gusts. Leaves scattered before them, pushed and pulled by invisible tendrils of wind.

Carol Anne stopped. They were at the edge of the orchard. "What if Angelica doesn't want to go?"

Meda looked at Carol Anne with admiration. This child should have been born a Lakota. She was smart and brave; it was hard to believe that she was only four years old.

"I don't think Jean Claude will care..."

She was cut off by a bellow of rage that came from down at the creek.

"Quick," Meda told Carol Anne, "run back to the house and stay close to Angelica. If there is danger, then you need to hide until you know that it is safe."

With that, Meda turned and sprinted back down the path toward the creek. Carol Anne ran in the direction of the house.

•••

Jean Claude rooted through the reeds until his fingers clasped around the chain that he had tethered his trap too. Pulling on the chain, he watched as the trap sliced through the water, with a piece of wood caught in its tines.

"Son of a bitch," he snarled.

This was the fourth trap that he had checked on that had a piece of wood in it. Only human interference could have caused this, and as anger shot through every cell of his body, he knew that it had to be that squaw. No one else would have dared touch his traps. Opening the jaws, he removed the wood and flung it back into the stream. Resetting the device, he placed it back among the reeds.

The anger was turning to rage, and all he wanted was to find the meddling bitch. Show her that she couldn't mess with his traps or him. He actually took a few steps toward the tepee before some semblance of a thought penetrated his brain. Damn filthy squaw needed to be shown her place, but that would have to wait. Ghost would be here tomorrow night, then the brats and the meddling Indian bitch would be gone.

Unclenching his back teeth, he enjoyed the thought of watching Ghost take Meda and the children away, knowing that he would never see them again. Best of all was knowing that there would be no one left to challenge his claim to Angelica or her ranch.

He just needed to bide his time, and then Angelica would be all his.

•••

Carol Anne bolted through the door and ran to Angelica. Flinging her arms around Angelica's leg, she buried her head in the folds of the older woman's skirt.

Angelica's heart was racing. "What's wrong?" she asked, trying to pull the small girl back so that she could see her face.

Carol Anne let out a sob and clung tighter. Pulling her along, Angelica crossed over to the rocker and sat down. She maneuvered the child so that she was cradled on her lap. "All right now, what are all the tears about?"

Carol Anne continued to cry as Angelica rocked her. Angelica had never seen Carol Anne cry before, and it made her nervous. Finally, the shaking shoulders subsided, and Carol Anne was reduced to hiccupping.

"Are you ready to talk now?"

Teary eyes turned up to her, and they seemed to take up Carol Anne's entire face. Even though she was only four years old, her eyes had seen their share of pain and suffering, and now they showed every moment of it. Angelica felt her heart twist painfully. "What is it?" Angelica whispered.

"Meda says that Jean Claude is going to take you away. I don't want him! I want Luke! Please say that you won't go away with Jean Claude and leave us! Please!"

Once again, the little girl was reduced to tears. Angelica held her close and made comforting sounds as she stroked Carol Anne's hair, but her mind was racing. Meda was not one to frighten a child unnecessarily. Had Jean Claude said or done something to warrant Meda to warn Carol Anne? Where were Meda and Jean Claude now? Where were the boys?

Holding Carol Anne so she could wipe away the child's tears with her apron, Angelica said, "Don't worry sweetie. Jean Claude isn't taking me anywhere. We are a family, and families stay together. I'll go and have a talk with him and Meda and get it all straightened out. Okay?"

| 151 |

Wiping away at the tears, Carol Anne looked far from convinced that Angelica could make things right. Angelica put a smile on her face and placed the small girl on her feet. "Now you go and find the boys and tell them to go finish up any chores and that dinner will be ready when they are done."

Opening the front door, she let Carol Anne walk out ahead of her. She was thoughtful as the child headed for the barn and disappeared inside.

Fear started to churn in the pit of her stomach. Squaring her shoulders, Angelica turned and headed for Meda's tepee.

•••

Meda watched as Jean Claude stalked from the river, heading up the opposite bank after glaring in the direction of her tepee before moving out of sight. It wasn't hard to figure out that he thought she was the one that had sabotaged his traps. That was good. She would rather have him focused on her than Carol Anne. She willed her heartbeat to slow. It was time to start putting her plan into action. She had known from the minute he had arrived that everything her grandmother and mother had taught her would be put to the test.

Moving briskly, Meda started up the path toward her tepee. Wolf was waiting for her when she reached it. He had been pacing back and forth and gave a small yip when he caught sight of her. His coat was matted and dirty, and his once full frame was thin and gaunt.

"I too am glad to see you, my friend," she told him before slipping into the tepee and then reappearing with two wooden bowls. Crossing to a small iron pot that had been placed in the middle of some hot coals, Meda ladled some stew into the dishes. She placed one in front of Wolf and squatted down next to him.

"Eat," she told him. "Jean Claude is angry, and the children are in danger." Taking a spoonful of the stew, she ate but didn't taste it. Her mind was going over all the preparations that she had been working on. "Stay close to Carol Anne. We must be prepared for anything."

Wolf followed her movements with his gold eyes. Nosing at the bowl, he took a tentative lick at the stew. Hunger took over and he dove into it.

Meda continued to talk. "There will be no moon tomorrow night. It is the time when a predator would strike." She furrowed her brow. "I found tracks down by the river, and I feel that Jean Claude has not come here alone."

Wolf looked up at her and yipped.

"You know who it is, don't you? I believe it is the shadow man that sells captives to other tribes. That would make sense. With us gone, there would be no one to stop Jean Claude from taking Angelica."

Usually, Meda missed Jean Claude's visits. The few times she had seen him, she had noticed the lust he had had for Lillian, and it wasn't a giant leap to see that he wanted Angelica too.

She stood up and refilled Wolf's bowl. "I must go find Luke and bring him back."

Wolf had begun to eat, but at her words, he stopped and growled.

"I am not strong enough to fight a man, and the wolf spirit said that we needed Luke to be victorious," she told him. "I don't know what else to do."

The light was fading, and the wind had doubled its efforts since the afternoon, making branches bend back and forth. Yet through the noise of the rustling leaves, Meda could hear someone heading her way. Closing her eyes, she listened and knew that it was Angelica's footsteps that she heard.

A few seconds later, Angelica entered the clearing. Meda did not acknowledge her but instead turned back to the hot coals and poured a bucket of water on them. They sizzled and hissed as a cloud of steam rose, only to be pulled apart by the strong wind. For a moment, Meda thought that she saw a face in the vapor, but it was a face that she didn't recognize.

Angelica was out of breath by the time she reached the tepee. "Carol Anne said that you warned her about Jean Claude. Why? What has happened?"

Small bits of sleet had begun to pelt their faces as Wolf turned and trotted down the path. Meda motioned for Angelica to enter the tepee.

The smoky interior was dark and quieter. Meda knelt next to the fire pit and stirred the embers. Feeding small bits of kindling to the coals, she soon had a flame that she added some small logs too. Only when she was satisfied that the fire would not go out did she turn and look at Angelica. "I think Jean Claude plans on taking you away with him. My guess is that he plans on having a renegade, who the white man calls Ghost, sell me and the children into captivity."

Angelica's mouth fell open and she could only stare at her friend.

"I found prints of a man's moccasins down by the stream, and there is no reason for Jean Claude to have brought the remainder of the wood until spring. There will be no moon tomorrow night. It is the perfect time for an attack, because there will be no shadows to give them away."

"But that is ridiculous!" Angelica sputtered. "Jean Claude just can't kidnap anyone or force me to go with him. There are laws in this country. All I'll have to do is tell someone and they will have him arrested."

Meda shook her head at her friends' innocence. It wasn't Angelica's fault that she was so naïve. Living out on the prairie alone did not give much opportunity to socialize or learn human behavior, good or bad.

"Jean Claude will not give you the chance."

Meda sat down next to the fire and held out her hand. The fire light flickered and made shadows dance around them. Angelica sat down, facing her friend.

Meda's voice was soft. "At first, I thought it was the Long Knives that were after your land. I was blind to what was in front of my eyes. Jean Claude wanted your mother. We both knew that, as did she. Remember back. He would seek her out and she would stay very close to you and your father. She knew that he was dangerous, that he wouldn't hesitate to harm you or your father and take her away."

Angelica stared into the fire, and Meda knew that she was thinking back. Unfortunately, a child's memory is usually filled with inaccuracies. The innocence of the child's mind latches onto only those memories that had strong emotions attached, and Lillian had protected her child well. She had hidden her fears from her daughter, never conveying the danger that Jean Claude had presented. Angelica's face was very readable, and Meda knew that she didn't remember the things the way that Meda did. The Lakota did not write things down; they were known for their storytelling. Every village had a storyteller that could recite every word, every aspect of their history going back hundreds of years. Meda was one for whom details were very important. They could mean the difference between life and death.

Angelica shook her head and confirmed what Meda had already known. "I'm sorry. I just don't remember my mother telling me anything bad about him. He's always brought us wood for as long as I can remember. I know that he is uncivilized, but that doesn't mean that he's out to hurt anyone." She stood up and began to pace the small space. "You've said it yourself that the spirits speak in riddles. I don't think that they are warning you about Jean Claude. Maybe the prints that you saw are from this ghost person, and he is the one that they are warning you about. Maybe Jean Claude showing up forced whoever it was to change their plans."

Meda rose slowly. Angelica was grasping at straws, and Meda did not have the time to try to change her mind. "We are blood sisters," she said as she walked over to her friend. "I have learned from your family, and you have learned from mine. You are more Lakota than you know. Put aside the white man's voices in your head and listen with your Lakota heart. You know that it is telling you that Jean Claude is dangerous and what I say is true."

Reaching into her pocket, Meda pulled out a beaded necklace that had a leather pouch attached to it. She placed the necklace around Angelica's neck. "I have made this for you. It is filled with strong medicine that will help protect you. Just in case," she said solemnly.

There was confusion on Angelica's face, plus something else that Meda had a hard time deciphering by the limited light cast from the fire. Anger? Determination? Denial? Here was the moment that Meda always knew was coming. They had become blood sisters when they were children. The ceremony had been a sacred one for Meda. To bond to a sister for life meant that they had become of one blood—family. To Meda, that meant that she would die for Angelica if that meant Angelica could live. What did it mean to Angelica? Did she take it seriously and understand the ramifications of their childhood action? Would she give up her life for Meda, an Indian that most white men considered filthy savages?

"I still think that you're wrong," Angelica told her as she turned to go. "I don't think that Jean Claude is dangerous to us at all, but I will trust your instincts that something is wrong."

Meda watched as she fingered the pouch, pausing as she appeared to search for what she wanted to say. Taking a deep breath, she stood straighter and grabbed Meda's hand.

"I have always considered you a sister too. I trust you, and we will face whatever this is together."

Meda smiled. It was the blessing that she had been looking for.

●●●

Jean Claude leaned against the side of the tree and observed Angelica leave the tepee. The wind and snow were picking up, but he waited in his hiding spot, watching as Meda came outside to pick up the pot and bowls that were around the fire pit. He was about to leave when she straightened and looked directly at the spot he was standing. Her gaze never wavered and she angled her chin so that he got the feeling that she was looking down her nose at him. As anger began to overtake him. He noticed the small smile on her face, and he suddenly knew that the interfering bitch had figured things out and was about to ruin his plans. Now he would have to move without Ghost. There was no time to wait for him. Somehow, he would have to stop the squaw from keeping him from Angelica.

CHAPTER SIXTEEN

As Luke looked out at the driving snow, he figured that the wind must be coming from the north, bringing the arctic cold with it. Though it was early morning, Luke knew that the ranch hands would have already checked on the herd in the lower pastures. There, the cattle would huddle together, using their numbers to keep warm. It would be easier to haul hay to them than to the higher elevations where the snowfall amounts would be doubled.

Ice was beginning to form on the edges of the glass in a lacework pattern, and Luke could feel the cold seeping through. He could see the reflection of the fire that was trying to warm the room behind him. It sputtered and hissed as wind-driven snow forced its way down the narrow flue.

Luke was about to step away from the window when movement from outside caught his attention. Narrowing his eyes, he scanned the blinding white landscape. There, to his left, was a small shadow that stood still against the gusts of wind and pelting snow. Luke figured only a human would be out in weather like this, animals having a much more sense of survival. His eyes hurt as he tried to focus, willing the shadow to come closer and reveal itself. It was most likely just a few seconds, but it felt like a lifetime before the shape moved forward and Luke's heart stopped for a moment as he recognized Wolf. He knew that the animal wouldn't have traveled during a blizzard unless there was something terribly wrong.

It took several strides for him to reach the door and wrench it open. Stinging snow whipped his face, and the wind stole his breath away. Shielding his eyes, Luke watched as the canine came into view again, but he wouldn't come any closer. Luke stepped out onto the porch, but it seemed that Wolf stayed the same distance away. "Come on!" he shouted, but the wind flung his words away.

Luke took another few steps forward, but he didn't dare go too far. He hadn't grabbed a jacket or gloves, and the wind chill had to be below zero. It would be sheer foolishness to venture farther. Going back to the door, which was hanging wide open—in his haste, he had forgotten to latch it—he stood inside the threshold. Scanning outside, he didn't see Wolf anywhere. Quickly, he shut the door against the brutal cold and relentless wind-driven snow.

Back in Landon's study and standing in front of the fire, Luke pondered the sudden appearance. Last time he had seen Wolf was when he had left Angelica's. It didn't bode well that the animal would show up in a blinding snowstorm. Normally, Wolf would have found a place to hunker out the storm and appear when the storm was over. That wasn't the only thing that bothered him. There was something different about the way Wolf acted. It wasn't like him not to come into the house when Luke called. Moving back to the window, Luke scoured the area, but all he could see was white. Running a hand over his face, he debated about what to do. Going out in this weather was foolhardy, but it bothered him that Wolf would brave such weather to get to him and then wouldn't come in for shelter. Maybe he could get to the barn and see if Wolf would follow him there.

With the decision made, Luke turned toward the back of the house, but was stopped in the kitchen by a yell from upstairs. It was Landon.

"Luke! Goddamn it, where the hell are you?"

The panic was evident in his friend's voice. Running back to the front of the house and to the staircase, Luke nearly collided with Landon, who had flown down the stairs. Landon's hair was sticking up straight and he was only half dressed. His pants were unbuttoned, and his shirt hung open and loose. He had one sock on and still held the other in his hand, but Luke figured that he didn't know that.

Landon grabbed Luke by the shoulders and practically threw him up the stairs. "It's Mary! I think the baby's coming right now!"

Luke took the stairs two at a time and turned down the hallway to the last bedroom on the right. Stepping inside the room, he found Old Kate stripping the sheets off the bed and replacing them with an oilcloth and some clean blankets. She turned and looked at the men as they entered, and before Luke could ask where Mary was, Old Kate spoke. "Miss Mary is changing because her water broke. This babe is ready to come into this world, though with Mr. Landon yelling loud enough to raise the dead, I'm not sure this wee one is gonna want to come see his papi!"

Landon's face was pale, and there was a green tinge around his mouth. Luke silently willed himself to relax. Landon was going to feed off any emotion in the room, and he needed everyone to be calm.

"Well, it looks like you'll be a daddy sooner than we thought," Luke said, slapping his friend on the shoulder.

Landon almost landed on his face by the unexpected contact. His mouth gaped open like a fish searching for much needed air. Luke squeezed his friend's shoulder as he turned to Old Kate. "My instruments are in my room on the dresser, along with the bottle of carbolic acid to sterilize them. I'll also need a basin and some hot water to wash up with."

A look passed between them. It went without saying that he was ready to use those instruments, if necessary, to go in and get the child. He had talked a long time with Mary regarding the risks, and he had planned on easing into the conversation with Landon, but now they had run out of time. This child would definitely be like his father—impatient.

Old Kate left the room just as Mary came around the corner of the changing screen. She looked incredibly small in comparison to her bulging abdomen. Her face was set like that of a gladiator, ready to face the enemy and prepared to do whatever was necessary to emerge victorious. Her hands rhythmically rubbed over her stomach, as if to give comfort to the child.

Luke turned to Landon. "We'll need to stoke that fire and keep this room warm. Bring enough firewood to last for a couple of days." At Landon's panicked look, he added, "Mary and the baby will need to be kept warm."

Landon looked relieved to have something to do and to have an excuse to escape the confines of the room. Once he was gone, Luke's attention shifted to Mary. She had seated herself on the side of the bed.

"The pains are about every ten minutes," she said. "I didn't want to worry Landon until they were closer, but then my water broke." She gave him a weak smile. "It was impossible to hide that."

Just then, one of the contractions came along and she bent over, clenching her teeth. Luke moved and squatted down before her.

"Don't fight the pain," he told her, taking her hands. "Breath like you're blowing out a candle. There you go. Concentrate on the breathing and let the pain go. Good."

Easing her back against the pillows, he was aware of Old Kate reentering the room and setting his bag of instruments down on the bureau before she hurried out again, no doubt to heat and bring up the water.

Landon appeared in the doorway with an armload of wood. Seeing his wife lying comfortably on the bed seemed to add some color in his otherwise pale face. He placed a few logs on the brightly burning fire and set the others to the side. With a quick glance at Mary, he headed back downstairs for another armload.

Grabbing his stethoscope, Luke placed it against Mary's abdomen and listened. The baby had a very strong heartbeat, yet it seemed a little fast. Setting the stethoscope aside, he began to palpate Mary's abdomen, trying not to press hard enough to hurt, but he wanted to get an idea what direction the baby was facing. He wasn't surprised to feel arms and legs, but he couldn't tell if the baby was breech or not, and that worried him. Straightening, he caught Mary's gaze. There was complete trust in her eyes, along with an unshakable confidence.

"I can explain to Landon, if you want me to," she spoke softly.

Luke shook his head even though he was tempted by the offer. Landon needed to know all of it, things that he had fully explained to Mary, things that she understood and had accepted.

Old Kate arrived with a basin of hot water, a cake of soap, and a handful of towels. Placing this on the washstand, she turned to plump Mary's pillow, fussing over her charge.

"I'll be right back," Luke said to them.

The hallway was cooler, and as he headed down the stairs, Luke wasn't sure if he was sweating from the heat of the room he had just left or from the task before him. He entered the kitchen just as Landon was coming through the kitchen door with another load of wood. Landon hadn't bothered with a hat, and snow and ice covered one side of his face, setting his features.

Seeing Luke, Landon stopped dead in his tracks. Luke reached behind him and shut the door against the punishing wind and snow.

"Is Mary…the baby…?" Landon couldn't finish.

Luke clamped a hand on his friend's shoulder and directed him to a chair at the kitchen table. Landon set the wood down before sitting, but he never took his eyes off Luke's face.

"Mary is doing fine right now," Luke began, taking a seat across the table. Bending forward, he pinched his nose between his thumb and pointer finger. Taking a deep breath, he raised his head and looked at his friend. Landon needed to know.

"I'm afraid that this baby is also trying to come out breech. I can wait and see how this labor progresses, but if Mary is unable to pass this child, I don't have many options." He paused. The crackle of the fire in the old cooking stove was the only sound in the room.

"There's a surgical procedure called a caesarian that I can do, but it's very dangerous. The anesthesia is always risky, and it alone could kill them both. You should also know that most women only survive for about three weeks after the procedure due to infections. If I let this labor progress and one of them is in distress…well, I could lose one of them, possibly both, trying to put them under to operate. The only other option is to," Luke stopped and took a breath, "terminate the baby and save Mary."

There—it was said. Luke had hoped that there had been time for the baby to turn and present itself in the normal way, but he knew nature had a mind of its own.

Landon just stared at him like a man who was watching the lifeboats leave without him. "So, it's the baby's life or Mary's?"

This was the hardest part of the conversation; to give hope but not to build up too much. Luke chose his words carefully.

"I want to perform the caesarian before the labor progresses too far. I've studied the procedure a lot over the last month, and I think I know where the problem lies. Most surgeons don't close the womb; they leave it open because they feel that the sutures will cause an infection. I don't think it's the sutures that cause the problem. I believe it's because they don't close it up that it gets infected. So, I want to suture it closed. If I need to go back in and take out the sutures after she's healed, then I'll plan on doing that." He took another deep breath. "Mary knows all the risks, and she's prepared for whatever happens. She wants me to save this baby, for you, at all costs."

Landon dropped his head into his hands. He was a man drowning, and he had to make a decision that could result in the death of his wife, child, or possibly both. Luke knew decisions like this weighed heavy on a man's soul. Unfortunately, a decision had to be made, and fast.

Landon had been a successful soldier because he could read a situation better than anyone else Luke had ever known. He had that unique ability to see all the sides and come up with the best course of action, even if he didn't like the decision.

Luke let Landon take a few minutes to absorb the information, but the clock was ticking and time was not their friend. Getting in and getting the baby out as soon as possible was his plan, but he needed to make sure that Landon understood all the possible ramifications. Just when he was about to prompt his friend, Landon lifted his head.

Anguish was in his face, but his eyes were filled with determination.

"I fully trust you, Luke. You do what you have to save both of them, but I'll understand if you can't. It'll be God's will." His words were low and full of unspent emotion. "I'd like to go up and have a moment with Mary."

Luke nodded.

Landon gathered the wood from the table and headed to his wife's bedside.

Luke once again pinched his nose between his fingers. He wanted to yell, scream, and curse a god that everyone said was merciful and good. If this god was so good and kind, then why was he here, holding two lives in his hands? Where was the mercy in telling his best friend that he might—*might*—be able to save his loved ones? What if he couldn't save either one of them?

He shook himself. This was no time for self-doubt. He would save them both, God be damned. Mary would survive to have more children and to see her grandchildren. There was no other option to consider.

Taking a deep breath, he stood and headed for the front stairs.

• • •

Angelica left the tepee and made her way toward the house. She needed to find the children. While she wasn't convinced that Jean Claude was the threat that Meda thought he was, it would be foolish not to heed the warning. Unfortunately, the snow had increased in intensity. There was no way that she could send the aging trapper away in a storm. Even if Jean Claude was the fiend that Meda thought he was, if something happened to him on his way home, she wasn't sure if she could get over the guilt.

Out of breath, she reached the barn. Calling the children's names produced no result. Since she was already there, she checked the animals' hay and water before closing the doors and turning to the house.

Angelica's ears and face were painful from the brutal cold. Shivering next to the stove, she took a few minutes to turn, like a rabbit on a spit, to warm herself. Again, calling the children's names produced only silence.

Where could everyone be? They weren't in the barn or the house, and the weather outside wasn't conducive to staying out very long. Even Purrsistence wasn't to be found. Well, she'd give them a few minutes while she started dinner. If they weren't back by the time it was ready to eat, then she'd go looking for them.

A small ripple of fear ran down her spine, but she squashed it. Meda seemed to think that Jean Claude was waiting for someone before he would make his move and that they would wait until the dawn of the new moon. Besides, it wasn't like this mysterious accomplice could travel with a potential blizzard coming. No, the children were just busy with something, and they would be in shortly. Then they would eat with Jean Claude. After dinner, there would be time to talk to the children and make some plans. Until then, everything should appear as normal as possible.

Straightening her spine, Angelica ladled some warm water from the stove reservoir so that she could wash her hands. The sooner she started, the better.

•••

When he was sure that Angelica was out of earshot after she'd left Meda's tepee, Jean Claude stepped tentatively out of his hiding space. He waited a few minutes to see if Meda would follow, and when she didn't, he slipped inside the dark interior. Once his eyes adjusted to the gloominess, he spotted Meda kneeling next to a small fire. Her arm was outstretched as she dropped several plants onto the flame. The smoke gave off a sickly-sweet smell that made his eyes water. He noticed that she was softly chanting.

His knuckles whitened as he pulled on the rope that he held. Her eyes opened, and she looked straight at him. It surprised him that she showed no fear. It seemed as if she had been expecting him, and that gave him pause. He had anticipated her to be like the animals that looked up at him from his traps when they knew that there would be no hope of escape, their terror palpable. Instead, she looked as if he had done exactly what she had expected him to do and was amused. The thought of her laughing at his expense made him angry.

Moving swiftly, Jean Claude crossed the small space and shoved her backwards. "You laugh at me, bitch?" he snarled as he turned her over and began to bind her hands behind her back. "We shall see how amused you are when you are sold to your enemies. They will treat you like the dog that you are."

Using a technique that he had learned from an old slave trader, he tied her legs with her knees bent and twisted the rope so that a hangman's noose encircled her throat. If she tried to straighten, the rope would tighten around her neck, thus strangling her. In fact, any struggle would tighten it. Her hands were bound behind her back, also creating tension on the noose. No one had ever escaped from it. Her head was stretched back as he checked the tautness of the line.

Surprisingly, the squaw hadn't said a word. In fact, she hadn't struggled in any way. His plan had been to immobilize her first, because he figured that she was the one that was going to put up the biggest fight. He should have known that she was as worthless as the rest of her people. They were always talking about their victories and bravery and acting like they were the superior race. Hell, if he had known how easy this all would be, then he would have taken Angelica when he had brought the first wagon full of wood.

Meda started to chant softly. Drawing his foot back, Jean Claude kicked her hard in the ribcage. It annoyed him when she didn't make any sound of pain but just kept chanting.

"Shut up," he told her as he kicked her again.

The infernal noise stopped, and it gave him a moment to think about his next move. He had planned on hiding her, just in case someone came looking for her. Ghost needed his captives alive to get a good price for them. This weather limited where he could keep her. Looking around, he noticed that there wasn't much by way of personal items. This didn't surprise him, as most Indians traveled light unless they were moving the village. Then there would be travois filled with the buffalo hides for the tepees, hundreds of tent poles, food, and other provisions necessary for life on the plains. Women could pack up a village and be on the trail in a matter of hours.

Seeing nothing that he could use to hide her, he decided that he would just have to leave her there and make sure that no one came looking for her.

Bending down, he leaned his face close to hers. Spittle flecked from his mouth, landing on her, as he spoke. "If it were up to me, I'd just cut all your necks and be done with it. But the four of you are going to help pay off an old debt." Straightening, he looked down at her. She showed no fear at his words. In fact, her eyes didn't even follow his movements. As he headed out the door flap, he almost got the impression that she was not there but somewhere far away. Of course, that was ridiculous. She wasn't going anywhere.

•••

William sat behind a bale of hay in the loft of the barn. He and Matthew had taken refuge there after Meda's cryptic warning to William. They had been arguing for the better part of an hour.

"I'm not going to hide out like some coward," William told his brother for the umpteenth time. "I can handle Jean Claude. I just need to know that you will take Carol Anne and hide till this is all over."

Matthew rolled his eyes. "You can't fight a grown man by yourself, especially someone as big as Jean Claude, and besides, you said that Meda told you someone else was coming too. We need to do this together or it's not going to work."

William ran his fingers through his hair in frustration. Matthew was just being stubborn. He had found his brother right where he thought he would, upstairs on his bed, nose pressed into a book. He explained that he wanted Matthew to find Carol Anne and be ready to hide till any danger had passed, but Matthew had surprised him. Matthew wanted to help, which was a damn foolish offer. What could his brother do? Recite some poetry or tell Jean Claude a story? No, his brother needed to find their sister and hide out of harm's way until William had dealt with Jean Claude and anyone else that showed up.

"I'm done arguing about this, Matthew. I want you to find Carol Anne, and I want the two of you to hide and not come out till I yell for you." His tone was that of his father's, the one that said the conversation was over.

Unfortunately, Matthew was not intimidated. "I'll make sure that Carol Anne hides, but I won't. I can go to town for help, I'm pretty sure that I remember the way, or maybe I can distract Jean Claude so that you can get the drop on him."

William shook his head. His brother had read too many of those dime store novels. It made him angry. "Grow up, Matthew! This isn't some made-up story where the good guys win just because they are the good guys. Sometimes the bad guys win, because life isn't fair. Jean Claude is dangerous, and if what Meda thinks is going to happen is true, then we're going to be sold as slaves to the Indians. This is real, not some stupid book!"

They glared at each other for a moment. William wanted to take the words back, but he also needed Matthew to listen and do what he asked.

Tears glistened in Matthew's eyes. "You think just because you're older that you're always right. I'm not stupid just because I read books. I know what's real." He took a shaky breath. "Like I said, I'll hide Carol Anne, but I won't promise to stay hidden. If I can do something, then I'm going to do it."

With that speech, he crossed to the ladder and left the loft. William lay back in the hay. Damn. Now he had to worry about what his brother was going to do. Not for the first time, he wished that his father or Luke were here. They would know how to deal with Jean Claude.

•••

Carol Anne arrived just as Angelica was about to go looking for the children. Lighting the lamp, she had turned at the sound of the kitchen door opening. Relief flooded her body as she saw the little girl.

"Where have you been?" Angelica lightly admonished, pulling Carol Anne into the warm room and shutting the door.

Carol Anne wore her jacket but no mittens or hood. Her blonde hair was windblown and snarled around her head, like invisible hands had pulled it into every direction. Her skin was colorless as porcelain, except for two bright red spots on her cheeks and a blue tinge around her lips. As Angelica grabbed one of the girl's tiny hands, she noticed how cold it was. "You shouldn't be out in weather like this without mittens or a hood. You'll catch your death with pneumonia!"

Placing Carol Anne near the stove, where she had warmed herself not long before, Angelica stripped off the child's coat and began to rub her hands. The four-year-old was listless, and there was a glazed look in her eyes. Angelica felt fear in the pit of her stomach. It was the look of someone that was succumbing to the cold and was beyond helping themselves. It was the look her parents had days before they succumbed to pneumonia.

Leaving Carol Anne for a moment, Angelica hurried to grab the quilt off of her bed. She bundled it around the child's small frame and sat her in a chair pulled up as close to the stove as she dared. Next, Angelica ladled some hot water from the stove reservoir into a cup, and after retrieving the whisky bottle, she measured several teaspoons, which she added to the water. She filled the rest of the cup with milk and pulled Carol Anne onto her lap. Using a spoon, she managed to get some of the mixture into Carol Anne's mouth. She alternated rubbing the child through the quilt and spoon-feeding her. It seemed a long time till the bluish tint started to recede. Relief again flooded through Angelica when Carol Anne was warm enough to start to shiver.

"What were you doing outside in this weather?"

She really didn't expect an answer, but Carol Anne surprised her. "I was following Jean Claude. He put out some traps, trying to get Wolf."

Angelica's stomach twisted at the mention of the traps. Jean Claude would know that she would never allow him to set up traps on her property. That he would dare do such a thing seemed to support Meda's theory. Damn him! What right did he have to come here and decide her fate? She wasn't a child who needed to be looked after or cared for. She was a grown woman who wanted to decide her own destiny and choice of a husband, if she ever decided to get married.

"I threw wood in most of them, but I think he found out," Carol Anne continued.

"What do you mean that you threw wood in them?" Angelica couldn't believe her ears. "How did you manage to do that, and did Jean Claude see you do it? You could have been hurt." Her voice rose a few octaves.

"No, I think he blames Meda. He went into her tepee, and he looked mad."

Angelica closed her eyes. Meda thought that they had till dawn of the next day, but it seemed that time had run out. Carol Anne had no idea of the danger that she had just put them all in. Jean Claude was not a man that would allow his traps to be fooled with. If he thought Meda had been the one to trip the traps, then he would be angry. The question was how angry and what he would do to Meda.

Angelica rose from the chair and began to pace the kitchen. Meda believed Jean Claude was waiting for someone, possibly some Indian, that would sell Meda and the children into slavery. If she was right, then that meant that for now they just had Jean Claude to deal with. That was better odds, and they had the benefit of surprise on their side. Jean Claude wouldn't be expecting any sort of rebellion, because he would think that they were unaware of his plan. The trouble was that anything she did could backfire on them. The thought of them being enslaved by Indians was frightening enough, but the thought of one the children being hurt or worse, being killed, was unimaginable. Would Jean Claude kill them if his plan didn't go his way? Angelica wasn't sure.

Grabbing a plate, she dished up food for Carol Anne and set it on the table. Turning the chair with the child in it, she pushed it closer to the table and was heartened to see the girl begin to eat. It seemed that almost freezing to death didn't have any effect on Carol Anne's appetite.

Once Carol Anne had finished, she was put into her nightgown and tucked into bed, while Angelica ignored the child's protests. "It's too early to go to bed! I have to check on Wolf and make sure that all the traps didn't hurt any animals."

Angelica sat down on the side of the bed and tried to look stern. "You are not going out of this house tonight. Wolf and the animals will just have to take care of themselves, and I forbid you to go near any of those traps. They are far too dangerous, and they are not something that a four-year-old should be playing with." She put up her hand to stop the protest that was on Carol Anne's lips. "No. Nothing you say is going to change my mind. I want you to stay here, get some sleep, and stay warm. I will deal with Jean Claude and the traps."

Carol Anne looked mutinous, but she didn't say another word. Instead, she crossed her arms over her chest and glared at a spot behind Angelica's head. Hiding a smile, Angelica leaned in and kissed her forehead. "Goodnight, sweet dreams," she said, heading back to the kitchen.

There was no answer from the form in the bed.

•••

Angelica glanced at the clock and was alarmed to find how late it was and that there was still no sign of the boys. The sun had set hours ago, leaving an unsettled darkness in its wake. The light from the kerosene lamp on the table pushed back some of the gloominess of the room, but shadows still lurked in the corners.

Where were the boys? she fretted. Even with the evening chores, they should have come in for dinner by now. What if they were like Carol Anne and frozen to the point that they couldn't make it back? Had they had a run-in with Jean Claude? All sorts of scenarios played in her mind, each one more terrifying than the one before.

Glancing out the window proved useless, as the swirling snow acted as a curtain. Angelica had hoped to see a light coming from the direction of the barn, but there was only darkness. Did she leave Carol Anne alone and go in search of the boys, or did she wait them out? It was unlikely that Jean Claude had done something to them without his cohort, but then again, it was possible. Had he done something to Meda and was systematically eliminating them one by one? The indecision and waiting were getting to Angelica. Knowing what she was facing and dealing with it head on was preferable to this inaction.

A noise outside the door made her jump. Her heart dropped as the door opened and the burly form of Jean Claude entered the house. There was no sign of the boys behind him.

The trapper was covered from head to toe in furs, and his usual offensive aroma wafted across the room to her. Dark hair, from his beard to his greasy hair that poked out from underneath his cap, made his face hard to see. The resemblance to a black bear was startling, right down to the beady brown eyes. It crossed her mind that she might want to take her chances with a bear instead of him, but she knew that wasn't a realistic thought. Jean Claude was here, and she would have to deal with him.

Angelica straightened her posture and placed a smile on her face. "Jean Claude, you startled me. I was just wondering where everyone was. Have you seen the boys at all? They're late for dinner and I was getting worried."

He looked around the room as if she had misplaced the boys and they would magically appear. Fighting the annoyance that rose up, Angelica turned to the stove.

"Haven't seen them," he replied, "or the little…girl."

There was a slight hesitation before the word "girl," and she wondered what he was going to say instead. She looked over her shoulder at him.

"Carol Anne is already in bed. She took a little chill and I insisted that she get some rest. I haven't seen the boys since this morning, and I was just thinking that I should go out and look for them. They might be with Meda."

It could have been a trick of light, the way he started, and his eyes darted in the direction of the window that faced Meda's tepee, but she wasn't sure. He looked guilty. That made her nervous. Meda would be worthless in Jean Claude's eyes, and he could do anything he wanted to her and not fear any consequences.

While there were some laws protecting white women, there were no laws that protected Indians. They could be raped, beaten, or murdered, and no one would bat an eye. Angelica should have gone and checked on Meda when Carol Anne had told her about Jean Claude's visit. Now it was too late.

The kitchen that once seemed so big when she was living here by herself now felt very small and confined. The flickering lantern cast Jean Claude's face into shadow, making it impossible to read. The eyes were the windows to the soul, her mother always said. Right now, Jean Claude's eyes were soulless black holes.

It did nothing to ease her nervousness as he moved closer. Pretending to need something from the pantry, she crossed the kitchen. It was a mistake. Jean Claude moved farther into the room, blocking her exit, effectively cutting off any chance of escape.

Pretending a calm that she didn't feel, Angelica took a few cans of peaches from the shelf. She caught sight of the knife that she used to open the burlap bags of flour and sugar. Leaning forward, she let one of the cans slip and fall to the floor. As Jean Claude's eyes followed the can, she slipped the small paring knife into the pocket of her skirt.

"I'm sorry," she said as she moved forward. "I can be so clumsy sometimes."

Leaning down, she picked up the can, causing Jean Claude to step back out of the doorway to give her some room. Taking the opportunity, she squeezed out the opening before he had a chance to recover.

Her heart felt like it was about to jump out of her chest. She felt an urge to go running out of the house screaming. Of course, she couldn't do that. One, she couldn't leave Carol Anne alone with Jean Claude, and two, she had to keep up the pretense as long as she could. Meda had told her that she had a plan, and Angelica's job was to buy as much time as she could.

Her friend had been vague, but Angelica trusted her. Now she was unsure if Meda was able to carry out her plans, or if it was now up to her to stop Jean Claude.

Jean Claude was visibly not pleased that she had slipped past him and that the table was between them. His left eye had developed a tic, and he practically growled when he spoke. "I have decided to take you as my mate." He practically spat the words. "You will be my Lillian. I give you fine strong sons, yes? Then you will be happy."

Happy? He talked about kidnapping her and making her a substitute for her mother, and he thought she would be happy? She had been a naïve fool all these years. Meda had been right. Her mother must have recognized the danger that Jean Claude had presented and had sheltered and protected her. In the end, it had done her a disservice. Even the children had recognized him for what he was.

Now there was no one that was going to come to their rescue. The time for believing in fairy tales was over.

Her fingers gripped the knife handle. There was no way that she would win a struggle with him. It would be foolish to even try.

"God gave women brains and men brawn," her mother used to say.

Well, if she couldn't hope to win physically, then she would have to outsmart him. Unfortunately, panic was clouding her mind, she had no idea what she could say or do that would deter him. Warily, she watched as he started to move around the table towards her. As he moved to the left, she had managed to keep moving as well, like two dancers, keeping the same amount of space between them. Why hadn't she realized how big he was? It wasn't that he was much taller than her, but his shoulders were wide, and his hands seemed very large.

"I won't go with you, I am Angelica, NOT Lillian!" She knew that the words fell on deaf ears. She was unaware of how her eyes crackled with fire and passion as she spoke and how her hair, which had been pinned back and neat that morning, was cascading down over her shoulders, making her look exactly like her mother. Jean Claude stared open-mouthed at her before taking a step forward. For a moment, Angelica panicked as she thought he was going to send the table flying and rush forward to grab her, but surprisingly, he stopped and glared at her instead.

"I will be back in the morning. There's nowhere you can go that I can't find you. You will be mine. If you fight me, then I will kill the squaw and the brats."

Leaving her speechless, he turned and stalked out the door.

CHAPTER SEVENTEEN

Luke felt like an intruder as he entered the room. Landon was clasping Mary's hands between his own as he kneeled beside the bed. Their foreheads were touching as they talked in low tones. It was a private moment, one that was as old as time, the birth of a child, an expected miracle. There was no fear felt in the room, only that of unwavering faith, and that shook Luke a little. Having lost his, it was humbling and a little intimidating to note that while he was the one trained to heal the sick or injured, it was not in his ability to give such unshakeable conviction.

The room was hot, thanks to the firewood that Landon had brought up. Old Kate had stoked the fire and was waiting near the hearth. Luke crossed the room and rolled up his shirt sleeves. The water in the basin was steaming. Wetting his hands first, he picked up the bar of soap and began to lather up. It gave him a reprieve and gave the couple a chance to finish their conversation.

"What are you thinking?" Old Kate had moved to his side, holding out a towel for him to dry his hands. Her voice was low so as not to carry.

"I'm planning on getting this baby out quickly and have mother and child be doing just fine in time for supper." He glanced at the couple as Mary doubled over with another labor pain. "Landon and Mary both know the risks. I'm going to have to do what I think is the best option and hope to hell that I made the right decision."

Old Kate laid a hand on his arm. "You listen here." Her voice brooked no argument. "You are the finest doctor that I know. The Lord Almighty gave you a gift, and just because you lost your faith in the Lord don't mean he lost faith in you. We've all been put on this earth for a reason, and your reason is to save those that the good Lord has chosen to be saved. Let him guide you. Open your heart to him again, and he'll show you the way."

Luke felt like someone had punched him in the gut, and he turned his head away from her before she could read his expression. She couldn't be serious, could she? If the good Lord was choosing those that were meant to die, then why bother creating doctors? If they were going to live, then they would do that with or without his help.

He was spared having to reply as Landon kissed his wife and got up from the side of the bed. He walked over to Luke and slapped a hand on his friend's shoulder. There was no need for words; it had already been said in the kitchen, earlier. With a final glance at his wife, Landon left the room. Most likely he would head to the study to wait out his vigil.

Closing his eyes, Luke found himself almost mouthing a prayer. Anger surged throughout his body as he stopped himself and moved to the side of the bed. Standing next to Mary, he took her hand in his. Bending his head, he tried to let his mind clear for a moment. Now was the time to make the decision. Did he try to get this baby out the normal way, or did he go in and operate before mother and baby were both in danger? He had examined Mary, and the baby had not turned for a normal presentation.

Opening his eyes, he looked out the window at the wind driven snow. What the hell was he waiting for? A sign from God? It had been his experience that God was too busy somewhere else, so when he first saw the movement in the snow, he almost dismissed it. But there it was again, that dark shape in the curtain of white. The shape of a wolf.

Letting go of Mary's hand, he moved closer to the glass. He strained to see through the snow, but the image had disappeared. He was being sent a message. There was something wrong, and Wolf needed him. As if to confirm that thought, there was a lonely howl from somewhere outside.

Luke turned back to Mary, and he knew that he would have to perform the caesarian. If it wasn't God, then someone had just sent him a sign that time was of the essence.

"Mary," he began, but she cut him off.

"You've decided on the operation. I can see it in your eyes." Her voice was calm, like that of the Madonna. She squeezed his hand. "I trust you,

Luke. All that I ask is that you save this child for Landon. Let me go if you have to."

Her bravery made him feel like a coward. He hoped that Landon knew what this woman would sacrifice for him.

Leaning down, he gave her a kiss on the forehead. "I'm not letting anyone go. I fully intend to deliver your child safe and sound and make sure that you're around to give Landon a hard time into his old age."

Mary smiled. "I'd like that."

"Then it's settled. Let's get this little troublemaker out so that he can start terrorizing his daddy."

•••

Old Kate placed the mask over Mary's mouth and nose, then Luke showed her how to count the drops of chloroform. It took almost ten minutes before Mary became unconscious. At his instruction, Old Kate lifted the mask off and let Mary breathe in room air. Luke had about five to ten minutes until Mary started to come around. If he wasn't finished by then, Old Kate would put the mask back over her nose and mouth and add more drops. It wasn't an exact science, this job of anesthetizing the patient, and unfortunately because it wasn't, many patients were overdosed and died, some by suppressing the respiratory system and others by causing liver failure. It was a terrible thing to have a patient survive the procedure only to turn jaundiced and die weeks later. Years ago, Luke had learned that the trick was to make sure that only enough drug was given to make the patient unconscious, then room air was introduced to help dilute the drug in their system, therefore making it safer.

Pressing the scalpel against Mary's abdomen produced no reaction. Luke had already washed the area with soap, water, and a little whiskey. Every precaution that he knew was in place. It was time. Clearing his mind of everything but the procedure that he had studied over the last month, he made his incision.

The fire crackled in the fireplace, interrupted by an occasional hiss as some snow tried to make its way down the chimney. Old Kate had brought in half a dozen kerosene lamps to help him see by, and they surrounded the bed, making it look like an altar. Occasionally, the windows would rattle as if to remind the occupants of the room that Mother Nature was waiting and watching, and she was not a patient bystander.

Luke clamped off some vessels that were bleeding and began to cut into the womb that protruded out of his incision. If all went well, he should be lifting out this child in less than two minutes. Being careful not to go too deep and risk cutting the child, he proceeded slowly. Once the opening was big enough, he reached inside and began to feel around. He cut open the birth sac surrounding the baby.

Mary made a groaning sound and Luke's eyes met Old Kate's. At his nod, she placed the mask again and administered more chloroform.

"I need a few extra minutes here," he mumbled. "I'm not sure what I'm feeling."

Carefully, he tried reaching around the child. His heart dropped as he felt lumps and bumps that normally shouldn't be there. It had been his worst fear that this baby was somehow going to be deformed and not survive—or worse, survive. He found a hand and was surprised when the tiny fingers latched on to his finger.

Reaching in with his other hand, he cupped the child. It had been his experience not to prolong things but to deal with them as soon as possible. This child was unusually heavy, and he grunted as he raised it out of the womb.

Old Kate removed the mask from Mary's face and gasped as she saw the bundle in his bloody hands. Crossing herself, she grabbed the clean blankets that she had set aside and tentatively moved in closer for a better look.

Luke placed the newborn into her outstretched hands. He clamped and cut the umbilicus, then turned back to begin sewing up Mary. He paid no attention to the small cries coming from across the room, but his subconscious categorized the sound.

"I'm going to show Landon," Old Kate said as she came up beside him. "I think he needs to know now." She looked down at the little fist that popped out of the blanket that she cradled.

Luke gave her a quick sideways glance and nodded. He had to finish stitching Mary up before she awakened. "Don't be long. I might need you."

Old Kate nodded and headed out the door.

•••

Landon stood at the window, watching the storm, taking some strength from it. He had recited every prayer that he knew and some that he created. It seemed that he had done the same thing the night that he'd lost his first wife and son. He learned a valuable lesson that night. No matter how much one threatened, pleaded, or begged, God could not be bought or changed. He'd been consumed for months afterwards. Nothing mattered, and he'd wanted to die too. Somehow, he made it through all the pain and depression, and it was only by forgiving God, putting his trust back in him, that Landon had gained some peace.

The sound of footsteps on the stairs made him turn from the window and head for the study door, but Old Kate was there before he could reach it. She carried a bundle, wrapped in a blanket, in her arms. Small cries were coming from the depths of the folds. Old Kate's face was a mask that even after all these years of knowing her, he couldn't read.

Emotions were coursing through his brain. So far, his child was alive, and that was more than he was allowed the first time. Like a man in a dream, he took several tentative steps forward. A small fist popped into view, and he was transfixed. Old Kate smiled and pulled back the fabric. Moving closer, he peered down and drew in his breath. There, cradled in the blanket, were two babies. One was bigger, about the size of a large pot roast off one of his prize steers, while the other was smaller, more delicate, like a small doll. They had their arms wrapped around each other; the smaller one snuggled up against the larger one's chest.

Landon could only stare.

"Are they…?" He was afraid to ask anything, afraid that this was all an illusion and that it would be fleeting.

Old Kate smiled. "The good Lord has blessed you with twins. A big strapping boy just like yourself, and a sweet little girl taking after her momma." Pride radiated from her. "I counted ten fingers and ten toes on both. They are perfect! Mr. Luke is tending to Miss Mary, and she is doing fine too. I'm going to bring these babies back up and clean them up proper like, so their mama can see them first thing when she wakes up."

Landon could do nothing but nod. Twins. His mind was still reeling that he had one surviving child, but to have two seemed like a dream. God had given him back a son and had added a daughter. It seemed more than he deserved. Then came a sobering thought. Was the daughter to lessen the blow if Mary didn't survive the birth? He shook that thought away. Luke had been pretty sure that he could save Mary along with the babies. That was what Landon would hold onto.

Heading back into the study, he sat in the leather chair next to the fire and said a prayer of thanks.

●●●

Luke watched Old Kate fuss with the babies. It had been over two hours since he had delivered the twins and finished sewing up Mary. She had woken long enough to see and try to feed her babies, and then he had given her a small dose of laudanum for the pain and to get some rest. Carrying twins was hard on the body, and the respite would do it good.

Besides, when these babies started making demands on her, she'd be lucky to get any sleep.

Old Kate gave one last look at the sleeping babies and tiptoed over to him. Her smile was from ear to ear. "I knew the good Lord would help us through. These youngsters are gonna be just fine! I'm feeling like cooking up a celebration."

Luke grinned as she sashayed from the room. It had been a long time since he had seen her so excited. Since the conflict, happy occasions had been far and few between.

Luke rose slowly from the chair and stretched. Peering into the cradle that Landon had made with his own hands, the mahogany wood having been carved with designs of vines and cherubs, he checked on the sleeping babies. He had examined them earlier and had found them both to be normal and healthy. In all his years of being a doctor, Luke had never seen two babies in one sac. He surmised that since the boy had been cradling his sister in the womb, it prevented them from turning and presenting in the usual way. It also kept him from detecting two heart beats. No matter what, without the caesarian, they all would have perished.

The relief that he had felt after Mary had woken was being replaced with sadness. Even though he and Landon weren't related by blood, they considered the other a brother, and these children would grow up to become his niece and nephew. The way he figured it, this would probably be as close to children of his own that he would ever have. No woman would want to live as he did, never staying in one place for more than a few weeks.

Angelica flickered through his mind. She was extremely attached to her ranch, she had made that clear, and besides, she had the children now. Children needed stability, and that was something he couldn't provide. Best for all if he just kept moving.

Landon's footsteps could be heard heading up the stairs. Luke turned from the cradle and met him at the door. Putting a finger to his mouth, he led his friend to his children.

Landon looked like a man who had been given riches beyond his wildest dreams, and in Luke's opinion, he had.

"I can't thank you enough Luke," Landon began, choked with emotion. "I had hoped for one child, but to be blessed with two…well…" He bowed his head. "I'm beholden to you."

Luke placed a hand on Landon's shoulder. "Brothers don't keep score. You would have done the same for me if you could have."

Landon nodded. It was true that they had watched each other's backs during their childhood and through the war.

"Just the same, it means a lot to have you here and that you saved my children." Landon glanced over to the sleeping form of his wife. "Mary and I talked about you being the godfather. Now that there are two, well I guess we would like you to be godfather to both."

Luke bowed his head. "I'm really honored, Landon, but you know that I can't."

Landon didn't get where he was by taking no for an answer, especially when he wanted something. "I know that you won't, not that you can't," he pointed out bluntly before continuing, "I'm thinking that a godfather is someone who will see that these babies grow, safe and sound. One who will teach my boy how to be honest and fair, and a man who will protect my girl. That man, my friend, is you." It was Landon's turn to slap Luke on the shoulder. "I know that you're running from the memories. No one knows better what those are than I do, but someday you're going to get tired, and you'll have to stand your ground and face them, like I did. I just hope that you don't regret all the things that you threw away." He cleared his throat. "Let the past go, Luke, you can't change any of it. These two babies are the future, and it's up to us to make sure that they grow up in a better world."

Luke couldn't respond. He was careful over the years to alienate himself from society; Landon had been the only one that he stayed close to. They were brothers in arms, and they made sure that the other made it out alive. Luke had tried to go home again, but home wasn't the safe place that he remembered. Loving people meant that he could lose them in the blink of an eye. The war had made him a coward.

Yet it seemed that while he thought he had walled himself off from people, they managed to slip through the cracks. Mary was like a sister to him, and it went without saying that he adored Old Kate. Now these babies were knocking on the wall of his defenses. It was going to be hard to stay here until spring and then leave them all behind.

"I'm sorry Landon, but…"

Landon wouldn't let him finish. "It's been decided. Officially or unofficially, I consider you to be my children's godfather." Then, whistling quietly, he turned and headed to the chair next to the bed.

●●●

Luke rubbed the back of his neck and looked down at the sleeping babies. Old Kate had wrapped them tightly in blankets that she had knitted. Even so, they lay facing each other, and the boy, Luke wondered what his name would be, had managed to get one arm free so that it touched his sister's blanket. It seemed that he was born to be his twin's protector.

The room was stifling hot, which made breathing difficult, and the walls seemed as if they were starting to close in on him. Nodding to Landon, Luke made his way out of the room. It was cooler in the hallway, allowing much-needed air into his lungs. He could hear Old Kate singing down in the kitchen, and the smells that wafted up to him set his stomach growling, making him realize that he had missed breakfast.

The upstairs hallway consisted of five bedrooms, three off the back of the house and two on the front. Luke had been placed in the last one on the left, close enough if Mary had needed him but far enough away so as to have some privacy. It was good sized, boasting a comfortable bed, dresser, washstand, and even white lace curtains. The comforter was a crazy quilt that either Mary or Old Kate had probably made from scraps of fabric.

The fire had died in the hearth and the room was chilly. Taking a poker and stirring the coals, Luke added some kindling, and after that caught, he added some logs. When he could feel some heat generating from the flames, he moved over to the window. Shutting the babies out of his mind for a few minutes, he thought about Mary. This would be the hardest part, the waiting. Waiting to see if going in and getting the babies was going to be her death sentence. There had been no way that they would have been born in the traditional way. The boy had just been too big, and with his sister in the way, they couldn't have turned. He made the right decision, he knew in his heart, but his head would wait and decide later.

Pushing the curtain aside, he watched as snowflakes drifted softly to the ground. There appeared to be a lull in the storm that had been raging since morning. The white snow was dazzling on his tired eyes. Maybe he should just lie down and take a nap before he went down and had some food.

Letting the curtain fall back into place, Luke moved to the bed and sat on the edge. Tension radiated across his shoulders and down his back. It was always like this; the adrenaline and stress seemed to catch up with him as soon as the crisis was over. It had been building up for a while; it would take a while to get rid of it. For now, he just wanted to sleep.

●●●

Howling. Who the hell was howling?

Luke was dreaming that he was back in South Carolina before the great conflict. Life had been simpler then. He'd just arrived home from medical school, and every mother in a fifty-mile radius was parading their daughter in his view. Marrying a doctor would ensure social status, though it wouldn't guarantee wealth like a plantation owner. Most country doctors were paid in vegetables, chickens, and such. Still, it was better than marrying a farmer or an overseer, where women would work hard from sunrise to sunset. He had been invited to more dinners than he could possibly eat in his lifetime, and women were dropping off pies and cakes to his mother's house by the dozens. He had just opened the door to another onslaught when one of the young women at the door started to howl. She looked just like Meda. He had been so surprised that he dropped the cake that she had just handed him and stared at her. He looked at the other women, but they just shrugged their shoulders and turned away.

Luke bolted to a sitting position on the bed. Sweat beaded on his forehead and he was breathing hard. Never in his life had a dream felt so real. In fact, he could still hear the girl howling. It took him several seconds to realize that there was howling, but it was coming from outside.

Son of a… Crossing to the window, he looked out. There below the window, staring up at him, sat Wolf, who about every ten seconds lifted his nose into the air and let out a howl. Seeing Luke at the window, Wolf got up and paced back and forth.

Luke spun around and started to grab some warm clothes. It didn't take much figuring out that Wolf wanted him to follow him to Angelica's. Something had happened, and they needed him. He should have trusted his instincts and brought them all with him to Landon's. He'd known that it was a bad idea to leave them out on the prairie alone.

Ignoring the voice in his head that tried to remind him that he was the one that had no intention of getting involved with Angelica or the children, he grabbed his saddlebags.

●●●

Old Kate was pulling a delicious smelling pie from the oven when Luke entered the kitchen. She placed it on the serving board and turned to him with her eyebrows raised as she noted the saddlebags.

Pinning him with a look only she could give, she asked, "Now where do you think you're going?"

Years of experience had taught him that when Old Kate got that look and crossed her arms in that way, then there was no putting her off. He would have to explain and hope to hell that she wasn't going to argue too much.

"So, you are going to head out into a blizzard because you think that this wolf being here means somebody is in trouble?" she asked after he had finished.

Putting it that way it did seem a little bizarre, but Luke knew Wolf and trusted his instincts where the animal was concerned. If the canine was here, it meant something.

"I don't have time to argue. It'll take me a day or two to make it to Angelica's, and depending on what is wrong, I should be there for a couple of days. I intend to bring them all back with me, so if this weather holds, it should take another day to get back. So I figure that by the beginning of next week, you should be looking for us." He shrugged into his coat. "I don't like leaving Mary, but I have to go. I want you to make sure that she gets up and moves around a little every day, but don't let her overdo it. Infection is the main concern for her. Also change the dressing twice a day and use rags that have been boiled clean with soap. I left the laudanum on the dresser in my room."

As he was talking, Old Kate ladled some stew into a bowl. "Now you sit down and eat something before you head out. Don't you be shaking your head at Old Kate," she told him as he backed away towards the door.

"I'm sorry, I don't have time. I'll be fine, and I'll have Angelica and the children with me when I get back. We'll celebrate then."

He fled out the door before she could get up the head of steam that she was working on and forcibly seat him at the table or bar the door.

The landscape was dazzling white and bitter cold. His breath hung in the frigid air. Looking to the north, he could see the storm clouds heading over the horizon. It was a damn foolish thing to head out onto the plains in this type of weather, but he couldn't ignore the fact that Wolf had tracked him down. His gut was telling him that Angelica and the kids were in trouble, and he knew that he had to follow that instinct. Regret was something that he lived with daily; he didn't want to add any more. This was a journey that he had to make, if only to ease his conscience.

He bowed his head against the cold and crossed to the barn.

•••

Landon arrived just as Luke was tightening the cinch. Luke was surprised that he had taken so much time.

"Here." Landon thrust a brown paper package at him.

"What's this?"

"Jerky. Old Kate is fit to be tied that you're leaving without so much as a bite to eat."

"Thanks." Luke put the bundle in his saddlebags.

Landon began to say something, but he stopped himself. Luke could see him out of the corner of his eye, and when Landon did speak, it came out raspy.

"We've named the boy Steven Lucas, after my father and you. The girl is Katherine Marie, for Old Kate and Mary's mother. It would be a shame if your namesake never got to meet you."

Luke bowed his head. Landon's words humbled him and shook him to his core.

Landon took advantage of his silence to continue. "If you wait till morning, then most of this storm should have passed and I'll ride with you. There can't be any harm in waiting till then. We'll make better time."

Luke turned to his friend. "I appreciate the offer Landon, I really do, but I have to do this now. You have no idea how long this storm will last and besides, you're needed here." He took the reins and headed for the door. "I told Old Kate to look for us at the beginning of the week. You take care of your family."

Landon, to his credit, didn't try to talk him out of going, not that Luke had expected him to.

Wolf was waiting a short distance away and gave a yip when he saw Luke, eager to be on his way. Luke stopped to wrap a scarf around his neck and mouth. After pulling the collar of his jacket up against the cold and tugging his hat down low over his ears, he mounted and then turned and nodded to Landon, who stood in the open doorway.

"If you don't see us in a week, then send someone to Angelica's ranch. Old Kate knows what needs to be done for Mary. I've left teas and herbs for her."

With that, he nudged the gelding forward and was lost in the glare of the landscape.

CHAPTER EIGHTEEN

William pressed himself up against the side of the barn and watched as Jean Claude exited the house. Swinging his arms wildly and talking to himself, the trapper headed in the direction of Meda's tepee and disappeared into the darkness. Running to the side of the house, careful not to slip on the collecting snow, William peered into the kitchen window. He could see Angelica sitting at the table with her head in her hands, but she looked unharmed. Relieved, he crossed back to the barn. It had only been several hours since the snow had begun, but already there were drifts against the buildings where the relentless wind had blown it. His tracks were disappearing, leaving depressions in the snow.

Behind him, unseen, the small shadow of Carol Anne blended into the darkness as she silently slipped out the front door.

William climbed into the hay loft, then made his way to the back where Matthew was waiting for him. A small kerosene lamp gave enough light to see by but not enough to be seen from below.

"Well?" his younger brother asked impatiently.

"She's fine. I don't think he intends to do anything until his friend shows up. Carol Anne is still in the house with her, so right now they're both safe."

He crossed to a bale of hay and sat. Rubbing his hands together, he was grateful for the relative warmth of the barn. The temperature had plummeted since that afternoon. Not for the first time, he wished that he had grabbed a jacket and mittens. "We need a plan. If Meda is right, we have till sunrise tomorrow to figure out how to stop Jean Claude. We're no match for him physically, so it's going to have to be by surprise."

"We could dig a pit and lure him to it. Once he falls in, he won't be able to get out."

William rolled his eyes. "We don't have time to build a pit, and I think that he would notice what we were doing. Besides, the ground is frozen solid."

Matthew looked undeterred. "How about we get him drunk, and when he passes out, we tie him up? Remember how Mrs. White used to drink, and she'd get all happy and then go to sleep on the stairs?"

Mrs. White was a woman who lived in the apartment below theirs, back when their parents were alive. William remembered how their mother would shake her head and remark on what an unhappy person Mrs. White was. Which didn't make much sense, cause as Matthew had said, Mrs. White was very happy when she drank.

Still, the idea had some merit. If Jean Claude passed out, then they could tie him up before he came to. The problem was that they didn't have any liquor. The other problem was that liquor could turn some people mean. Jean Claude obviously didn't need any help in that department.

William shook his head. "Maybe we could just wait till he goes to sleep. Meanwhile, we'd better keep an eye on him and wait for our chance. I'll take the first watch. You get some sleep, and I'll wake you when it's time. "

Matthew looked like he wanted to argue but thought better of it. With a nod, he blew out the lantern and curled up on a bale of hay.

William made his way down the ladder and out of the barn.

•••

The snow was being tossed by the wind and coming down thick, causing Jean Claude to almost walk into the side of the tepee before he saw it. Unlashing the ties to the door, he then stepped into the dark interior. The coals were faintly glowing, and the air was cold. Letting his eyes adjust, he could make out Meda's form, just as he had left her. Stirring the ashes, he tossed in some kindling, and when that caught, he added some logs. No sense letting her freeze to death. Dead captives didn't make money.

Squatting down next to her, he could see that she was breathing and appeared to be asleep. He picked up a lock of her hair and let it run through his fingers. It felt like silk, and for a moment he entertained the thought that this was how Angelica's hair would feel against his skin. His groin tightened and he closed his eyes, lost in his fantasy.

Jean Claude ran his hands over the exposed skin of her arms and marveled at how soft she was in comparison to his callused hands. She started to move under his ministrations, and he imagined that she wanted him to give her even more pleasure. His hands moved lower, and he was momentarily perplexed by the hard ridge that stopped him from lifting her skirt. Opening his eyes, he was brought back to reality as he looked into brown eyes that were unreadable. Meda was on her side, looking up at him; it had been the rope that he had felt, preventing him from groping her farther. Like before, there was no fear or any emotion in those eyes.

Rising, he walked to the other side of the fire, needing some distance to get his perspective back. Looking back at the squaw, he was surprised to see that she had closed her eyes again. Irritation rose up within him. Damn squaw was too dim-witted to be scared of him. He entertained the thought of giving her something to be worried about, but he stopped. He'd have his chance later. For now, he had to find the two brats and make sure that they didn't interfere with his plans. There weren't many places to hide in weather like this, though if they were stupid enough to get themselves frozen to death, that would take care of the problem. Although he figured that Ghost would be pissed about losing two healthy slaves.

He added more wood to the fire and went back out into the storm without a backwards glance.

•••

Angelica raised her head and listened for a moment. The only sound inside came from the old clock on the mantel. Outside, the wind whistled and rattled the door. Rising, she went to the stove and took the chicken, which was now overcooked, out of the oven. She placed it on the sideboard and began getting out the ingredients to turn it into a stew, but her actions were mechanical. This was how she got through the loneliness and despair after she had lost her parents, by keeping busy. The routine of the task slowly let her mind let go of the numbness that Jean Claude's words had created.

Cutting the meat off the bone, she began to think about everything that her parents had told her about Jean Claude. They had protected her, that was plain to see now. She had had a false sense of security because she had always known him and failed to see the warning signs that now were so obvious.

Whack! The cleaver cut through the carcass with the force of her rising anger. Even the children had known from the minute that they had met him what he was. She felt like a naïve fool. The anger felt good; it sustained her, kept her from feeling the fear that lay like a snake wrapped around her, ready to smother her.

After filling a large pot with water and dropping in the cut-up carcass, vegetables, and herbs, Angelica left it to simmer. She had better check on Carol Anne and make sure that the child wasn't running a fever. Pneumonia was always a fear in weather like this, and Carol Anne had definitely caught a chill. Maybe she should make a mustard poultice as a precautionary measure, she mused.

Stepping softly so as not to wake the sleeping child, Angelica reached the bed and pulled the covers gently back. Her heart nearly stopped as she realized that the mattress was empty. Carol Anne's pillow had been shoved under the blankets to give the impression that the girl was still there. For a brief moment, she feared that Jean Claude had taken the child but quickly decided against that. He had left by the kitchen door. There was no way that he had snuck back in and taken her, which meant that Carol Anne had left on her own. Maybe she had gone to join her brothers in hiding. That was at least a comforting thought, that they were all together safe, but was it the truth? What if Jean Claude had the boys already and Carol Anne was walking right into his trap?

"Sweet Jesus," Angelica said out loud, putting her hand to her mouth.

She had forgotten about the traps! With the darkness and snow, anyone could stumble into one of those blasted things. If Carol Anne stepped in one of them, she wouldn't stand a chance. Panic filled Angelica. She whirled, grabbed her cloak from the peg next to the door, and rushed out into the night.

●●●

Jean Claude stopped several paces from the tepee. William, who was several feet behind him, scrunched down deeper against the tree trunk as he watched Jean Claude scan the area. Seeming to be satisfied that no one was around, Jean Claude turned and made his way toward the creek. William wasn't sure if he should follow or go and check on Meda. It seemed strange that they hadn't seen her for a while, but she might have taken her own advice and hidden.

Waiting a minute or two, William decided that he should follow the older man, just to make sure that he didn't surprise Matthew or go back and bother Angelica. Wishing for the umpteenth time that he had thought to grab a heavier coat and some mittens, he proceeded down the path after Jean Claude.

●●●

Jean Claude had spent his life hunting and could smell game from a mile away. He knew right away that he was being followed, and he figured that it was the older boy.

He passed the path that would have brought him back to the barn and instead continued to the creek. Splashing through the fast-moving water, he crossed to the other side and up the embankment. Once he was over the edge, he walked parallel to the water before crossing back over. He had just enough time to take cover in a small thicket before the older boy came into view. Fading into the shadow of the trees, he watched as William followed his tracks to the water. The boy looked relieved to see that he, Jean Claude, had crossed the river, seemingly moving farther from the house, before turning back to head up the path to the barn. Jean Claude waited a few minutes and then followed.

••

Carol Anne kept to the well-trodden path around to the back of the house, and when she reached the point where it came adjacent to the small door that was at an angle in the ground, she jumped as close as she could get to it. With any luck, the blowing snow would cover her tracks, and no one would notice them. Pushing the door shut behind her, she crouched and retrieved a small candle and box of matches that she had left for the occasion. It was warmer here, out of the whipping wind and snow. Striking a match and lighting the wick, she was able to navigate the narrow tunnel that loomed in front of her. Rock columns held up wood beams that created the ceiling, allowing enough room for her to stand up in. At the end, it opened into a larger room that was laden with canned goods and barrels of apples and cider. Onions and garlic hung from the rafters of the ceiling. Circles of cheese were stacked on wooden shelves covered in cheesecloth. This was the root cellar that ran under the kitchen of the house. She had discovered it one day when she had explored the grounds.

Left of the tunnel's opening stood half a dozen empty large barrels that she had managed to maneuver until there was a small area for her to crawl into and have enough space to be able to lie down. Whenever she could, she brought things and stored them in her secret hideout. Several purloined tins held food and glazed jugs held water. This was her private retreat, a luxury that she had never had. She'd had to share everything with her brothers for as long as she could remember. Maybe that's why she hadn't told them about this place. William had taken over the barn loft, while Matthew stayed mostly in the loft at the house, reading books.

It was safe down here, away from Jean Claude. There was something in his eyes when he looked at her. It was the same glint as the bullies' eyes at the orphanage. They enjoyed taunting and torturing the weak and young, stealing everything that they could get their hands on. They had soon learned to stay away from her and her brothers. They had thought because she was little that she wasn't able to understand what they were doing. They had been wrong. Jean Claude was no different, just more dangerous. She hadn't understood all the things that he had said to Angelica in the kitchen, but she knew that he had threatened to kill her and her brothers. Well, he couldn't hurt them if he couldn't find them. Unfortunately, she hadn't been able to find her brothers. It made sense to come to her hiding place until the snow lessened. She'd look for them in a little while.

The floorboards squeaked overhead, and she could hear Angelica banging things around in the kitchen. Smiling to herself, she pulled the blankets that she had gathered over her, blew out the candle, and drifted off to sleep.

•••

A loud crash woke Carol Anne from the depths of a dream. For a moment, she had no idea where she was, but as her hand touched the wood of the barrel, it came back to her. Normally, it was almost pitch dark down in the cellar, with a few threads of light coming through the floorboards, but now the room was definitely brighter. Moving quietly, she stuck her head out of the opening and saw that the light was coming from the open trap door by the stairs. Expecting Angelica to come down the stairs, Carol Anne jumped as two bundles tumbled down the steps instead. Then the trap door was slammed shut, plunging the space into darkness.

Carol Anne fumbled around, looking for the matches, and as her hand wrapped around the small box, there came a sound of hammering from above. She shakily lit the candle and moved cautiously toward the bundles that were now lying on the dirt floor at the base of the stairs. In the dim light, she recognized Matthew first. Putting a hand to her mouth, so as not to give herself away, she knelt by him. There were several bruises on his face, and blood was dripping from the back of his head. William was lying face down next to him, and he too was bleeding from the head. Both were unconscious. Someone, most likely Jean Claude, was nailing the trap door shut.

Hopefully he didn't know about the back tunnel.

Carol Anne waited several minutes after the hammering stopped and she heard footsteps walking away before trying to shake, first Matthew then William awake. Neither woke up. Tears streamed down her face. What if they died? Where were Angelica and Meda? Had he hurt them too? What would happen to her? To all of them?

Failing to get a response from either brother, Carol Anne ran back to her hideout and grabbed the blankets. She was too small to move her brothers but knew that she needed to keep them warm. It didn't seem that Jean Claude would be checking on them for a while. With any luck, the boys would wake up and they would all be hiding somewhere else by the time he came back.

Right now all she could do was wait.

CHAPTER NINETEEN

The storm clouds raced behind Luke and unleashed their fury about an hour from Landon's. The wind flung snow in all directions, making it impossible to see more than ten feet in front of him. Wolf had kept a steady pace that the gelding was able to maintain, even with the drifts of previous snow. Now the punishing wind pushed them onward, only to wrap around the front and push them back after snatching their breath away. It played with horse and rider, making them as substantial as a leaf caught in a tornado.

Wolf's tracks were barely visible in front of Luke, and every so often the canine would backtrack to check and make sure that horse and rider were still following. The gelding's sides started to heave from the exertion of plowing through the drifts and wind. Several times, Luke stopped him, dismounted, and used his own body as a windbreak so that the horse could catch its breath. Wolf would pace a short distance away until Luke mounted up again and continued.

There had only been a few times in his life that Luke had reacted from the gut instead of the head, and he knew that it was plain stupid to be out here, on the Dakota plains, in the middle of a blizzard, yet he couldn't shake the feeling that Angelica and the kids were in danger. That he needed to risk the weather to be there as soon as possible. There was no other explanation for Wolf coming to get him.

In good weather, it took nearly a full day to get to Angelica's. In weather like this, the best he could hope for was to get there some time in the night, yet he was worried. He had only been riding for roughly three hours, and already the horse was spent. Reining the gelding to a stop, he dismounted. There was no respite from the wind, so once again Luke went to the horse's head and cradled it against his body. The horse acted grateful for the chance to catch its breath. Once the equine had rested, Luke turned and started walking, with the horse following. They needed to keep moving. To stop out here meant certain death.

Wolf's prints had become slight impressions in the snow and were totally wiped away in some places, which meant that Luke's guide was a good distance ahead. With all the blowing snow, there were no landmarks to be seen to determine where he was.

Luke's movements were becoming slow and clumsy. The loss of feeling in his feet, ears, and nose meant that frostbite was starting to take hold, and he needed to do something about it. As if he had conjured him with his thoughts, Wolf came back and circled him.

"We need to stop and rest!" he yelled to the canine. "I need some sort of shelter to start a fire."

Wolf gave a yip and veered off to the right, stopping to look back at him. Luke bent his head and followed him into the driving snow.

●●●

It felt like an eternity before a large shadow loomed in front of him and the wind seemed to lessen. Luke held on to the pommel and managed to stay in the saddle only because he was frozen to it. The gelding trudged forward and perked up as the large shadow began to take shape and took on the appearance of solid rock. Wolf stayed close to them and led the way into a narrow canyon that had just enough room for him to ride through. The high walls on either side blocked the wind.

It took Luke several minutes to realize that the gelding had stopped. Prying the reins from his stiff fingers, he pushed his hat back and looked around. His ears still rang from the fury of the wind. The canyon was actually a crack in the rock's wall, and it ended in a space wide enough for him and his horse to be able to turn around. It was enclosed on three sides, with an overhang of rock that served as a roof. The wind couldn't make its way down the narrow passage, and only small flakes of snow fell gently around him.

Working on sheer instinct, Luke dismounted and led the horse to the back of the space and began to unsaddle him. His movements were clumsy, yet he managed to pull off the saddle and rub the horse down with the blanket that had been under it. Then he re-covered the horse with the blanket and placed a feed bag with some oats on the horse's head. Only when the horse was settled did he start looking around for anything that he could use to start a small fire.

Hypothermia was setting in, and if he didn't get warm soon, he knew that he would be beyond helping himself and he would succumb to it. Unfortunately, there were no small sticks or anything that he could see that would make a fire. Grabbing his bedroll, he sat down on it and began to remove his boots. His feet had become numb miles back. Rolling himself in the rough fabric, he scissored his legs back and forth in the effort to create some heat. A heavy weight pressed up against his side, and when he popped his head out and looked, he saw Wolf lying up against him. Slowly, the canine's body heat began to seep into his frozen form. Both his hands and feet began to throb with pain, and he welcomed the sensation. It meant that he hadn't lost them to frostbite yet. Inch by grueling inch, his body began to warm, and soon he started to shiver.

Turning onto his side, he backed his back up against the solid form of Wolf and thought about his next move. He had been rash in leaving Landon's in such weather, but he knew that he would do it again. Something was telling him that time was of the essence. Yet it was the brutal cold and wind that was slowing him down. There was no way of knowing how long this storm was going to last, so there wasn't much choice but to continue and hope that he made it in time.

At some point, he was warm enough to sleep, and when he awoke, it took him a few minutes to get his bearings. Taking the covers from his head, he peered out. The gelding was tethered nearby, its head hung as it took advantage of the respite. It was hard to tell if the snow and wind had lessened in such a sheltered place. Every muscle in his body protested as he threw the covers back and untangled himself from the bedroll. His feet were sore, and it was difficult to get his boots back on. Wolf was nowhere to be seen.

Walking out to the narrow path, he looked up but saw nothing but gray sky. A few stray snowflakes manage to find their way down the crevice to fall around him. The walls of the fissure must have been at least seventy feet high. This was no small rock outcropping in the middle of the prairie; it was a substantial formation, yet he could not place it. He could have sworn that he knew every hill and valley between Landon's place and the town of Newcomb, yet he had never seen anything like this except in the Black Hills, and they were at least fifty miles to the west.

Flexing his stiff fingers, Luke made his way out to the opening. With the clouds, it was impossible to pinpoint the time of day, but he got a sense that it was late afternoon. Swearing, he scanned the landscape, but there was no sign of Wolf. In fact, there was nothing as far as the eye could see. So what the hell did he do now? It would be suicide to head out without Wolf as a guide. Without landmarks, he had no idea which direction to even travel. Turning, he went back into the shelter of the rocks.

Reaching into his saddle bags, he pulled out the brown package that Landon had given him and silently blessed Old Kate. Inside was the dried jerky, and he almost broke a tooth trying to take a bite of it. It was frozen solid. Using his molars, he was able to break off a chunk. Rolling the jerky around his mouth for a few minutes, he was rewarded with a rich hickory taste as it began to thaw. It was enough to quiet the hunger pains that gnawed at him. It also gave him something to think about other than being stranded in the middle of the prairie, wondering what the hell he was going to do. Common sense told him to wait for Wolf, but if he had listened to that, he wouldn't be out here in the first place.

The only thing he could do was to make a plan of action and do it. There was nothing to be gained by second guessing himself. Looking back at the sky, he decided that he would wait a half hour for Wolf. After that, he would head out and head east. With any luck, he would find a landmark that he knew before it became too dark.

•••

The gelding balked at leaving the relative comfort of the rocks, and Luke couldn't say that he blamed him. No creature in his right mind wanted to leave the comfort and warmth of shelter to head out into bitter cold and winds, but the horse was well trained and soon settled into a gallop. Luke had waited forty-five minutes, but there had been no sign of Wolf.

Figuring that he had wasted enough time, they had set out. At first, it was relatively easy going. The wind had died down, making it feel warmer and easier to see distance. Yet there were still ominous black clouds all around him, and he knew that this respite was going to be brief. Pushing his hat down more firmly over his ears, he urged the gelding on.

•••

Dusk was settling when Luke came along the remains of an Indian village. From the look of it, it had been abandoned for several months. He found buffalo heads halfway buried in the shifting snow. They had been placed in a ring, each sun-bleached, eyeless skull facing to the east where the morning sun would rise. He knew that it was a Sioux ritual that they believed helped ward off evil spirits. The tribe would search the surrounding area and bring back the skulls before making camp. For some unexplained reason, the skulls gave Luke comfort.

The wind was picking up again, and a glance behind him proved that the clouds that had been slowly gaining on him were about to overtake him. Looking at the darkening landscape, Luke was aware that he still had no idea where he was. He pinched the bridge of his nose between his fingers and tried to think. Angelica's ranch had been southeast of Landon's. He figured that he had been at least halfway when Wolf had brought him to shelter, so that would have taken him to the west by a few miles. Traveling east should have brought him back to familiar territory. That it didn't meant that he had probably gone past the split in the trail and had gone too far south. The question was, did he continue to go east and hope to run into the trail, or did he backtrack north and meet up with the trail there? Either way, he would lose precious time. Lifting his head, he was about to turn the gelding and head east when he saw movement in the distance to the south. Then the clouds were upon him and the snow started falling in earnest.

Urging the horse forward, Luke was relieved to spot Wolf standing on a small rise, waiting for him. As he got closer, he began to recognize the surrounding land. They were still over four hours, on a good day, away from Angelica's, but the familiarity of where he was gave him a surge of confidence.

Wolf had been keeping a certain distance from Luke during this trip, but now as he drew abreast of the animal, he began to notice things he hadn't before. Wolf wasn't as big as he remembered; in fact, he looked to be much smaller. Reining next to the canine, Luke looked down into the animal's brown eyes. It took him a minute to register that Wolf had gold eyes and that he had seen these brown eyes before. An image of Meda, talking to him the night he had been fixing the fence when the light had flickered giving her the appearance of a wolf, flashed through his mind.

His common sense told him that it was impossible to believe that this wolf could be Meda. He wondered if he had perhaps succumbed to the elements and now was having a hallucination, but he quickly rejected that thought. There must be some other explanation.

The wolf watched him without so much as a blink.

CHAPTER TWENTY

Reaching Meda's tepee, Angelica silently prayed that the children and Meda would all be there, safe and sound, waiting for her. Her boots slipped on the icy snow, and she clutched her cloak tighter around her against the wind-driven snow. As she approached the tent, a white mass stepped in front of the opening, startling Angelica so that she cried out as she placed a hand to her throat and retreated a few steps. "Good heavens, you scared the daylights out of me," she scolded the large wolf.

As she stepped forward, she was surprised when the animal began to growl and snarl.

"What's gotten into you? Shoo. Move." Wolf ignored her words and continued to guard the door. Angelica didn't know what to make of the unusual behavior. Luke had assured her that the wolf was harmless. "Meda! William! Anybody! Can you hear me?"

No one came to reassure her that they were all right. Wolf continued to stand his ground and only relaxed when she took a step or two backwards. Glancing around, she couldn't make out any tracks in the snow other than her own. Were they inside, unable to let her know? Why wouldn't Wolf let her pass? It was all overwhelming. If they weren't inside the tepee, then where could they be? There weren't many indoor places to hide. She had a mental image of the children out in the storm, possibly freezing to death.

Tears welled in her eyes. Carol Anne had already caught a chill; pneumonia could set in very easily, especially for a small child. She had just begun to love the children, and now everything was in jeopardy.

Falling to her knees, mindless of the snow saturating her skirt, Angelica bent her head as if in defeat. It seemed as if Jean Claude was going to get away with his plan.

Wolf came forward and nudged her with his nose. She wrapped her arms around his neck and buried her head in the thick fur. "Help me find them, Wolf. I couldn't bear it if I lost them too."

Wolf backed away from her so quickly that she almost fell forward into the snow. He sat down on his haunches and stared at her. His gold eyes were unreadable, but for a split second she thought she saw a flash of understanding in them.

"Do you know where they are?" Having been alone for so many years, she had gotten used to talking with the animals. Conversing with them had been better than the endless silence. There had been times that she thought she would go mad, longing for the sound of another human voice. Right now, she would give anything to hear the children's or Meda's voices. to know that they were safe, for the moment at least. But reality was setting in, and she began to feel foolish for thinking that a wolf could understand her, like a well-trained dog.

Her skirt was soaked, and she began to shiver. Rising, she looked down. "You can't help me, can you? I guess at this point, no one can." Tears stung her eyes. "Jean Claude is going to get away with this, and there isn't anything I can do to stop him."

Once again Wolf stared at her with those inscrutable eyes.

Clutching her cloak tighter around her, Angelica turned but stopped as she felt something. Looking down, she saw that Wolf had stepped forward and pressed his muzzle into her hand. It felt as if he was reassuring her that all would be fine, but that was absurd, though the gesture did comfort her some.

Ruffling the fur on his neck, she said, "Thanks, Wolf."

•••

There was nowhere to go; Angelica had already checked the barn and any other place that she could think of to look. There was simply no sign of Meda or the children. The wind tugged at her skirts, directing her to follow its whim. So, it was a surprise to find herself standing in the small graveyard, at the wooden markers of her parents.

Once again, she fell to her knees into the snow, ignoring the cold and wetness of her skirt. Her mother's presence was strong here. It wouldn't have surprised her to look up and see Lillian appear in front of her. Instead, there was only darkness.

"I'm scared, Mom," she whispered. "I can't find anyone, and I don't know what to do." Bowing her head, she felt a stab of guilt at the sudden anger that she felt towards her parents. "You should have warned me about Jean Claude. I wasn't a child. I deserved to know the truth, and now it's too late."

"It's never too late, my angel." her mother's voice said inside her head. *"You're a strong, beautiful, and smart woman. You have never quit anything in your life, and I know you won't now."*

Tears came to her eyes. She missed her mother so much that it hurt. "What can I do, Mom? I don't know how to win this one. He's done something to Meda and the children." Her voice broke. "I can't do this alone."

"You are not alone, my love. We walk beside you every day. You need to have faith and hope. Trust in yourself and in the Lord."

Those words made Angelica think of the night that she had basically said the same thing to Luke. The words had come easily in her naivety. No wonder he had reacted so violently. She must have seemed like a pompous fool. Her faith had been shattered by Jean Claude's betrayal and realizing her own stupidity. It would take a herculean effort to get it back.

The wind brought the muffled sound of banging from the direction of the house, but she ignored it. Most likely it was something that had come loose in the wind. Before, the house and the land had become everything to her; they had been part of her soul. Now she would gladly give them to Jean Claude if it would bring back Meda and the children.

Angelica no longer felt the presence of her mother, and she was freezing. With great effort, she pushed herself up and turned toward the house.

CHAPTER TWENTY-ONE

The gelding managed to keep up a good pace as Luke took full advantage of the wind's lull. Occasionally, a gust would cause the falling snow to swirl around them, making the darkness even darker. Not for the first time, he wished that it had been a full moon. Even with the clouds, it would have helped illuminate his way. Right now, he figured that the bottom of a coal shaft would have been brighter.

The she-wolf kept close, making sure he didn't fall behind. Yet, Luke could feel the fatigue the cold created for him and his horse as each step took its toll. It barely seemed possible that he had delivered Landon's twins hours ago, not days. They would have to take a break soon, him to stretch his numb legs and the horse to rest. As if reading his mind, the wolf slowed her pace and the gelding followed suit.

This time, there was no miraculous shelter appearing from the dark gloom. Luke reigned in the gelding and dismounted, holding onto the pommel, as he couldn't put weight on his feet. They seemed to be blocks of wood for all the feeling that they had. It took several minutes, but finally he could feel the blood rush back into them. It was a painful process. Grabbing the canteen, which had been placed between the blanket and the sweating horse, therefore keeping the water from freezing, Luke hobbled to the gelding's head. He tore his glove off with his teeth. It took him several tries to unscrew the cap with his frozen fingers, yet when he finally managed it, he poured some water into the horse's mouth. The animal drank gratefully.

With the darkness and snow, Luke had no idea where he was but figured that they had made some pretty good time. It felt like dawn wasn't too far away, but that was a guess.

Luke's body was stiff from the cold, and his movements were slow and childlike. Once again, he pulled out some jerky and broke off a piece. Placing the frozen meat between his gums and cheek, he sucked on it, trying to defrost it while he contemplated his next move. The gelding was just about spent, and this endless cold was taking a toll on both of them. His eyes felt as if they were filled with sand, and he was having a hard time processing and concentrating. Unfortunately, there was no choice but to continue on.

"We need to slow down," he told the she-wolf, who paced back and forth nearby. "Or we need another shelter to rest in."

This time, there was no change of direction or mad dash off somewhere. She just increased her pacing.

"Guess that means no rest," Luke told the gelding as he remounted.

With a yip, the she-wolf once again set off.

●●●

Angelica awoke from her dream with a start, and it took her a minute or two to figure out where she was. Then it all came crashing back. Closing her eyes against the disappointment of reality, she tried to recapture the essence of the dream. Luke had been in it, as had the children. They had been happy, a family, everything that she had hoped for since she was a little girl. It seemed so real.

Something butted her head, and the remnants of the fantasy scattered like dandelion fluff on the wind. Opening her eyes, she reached out to pet Purrsistence. The fat cat meowed before settling down on Angelica's lap.

As Angelica leaned her head back against the wall, a tear slipped from her eye and made a slow descent down her cheek. Her life could have been so different except for the fates stepping in. What would happen to her beloved cat? Jean Claude hated Purrsistence and wouldn't hesitate to skin the feline alive. The thought was almost too much to bear.

There was no fight left in her, and Angelica bowed her head in defeat. It would seem that her destiny had been sealed a long time ago. What could she do now to change it? It would take a miracle.

Purrsistence growled as if reading her mistress's mind and not liking the turn of her thoughts.

"I'm sorry, Purrsistence," she whispered to the cat. "I'm so sorry."

•••

This time, Angelica didn't dream but woke up to the crash of the front door being thrown open. It must be just about dawn, she thought, crawling to the edge of the loft to peer over. Angelica could see gray shapes through the previous blackness. It was no surprise to see the outline of Jean Claude standing below. He looked around like he owned the place.

"Come out, Angelica. There is nowhere for you to go. I've wasted enough time."

Trying to make as little noise as possible, she scooted back, out of sight. Panic filled her and she grabbed the rifle, cradling it against her chest. It was just a matter of time before he climbed the ladder and found her. She felt like a coward, hiding in the loft, but she had enough pride left so as not to go to him. If he wanted her, then he would have to take her out of there, forcibly.

His footsteps echoed on the wood floor as she mentally followed his actions by the sounds. First, he checked behind the curtain next to her bed. Then into the kitchen, opening cupboards and then slamming them shut. It wasn't hard to picture him standing in the kitchen, trying to figure out where she was hiding. Then they returned to the living room, and she knew the second that he moved toward the ladder. Clasping her hand over her mouth so as not to cry out, she tried to make herself as small as possible in the far corner. Maybe in the semi-darkness, he wouldn't see her.

Purrsistence gave a low growl as she too watched the top of the ladder. The hair on her back stood on end and her body tensed as her tail flicked back and forth as if in anticipation. The moment Jean Claude's head appeared in the opening; she let out a combination growl and high-pitched scream as she launched herself forward. Jean Claude was taken by surprise and almost lost his grip on the ladder. Claws slashed at his face, causing deep scratches that drew blood. Swearing loudly, he tried to grab the fractious cat, causing him to get bit several times on his hand. Finally, he managed to seize Purrsistence and threw her, savagely, over the side of the loft to the ground below.

"No!" Angelica cried, rushing forward.

Jean Claude's face was smeared with blood as he turned and glared at her. Without a word, he grabbed her and dragged her down the ladder. The rifle fell to the floor below with a loud crash. A frantic glance around revealed that Purrsistence had disappeared. Hopefully the large cat wasn't badly hurt in the fall. Didn't God owe her at least one favor?

Jean Claude still had a tight grip on her arm as he too looked around for the cat. "I ever see that fur bag from hell again, I'll tack its bloody hide to the side of my cabin."

Fury rose in Angelica. "You had better not touch my cat, Jean Claude! And bring back my family, right now! There is no way that I'm going anywhere with you, and if you try, then I swear that I will cut your throat the first chance I get."

He looked at her like she was talking in a different language.

"There are laws in this country, and you can't just go around kidnapping women and…"

Letting go of her arm, he cut her off with a back hand across the face. The force of the blow sent her reeling, and she landed on her already damaged arm. Lying on the floor, Angelica tried to remain conscious as the throbbing pain in her ribs made black spots appear before her eyes. Her right cheek felt as if it was on fire. No one had ever laid a hand on her in anger before, not even her parents. Her eyes fell on the rifle, laying several feet away. Before she wasn't sure if she could shoot another human being, but now she'd give anything to have that rifle in her hands.

Towering over her, Jean Claude seethed. "Don't ever threaten me again. Where we're going, no one will find you, and without me you won't survive a day."

Hauling her to her feet, he crushed her against him. His blood smeared onto her face, and she felt the slickness of it and smelled its metallic scent. Bile rose in her throat.

"You will be my Lillian. I won't be denied again." His voice grew soft and more menacing. "Pack some warm clothes and enough food to last for a couple of days. Whatever is in my traps won't be safe for eating. Hopefully the pelts will still be good."

With that, he threw her away from him, grabbed the rifle from the floor, and slammed out the door.

●●●

Carol Anne listened to the loud crashes and Jean Claude's voice coming from overhead. The boys were still not moving, and she was very frightened. If only she wasn't so little and could haul the boys away from the steps and into her hiding place. Then maybe when Jean Claude came back for them, he would think that they had escaped and leave without them.

Earlier, moving as quietly as she could, she had searched the basement, but the only weapon that she could find was an old hammer. Lying between her brothers, she had placed the hammer next to her. She knew that Jean Claude could take it away from her, but it still gave her some comfort knowing that she could at least break a toe or two of his first. Satisfied at the thought, she snuggled up to Matthew and continued her lonely vigil.

CHAPTER TWENTY-TWO

Ghost paid no attention to the cold wind or pelting snow. There was no moon to cast shadows; that had been his plan from the beginning, but with the storm, it hardly mattered now. The old army coat that he had taken from a dead soldier, a trophy from his first battle, hung open. Its faded blue color helped him to blend into the shadows and become part of the night. His long black hair had been tied back with rawhide, yet the wind tugged at it like a child, relentless, causing stray tendrils to whip around his head.

Shadows would start to appear when the sun crested the horizon. He cursed silently as he heard Jean Claude yelling from inside the house. The stupid trapper hadn't kept to the plan. White men had no patience, no vision. They took what they wanted and left the Lakota and the Sioux with nothing. Robbing the land of buffalo and the Lakota's way of life, all for a shiny rock called gold.

Grinning to himself, Ghost knew that he would enjoy killing the trapper and seizing the white woman. She was a legend among his people. Living in the middle of the prairie, she had become a blood sister to the Lakota. She shared her crops with the tribe, and in doing so had fallen under the protection of the Sioux nation. Taking her and his Lakota sister, Sitting Bull's cousin, prisoner would undoubtedly cause Sitting Bull and the tribal council to search for them. But when they came, they would find evidence that the women were taken by their enemies, the Shoshoni. Ghost had heard that the Shoshoni had started going on raids against the Lakota with the Long Swords. Sitting Bull and the elders would have no choice but to declare war and wipe out their enemies for good.

Jean Claude stormed out of the house, dragging the woman with him. There appeared to be long scratches that were oozing blood from his cheeks. Ghost gave a nod of approval. It would seem that the white sister to the Lakota's' had some spirit after all. That would be good if he decided to keep her as his own. He would admire that spirit, as long as she knew her place.

Stepping back, deeper into the darkness, Ghost closed his eyes and began a silent chant of prayer to the Wakan Tanka as he prepared for battle.

•••

The snow was coming down fast and the wind whipped the flakes into a frenzy. Dawn wasn't far away, yet it was still dark and gray. Angelica slipped as Jean Claude pulled her by the hair towards the barn. The ground was icy, and she fought to retain her footing as they moved at a fast pace. If she fell, she knew that he would drag her. Pain coursed through her body as he yanked her forward, and her ribs protested as he threw her to the ground just inside the barn door. Sucking air into her throbbing lungs, she prayed for the hundredth time that the children were somewhere safe.

Jean Claude ignored her as he muttered to himself and began to bridle his horse. He had shut the doors, and the warmth of the space began to seep into Angelica's chilled body as her mind began to process her situation. She knew that she wouldn't be able to outrun him and that she was no match for him physically; he had already proved that. Glancing around, she spotted a shovel and a rake leaning against the far wall. She would have to get past him first to be able to reach them. Panic welled in her chest. If she could just reach the tools, she knew she would have no hesitation in using them; the problem was there was no room for error. If she missed, then he would beat her, tie her up, or kill her. Then she would be of no help to the children; they would be at Jean Claude's mercy. She couldn't bear to think about what he would do to them.

Closing her eyes, Angelica took several deep breaths. She'd need a clear head if she was going to save them all. Slowly she started to inch her way sideways.

"What were you thinking?"

His voice stopped her. For a moment, she thought that he knew what she had planned, but then she realized that he wasn't talking to her but her dead mother. Carefully, she moved sideways again.

"I've loved you since the day we met, yet you chose that imbecile over me! Waited for you to realize that it was us that should be together, but instead you bore him a child. It should have been my child! I would have given you sons!" His movements had become agitated, and his accent became more pronounced as he worked. "I would have been good to you. You would have had everything you could have ever asked for. You would have been wrapped in the finest furs, never wanting for anything."

Leaning his head against the horse, his voice became a mumble. Angelica slid sideways a few more inches and her heart stopped when he whirled around and glared at her. His eyes were unfocused and seemed to see through her. Taking a few steps, he reached down and hauled her to her feet and up against his body. The stench of him made her stomach roll in protest. His eyes had become focused again, and they bored into hers.

"You've been giving what should have been mine to that brat. My Lillian would have never done that."

Spittle flew from his face, which was just inches away from hers. His hand gripped her right arm where the healing fracture was still tender. Focusing on the pain helped her from passing out. Adrenaline shot like greased lightning through her veins, and with a sudden burst of strength, she took a step back. The momentum took Jean Claude by surprise, and they fell backwards against the wall. Angelica could feel the handle of the shovel digging into her shoulder blades. Unfortunately, the weight of Jean Claude's body pinned her against the wall, making it so that she couldn't get her left arm behind her to grab the tool.

"You are just like your father—a worthless, spineless fool. He was never good enough for my Lillian."

Anger and resolve began to replace the fear that had gripped her. If they were all going to get out of this alive, then it was going to have to be up to her. There was no knight in shining armor coming to ride to their rescue. Luke was miles away, and he had no idea that they were in trouble. No one would be traveling this time of year in this weather, as the soldiers would be holed up in the forts and most of the Indians would winter over on the reservations, if they hadn't already headed south.

Though it seemed unlikely that his accomplice would travel in this weather, it appeared that Jean Claude had easily disposed of Meda and the children, alone. Unless he hadn't done it alone, a little voice whispered in her head. Angelica hadn't thought of that before. Maybe his accomplice had already taken Meda and the children, and they were miles away. How would she find them? The panic began as a dull ache in her stomach and made its way up to her throat, making it hard to breathe.

"*Stop it!*" she told herself. Nothing would be gained if she panicked. She could only deal with one problem at a time, and right now that meant getting away from Jean Claude. The man was obviously a lunatic who had lost his grip on reality.

Using her mother's tone, she commanded, "Jean Claude, let go, you're hurting me!"

Jean Claude's features softened as he stepped back, lifting his weight off of her, to look into her eyes. "Lillian?"

Angelica felt a pang of guilt that she quickly quelled. There was no room for sympathy. Taking the moment, she reached behind her and wrapped her fingers around the shovel's handle.

"Why are you hurting me, Jean Claude? I thought you loved me?"

"Oh god Lillian, I would never hurt you. I've missed you so much. I thought you were lost to me forever."

Without warning, he pulled her towards him and tried to kiss her. Moving her face just in time, his lips found her temple. Revulsion was her first response, yet she had to keep up the pretense of her mother if she hoped to get out of this situation. Smothering the urge to back away from him, she let him ramble on for a few minutes before gently pushing him away. "I need to find my children, Jean Claude. Take me to the children. I need to see them now."

He didn't seem to understand her words. She shook him. "What have you done with the children?"

Jean Claude stepped back and, as she watched, his face twisted as reality came back to him.

"Bitch," he hissed as he cuffed the side of her head.

The force of the hit made her slam up against the wall and fall to the floor, taking the shovel with her. Jean Claude loomed over her.

"You will never see those brats again. Ghost will take them away when he comes, and that Indian whore too."

Relief and hope coursed through her veins. That meant that this Ghost person hadn't shown up yet and they weren't miles away as she had feared. They must still be somewhere hidden on the grounds.

The right side of her face again felt like it was on fire. Her eye, already bruised, was swelling shut, yet she looked up at him with all the loathing and hate that she was feeling. "If you've hurt them, I'll kill you."

He laughed at that. "You will be my slave, my Lillian, and everything you have will be mine. You can't escape from me, and in time you will come to desire me. The way Lillian should have."

The man was clearly insane if he thought for one second that she was going to ever desire him. How the hell was she going to get away from him? What would happen when his accomplice showed up? There was no way that she could fight two men. Her mind skittered over that thought. She needed to keep hope alive; it was all she had left. First, she had to get Jean Claude out of the way.

With a snort, he turned back to finish saddling the horses. Gripping the shovel handle firmly, Angelica inched her way up the wall. Using all her strength, she swung the shovel at his head. A satisfying thunk sounded as the metal collided with his skull. Jean Claude started to turn, with a surprised look on his face, so she hit him again. Wordlessly, he crumbled to the floor.

Dropping the shovel, she wasted no time in heading for the barn door.

•••

At first Angelica ran blindly, heading toward the creek. Reaching the edge of the water, she was forced to stop—she had no idea where to go. There was nothing but open prairie all around her. The snow seemed to lessen but it was hard to tell with the wind still howling.

"Breathe, Angelica, breathe." Her mother's voice. *"You need to stop and think."*

It took everything she had, but Angelica closed her eyes and concentrated on breathing. Her heart slowed, helping to clear her mind. It had been foolish to leave Jean Claude back there; she should have tied him up. He could gain consciousness anytime and come after her again, and this time he wouldn't let her get the better of him.

Pacing back and forth, Angelica tried to come up with a plan, but the only thing that she could think of was to go back and tie Jean Claude up. Maybe if he stayed unconscious, she could hide him in the barn, then she would have only his accomplice to deal with. Without Jean Claude calling the shots, she might be able to buy his friend off. There were six five-dollar gold pieces still tucked away in the sugar bin in the pantry. Then she would be free to find Meda and the children. She had no idea what she would do if he said no.

Having no other choice, Angelica turned and returned to the barn. Approaching from the rear, she waded through knee high drifts of snow and pressed herself to the side. Pulling on the back door, it didn't budge. It was frozen shut. That meant that the only way in was through the front.

Inching her way along the side of the barn, Angelica stopped several times to press her ear against the cold boards. There was no sound from inside other than Gracie, who was impatient to be milked. As quietly as she could, Angelica made her way to the front corner. Crouching, she peered around. The barnyard was empty, and the barn door swung wildly in the wind. Blowing on her freezing hands, she toyed with the idea of heading to the house first and getting her shawl and mittens. Deciding that there wasn't time to waste, she stood and made her way around the corner. It seemed like ages before she reached the barn door. Steeling herself, Angelica peered around the door.

•••

Luke swayed in the saddle, lost in a daze. He no longer felt the cold and time had ceased to exist. The gelding plodded slowly through the drifts of snow with its head down. It was near dawn and the wind had escalated, causing the falling snow to become an impenetrable curtain of gray. Luke had no idea where he was, and he was beyond the point of caring. The she-wolf would disappear and then show up occasionally to check on his progress. Once she had bared her teeth at him when he told her that he was too exhausted to go on. Another time she had nipped at the gelding's hind legs when the horse had stopped, causing it to start walking again.

Memories flooded Luke's mind as the horse lumbered forward. He could hear his mother calling him to breakfast. Feel her kissing him on the top of the head as he tried to duck underneath her arms on his way out the door to head for school. Remembering his first operation. It had been a neighbor who had slipped with an ax and had nearly cut his foot off. Luke had been scared to death, yet he had managed to save the foot. There were other memories, but they came in flashes. Then he remembered the day that he rode into Angelica's.

His head lolled forward, and he shut his eyes.

His gut clenched as he remembered how she had looked up at him with those huge eyes and fainted in his arms. For a little bit of a thing, she had to be one of the most self-sufficient, fearless, and beautiful women that he had ever met. She hadn't even blinked when he brought the children to her. Guilt stabbed at him as he remembered her face as she bid him goodbye. He wondered, inanely, if she had read the book that he had given her for her birthday and if she thought of him when she read it. He hoped so.

"*You're a fraud,*" a voice in his head scolded.

Luke opened his eyes and tried to ignore the voice.

"*You fell in love with her,*" the pesky voice continued, "*yet you left her. She could have been the best thing that ever happened to you, but you threw her away.*"

He shook his head. The voice continued. "*If you're not in love with her, then why the hell are you out here, against all odds? Willing to brave a blizzard at the mere hint that she might be in trouble? Willing to die trying to reach her?*"

Denial welled up in Luke. There had been no thought when he had seen the wolf; he had just reacted. Somehow, he had known that the wolf had come to get him because Angelica needed him. But that didn't mean that he was in love with her. It just meant that he felt responsible for her and the children, was all. Any man would do the same in his shoes.

The voice snorted—or was that the horse? "*You can't even be honest with yourself. You've hidden yourself away from everyone that you could come to care for. You've even forsaken God, for god's sake!*"

That did it. Anger replaced the denial, and he welcomed it. He felt safer when he was angry. "I did not forsake God. God abandoned me!" he growled out loud.

His lips were dry and cracked, and the snow and ice had settled into the lines of his face that hadn't been covered with his bandana. His throat was raw and dry, and his voice sounded brittle and hollow even to his own ears.

Yet, that pesky voice wouldn't relent. "*Do you really think that God deserted you? Did it ever occur to you that bad things happen to all of us and that it's our faith that sees us through? No, you took it as a personal attack. Somehow you think you are above the average man. Nothing bad should happen to you or anyone you care about. That's why you became a doctor, wasn't it? To save everyone, and when you couldn't, you blamed God.*"

He wouldn't listen to any more of this. Pulling on the reins, Luke stopped the gelding. Swinging his leg over the saddle, he dismounted and immediately wished he hadn't. Waves of pain radiated up his legs and into his back. As before, there was no feeling from his feet. Focusing on the pain kept the voice at bay, for a few minutes anyway.

Hanging onto the pommel, he wondered if he had gone crazy. The relentless shrieking of the wind, the isolation and the bone chilling cold were taking their toll. Now he was hearing voices in his head and was even answering them. Couldn't get much crazier than that.

"Just as loco as following a wolf through a blizzard," he muttered.

The she-wolf appeared then as if summoned. Her eyes were questioning as she paced back and forth, watching him, mocking him.

"You brought me on a fool's mission, didn't you?" he accused the wolf.

"I'm too late to save them, aren't I?"

The she-wolf watched him.

All his anger and fear came rushing to the surface. "Angelica, the children…they're dead, aren't they?" he yelled. "I thought that if I left, then they would be safe from…from…" Bowing his head, he couldn't finish.

"*From you?*" that relentless voice chimed in. "*Did you really think that you were the one that they had to fear? Stop lying to yourself. You didn't leave because you were afraid of hurting them; you left because you were a coward. To stay meant that you would have to face everything that terrifies you.*"

It was Luke's turn to pace. Why wouldn't the voice go away? Was this it, then? Had he finally gone mad?

"*To love them meant that you had to run the risk of opening yourself to pain.*"

He shook his head.

"*To love them means that you might have to—*"

"Might have to what?" he railed, stopping the voice. "Watch them die because of some whim of God or man? Might have to watch them come to hate me? Have them realize that I'm not a hero but only a liar that makes empty promises to keep them safe, knowing that I can't do a damn thing to save them?"

Dragging fingers over his face, Luke stared at the bleak landscape without taking in any detail. All he could see were young boys who had had their whole life in front of them, alive one moment, dead the next. Blood and death everywhere he looked. Luke had agonized over their loss, feeling like his soul had been torn from his body, unable to be repaired, the scars running too deep.

"*To love again means that you might have to feel again, take a chance at happiness. Something that you don't feel that you deserve. You've martyred yourself for years, and it's a role you play perfectly.*"

"I won't listen to this!" he bellowed.

The she-wolf continued to watch from a distance, circling him, as the voice continued.

"*You don't need to listen—you need to feel. Feel the pain that you've been bottling up inside you for all these years. You survived that attack, and the guilt has eaten away at you ever since. Let it go. It's time. Those boys died for a cause. They're in a better place now. They never asked for your guilt, and they wouldn't have wanted it.*"

Luke grabbed the reins and started walking. Anything was better than freezing to death out on the plains while he slowly lost his mind.

The voice's words echoed in his head. Those soldiers had died for a cause even if the cause had been a flawed one. But were they in a better place? To believe that meant that he had to trust in life after death and that God did exist. Luke wanted to accept that they were in some sort of heaven, but he couldn't get past that they were just boys, young men that had had their whole lives in front of them. Most of them hadn't even been old enough to shave. They would never grow up to dance with a pretty girl or get married and hold their sons or daughters in their arms. That was the part that burned like acid in his mouth. The part that made him feel that he didn't have that right either. He cursed out loud. Landon should have left him there to die that day, because the voice was right—he did feel guilty for still being alive. Why had he survived when they had all perished? That was the question that haunted him the most.

The gelding, which had been plodding along, perked up his ears and shook his head. The snow was slowing, and the wind appeared to have lessened. Climbing back into the saddle, Luke let the gelding lead. Out of the two of them, he figured that the horse probably was the sanest. The she-wolf had disappeared again, but he paid no attention.

With renewed energy, the gelding set off.

CHAPTER TWENTY-THREE

Carol Anne awoke to the sound of loud voices and things thumping on the floor from above. Biting her lip, she once again tried to wake her brothers. Relief flooded through her veins when William groaned and began to move around. Getting him to sit upright, she helped him lean back against the dirt wall.

William's movements were slow and shaky as he reached up to touch the back of his head. There was still some seepage from the jagged wound, and his hand was bloody as he brought it back down to look at.

The sounds from upstairs stopped abruptly. It was so quiet that Carol Anne could hear the blood pounding in her ears.

"William," she whispered. "I think Jean Claude took Angelica. We gotta hide."

Confusion clouded William's eyes as he turned in her direction at the sound of her voice. "Carol Anne…what happened? Where's Matthew?" He looked around in the dim light. "Where the heck are we?"

Sidling up beside him, she tugged on his arm. "We gotta hide," she repeated slowly. "Matthew is right here. We're in the root cellar. Jean Claude locked us in, but I know how to get out."

William tried to stand. It took several tries, but he finally was able to gain his feet, although he leaned heavily against the wall. Meanwhile, there came a groan and movement from Matthew.

Carol Anne was feeling better by the minute. Her brothers would make everything right.

"We need to hide," she reiterated. "Behind the barrels."

Nodding his assent, William tried to step forward. It took a few moments of wobbling and bracing himself with a hand on the wall, but eventually he was able to stand.

Between the two of them, they half carried, half dragged Matthew to her little hideaway. William had to move some barrels to make them all fit, but soon they were hidden in the small space. Matthew was half conscious, leaning against the wall.

"All right," William said to Carol Anne now that they were settled. "Tell me everything."

•••

Angelica tried to turn and run, but it was too late. Jean Claude, blood covering the right side of his face, stepped forward from the shadows and snatched her by the arm. Pulling her into the barn, he grabbed some rope lying nearby and forced her to the ground. Binding her hands behind her, he hauled her back up and dragged her over to where two horses were tied and threw her into a stall.

With over a foot of snow on the ground, and deeper in the drifts, there was no way the horses could pull a wagon. Jean Claude rooted around and found a moldy saddle in a corner of the barn. Not bothering to dust it off, he placed it on one horse and tightened the cinch before loading the other horse with bags of supplies. He would ride with Angelica in front of him. With the stunt that she had just pulled, he wouldn't put it past her to try to escape, if she had her own horse.

Angelica fought as he tried to lift her onto the horse. He let her struggle against him for a few seconds before gripping her face hard and turning her to face him. "Don't think that I'll forget what you did. Keep fighting me, and I might decide that you're more trouble than you're worth. Get on this horse and do as you're told, or I'll gut those brats one by one."

It pleased him to see the fear and surprise in her eyes. Good. A woman should always be a little fearful. It kept them in their place. Jean Claude knew that Angelica wanted to defy him, but in the end, she dropped her gaze and turned back to the horse. So that was the secret of keeping her in her place. All he had to do was to threaten the others and she became compliant. Maybe he should go and find the little girl and bring her along.

Turning, Jean Claude looked toward the house. Problem was, he had no idea where the girl was, and he had already wasted too much time. They needed to go now if he hoped to make it to his cabin by dark. With the snow slowing them down, never mind riding double, he decided that he couldn't spare the effort. Maybe when Angelica had settled in, he would go find another little girl. Bring her home as a present.

Lifting Angelica into the saddle, he led the horses out of the barn.

"I don't have a coat, hat, or mittens," she told him. "I'll freeze long before we get there."

Wrapping the reins around his hand, he pulled the other horse alongside. Rummaging around in one of the packs, he brought out a well-worn fur lined coat. Turning, Jean Claude tossed the jacket to her, being careful to stay away from her feet.

She glanced down at the jacket, wrinkled her nose, and glared at him. "I won't leave my horse and cow here. "

"You don't have a choice," he told her bluntly. "Besides, Ghost's tribe will probably have them stewed up before sunset. Say another goddamn word, and I'll save them a few bullets and shoot them myself."

Tears filled Angelica's eyes as she glared at him, but she stayed quiet. He mounted up behind her and chuckled when she tried to move away from him. Jerking the coat firmly around her, he then pulled her tight against him. He clicked to the horses, then they headed around the barn to the path that led to the creek. Jean Claude had meant to fill his canteens earlier but hadn't had time. The horses moved quickly through the drifts, eager to get to the water.

The snow had stopped, and the wind came in gusts, causing the snow to swirl up and hang in the air for several seconds before getting whisked off by another gust. The sky was brightening, and the white landscape glowed.

The horses reached the creek's edge. Jean Claude was about to dismount, intending to fill his canteen, when a streak of color caught his eye. Turning his head, he was just in time to see his feline nemesis Purrsistence running through the snow, and before he could kick the horse forward, the mangy cat had leapt up onto his horse, sharp claws digging into its rump. The horse began to buck, almost causing Angelica to fall off. Jean Claude swore as he turned around to grab Purrsistence. The cat was too quick for him as she jumped onto the pack of the other horse and sank her teeth into the equine's neck. The pack horse reared in terror and pulled the reins free. Purrsistence jumped to the side as the equine took off, back up the path that led to the barn.

Jean Claude had almost gotten his horse under control when he noticed another movement to his right. Thinking that it was that blasted cat again, he swung the horse around. It took the trapper a second longer than the horse to realize that there was another animal in front of them. A white wolf was crouched, as if ready to spring, and baring its teeth, growling as it inched closer. The horse began to thrash and buck in earnest, causing Angelica to lose her balance. Jean Claude grabbed her arm and felt the bone break with a loud snap. He lost his grip, and she tumbled to the ground. She showed no evidence of pain as she swiftly rolled out of range of the frightened horse.

Everything happened in a split second after that. Dismounting, Jean Claude tried dodging the bucking horse's hooves but lost his footing in the slippery snow, causing him to land flat on his back in the frozen weeds at the edge of the creek. With the shock of the cold water taking his breath away, it was a moment before he realized that there was a searing pain in his right arm. Sitting up, he looked down in surprise to see one of his own traps digging into the flesh on either side of his elbow. His worn coat had offered no protection to the steely jaws of the trap, and the rusty tines were embedded into his bone. Blood dripped into the moving water as it flowed down stream. Another surprise was that he had been able to hold on to the reins of his frightened horse.

Cradling his arm, Jean Claude managed to stand and stumble to the shore. Angelica had had the wind knocked out of her and looked dazed but was trying to sit up. Dragging himself closer, Jean Claude lay against her, using his body weight to pin her more firmly to the ground.

The horse was frantic with the wild wolf's smell so close. The animal's eyes were rolled back so that just the white showed, and it pulled desperately on the reins, trying to break free, ready to bolt. Jean Claude struggled, holding on to the leather straps with his good arm. He grunted in discomfort every time the horse pulled at him as the trap drove deeper into his flesh, causing searing pain.

The wolf continued moving slowly forward as the hair stood up on its back and its gold eyes bore into Jean Claude's. The trapper was finding it difficult to try to keep Angelica pinned down and maintain his hold on the frightened horse at the same time. He needed to quickly make a plan.

The decision was made for him when the horse reared, yanking him off Angelica and dragged him backwards by several feet. It also gave the wolf the opportunity to place itself in front of Angelica. Gritting his teeth against the pain, Jean Claude managed to get on his knees and then into a standing position. Blood was dripping from his fingers, and the smell seemed to make the horse even more agitated. He needed to get the damn trap off his arm.

Swearing loudly, Jean Claude let the roan back up a short way to let it calm down a little. Bracing his right arm against his chest, he tried to pull the jaws apart with his left hand, but the rusted tines wouldn't budge. The only thing he accomplished was to have the steel tines dig deeper into his arm. Meanwhile, Angelica had regained her footing. Without a backward glance, she made her way through the drifts to the path that led back to her ranch.

"Get back here!" he snarled to her.

Stopping, she turned and looked back at him. Her hands were still bound behind her back, and she had lost his coat when she had fallen. "Go to hell," was all she said as she turned to make her way up the path.

●●●

The gelding was passing the orchard before Luke realized where he was. He hadn't seen the she-wolf in over an hour. The snow had stopped, and now he could see the ranch house. Relief flooded through him until he noticed that there was no smoke rising from the chimney. Had Angelica run out of wood? The sod house was extremely tight to the weather, and if she and the children had bundled up together, they should have been able to ride out the storm.

The horse stopped in front of the barn and Luke dismounted, mindless to the pain in his legs and feet. The barn doors were swinging in the wind, and the cow was making enough noise to raise the dead. There were impressions in the snow, but the blowing snow had partially filled them in, so it was hard to tell how old the tracks were. Leading the gelding into the barn, the first thing he noticed was the large spot of blood on the ground. The second was the horse that he didn't recognize was packed and acting terrified. Placing his horse in a stall, Luke grabbed his rifle from the scabbard and made for the house.

Halfway there, he knew that there was something very wrong. The front door was ajar and there was an air of desertion about the place. Moving slowly, he pushed the door the rest of the way open and peered inside. The place was in shambles. Chairs were turned onto their sides and lamps lay broken on the floor. Someone had been in a hurry.

In the kitchen, the table and chairs had been flung to the side and a pot of what looked like chicken soup sat on top of the stove. Touching the side of the metal confirmed what he already suspected; it was ice cold. There were several logs and kindling in the wood box next to it. Heading to the kitchen door, Luke opened it to see a wood pile that was neatly stacked with at least a cord of wood.

Turning and placing his rifle on the table, Luke once again surveyed the room. His mind was sluggish, and he knew that he needed to get warm. His movements were slow and clumsy as he grabbed some kindling and proceeded to light the stove. Once he thought he heard a sound, almost like a whisper, but it wasn't repeated, and he had no idea where it had come from. Going through the motions, he made himself a pot of coffee, and when it was hot, he poured a mug full. Wrapping his frozen hands around the warm metal, Luke sat down at the kitchen table.

Between the light warmth from the stove and the heat from the coffee, Luke's brain started to come alive again. Before, he had been in survival mode, fearing the worst, but now that he was here, at Angelica's, he needed to reassess. Meda's tent was gone from behind the barn. That surprised him; he had thought that she had intended to stay through the winter here.

It appeared as if Angelica and the children had left in a hurry, yet Luke couldn't imagine that she wouldn't have banked the fire or closed the door. He took a couple of gulps of coffee. The warmth spread like lightning along his veins. Would she have left the cow and the horse in their stall? It seemed unlikely unless she expected to be back shortly. Then there was the blood and the unknown horse in the barn. It seemed improbable that she would have packed up a wounded person and tried to reach town in a blizzard.

Getting up from the table, he went back into the living area and looked around again. Now that the caffeine was reaching his brain, he could see the obvious signs of a struggle. His heart dropped, and he could feel fear take hold deep down. He was too late. Somebody or someone had taken Angelica and the children, and there was no way of knowing when or what direction they had gone. The wind and snow would have obliterated any trace of their tracks. For all Luke knew, they could have passed within feet or each other with the blizzard conditions and not have even known it.

Luke's fingers, toes, and face were beginning to throb as he retrieved his rifle from the kitchen and started back to the barn to take care of the livestock. He was halfway there when he saw movement at the edge of the trees. At first, he wasn't sure what it was, but as he watched, he realized that it was Angelica, stumbling through the drifts of snow.

He was about to break into a run when another movement caught his eye to the left. The she-wolf was running full at him, teeth bared and growling. She was almost upon him when she leaped into the air, straight for him. Jumping to the side, Luke rolled in the snow and turned to watch as the canine flew by. She disappeared, turning into a flurry of snow, surprising the Indian that had been just steps behind him. The Indian held a large knife, raised in one hand. Had it not been for the wolf, Luke was sure that that knife would now be in his back.

His attacker recovered quickly. Before Luke could blink, the Indian launched himself at him. Grabbing the arm that held the knife, Luke pulled the man forward, rolling backwards while lifting and placing his foot into the Indian's stomach. The Indian flipped over Luke's head and landed flat on his back. By the time his attacker had regained his footing, so had Luke. They circled each other, sizing each other up.

Luke had dropped his rifle in the snow when the she-wolf had leapt at him, but he didn't dare take his eyes off his opponent to look around for it.

"Did you come to be the hero?" the Indian taunted. "You're too late. Their scalps will bring me a good price, as will yours."

Luke was exhausted, and he knew that he wasn't in any shape to take on an Indian warrior. His mind skittered over the taunting words. Was he too late? He had seen Angelica, but she had collapsed in the snow. Could she have been mortally wounded? Were the children wounded as well? And Meda? His breath was coming in gasps.

The Indian lunged at him again, aiming at his stomach. Jumping back, Luke could feel the tip of the blade tug on his jacket. His reaction time was slowing, his vision was starting to blur, and he had no doubt that the Indian would soon go for the kill. Without thinking, he stepped forward and grabbed the arm that held the knife. Using two hands, Luke brought the Indian's arm forcibly down on his raised knee, trying to knock the knife from the attacker's grip. Driven by pure adrenaline, this was a match that he couldn't afford to lose.

Muscle strained against muscle. Slowly, the Indian managed to move the knife up. Between his two older brothers and Landon, Luke had learned a few tricks of fighting. Quickly letting go of the Indian's arms caused his opponents hands to suddenly be free and be thrust up above his head, still clutching the deadly blade. Using all his strength, Luke threw a punch into the Indian's exposed middle. The Indian grunted as he doubled forward. Luke stepped to the side to miss the swinging blade and used his knee to connect with the Indian's face. Blood poured from the warrior's mouth as he was propelled backward. Luke had hoped that the force of the blow would have caused the Indian to fall flat, but he was disappointed. His opponent caught his balance, and there was no amusement in his grin.

"It'll be a pleasure to kill you, white man," the Indian taunted.

Luke was breathing hard, his eyes refusing to focus. It took a few seconds to realize that there was a voice coming from behind him. Without turning his head, he recognized that it belonged to Carol Anne, and she was calling his name. Relief warred with dread. He was relieved that she was alive, but she had now put herself in harm's way. She could be used as leverage, and that knowledge showed in the Indian's face.

Everything seemed to move in slow motion after that. The Indian shot his leg forward, hooking one of Luke's, pulling it out from underneath him. Falling backwards, Luke watched as the Indian advanced with the knife raised high. Regret washed over Luke. It seemed as if he had failed Angelica and the children after all.

From the right, a large shadow glided across the snow, causing both Luke and the Indian to turn and look. A large horned owl swooped down, making the Indian jump back and take a swipe with his knife at the low-flying bird. Luke took advantage of the distance to crawl backwards in the snow and get to his feet. The bird landed on the roof of the house. There was a loud wolf howl from the direction of the creek. Cursing, the Indian backed away again and made a clicking noise with his tongue. A horse came out of the woods behind the barn, breaking through the thick drifts of snow. The Indian kept his eye on the owl until the horse reached him. Grabbing the horse's bridle, he swung up onto the equine's back.

Using pressure from his knees to turn the horse, the Sioux looked at Luke. "You won't always have her protection. I will come and kill you all." With that, he let out a high-pitched cry and kicked the horse into action. Luke watched as they disappeared into the trees.

Dazed, Luke looked around and found his rifle. Picking it up, he heard a horse behind him. He turned with his gun raised. He supposed that he should have been surprised to see Landon trotting into the yard on a horse not more than a few seconds after the Indian had disappeared from sight. He lowered his rifle.

"What took you so long?" Luke asked after Landon had dismounted.

●●●

Carol Anne ran through the snow and launched herself at Luke, almost knocking him over as he crouched to catch her. Burying her head into his neck, she wrapped her arms around him and clung. "Jean Claude took Angelica, and he hurt the boys. They had blood on their faces, and they were sleeping, but now they're awake. I think he did something bad to Meda too."

The words came out in a rush, and it took Luke a moment to decipher them. At the mention of Angelica, he rose to his feet and looked in the direction that he had last seen her. Silently, he pulled Carol Anne from him and passed her to Landon.

"What is it, Luke?" Landon asked as Luke took off running.

•••

Angelica was lying in the snow on her side, unconscious, her hands bound behind her. Kneeling down beside her, Luke removed the knife from his boot and cut her bindings. Then he lifted her onto his lap and turned her towards him. Bruises covered the right side of her face, and her arm was at an unnatural angle. Rage boiled up inside of him. Lifting her into his arms, he turned and swiftly headed to the house. Landon, who still carried Carol Anne, fell in step with him.

The stove's warmth hadn't reached the living area of the ranch house as Luke placed Angelica on her bed and turned to Landon. "Get some more firewood and get the stove and fireplace heating up this place. I'll need some hot water, so check the reservoir and fill it if you have to."

Landon nodded in Angelica's direction. "She going to be all right?"

"I have to get these wet things off her. My immediate concern is she's suffering from shock and hypothermia, but I'll know better after I examine her. She took a nasty fall several weeks ago. I'm hoping that her ribs aren't fractured again."

Landon nodded and turned.

"Landon?" His friend spun around. "After, take Carol Anne and get the boys. She said that they had been hurt but be careful. I'm not sure what happened here, but there might be more Indians around."

"More Indians?" Landon asked.

Luke nodded. "I'll explain later. Just keep an eye out."

Landon saluted and then was gone.

Luke looked down at Carol Anne and somehow conjured up a semblance of a smile. "Let's get Angelica warm, okay? My friend will be back to get your brothers, and I'll take care of them too."

Carol Anne looked relieved and nodded.

•••

Slipping into his doctor's persona had been easy. Maintaining an air of detachment had been excruciating. Luke, with Carol Anne's help, undressed Angelica, leaving on her underthings, before piling quilts on top of her. Her ribs were fine, with no sign of refracture, but her arm had obviously been rebroken. Since she was already unconscious, he took the opportunity to reset the bone.

Landon had left with Carol Anne a while ago to retrieve the boys. Luke had just finished tying Angelica's splint when Landon arrived with them. William was walking under his own power, but Matthew was leaning heavily on Landon. Dried blood caked their hair and covered their jackets. They looked like the boys that had been brought into the medical tents on the battlefield. Bile rose in Luke's throat as those memories threatened to pull him into a dark abyss. Carol Anne inadvertently pulled him back when she innocently took his hand and looked up at him with such trust.

Landon talked as he examined Matthew. "They were down in the root cellar. According to Carol Anne, this Jean Claude person had knocked them out and then threw them down the stairs. Nailed the door shut. Seems he didn't know about the tunnel entrance."

"Carol Anne had a hiding place down there," William added weakly.

Landon was already in the kitchen. "I'll go take care of the horses. Sounds like I need to milk that cow too before she bursts."

Carol Anne ran after him. "I know where the milk bucket is, and I can get the eggs all by myself," she said proudly.

"That right?" Landon answered. "I could use a ranch hand like you over at my place."

Their voices faded as they closed the door behind them.

Luke hadn't been listening. Matthew's pupils were slightly uneven, and he was slow to answer the questions that Luke put to him.

Luke eased Matthew back onto the couch and covered him with a blanket before moving over to look at William. The younger man wouldn't meet Luke's gaze when Luke bent down to examine him.

"What's the matter, William?" Luke asked, although he was sure that he already knew.

William licked his lips. "Jean Claude took Angelica, and I couldn't stop him." It came out in a whisper. "I promised you that I would take care of her, and I couldn't do it." Tears filled his eyes and his voice broke. "He's got her...out there...and there was nothing I could do."

Luke squatted down in front of him. The anguish in the boy's eyes was almost his undoing. "Angelica isn't with Jean Claude, William. I found her. She got away from him. She's over there in the bed and she's safe. All right? It's not your fault. You did the best that you could."

William broke down then and began to sob. He kept repeating "I'm sorry," over and over again.

Luke was at a loss as to what to do or say.

"William." The whisper came from the bed. Angelica was awake and she was trying to sit up.

Luke led William over to her. Propping the pillows up behind her, he helped her to lean back against them. William sat on the bed beside her. Weakly, she reached out and grasped the boy's hand.

"This wasn't your fault," she told him tearfully. "It's mine. I didn't understand how dangerous Jean Claude was." She gave a fragile smile. "You all tried to tell me, but I didn't see it. Forgive me."

William started to speak, but she squeezed his hand to stop him.

"No arguments." She then looked at Luke. "I heard Carol Anne's voice, and I see that you found both boys. What about Meda?"

Luke shook his head.

She started to rise again. "We need to find her."

Luke gently pushed her back. "Slow down. You're in no shape to get up. Landon and I will look for Meda as soon as I have you all settled. But first, I need to know what happened here. Isn't Jean Claude the family friend you were waiting for to bring the firewood?" She nodded. "So, he brought the wood, but something changed, didn't it?" Again, she nodded. "Did it have something to do with the Indian that attacked me when I got here?"

Angelica's face was pale in the places that weren't covered with bruises, and she had a tint of blue around her lips. At the mention of the Indian, Luke could have sworn that her face had gone even paler.

"Meda was right then," she whispered. "You need to find her, Luke. I know that they did something horrible to her." Her voice rose. "She's been gone for two days, and I know that she would never have left willingly."

The tears that she had been struggling to hold back came to the surface. Great sobs, from deep within, were wrung out of her as all the emotional turmoil from the last few days caught up to her. The sound tore at Luke's soul. These were not the gentle tears that he had seen women use to get their way. These were tears of loss, hopelessness, and gut-wrenching grief.

Not sure what to do, Luke gathered her close and held her. Her small frame shook as she released everything that had been bottled up. It was a while before the sobs subsided and became hiccups.

Once again, Luke placed her gently back against the pillows. "I need to know what happened so I can help Meda. I'll find her, I promise, but I need to know what I'm facing."

Angelica nodded, and with William's help, she told him about Jean Claude's betrayal.

CHAPTER TWENTY-FOUR

The pain in Jean Claude's right arm was unbearable, and the damn horse wouldn't slow down. He kicked the animal as hard as he could with his heels, but that just spurred the horse faster. He tried leaning down and using his left hand to reach out and grab the reins, but the trap on his right elbow only dug in harder, scraping the bone. Finally, he was able to grab the bridle, and with an agonizing cry, he yanked the horse's head to the side so that it came to a jolting halt. The force of the sudden stop propelled Jean Claude forward, and he was flung over the horse's neck and onto the ground.

"Stupid son of a bitch!" he railed as he tried to regain his footing. His entire body screamed in pain.

The horse stood nearby, its sides heaving. Stumbling over to it, Jean Claude took out his Winchester from the scabbard on the side of the saddle and tried to raise it with his left arm. He aimed the barrel at the horse's head and considered pulling the trigger before some semblance of rationale kicked in. If he shot the equine, then he would be stuck out here on foot. He was lowering the gun when he felt the prickle on the back of his neck. Turning sharply, he could see a large pack of wolves about a half mile off, running in his direction. As he watched, they started to fan out.

"Shit," Jean Claude muttered. Turning back to the horse, he sheathed the rifle and grabbed the dangling reins. The horse balked at the sudden movement and jumped away, pulling Jean Claude off balance. Once again, the trapper fell to the ground, this time landing on his right arm, the trap digging into his chest and puncturing the skin.

The pain caused his vision to blacken down to a pinpoint of light. He gasped for air and flipped over onto his back. Unfortunately, he didn't have the luxury of time as a quick look showed that the wolves were closer and starting to surround where he lay. It took everything he had to roll over and get to his knees. The reins were still in his hands, and he used them as leverage to gain his feet. Leaning against the horse, Jean Claude tried to lift his leg and put it into the stirrup, but the horse could smell the wolves and started to sidestep, wanting to bolt.

"Whoa!" Jean Claude snarled as he once again tried to mount, but the gelding kept turning away, circling him.

The wolves were upon them. Jean Claude had no choice but to grab the rifle again and make a stand. The horse wanted to run, but Jean Claude held onto the reins. Hopefully the horse would help even the odds, as it too would have to fight. His Winchester held seventeen shots, and he hoped that if he got enough of the mangy bastards, the others would back off. He knew that he couldn't aim very well, so hopefully that would give him some time to get on the horse and get back to Angelica's. He also knew that he wouldn't be able to outrun a pack of wolves, as they'd run their prey to exhaustion before they came in for the kill.

One wolf came in and nipped at the equine's legs, causing it to kick out and scream in terror. As the horse tried to run forward, another wolf lunged, causing the horse to rear up.

"Get back, you bastards!" Jean Claude yelled. He couldn't hold the rifle steady as the horse was pulling him all over the place. The wolf in front of him came close enough that he raised the rifle and was able to get one shot off. The wolf fell, and the others retreated for a moment. Jean Claude's horse bolted, ripping the reins from his hands, and he fell to his knees. Putting the rifle's stock on the ground, he tried to cock the gun so that the next bullet would be pulled into the chamber, but the mechanism was stuck. Sweat began to roll down Jean Claude's face as he tried to move the frozen lever. It wouldn't budge.

• • •

Up on a small rise, Ghost sat on his horse and watched as the wolves moved in for the kill. The trapper got a shot off and one of the wolves fell in place. The rest of the pack ran off a short distance away, scared of the shotgun blast, but when no new sound followed it, they circled back to surround the trapper again. The horse finally broke free from Jean Claude's grip and ran for its life. Jean Claude was down on his knees. It looked like he was trying to get his rifle unjammed, but Ghost knew that it would be too late. Without the horse to act as some protection, the wolves increased their effort.

Ghost gave a grunt of satisfaction as the pack moved in at once. He could hear Jean Claude's death cry and saw the spurt of red as a wolf tore into his neck. Then the trapper was lost from view as the wolves swarmed over him.

Ghost looked back at the direction he had just come from. He hadn't anticipated the level of protection surrounding the white woman. It surprised him that Meda had such power, and it gave him pause. It was best to leave the white woman and Sitting Bull's cousin alone for now. He would go to Jean Claude's place and see what he could trade or sell. White man money meant little to him, but he wasn't stupid. It could be used to buy food, weapons and loyalties.

Without a backward glance at the carnage behind him, he set off.

•••

Luke arrived at Meda's tepee, with Landon a few steps behind. There was no smoke coming out of the top, and Luke took that to be a bad sign. According to Angelica, Meda hadn't been seen for over two days. If Jean Claude had left her alive, well, the chances were that he let her freeze to death. Flinging open the flap to the tepee, they stepped inside. The interior was dark with limited light.

"Meda?"

Luke moved slowly toward the center, allowing his eyes to adjust to the gloom. There, to the left, was the dim outline of something stretched out on the floor. Moving closer, he recognized that it was Meda, lying on her side. He didn't see the rope until he knelt beside her. Pulling the knife out of his boot, he sliced away the piece that pulled at the noose around her neck first. Anger burned in the pit of his stomach as he worked, along with guilt. She had tried to warn him, and he hadn't listened. They would have all been safe if he had just stayed. Feeling for a pulse, he noticed how cold she was and by some miracle, there was a faint thump under his fingertips.

Landon had found the kindling and began a fire.

"She's alive, but she's ice cold," Luke told his friend. "We'll need to get her warm." By now his eyes had adjusted to the darkness. Peering around, he found several blankets and a fur-lined jacket. Snatching them up, he piled

| 231 |

the coverings on the pallet that was nearby. Carrying her to the makeshift bed, Luke laid her on top of the blankets and tucked the jacket around her.

The kindling caught hold and Landon added several pieces of wood. Smoke filled the tent until the flames became hotter and caused the smoke to rise and clear.

"What's the plan?" Landon wanted to know. "And I'm not talking about just the next few days."

Luke ran a hand through his hair and looked around the small space. What was his plan? Hell, if he knew. It seemed that all his energy had been to just get here and make sure that everyone was all right. By some small miracle, he and Landon had found them in time, and they were alive. He hadn't had time to think about what would come next.

"I'm really not sure," he replied after a short silence. "I was thinking that I'd try to get Angelica to go to your place for the winter. That way you, Mary, and Old Kate could keep an eye on her and the kids. Make sure that they recover all right." He couldn't meet his friend's penetrating gaze.

Landon stared at the fire for a few minutes before he answered. "I have to say that I've never seen you take a chance like you did getting here. Seems that Angelica and those kids are mighty important to you, so important that you were willing to risk your life to get to them. I thought that almost losing them might bring you to your senses, but I see that it will take more than that."

He crouched near the fire and stared into the flames some more before turning his head and pinning Luke with his gaze, hard and unwavering. "I said it before, and I still believe it. You're so scared of caring for that little lady and those kids that you can't even see straight. Well, you'd better start thinking long and hard about what you're giving up. A woman like Angelica won't be alone long. The men will be courting her hard and fast the moment that you head out."

Landon stood and drove home his point. "Can you live without them? Without her?"

The picture that Landon was painting with his words was too painful to think about. Pacing back and forth, Luke tried to wipe the images out of his mind. The problem was, he could picture Angelica pregnant, only it was with his child; it was his name that fell from her lips. He wanted nothing more than to watch all the children grow and thrive together.

He stopped pacing and realized that that was the problem. What if they didn't thrive? The world was filled with all sorts of dangers and diseases. Wasn't his trek through the blizzard to get here proof of that? Didn't he just deliver Landon's twins, leaving Mary's life in jeopardy? The thought of opening his heart, his soul, to loving Angelica meant that he opened them to immeasurable pain too. Tamping down the panic that was starting deep in his chest, he bowed his head and closed his eyes. Maybe he was a coward.

Landon was waiting for an answer, his stance impatient.

"What if I have one of my episodes and hurt her or the children?" Luke asked. "She'd never love me if she knew the real me. Knew of the terrible things that I've done. I'm too damaged, Landon."

Landon gave a snort of disgust. "That's all a bunch of bullshit and you know it. I know you better than anyone. You'd never hurt her or those kids, and deep down you know that too. We were in the middle of a war, Luke. It was kill or be killed. For god's sake, forgive yourself! You deserve to be happy, to love Angelica and let her love you back. Give those kids a father. And I swear to God almighty that if you start spouting off again about how you're a doctor and you took a damn oath to do no harm, I'll break your nose."

Luke grinned despite himself.

Changing the subject, he asked, "How did you find me, Landon? I almost froze to death and if it wasn't for…" He stopped before saying *without Meda guiding me*, as he still wasn't ready to think about that. So he continued with, "…sheer luck, I probably wouldn't have made it through."

Squatting down next to Meda, he checked her color. Her lips were still blue, but her face was starting to pinken.

Landon gave him a look that said the former conversation was far from over. "After you left, I wasn't sure what to do. Half of me wanted to head out after you, and the other half knew that I should stay with Mary and the babies. Couldn't make up my mind. Then just after supper, there was this scratching at the door. Looked out and saw the wolf that you had been following. Thought that you had run into some trouble, so I grabbed my gear and headed out too. Most of the storm was ahead of me, and every time that I thought I was lost, that wolf would show up again and lead me on."

Luke looked down at Meda and shook his head. There were things that people couldn't explain happening all the time. Some people even called them miracles. His mind shied away from that thought. Believing in miracles meant that he had to believe that there was a higher power causing them, and he wasn't willing to go there. There had to be a rational explanation.

Landon's voice cut into his thoughts. "We gonna leave this little lady here, or are we taking her back to the house where we can keep an eye on everyone?"

That was a good question. The tepee was warming up, but someone would need to stay and keep the fire going and watch Meda. Bringing her back out into the cold for the walk back to the house wasn't ideal either.

Rubbing a hand over his face, Luke realized how tired he was. It had been over twenty-four hours since he'd had any sleep. Was it possible that it was just yesterday that he had delivered the twins? "We'll need to bring her back to the cabin," he decided. "I have no idea where this Jean Claude character is or if he'll try to come back. I'm hoping he's seen our tracks and has hightailed it back up north, but he doesn't sound that smart."

Landon gave him a grin, but there was no humor in it. "I'm praying he isn't, 'cause if I get my hands on that son of a bitch, I'll tear him apart."

"Not if I get to him first," Luke replied.

•••

They bundled Meda in all the blankets, fur, and coats that they could find. Landon insisted on carrying her. They tried to use the path that they had created through the drifts, but it was still slow going. Finally, they reached the cabin and entered. Landon gently placed Meda on the floor in front of the fireplace.

"Is she alive?" a voice came from behind him.

Luke turned to see Angelica standing behind him. She had somehow managed to get dressed again. The comforter from the bed was loosely wrapped around her shoulders, and she held it together with her good hand. Scanning her face, he noticed that her lips still held a blue tint, but her face was beginning to brighten, and she was shivering. Relief flooded through him. Shivering was a good sign; it meant that her body was trying to warm itself.

"She's freezing," Luke informed her, walking over to Angelica. Gently grasping her elbow, he led her to a chair and sat her down. "But she's alive. Jean Claude had hogtied her up in the tepee, but it doesn't look like he hurt her beyond that."

Angelica's teeth were chattering so much all she could do was nod in reply.

Matthew was sleeping on the settee, and Luke left Angelica to check on him. Bending, he shook the younger boy by the shoulders and called his name loudly. The youngster looked up groggily at him and answered the few questions that Luke put to him. Satisfied, Luke let him go back to sleep.

As long as Matthew didn't fall into a coma, sleep was the best thing for him. He made a mental note to wake him up again in a half hour.

William sat on the floor in front of his brother and stared at the fire. Luke was sure he was silently berating himself about not being able to protect Angelica or his brother and sister. Luke could sympathize. He felt the same way.

Only Carol Anne seemed to have come through unscathed. She was sitting in the rocking chair, listening to Landon tell her about his ranch. Luke chuckled to himself. She was something else.

A meowing sounded at the door. Luke opened it and Purrsistence sauntered in, her tail raised high. Angelica had told him how the cat had jumped on the horse, helping her to get away from Jean Claude. The feline wound herself around his legs before making her way over to William and plopping her fat body into his lap. Her purring could be heard throughout the room. She pushed her head against William's hand until he began to pet her.

Everyone was accounted for and safe, if not totally out of danger, but Luke was restless. Jean Claude and the Indian warrior were still out there, and there was no doubt that they were dangerous men. Men like them didn't give up when they wanted something, and it was obvious that Jean Claude had coveted Angelica, going to great lengths to try to have her. The Indian known as Ghost was a wild card. No doubt he would be back to try again. Luke hated waiting. He'd wanted to head out and track down both of the sons of a bitches, but Landon had talked him out of it.

"Don't be stupid, Luke," Landon had said, as blunt as ever, when they'd been alone for a few minutes. "Jean Claude is a trapper who's most likely lived his entire life in the wilderness. He could lead us away from here for days while this Indian renegade came back for Angelica, Meda, and the kids while we're out chasing our tails."

As much as he hated to give up the chase, Luke knew that Landon was right. They couldn't leave the ranch unprotected. It didn't lessen his frustration though. He felt emotionally raw, like the inside of him had been scraped as thoroughly as the bottom of a barrel.

●●●

Hours later, everyone but Matthew and Meda were sitting at the kitchen table eating dinner. Meda and Matthew had fallen into healing sleeps, and Luke figured that they could eat when they woke up. Several jars of stew from the pantry were heated and served with bread. It was late afternoon, but the sky was already darkened.

No one spoke much. Carol Anne had practically fallen asleep at the table, and Luke had carried her to bed. He had tucked her in, clothes and all. Then he and Landon heated water for William to take a bath. Luke wanted to get a better look at the boy's head to see if the wound would need to be stitched. Angelica retired to the living room to sit in the rocking chair and keep an eye on the two sleeping invalids.

The copper tub was brought from the pantry, set in the kitchen, and filled with warm water. William stripped out of his bloody clothes and stepped in. He used the caked soap to wash the blood from his body, his movements slow and clumsy. Using a small metal cup, Luke poured warm water over the boy's head and worked the clotted blood out of his hair. The gash was roughly two inches long, and blood seeped after the clot was washed away.

"You're going to need some stitches," Luke told him. "I'm going to have to clip some hair before I try to clean it, and it's going to sting some, but it'll keep the infection out."

William nodded, then Luke got to work.

•••

Staring into the fire, lost in her thoughts, it took Angelica a few minutes to realize that Meda had awakened.

"How do you feel?" Angelica asked her friend.

Meda sat up and winced. The bruises around her neck and wrists were in stark contrast to the rest of her coloring. Red streaks ran through the blues and purples.

"I feel blessed to have another day on Mother Earth," she replied.

Angelica was solemn. "Well, we all have you to thank for that. (I know somehow you brought Luke and Landon here. Without you, we would have all been in serious trouble.) Without you bringing Luke and Landon here, we would have all been in serious trouble."

Meda stretched out her legs and moved her shoulders back and forth. "It was not me that brought these men here," she replied in her soft voice. "You were the one with the connection to Luke and through him, the other man."

Angelica was confused. "What do you mean? I have no mystical powers."

Meda's eyes were serious. "We made a blood pact. My blood runs through your veins as yours does mine. Your love for the man named Luke and his love for you was a connection that I could use to call him, by means of the appearance of a white wolf. His connection to the other man allowed me to bring him also."

Angelica was speechless. They had been children when they had become blood sisters. Angelica hadn't thought that the small ceremony, where they had sliced their forefingers with a small knife then smearing the bleeding cuts together and chanting, had meant anything more than two girls dreaming of being real sisters. She hadn't realized that there had been any type of magic involved. Then Meda's words penetrated her brain.

"What do you mean my love for him and his love for me? I barely know the man. Besides, he left me…us. He only came back because he felt responsible for the children…." She trailed off.

Meda continued as if Angelica hadn't said a word. "I don't believe that Luke knows his feelings for you yet. He continues to lie to himself even though his heart is starting to believe. It is hard for him to understand that someone could love him when he is at war with himself." She shook her head and let out a small sigh. "His is a broken soul that has turned his back against his true self."

Leaving Angelica shaken, Meda pushed herself slowly off the floor and made her way over to where Matthew lay sleeping. Reaching down, she placed her hand over the wound on his head. A look of pain crossed her face. "I have some healing herbs and barks. It will help with the ache." Wrapping the blanket around her, she went out the door.

Angelica felt as if she had been the one smacked in the head, for all reasonable thought had left her brain. She couldn't move on from Meda's words. What if they were true? What if Luke was starting to care for her? Would it be enough? He had been a soldier in the great conflict, that much she knew, and he still had nightmares about it. No surprise there. Battle fatigue is what she'd heard it called. Thousands of soldiers had returned home, but some couldn't bear what they had seen and done. Suicides were common in the months after the final battle.

But he hadn't been in the battles. He was a doctor; he would have been back in the field hospital. Maybe that had been worse, knowing that he couldn't save everyone. Having to cut off damaged limbs must have been a nightmare for him. There had been several soldiers that had stopped at the ranch over the years, some missing arms or legs or both. They all had the same haunted look. Some had told the horrors of the battle to her father when they thought she was out of listening range. It had been hard to comprehend that men could stand in fields and shoot each other.

What did it take for a man to come back from such carnage? Would they even be whole again? Luke refused to believe in God because of what he'd experienced, whereas she relied on God to see her through.

Rubbing her temple, Angelica let out a sigh. None of it mattered. Luke wasn't one to stay in one place for too long and she couldn't go with him, knowing that he might never settle down and face his past. It might be selfish of her, but she wanted the whole man, the man that she had glimpsed when he had tended to her wounds, the man she had shared time with, the man who didn't exist except in her dreams. The sooner that she accepted that, the better.

•••

Luke finished stitching William and helped the boy get dressed. William almost looked like his old self if one didn't examine him too closely and see the traces of shadows deep in his eyes.

Angelica had traded his bloody clothes for clean ones, and Landon helped him out of the kitchen and into the loft. Luke lugged the tub of bloody water to the kitchen door and emptied it off to the side. Using handfuls of snow, he wiped the inside clean. Landon had filled the stove reservoir while William was bathing, and the water would be well heated for when Matthew woke up.

Setting the tub back into the middle of the kitchen, Luke took a deep breath. It bothered him that Matthew was sleeping so much. Part of him knew that sleep was the best thing for the younger boy, but he would have felt better if Matthew was up and talking, like William. Not for the first time, he wished that he could go find Jean Claude. His jaw and fists clenched at the thought of what could have happened if the she-wolf hadn't summoned him and subsequently Landon too.

But she did, the voice said in his head. *You were meant to save them. That's why you lived that day, so that you could be here for them. Have a second chance.*

A sharp pain ran through his back molars, reminding him to unclench his jaw, though it took some effort to do so. He hadn't saved them yet. Jean Claude and Ghost were still out there, and there was no doubt in Luke's mind that they would be back. The sooner that he and Landon got them all back to Landon's ranch, the better. His mind skittered from the thought that he would be saying goodbye once they were there.

It was time to check on Matthew, so he made his way into the living room. Matthew was still asleep on the settee, and Angelica was staring into the fire with a faraway look on her face.

"Where's Meda?" he asked, though he was sure that he already knew the answer.

Angelica looked up at him as if he had sprouted out of the floorboards.

Then her expression cleared. "She went to her tepee to get some medicine for Matthew's head."

Luke's gut tightened. He went back into the kitchen and grabbed his jacket and his rifle.

"How long has she been gone?" he asked Angelica as he came back into the room.

"About ten minutes. Why?"

"Jean Claude and Ghost are still out there, and if they are watching the house, they could have grabbed her, and I doubt this time they are looking for prisoners." With that, he bellowed for Landon.

Landon appeared at the top of the ladder.

"Meda has gone back to her tepee," Luke told him. "I'm going to find her and make sure she's okay. If I'm not back in ten minutes, then you'll know that at least one of them is back, if not both."

With that, he stormed out the door.

* * *

Angelica stared at the door. Her thoughts were jumbled. She hadn't considered that either Ghost or Jean Claude would return. With Luke and Landon here, she had assumed that Jean Claude would have given up and gone back to his cabin. Obviously, Luke didn't.

Landon came down the loft stairs and grabbed his rifle and saddle bags. With swift movements honed from years of practice, he checked the rifle to make sure it was loaded. Then he turned down the wicks in the lamps so that most of the light came from the fire in the fireplace. His face was set and calm, yet Angelica felt the energy pulsing from him.

Taking one of the kitchen chairs, he set it on the side of the window. Sitting down, he scanned the landscape outside. Angelica almost got the impression that the large man would have relished seeing Jean Claude out there.

Her suspicions were confirmed when, never looking away from the outside, he said to her, "Wouldn't mind putting a few bullets in that son of a gun's backside if he presents it."

"You and Luke seemed to think that Jean Claude is still around. I don't think he will stick around once he knows you both are here. I can't see Jean Claude being brave enough to take you both on."

Landon's gaze never wavered from the window. "Most likely he'll bide his time and try to catch us by surprise, probably after dark. Men like him always come at your back. So, we can't be sure that you'll be safe until we get you all to my ranch. He wouldn't dare try to get to you there. Not sure about the Indians' motivation."

The crackle of the fire was the only sound for a few minutes as Angelica let his words sink in.

"I'm not going anywhere," she said finally. "This is my home. The children and I are staying right here." Her voice had a slight edge to it.

Landon looked back over one shoulder at her. "Luke's decided that it would be much safer for all of you if you come back to my ranch. Besides, my wife, Mary, would love the company. Once you are all healed up, you can decide whether you want to stay on or come back."

Angelica felt as if she had been pole-axed. Luke had decided? Did he think that she was unable to take care of herself or the children? Anger began deep in her chest. For three years she had been on her own, making her own decisions, and she had done just fine, thank you very much.

Meda was wrong. Luke didn't love her. If he felt anything, it was an obligation.

CHAPTER TWENTY-FIVE

Clinking dishes and hushed voices could be heard coming from the direction of the kitchen the next morning when Angelica opened her eyes. Someone had covered her in the night with a quilt, and the cabin was warm. She was warm. Her muscles protested as she sat up, but she felt better from the rest. It had been several days since she had had such a restful sleep.

Standing, she checked her reflection in the mirror. Her hair and clothes were both rumpled. The bruises on her face were vivid blue and black, with a tinge of yellow around the edges. Her broken arm throbbed but it was bearable. Lifting her good hand to her head, she began to fix the strands that had become unpinned but stopped herself. Who would care if her hair was mussed? The children probably wouldn't even notice. Certainly not Luke and Landon, who was a married man, wouldn't care what she looked like. She studied her reflection again.

She was passably pretty, she decided. Her mother had always told her that she was beautiful, but she figured that all mothers said that to their daughters. Lillian had also said that any man would be blessed to have her as his wife. What her mother had failed to point out was that sometimes the one that you fall in love with doesn't always love you back. Not that she was in love with Luke, Angelica told her reflection silently, as she unpinned and brushed her hair. She'd have to leave it loose until she could have Carol Anne pin it back for her. It was just that he had seemed like he had cared, and they had had so many things in common. It had been easy to picture herself making a life with him.

"Well, time to move on," she told her reflection as she straightened her spine and unconsciously smoothed her skirt.

•••

Luke knew the second that Angelica appeared, behind him, at the doorway, even though she never made a sound. The air somehow changed and became charged with her presence, like heat lightning on a summer night. With one hand stroking Wolf's head, he waited a moment before turning and looking at her. Her dress was rumpled, and her face still held the remnants of sleep. He couldn't remember her looking more beautiful.

"Would you like some tea?" he asked as he stood. "It's been steeping for a while."

Right away, he could tell that she was uncomfortable with being alone in the kitchen with him. Her eyes darted everywhere but at him. Silently, he sighed. Landon had told him last night when he had returned that Angelica hadn't taken to the idea of going back to Landon's. Obviously, she hadn't changed her mind overnight.

Wolf walked around the table and nosed her hand until she began to pat him. A small smile tugged at her lips. For the first time, Luke found himself envying the canine.

"Please," Angelica answered him as she gingerly sat down at the table, with a quick glance at him. "Where is everyone?"

Bringing her the mug that he had been keeping hot, Luke placed it in front of her and sat down on the other side of the table.

"Landon, Carol Anne, and William just left for the barn to take care of the chores. Meda and Matthew are out on the front porch getting some fresh air."

Relief flooded her face. "Then Matthew is doing better?"

Taking a sip of his own coffee, he watched her over the rim. The bruises stood in such vivid contrast to her lighter complexion. They were so out of place on her. It was like someone had defiled a work of art.

Shifting his thoughts away from the sudden anger he felt towards Jean Claude, Luke sat back and answered her. "Meda gave him some herbs, and they seem to be helping. He was able to get up this morning and take a bath. I cleaned the wound, so we'll just have to see how he does."

Nodding, she took a sip and kept her eyes down. Sighing inwardly again,

| 242 |

he figured that they might as well have the argument and get it over with now. "Landon said that he told you about my plans to bring you and the children back to his ranch."

Her head snapped up and he could see the argument brewing in her eyes. Lord but it was going to be hard to leave her when the time came. He had done it once already, and he hoped that he was strong enough to do it again.

"Before you tell me that you're not going, hear me out. Jean Claude is still out there, and he tried to kidnap you once. He will be back. Men like him take what they want, and he's already shown that he wants you. Next time, he won't hesitate to kill anyone that gets in his way, and that includes the children. He damn near killed them this time. You going to Landon's for the winter gives me time to track him down and make sure that he can't harm you again. Then I'll have to see what can be done about this Ghost renegade."

She stared at him. "You plan on killing Jean Claude?"

Wolf, who had lain down beside her chair, lifted his head and whined.

The thought had crossed his mind, and he honestly couldn't say he wouldn't if he caught the bastard alone. It took him a moment to answer, and when he did, he didn't meet her gaze. "I intend to track him down with some soldiers and have him arrested and brought to trial. But until that time, I need to know that all of you are being protected. Landon is family, and I trust him completely. You'll be safe there."

Her clipped words surprised him. "I appreciate your concern for our well-being," she told him, her voice dripping ice. "But the children and I will be staying right here. I'll have Landon wire the army to pick up Jean Claude, and I'm sure that they are quite capable of bringing in him. I will also have him talk to them about Ghost. You can leave with a clear conscience knowing that you did everything you could and that we are no longer your obligations."

With that, she pushed her chair back and rose. Luke was sure that he had heard her wrong. Had she just politely told him thanks for your help but you can leave now?

"Wait a damn minute…" Rising, he had moved to block her way, but the sound of a horse entering the barnyard caused him to stop and turn. Grabbing his rifle that had been within easy reach, Luke hurried for the door.

His command of "stay here" went unheeded as he felt Angelica right on his heels.

Landon stood in the barn door with his shotgun aimed at the roan that stood panting in front of him. Lather covered the horse's body, its sides heaving. It was obvious that the horse had tangled with something, as there were gashes on its legs and haunches. Luke moved forward cautiously with his own rifle raised, searching the tree line for any movement.

Angelica recognized the horse right away. "That's Jean Claude's horse," she said as she drew closer.

Landon scanned the area before he walked forward and approached the horse. Its eyes were wide with terror, and it took him a few minutes of talking softly and moving slowly before he could grab the reins. Once he had them, the horse began to calm. Looking around again, Landon turned and led the exhausted horse into the barn.

Cupping one of her elbows, Luke turned Angelica and guided her back toward the house, all the while keeping his rifle and eyes trained on the landscape around them.

"Shouldn't we stay with Landon and see how the horse is?" she asked.

"No," came his terse reply.

"Why not?"

His face was set, and he gave her a glance that could scorch wood. Ignoring her question, he opened the side door and guided her through. Leaving her in the kitchen, he went into the front room and opened that outside door. She could hear him say a few words to Meda and then he was back, glaring at her.

She had never been afraid of him, but this was not the Luke that she knew. This man was angry, very angry.

"The next time that I tell you to stay put, lady, you better stay put. The damn horse could have been a diversion to get us all out to the barn and gun us down. I don't know what you've got going on in that brain of yours, but until I know that you're safe, I'll be giving the orders around here. Got that?" He had crossed the room and was standing less than two feet in front of her, using his finger in a jabbing motion to make his point. No one had ever talked to her like that before, and for a few seconds she was speechless, but before she could reply, he continued. "And another thing, what is all this nonsense of I appreciate your help, but we'll be fine bull? I never made any promises, Angelica. I told you from the start that I wasn't the type that could forget my demons and settle down."

Stepping back, he ran his hands through his hair and began to pace. Anguish was written all over his face. Stopping, he looked at her, and there was a plea in his eyes. "Don't you think that I want to stay? Want things to be different? I curse God every day for putting me through this hell. I can't afford to love you or the kids. I can't watch any of you die and know that there is nothing I can do to stop it. I'm not a hero, and I'm not strong enough to watch your love turn to hate and resentment. I need to know that you're safe, at Landon's ranch, until I hunt down Jean Claude. Please, promise me at least that."

Without waiting for a reply, he walked past her and out the door.

Shaken, she stood there letting his words sink in. She was beginning to realize how deep his fears ran. Closing her eyes, she said a prayer, but it seemed inconsequential in the face of such insurmountable odds.

•••

Kicking himself mentally, Luke wasn't sure where to run. Landon and the kids were in the barn, and he wasn't up to talking to anyone right now. Angelica must be thinking that he was an idiot.

Walking around the side of the house, the glare from the sun on the snow blinded him for a moment. Then he spied the little graveyard in the distance. At least the dead couldn't tell him what he already knew, that he was a fool for letting the woman that he loved go.

The wooden grave markers peeked out of the snow. Removing his hat, he stood in front of Angelica's mother's grave, and for some strange reason, it gave him a moment of peace. Closing his eyes, he swore he could almost hear a woman's voice whispering to him. He couldn't make out the words, but he figured it was the wind.

Noises behind him made him turn with his gun raised. Two riders had ridden into the barnyard, and they were dismounting in front of the barn. Landon was there, and Luke could see that he knew the two men by the way he greeted them.

As Luke approached, he recognized the men. They worked as ranch hands for Landon. Their boss was smiling and slapping them on the back.

"Luke," Landon greeted him. "Tom and Joe said that Mary and the babies were doing fine. Just fine."

Luke nodded to the two men. Tom was in his early thirties, tall and thin. His eyes were gray, and his brown hair was thinning on top. Joe, on the other hand was young, around eighteen, with dark eyes and dark hair that hinted at a Mexican heritage.

Tom delivered his message. "Old Kate told us to high tail it here and make sure that everyone was safe. Then we're to stay if need be and send you both back."

Landon met Luke's eyes for a moment, but his smile never changed. "Well, let's get your horses settled and we'll make plans over some coffee." Landon led them into the barn. Luke followed along silently.

It took a minute for Luke's eyes to adjust to the dimness after the brilliance of outside. The men kept up a steady stream of chatter, updating Landon about the happenings on his ranch as they rubbed down the tired horses. Carol Anne and William came forward and were introduced. Since there weren't enough stalls in the small barn, the men tied their mounts to some posts.

"Hey," Joe said, spying the injured horse. "We saw that horse being chased by wolves, came up on them about four or five miles north. We ran the wolves off, but we couldn't catch the horse. Took off like a shot."

That caught Luke's attention. "Any sign of a rider?"

Joe glanced quickly at Carol Anne and nodded.

Luke turned to the girl. "Carol Anne, why don't you run to the house and tell Angelica we have company and to put a pot of coffee on. We'll be in shortly."

She gave him a look that said she wasn't fooled but smiled at Landon before heading off, skipping to the house. Once she was out of earshot, Luke turned back to the ranch hands.

"It was a bad scene," Tom said solemnly as Joe nodded. "We saw the horse and the wolves. Figured that someone was in trouble, so we tracked the direction that the horse had come from. Came over a rise and there was a good twenty to thirty wolves fighting over something. From where we were you could tell that there wasn't much left of whoever was riding that horse."

"You saw a body?" Landon asked.

Tom swallowed visibly. "All I can tell you is that it looked like a man. I saw a boot and an arm with," he looked at Joe, who nodded again, "what looked like a steel trap on the arm. I know that sounds crazy, but that's what it looked like. There was blood everywhere."

Closing his eyes, Luke wasn't sure what he felt. Ghost was still out there, but would he bother coming back with Jean Claude gone? Relief warred with disappointment. Angelica and the children never had to worry about Jean Claude again. Not that there weren't other dangers out here, alone on the prairie.

Once Angelica found out that Jean Claude was dead, there would be no chance of her going with them to Landon's ranch, and there would be no excuse for leaving her, other than the truth, as inadequate as it was.

Time seemed to move faster after Tom and Joe arrived. Knowing that the threat of Jean Claude was gone, Landon wanted to get back to his ranch as soon as he could, and he made no secret that he expected everyone to go with him. Angelica thought that the man should have been a lawyer or a politician. For every argument that she gave to him for staying right there on her own ranch, he had three reasons that she should go back with him. She had to admit, he painted a wonderful picture of being part of a large family, as he put it. Luke, however, became more distant. He, Landon and the two ranch hands slept in the barn. It seemed that he went out of his way to avoid not only her but the children as well.

The weather had warmed, causing the snow to melt, and with every passing day, more of the bare ground was exposed. It had been four days since Luke and Landon had arrived, and Angelica knew that she had to make a decision. While Luke hadn't said anything else about her and the children going back to Landon's, Landon had given her a deadline, and that deadline was in two days. Angelica couldn't blame him for wanting to go home. After all, his wife had just delivered twins, and he was anxious to get back to them. It was just that she was afraid that if she left the ranch that she would never see it again.

The ranch had been her whole life, her world. Her parents were buried there, along with her brothers and sisters that she never had had the chance to know. Her family's blood and sweat, along with her own, had built a home in the middle of Indian country and had thrived, but it had come at a large price. Maybe now was the time to venture out and try those new horizons. Climb those mountains that had always been in the distance just out of reach, the ones that she had been dreaming about her whole life. Make a new start and forget about the past.

A sigh escaped Angelica, and she leaned back into the chair on the front porch where she had been banished to. She kept thinking of all the things that Landon had talked about. The wonderful picture he had created of her and the children becoming part of his extended family. Lord knew that it was more than she had had, more than she felt she deserved, but she also had a selfish desire to have more, and the thought shamed her. She had no right asking for more. The Good Lord had a plan for her, and she should be grateful that he had blessed her with three wonderful children. As for Luke, she had to believe that he was just a messenger, an unlikely angel just passing through.

Sitting in the chair was causing her back to stiffen, so she rose and walked to the edge of the porch and leaned against a post. It seemed that everyone was busy. Voices could be heard coming from the barn where Landon and his men were getting the wagon ready for the trip back.

Thanks to the bark and herbs that Luke, with some additions from Meda, had mixed up for her to drink, Angelica was not in pain. She just felt useless. It was not like her to be idle, but every time she tried to do something, someone led her away and made her sit.

Carol Anne rounded the corner of the house, and Angelica had to smile. The snow had mostly melted, and the little girl was skipping and humming to herself. Her blonde hair looked white in the bright sunshine. She wore a blue gingham dress that Angelica had sewed for her.

"Hello," Carol Anne said as she jumped onto the porch. "I'm supposed to check on you and make sure that you're not over…over…exturning yourself."

Angelica hid a grin. "You mean overexerting myself?"

The little girl beamed. "That's the word!" she cried. Then she wrinkled her forehead. "You're not, are you? You know, doing what you just said?"

Angelica couldn't contain her laughter. Yes, she was truly blessed, and she was a horrible person for wanting more.

Hugging the child, she replied, "No, sweetie, I'm resting like everyone has been telling me to."

Carol Anne's smile beamed even brighter, if such a thing was possible. "Good, that means you'll be better by the time that we go to Uncle Landon's place. He has horses, and in the spring, he said that I could pick one out to be my very own! He has real cowboys on his ranch and one of them will teach me how to ride!"

Angelica glanced involuntarily in the direction of the barn. Uncle Landon, was it now? When had that come about? She should have guessed that Landon would have told the children about the plan and that they would be excited at the prospect of an adventure. Though offering the child a horse, well, that was just plain unfair and underhanded. She sighed again, this time from deep down in her soul. Might as well give in, she thought. They had already decided that she was going, so why not be gracious and admit defeat?

As if summoned, Landon appeared in the doorway of the barn and looked in her direction. When he saw that she was talking to Carol Anne, he ducked back inside.

Sent a child to do his talking, Angelica thought, but not unkindly.

She liked Landon. He was a big man that spoke very little, yet he always seemed to know the right thing to say, though he laughed at that when she mentioned it and said he wasn't sure his wife would agree. His presence created a buffer between her and Luke. Without his friend here, Angelica was sure that Luke would have avoided her entirely, but Landon made sure that they all sat down at mealtimes together. Landon shared stories of Luke and his life before and after the war, but he never mentioned their time *in* the war. It saddened her to hear about the carefree boy that Luke had once been and how fractured the war had made him.

Landon also talked about his wife and how Luke had saved her and the twins that had just been born. It was obvious that he wanted to see his family again and start raising his children.

"Angelica?" Carol Anne tugged on her sleeve, bringing her thoughts back around. "Is Luke mad at us? When I told him about Landon's promise about the horse, he got this sad look on his face. I asked if he would help me name the horse and he said that he didn't think he'd be around when I got one. I thought he was going back to Uncle Landon's with us."

Angelica closed her eyes. This was one of the moments that she had been dreading. The children had created a strong bond with Luke. They were going to be hurt and confused when he did leave for good.

Clearing her throat, she placed a hand on the little girl's shoulder. "Luke is going to go back to…Uncle Landon's ranch with us. He has to check on Landon's wife and new babies. I'm not sure how long he is going to stay, but one day he is going to ride out and I don't know if we'll see him again for a long, long time. It has nothing to do with us or how much he cares for you and your brothers."

"Then why can't he stay? With us?" The tears in Carol Anne's voice were unmistakable.

It was hard to keep her tone light when she too wanted to sit down and cry, but somehow, she managed it. "There are things in Luke's past that he can't face, honey. He's afraid if he slows down and stays in one place for too long, that those things will catch up, and that scares him."

Angelica could literally see the gears churning inside Carol Anne's head as she absorbed this information.

Finally, the little girl said, "I was scared once too. Do you think if I told him that I love him that that would help?"

Tears filled Angelica's eyes, and she nodded. "I think that would help a lot."

Smiling brightly again, Carol Anne jumped off the porch and headed on her mission to find Luke.

When Carol Anne found Luke, he was outside, next to the barn with Ranger. The horse had been mainly used for plowing in the spring and fall or hitched to the wagon for the occasional trips to town. The horses' hooves had overgrown, and they needed to be cut back if the horse was going to make the trip back to Landon's with them.

Bending over and facing the backend of the ancient plow horse, Luke had the animal's rear left hoof wedged between his knees as he ran a file over the sharp edges that he had just cut. Sweat poured down his face and beaded off his nose. The sound of humming made him glance up. Carol Anne, looking like a china doll in her pretty blue dress, stood in front of him with a solemn look on her face. Finishing the hoof, Luke placed it back down on the ground and stood up straight. There was a low throbbing pain in his lower back that reminded him that he wasn't as young as he used to be.

He expected Carol Anne to start chattering like she normally did, but she just stared at him with a slight tilt to her head and a quizzical expression.

Grabbing the ends of his shirt, Luke wiped his face and asked, "Something on your mind?"

"Angelica said that you were scared and that you can't slow down and that's why you don't want to stay with us to name my horse. I wanted to tell you that I've been scared too. My mother would tell me that she loved me, and it always helped me not to be scared anymore. So, I just wanted to tell you that I love you so it would help you not to be so scared anymore too." Carol Anne took a deep breath and then continued, "I know that you like us and Angelica, and I want you to stay and be my daddy cause my real daddy is up in heaven with my real mommy. William says that they can still see me, but I just can't see them. But I want a real mommy and daddy, who will tuck me in at night and read me stories like you and Angelica do."

Her words came out in a rush, and it took Luke a few moments to decipher what she had just said. He guessed that they made sense in a four-year-old sort of way. Her words had the same effect as a prize fighter delivering an uppercut to the jaw; they blindsided him and knocked his breath away. Rubbing his hand over his eyes, he wondered how to answer.

He had never been good at goodbyes, so he generally didn't say them. Simply riding out was easier, and Luke guessed that in the back of his mind that without the words, it never made it final. It left the door open in case he ever saw the person again. No doubt his family was used to him just up and leaving, but he hadn't thought about Carol Anne or the boys.

Taking a few steps forward, Luke crouched down so that he was eye level with the small child. Carol Anne's blue eyes were clear and bright, not shadowed by any of the terror that she had been through for the last few days. Yet there was a deep intelligence to her gaze that seemed to see deep into his mind, as if she was taking his measure. It was a bit unsettling.

Taking a steading breath, Luke lowered his eyes and studied the ground. The sun was warm on his back, and he could hear Landon and his ranch hands talking in the barn as they worked, their voices a low murmur. Water dripped from the barn roof, sounding loud in the relative quietness. Chickens squawked and clucked as they scratched in the dirt, unaware of the conversation between the man and girl. Luke envied them for a split second.

After a moment, he met her eyes again. "I can't stay, Carol Anne. I have too many things from my past that make that impossible."

Her face clouded and her eyes filled with tears. "But I don't want you to go. You belong here with us. William once told me that the past is gone, and we should forget about it and move on and we did. You can do that too, can't you?"

God, his heart was breaking. A tear slipped down her cheek, and he wiped it away with his thumb. He couldn't bear that she was crying because of him, but his life was what it was, and there was no turning back. No doubt she'd thank him some day if they ever met again.

His voice came out as rusty as an old bucket and just as hollow. "I don't want you to cry for me, sweetheart. I'll be just fine, and someday soon I'm sure that someone will come along and take a shine to Angelica and want to be a daddy to you. I'm also sure that by then you won't even remember me."

Even as he said the words, he knew them for the lie they were, and from the look on Carol Anne's face, she did too. Now she was mad. She said, "Why do grownups think kids are stupid?"

"I don't think you're stupid—"

She didn't give him the chance to finish. "Yes, you do! You don't want to stay because you're afraid of memories, but I've heard you talk. Not all your memories are bad. And just because you won't be there doesn't mean that my heart won't still love you. My mommy and daddy died in a fire, and I still love them and they're in heaven. Distance doesn't mean anything, that's what William says. He said that no matter how far apart we are, he'll still love me and Matthew."

The voices in the barn had stopped as Carol Anne's voice had risen. Luke didn't know what to say to her, but Carol Anne wasn't having the same problem. It seemed she had more to say to him and she was determined to say it.

"I know that you love us and Angelica, and you want to stay. You're just being a fraidy cat! You can't stop me from loving you, no matter how hard you try, and you'll still love us no matter where you are!"

Having said her fill, she turned and fled into William's arms. The boy had arrived earlier, standing at the corner of the barn, letting his sister have her say. Wrapping his arms around her, he scooped her up and with a final glance at Luke, he turned and carried the sobbing girl back toward the house.

Luke sat back on his heels and let her words wash over him as he tried to convince himself that she was simply too young to understand what she was asking of him.

Landon had come around the corner too and was now leaning up against the side of the barn, arms folded across his chest. "Damnation!" he said. "That little lady has a way with words. She's got my vote if she ever wants to run for mayor, or even territorial governor for that matter!" He leveled a look at Luke. "She'd make a good hanging judge too, don't you think?"

With that, he walked around the corner and Luke was left alone once again.

CHAPTER TWENTY-SIX

Lord almighty. Old Kate was struck speechless when she saw the young woman, carrying a large cat, who preceded Landon through the door. The purple and red bruises that marred the woman's features couldn't hide the fact that this was one beautiful woman, and that made Old Kate nervous. Living as a slave until Landon's daddy came and bought her freedom, Old Kate had seen plenty of beautiful ladies. Oh, they spoke pretty and acted shy and sweet, but she had seen the cruelty and meanness behind their façade. They thought nothing of having another human being whipped for some imagined slight. She had seen young slave girls slapped across the face because the mistresses' hair hadn't been styled the way they wanted, even though it was done perfectly. Yes sir, Old Kate knew that beauty was only skin deep.

The question was, was this one beautiful only on the outside? Only time would tell.

The two boys had arrived earlier and now sat at the table, eating the beef stew that she had served them. The poor things were trying their best not to shovel the food into their mouths. Old Kate watched as the woman's eyes took in her sons and showed relief. Then those eyes turned to Old Kate.

With a shy smile, the woman held out her left hand; the other was encased in a sling. "I'm Angelica Barnes. I hope that we're not troubling you in any way."

Old Kate took the woman's hand in hers and realized how cold it was. That Angelica didn't pull her hand out of the black woman's grasp spoke volumes about her.

"Goodness gracious but you're as cold as ice," Old Kate exclaimed, pulling the newcomer towards the large stove. "You sit down, and I'll get you a hot bowl of beef stew."

Turning, the housekeeper saw a small blonde girl step from behind Angelica, staring at the boys' stew with longing.

"You sit yourself down, young missy, and Old Kate will fix you up too. Lord have mercy! Travelling in this here weather could catch a body pneumonia!"

Bustling around the large kitchen, Old Kate set about getting bowls and ladling up stew. She cut up large hunks of bread and set them on a plate in the middle of the table, then retrieved the butter dish from the lean-to that was attached to the kitchen. Nothing pleased her more than having people around to fuss over and feed.

"You don't need to wait on us," Angelica protested, rising from her chair. "Here, let me help you."

Old Kate turned to face her. Putting her hands on her hips, she drew herself up to her full diminutive height. "I've been running this kitchen myself for years. You are a guest in this here house, and no one's gonna say that Old Kate made a guest work for their supper. No ma'am, I've got a reputation to think about." With that, she turned and started fussing over the children again.

Angelica sat back down. After a few minutes, she accepted a bowl of hot steaming stew with a murmured thanks and settled back to eat. Old Kate set a bowl of meat scraps down for the feline as well. It ate hungrily.

Old Kate looked pleased with everyone's appetite.

Landon had silently watched the exchange from the doorway. Old Kate had known him since the day he was born. He looked tired, and she guessed that he wanted to get upstairs and check on Mary and the babies, yet he paused.

Catching her eye, he smiled at her, shook his head at some private thought, and continued on his way into the interior of the house. Turning back to her new charges, Old Kate hid her smile and continued to fuss.

●●●

As Luke made his way out to the barn a week after returning to Landon's, the sun crested the horizon, but its rays were too young to create any warmth in the early morning. There was a light dusting of snow on the ground, and Luke's breath hung in the air as he stopped and took in the landscape. Winter was coming hard and fast in the Dakotas. Travel was becoming too uncertain and dangerous. He had planned on staying at Landon's till spring, but with Angelica here, it was increasingly difficult to see her every day and keep his distance. She was everywhere he looked.

Mary and the babies were thriving. He had removed her stitches, and there was no sign of the infection that he had worried about. With the winter basically knocking on their door, and the herds in the lower pastures closer to the house, there wasn't much to do unless there was more than a foot of snow on the ground, then Landon and the ranch hands would load up the sleigh and bring fresh hay out to them. They broke holes in the ice of the watering hole so the animals could drink. Winter was usually a time to repair equipment and keep close to the home front. Blizzards came without warning out here, and no one wanted to be caught unaware.

Entering the barn and pulling the door shut behind him, Luke allowed his eyes to adjust to the dim light. It was warm in the barn. A few of the horses neighed in greeting. Taking a quick look around, confirming that he was alone, he removed his hat.

He'd done his best to avoid Angelica and the kids the past week. It was too hard to think when they were close, so he had created some distance and had come to some hard decisions.

The gelding stuck its head over the side of the stall door and nickered. Luke rubbed the horse's nose. As if sensing that his companion was troubled, the gelding pushed his head against Luke's chest several times, seeking reassurance, causing him to smile. The two of them had spent a lot of years roaming the wild, untamed west alone; sometimes Luke swore that the horse could read his mind.

"We'll be leaving in the morning," he said out loud, just to give the words weight. "Time for us to move on."

The gelding tossed his head hard against him. It seemed that the animal didn't like the thought of moving on, and Luke couldn't blame him. It was warm here in the shelter of the barn, after all. Only a damn fool would leave such a snug place at this time of year. Purrsistence watched down at him from the rafters.

Running his hand through his hair, Luke let out a shaky breath. There hadn't been much to do on the ranch for the past week but face some hard truths. He knew that he was running away because somewhere along the way he had fallen in love with Angelica and the kids. He also knew that he didn't deserve them. It wasn't just the fear of losing them; it was the fear of losing himself, for just even an instant. The minute that he forgot the monster that lay inside him, he knew that it would rear its ugly head and remind him. Deep down, in the depths of his soul, that's what scared the hell out of him. One had to care about someone to fear losing them, and he knew that he didn't have the courage to lose any of them.

The war had tainted his soul. It had shown him a side of himself that he hadn't known existed, and he was ashamed of it. Ashamed of himself.

Quick footsteps could be heard heading for the barn. Turning as the barn door opened, Luke was both relieved and resigned when he saw Old Kate. It was no surprise that she had tracked him down. She'd held her tongue all week, but Luke could see it in her eyes that she was priming up to give him a long lecture. It seemed that she had decided it was time.

Wrapped in her shawl, her back was so ramrod straight that he thought it might break, but it was her eyes that snapped at him as she neared. "You fixing on leaving again?"

Luke almost laughed out loud. Old Kate never wasted any words. When she had something to say, you could bet your last dollar that she was going to say it and you were going to listen.

"Don't you be thinking that this here is a joke!" she told him, wiggling her finger under his nose. "I've watched you and I know you have feelings for Miss Angelica and those young'uns, so don't you even dare lie to me."

She pushed her shoulders back. Luke thought for a moment she looked like a rooster, priming for a fight. Lowering his eyes, lest he broke into a grin, he waited for the rest of the tirade. It was always best to let Old Kate have her say first. He wasn't disappointed.

"It's time to stop running, and it's time to settle down. Miss Angelica is a fine woman, and she'll make you a fine wife. And those young'uns think the sun and moon rise and set for you."

The gelding nudged him with his nose as if in agreement.

Old Kate continued. "I've known you your whole life, Luke, and you've been like a son to me. You've been running since the war, and it's done nothing but brought you loneliness. Now Mr. Landon, he's got it right. Found a wonderful woman and is building himself a family. He ain't letting the war ruin his happiness, not like you've been doing." She wagged her finger at him again. "The Lord brought you straight to Miss Angelica and those young'uns, and you are just gonna throw them away? Women like Miss Angelica don't come along very often. I'm sure Angelica would tell you..."

"Thank you, Kate, but it's all right, I can speak for myself."

Old Kate wheeled around. Neither one of them had heard Angelica enter the barn. She stood just inside the door, her shawl wrapped tightly around her. Her cheeks were pink, and Luke wasn't sure if it was from the cold or embarrassment.

The older woman got over her surprise quickly and smiled. Throwing Luke a quick look, Old Kate crossed to Angelica, gave her a hug, and left the barn without saying another word.

•••

Angelica stood looking at Luke for a few minutes. He'd lost weight in the past week, and there was a desperate look hidden deep in his eyes, if one looked closely or knew him well. Clean shaven when they had arrived, he now sported a beard that did nothing to detract from his good looks.

She'd been avoiding him all week, but she knew where he was most of the time. It was like they were connected with an invisible cord. Landon, Old Kate, and Mary also made sure that they tried to throw the two of them together whenever they could. The three of them seemed to think that Luke would suddenly realize that he loved her and would want to stay. It was obviously wishful thinking on their part. The war had scarred this man worse than any of them knew.

"You know that she means well, right?" She moved one step closer and stopped when he flinched.

"I know that they all mean well, it's just..." His voice trailed off.

She finished the sentence for him. "It's just that you are afraid to settle down. Not just with us, but with anyone, because it means that you might have to care for someone. And caring means that you'd have to confront your fears." Another step forward. "What?" she asked at the look he gave her. "Did you think that we didn't know? It's obvious that you care for us but that you don't want to. Landon told me a little bit about what happened to the both of you in the war, but I'm sure that he left out a lot of things."

She had stepped forward another step as she had talked, making sure to keep her voice low and calm. There was a wariness in Luke's stance when she had mentioned the war, but he stood his ground. He reminded her of a deer—watchful and wary, ready to bound away at any moment if someone got too close. Her heart ached for him.

"Of course, I care for you and the children," he said, his voice raspy. "I'd give anything to be able to stay. But I can't."

She had crossed halfway to him. "Then tell me why you can't. Make me understand what it is that scares you so much."

It was a risk to ask him outright. There was a real possibility that he would bolt like the deer, heading for the proverbial hills, literally. Yet, there didn't seem to be much to lose since there had been signs that he was planning on leaving soon anyway, and she needed to know why. Regret was not something that she wanted to live with, and she figured that if she was at least able to understand what drove him, it would help lessen the pain when she thought back on what could have been. He also needed to hear what she had to say. She wasn't under the illusion that she could change his mind like the others, but if there was a tiny glimmer of hope, then she wanted to make sure he understood her feelings for him.

Luke had held her gaze for a few seconds before looking back at the gelding, who was nudging him forward. Angelica took the opportunity to take two full steps forward. The look that he gave her when he turned back told her that she wasn't fooling him.

It was several beats of silence as they just held each other's gaze. Just when Angelica was afraid that he wasn't going to answer her questions, Luke glanced away from her and cleared his throat. "Everyone thinks that I should just get over what happened, but it's just not that simple." Dragging his hand through his hair, he focused on a spot behind her head. "I have to live with myself with what I did there, and I'm not sure that I can. The war changed me, and I became someone that I didn't recognize. Someone that was capable of forgetting everything that they believed in." His voice became low and halting. "I took an oath to do no harm and to save lives, no matter what my feelings may be, and in a second, I threw that oath away."

"So, you should have stood aside and let all those boys be butchered? Yes, Landon told me about the hospital being overrun," she said at his sharp look.

Anguish was evident in the set of his shoulders and the lines on his face. She reached out her hand to him as she took another step closer. "No one could have stood by and watched that, Luke. I know that I couldn't have. You need to forgive yourself and find peace."

Luke shook his head. "I don't think I'll ever find peace," he told her bluntly. "And I'm not the man you think I am. I wouldn't be able to live with myself if I hurt you or the children." He swallowed hard. "I just can't take that chance."

Tears filled Angelica's eyes. Did he really think that he was capable of harming them? He had traveled miles through a blizzard to get to them when he had sensed that they were in danger. She felt safe with him, and she knew with her whole being that he could never hurt them. But it seemed that he didn't know that, and she doubted that her words would convince him but she had to try.

Her heart was beating as fast as a hummingbird's wings as she took a deep breath and crossed the last remaining feet that separated them to touch his arm. He flinched but didn't pull away. "I know who you are, Luke, not just on the surface but deep down. You've saved my life twice now, and that's not the actions of a man that wants to hurt others. It's the actions of a man who did what he was born to do and who is protecting and healing the sick and wounded. You feel that you have to pay some sort of penance for what you did, and in a way, I can understand that, but how long must you pay for being human?"

Leaning forward on tiptoes, she kissed his cheek. He didn't move as she leaned back and smiled sadly. "Whether you believe it or not Luke, we all love you. I love you. You are the one keeping yourself a prisoner. I hope you find the peace that you are looking for, because you deserve to be happy. I'm not going to ask you to stay; you have to want to on your own, but I need you to know that you will always have a special place in my heart. I'll wait a year for you to sort things out, but I won't put my life on hold any longer than that." Letting go of his arm, she half turned to walk away but stopped. "I don't know if you planned on saying goodbye to the children, but I do know that they will be heartbroken if you don't."

With that, she walked out the door, not once glancing back to see how her words had affected him.

•••

Old Kate and Mary were in the kitchen when Angelica entered, her breath coming in sobs. Old Kate turned from stirring something on the stove and Mary looked up from the rocker where she had been knitting. The two women exchanged looks as Mary rose from the chair. Opening her arms, the older woman embraced Angelica. The contact made Angelica lose any composure that she might have had. No one had hugged or comforted her since before her mother had died, and it felt good to have someone to hold her.

Mary led Angelica to the rocking chair that she had just vacated. Lowering Angelica onto the seat, Mary squeezed Angelica's hand before sitting at the kitchen table to resume her knitting. Old Kate offered a handkerchief, and the two of them kept a silent vigil as she cried. Angelica was grateful that they didn't offer her platitudes and meaningless reasons for Luke leaving.

They must have known, in that way that only women understood, that nothing they said would have made any difference, but their presence did.

Soon the sobs died down to hiccups. By suppertime, Angelica had regained most of her composure. She prayed that the children wouldn't be able to tell that she had spent the earlier part of the morning grieving over a lost dream.

When she woke up the next morning, Luke was gone.

CHAPTER TWENTY-SEVEN

The last of the spring snow fought both the rising temperatures and sun's rays as it clung to the shady places around the barn. Birds that had flown south for the winter began to appear at the ponds more frequently. They darted here and there, gathering old brown prairie grass to build nests. Crocuses and other flowers began to break through the warming earth and stretch their tiny blooms. Spring had taken its sweet time getting to the Dakota Territory, but now that it had arrived, it was glorious.

Angelica took a deep breath and reveled in the fragrant smell of the fresh plowed earth. Old Kate, Mary, and she had been up since just before dawn, weeding, turning, and preparing the soil in the garden. It was back-breaking work, but it was the women's to do. Landon had run a plow through it several days before, but there were tufts of grass and clumps of soil that needed to be raked out and composted material folded in. It was only April, but there wasn't a moment to waste. Old Kate had mapped out the garden, and as soon as the soil was ready, they would plant cabbage, snap beans, carrots, beets, onions, lettuce, potatoes, and peas. Turnips, spinach, and radishes would round out the first planting. At the end of the month, cucumbers, sweet corn, and squash would be added. Later, after May, it would be warm enough to finish off the planting of peppers, tomatoes, watermelon, and winter squash. Carol Anne was playing with the twins off to the side of the garden. Their laughter filtered through the spring air.

Old Kate was a seasoned gardener and knew the exact time to plant and harvest. With the first planting being picked in late June and early July, she would have time to plant a second crop and harvest in October. This garden was the one for the main house. Angelica could see wives of ranch hands and other workers hard at work in their own gardens.

It was amazing how self-sufficient Landon's ranch was. Everything that could be raised or made on the ranch was. The gardens needed to yield enough to feed them through the summer and then produced enough to be canned or dried to last the household through the brutal winters when travel was impossible. The thought of travel brought a fleeting image of Luke. Angelica wondered about him every day. He had been gone for over five months, and there had been no word from him. She hadn't realized how much she would miss him.

Meda appeared around the corner of the ranch house, leading an appaloosa horse, and stopped at the edge of the tilled soil. The horse was dragging a fully loaded travois. Angelica could see Meda's tepee's tent poles hanging off the back. Angelica recognized the look on her friend's face, and her stomach dropped. It was the look that Meda always got when she was ready to head out and back to her tribe.

She hadn't seen much of Meda during the past months, as the Indian woman didn't like to intrude into the "white man's domain," as she liked to call it. Meda had erected her tepee a short distance from the ranch house and had hunted for her own food. If Landon or Angelica brought her any provisions, she was careful to replace them with something comparable the next day.

"You're leaving so soon?" Angelica asked as her friend got closer.

Meda smiled. Her long black hair was tied back into a braid that hung down her back. She was dressed in a buckskin dress with deerskin leggings and boots that laced halfway up her calf. An old, faded blue army jacket, a relic from a long-ago skirmish, completed her outfit.

"I've received a message that Sitting Bull will be at the Greasy Grass in the month when the berries are good. I am expected to be there."

Angelica pondered for a moment. "I know that the 'berries are good month' is June, so I'm guessing that you have to be there by then, but where is the Greasy Grass?"

Meda took a moment to think. "It is a meeting spot on the other side of the Wolf Mountain and on the Little Big Horn River. We will be following the buffalo as they journey northwest in their migration. The Sioux nation will gather and honor our tradition."

A light breeze teased at Angelica's hair and pulled it from the bun that she had put it in that morning. The sun was warm on her face, and she put her hand up to shield her eyes from its bright rays. "But it's only April," she protested. "It won't take you two months to get there will it? Stay awhile longer, please."

Angelica knew that she was being selfish, and that Meda had most likely stayed longer than she had intended to. It was just that with her friend leaving, Angelica would feel alone, among strangers. Oh, she adored Mary, Landon, Old Kate, and the babies but they were Luke's family, and she felt like an uninvited house guest. They never treated her that way, and they had insisted that she was now part of their family. It would have been different if she was married to Luke, but that was not the case.

Meda smiled again, a knowing look in her eyes. "I will be going to the Rosebud reservation to meet up with Sitting Bull first. He will perform in the Sun Dance ceremony and look for a vision, and then we will head to the old Sioux camp on the river. It is a beautiful place that has hills and valleys where the spirit can soar and grow. I have many happy memories of childhood there, and it will be good to see my cousin and family again. Someday I will take you there, my white sister." Taking a few steps forward, she took Angelica's hands into her own. "I will be back during the moon of the ripening in time for the harvest, but for now it is time for me to go back to where I belong."

Angelica was surprised when Meda pulled her into a tight embrace. The Indian woman was not one for such a display of affection; they usually just shared a quick hug of greeting or farewell. This hug was different; it carried more weight somehow, as if Meda was trying to convey some message. Meda pulled back from the hug but kept a grip on Angelica's shoulders.

"I feel that you need to go home also, my friend. Your future is not here, and I think you know that deep down. I have given a sacrifice to the Wakan Takan to help guide you in your journey and to keep you safe."

There was a lump in Angelica's throat, and for a moment she couldn't speak. It wasn't a surprise that Meda was leaving, as she had been expecting it for a while, but for some reason this goodbye was different. There seemed to be an undercurrent, something that she couldn't quite put her finger on, yet the air fairly crackled with it. Whatever it was, it left her with a feeling of foreboding.

Mary, Old Kate, and Carol Anne, carrying the twins, came over to say goodbye, effectively stopping her from asking Meda to stay again, begging her if she had too. Too soon, Meda turned and mounted her horse and rode away. Angelica stood in the middle of the garden and watched until Meda was out of sight.

•••

It was a week later when Angelica asked the children to take a stroll with her. There was a rise on the south side of the property that leveled out into a meadow, and this was the direction that they walked. The ranch was laid out below them, with nothing but prairie beyond for as far as the eye could see. All winter, there had been nothing but barren miles of snow-covered land, but since the snow had melted, hints of color, flowers beginning to bloom, brought a subtle drama to the landscape. It was one of Angelica's favorite spots. Knowing that they could talk freely here, Angelica turned to her children.

"I'd like to go back to our ranch next week," she told them without preamble, waiting for their reaction.

They had thrived at Landon's, not just with all the responsibilities and chores that they had been given but also with all the attention that they had received. Having come from the city, they were used to a large number of people being around, whereas she was used to being alone. Angelica had rehearsed this moment in her mind because she wasn't really sure if they would want to go back with her. Legally, she was their guardian, and she could make them, but William was four years away from being eighteen. Once he turned, he could petition the courts to take the younger children away from her. As it was, he was the same height as she was, and being a boy, most likely stronger. There was no way that she could physically force them to go back, and that wasn't the way that she wanted them to return. She wanted them to love the ranch as much as she did. She wanted, and needed, them to go back freely.

Three sets of eyes stared at her in silence. Their expression gave nothing away, causing fear to slowly steal up her spine. It was what she was most afraid of; they didn't want to return with her. Closing her eyes, Angelica took a deep breath to calm the butterflies churning in her stomach, then looked back at them.

Carol Anne turned to look at William, as if he was the one that would make the decision for her. Matthew was solemn, but it was William that held her attention. His stare was intense, as if he was trying to read her mind or have her read his. His gaze unnerved her. It was obvious that the two younger siblings would follow their brother's lead.

The silence was deafening, and she started to prattle, her well-rehearsed speech forgotten. "We are only guests here on Landon's ranch, and I feel it is time to return home and get our garden plowed and planted. The fruit trees need to be pruned, and I have lots of things to catch up on if I'm going to continue to sell to the hotel." She swallowed. "Luke is gone, and I doubt that he'll be back, so it will just be the four of us. We are a family now, and we can't put off going back for much longer. I need to know what you want to do," she ended weakly.

William shot his siblings a quick glance, and at their nod, he turned back to Angelica. "We thought that you were going to leave us with Landon and Mary and go without us," he told her. A slight grin tugged at his lips. "I've been learning a lot here, and I can take on a lot of the responsibilities. We don't need anyone else. I can take care of all of us."

Relief surged through her veins, making her dizzy. "You mean that you want to return with me?" she asked incredulously. Now that Luke was gone, she hoped that William didn't think that he was now the man of the house, in charge, so to speak. She would need to explain things to him in regard to that issue. The question was whether this was the right time or not.

"We can't wait to get back to the ranch with you," he replied, Carol Anne and Matthew nodding in agreement. "We were beginning to think that you were too afraid to go back there."

It was more than she had hoped for. Flinging out her arms, she moved forward and hugged them all at once. Laughter bubbled up from somewhere deep inside her and escaped her lips. The sound came as a surprise. After everything that had happened, she had thought that she would never laugh again.

"There are so many more people and things to do here that I was scared that you wouldn't want to go back," she confessed as she stepped back.

"We're a family," Carol Anne said, "and families stick together."

Angelica leaned down and kissed the top of the little girl's head. "Yes, they do, sweetheart. Yes, they do."

Straightening, she looked at Carol Anne and Matthew. "Why don't the two of you go and give Old Kate and Mary a hand with some of the chores. I need to talk to William for a moment, and then we'll be right there to help."

To her surprise, they didn't question the request and ran back toward the ranch house, leaving her alone with William. When the two of them were out of earshot, she turned to speak but didn't know where to start.

"William, I…" she began, but he cut her off.

"I know that you are probably scared to go back, and I won't tell Matthew or Carol Anne, but I think it's for the best, and I can protect you this time. It'll be so much better, you'll see. I've been talking to some of the ranch hands, and they've given me some ideas on how to make the ranch more profitable." There was such hope and excitement in his voice. "Right now, you think of me as just a kid, but let me prove to you that I can run a ranch and make enough money to send Matthew and Carol Anne off to college. I plan on saving a hundred dollars by the time that I turn eighteen, and if I can do that, well, I hope you would consider me as a man of means then, someone that you would consider marrying."

Taking a steadying breath, she faced him. Nothing but the plain truth would work in this situation, she told herself silently. "I think saving a hundred dollars is a fine idea, and when you turn eighteen, you should decide if you want to take that money and go see the world or go to college yourself." She paused. "I'm flattered by your offer, but the answer is no. I won't consider marrying you, not now or then. Someday you'll understand."

"You think I'm just some stupid kid, don't you? That I'm too young to know what I feel?" His tone was flat and churlish. It was hard not to agree with his words, but she knew that his pride was on the line, and somehow, she needed to keep it intact.

"No," she told him gently. "I'm sure that you think that you care for me, but I am also older than you, and I know that this will pass. You're too old for me to think of you as a son, and I think of you as a younger brother."

He'd turned away from her, so she took a step forward, placing a hand on his shoulder. Reluctantly, he turned halfway to look at her.

"I understand what you're feeling," she told him. "Yes, I do," she continued as he shook his head. "I fell in love with Luke, and I asked him to stay. To marry me."

That got his attention.

She gave a wobbly smile. "He told me no. That he wasn't the type to settle down even though he had some feelings for me." She took a step back and wrapped her arms around herself. "It hurt, but I'm glad that he was honest, because I wouldn't want to love someone that didn't love me back. I'd rather let him go than keep him somewhere he doesn't want to be." A lone tear slipped down her cheek and she brushed it away impatiently. "If Luke is meant to come back, then he will, and if not, then only time will tell what the future holds for me. I have to believe that God has a plan for us. You were meant to do great things, William. All of you kids are, not to spend your lives on a ranch out in the middle of nowhere. But until that time comes, I'd like to go back and continue to be a family."

Half turning, she gazed out at the horizon. "I'm asking you to return to the ranch with me and help me to raise your brother and sister. All of you have become very precious to me, and I don't know if I can go back alone now that I know what I would be missing. If you don't think that you can do that, I'll ask Landon if you can stay here as a ranch hand, but Matthew and Carol Anne would come with me. I need you to understand that if you do come back with us, then I would consider you my younger brother. I would have control over you until you turn eighteen, and I would still be the legal guardian for Matthew and Carol Anne."

There was silence behind her as William digested her words. Everything relied on his answer. If he said no and wanted to stay at Landon's, then she had four years before he could come and try to take Matthew and Carol Anne away from her. How would she be able to stand the pain of watching them all leave her? It seemed that she was the only one that never left, never opened her wings and set out for those distant mountains that she had always dreamed about.

William moved to stand at her right elbow. "I'll go back with you, and I won't try to change your mind. But once I'm eighteen, if I still feel the same way about you then, I am gonna ask you again."

Angelica smiled at that. "Fair enough," she told him.

•••

The sight of her ranch house brought such a feeling of relief that Angelica thought that she might actually pass out from it. Over the last few days, she had worried that something bad had happened to the house, but there it was, still standing in the twilight, like an old friend to welcome her home. A light shone in a window, and a few wisps of smoke curled out of the chimney. It would be like Landon to send someone ahead and have the place warmed for them, since the spring nights still got chilly. It gave her a moment of peace knowing that there were people looking out for her. Then her brow furrowed as she looked at the house. Landon hadn't mentioned sending someone ahead, but he wouldn't have if it was supposed to be a surprise, she argued with herself. Then another thought jumped forward, causing her to catch her breath: could claim jumpers have moved in?

The two ranch hands that Landon had insisted on accompanying them must have been thinking the same thing, for they drew their rifles from their scabbards. Telling Angelica to stop the wagon and wait for them, they rode up to the house. Angelica watched as they dismounted and knocked on the door. When no one answered, they went inside. The silence was pressing against her chest as she waited for gunfire, shouting, something. Carol Anne and Matthew had fallen asleep in the bed of the wagon, along with Purrsistence, and William was riding the horse that had been Jean Claude's'. He reigned in next to the wagon and shared a worried glance her way.

The men left the house and disappeared into the barn. It felt like ages, but in truth it was only about five minutes when the men reappeared. The taller ranch hand waved her forward. Picking up the reins, Angelica urged the horses forward. Pulling up to the barn, she stopped and set the brake. Quickly she jumped down from the wagon before any of the men came to help her. The muscles of her legs and back gave little stabs of protest from sitting too long. In the waning light, she watched as the two men approached.

"Lamps lit and stoves going. Don't see no one," the tall ranch hand informed her.

Angelica was too tired to remember his name. Landon had introduced them both, but they had mainly kept to themselves, riding ahead and behind the wagon the entire trip. They had left well before dawn that morning and they had only stopped to have lunch. The men had politely refused the offer of sharing the meal and had sat off a short distance away, talking quietly to one another. Like most cowboys, they liked to keep to themselves and use the least amount of words to get their point across. Sometimes she felt as if she was playing charades trying to get answers from any of them.

The shorter ranch hand opened the barn doors wide. Finding a lantern on the post inside, he grabbed a match and lit it before setting it back on its nail. It took their eyes a moment to adjust to its light. William woke his brother and sister and began the task of putting the caged chickens into their coop. Purrsistence jumped down and began to explore the barn. Angelica unhooked the cow from the back of the wagon and led her to her stall. Bessie, her old cow, had been too old to make the journey, so Landon had given her a new cow that would calve in a couple of weeks. Although Angelica had protested that he should take money for the cow, the older rancher had admitted a fondness for the cheese that Angelica had brought with her and had struck a bargain. The cow was hers, and all that he asked was that she make him some cheese to bring home after he came for a visit, and he would make sure that she had wood for the winter. They had shaken on it.

It took Angelica a minute to realize that the stall had been cleaned and the dividers that had been rotted and half chewed over the years had been replaced. On further inspection, she noticed other improvements that had been made. Her heart sank. Someone had obviously been living here while they had been gone. Had they thought the place abandoned and moved right in? Again her mind thought of claim jumpers. There had been some talk in town of families being murdered by squatters when they had tried to take their property back. Nevertheless, the livestock needed to be fed and put away for the night. They would have to deal with whoever showed up later.

Entering the house, Angelica was grateful that someone had cleaned up the mess that Jean Claude had made and that her things were still basically where she had left them. Yet there were subtle changes here and there. At first her eyes skimmed over the room, unable to make out the differences before small things began to come into focus. Besides her rocking chair in front of the fire, there was another chair, one more masculine. Lamps had been moved closer to the chairs, as if the occupants sat there late into the night reading, or in the case of the rocker, knitting or rocking a baby to sleep. There were even logs in the fireplace ready to light. It was a cozy scene, yet it made Angelica's heart sink. It appeared that a couple had moved in and had set up the house to meet their needs. What if there were children involved? How could she throw out a family? Had they pinned all their hopes and dreams on this ranch, on this house that was her home?

Moving into the kitchen, she noticed that the stove had been blackened and polished, something she had been meaning to do before her life had been turned upside down. New shelves had been hung and filled with cans of food. There wasn't a pot or pan out of place. Looking at the floor, she could see that the nails that Jean Claude had used to seal the trap door had been taken out, the holes filled and sanded. It was almost as if they had never been there. The stove was warm, and she held out her hands to it as she closed her eyes and breathed in the familiar scent of her home.

Carol Anne's voice calling her name made her return to the main room. The little girl was staring at the back wall and pointing. Turning, Angelica was surprised to see a hole cut into the wall. A small hallway contained three doors. Grabbing a lamp and lighting it, Angelica entered the hallway and opened the first door on the right to reveal a small bedroom. Twin beds were set back against the wall, and a wooden bench, hand made by the look of it, sat against a side wall. Several pegs had been placed on the wall to hang clothes and such. There were no personal items in the room, and the beds were bare.

Leaving that door ajar, Angelica opened the door across the hall and gasped. A large, galvanized tub hugged the back wall. Carol Anne and the boys crowded the doorway behind her, causing Angelica to take several steps forward into the room. Behind the door was a washstand, but it wasn't like any wash stand that she had seen before. A shiny white, porcelain bowl was recessed into a polished oak wood counter on one side, and a small cast iron sink was set on the other. The cast iron sink had a hole in the middle that was attached to a pipe that disappeared down into the floorboards. The stand was attached to the wall in the back and had two carved wood legs in the front.

Running her hand over the cold porcelain, Angelica's thoughts were spinning. She had heard rumors of the White House in Washington, D.C., having a separate bathing room. The price had made it one of those items that one dreamed about but could never hope to own, which meant that this room was an expensive extravagance, and whoever had done this had spent quite a bit of money. That didn't fit with a claim jumper.

There was one more door at the end of the hall, and as Angelica moved to turn the knob, she had the feeling that she was like that character, the one in the children's book that had fallen down a rabbit hole and everything had been turned upside down.

Carol Anne and the boys stood a step behind her, and she could feel their excitement as she turned the glass knob and pushed open the door. The first thing that she noticed was her bed was set up against the back wall. She hadn't even noticed that it had been missing from the other room. The walls had been painted a pale yellow, and it played off the colors of the crazy quilt comforter that her mother had made. Two small tables flanked the bed and held kerosene lamps that were polished and filled, waiting to be lit. White curtains hung on the curtain rods. Her mother's trunk was set to her left, as was a rocking chair. Angelica recognized it as her grandmother's rocker, but that couldn't be, since it had broken, and her father had put it in the barn loft. Crossing the room, she looked more closely and saw where the rush seat had been repaired. Pegs were set behind the door, and several of her things hung from them.

It briefly crossed her mind that this was the room that she had described to Luke all those months ago. As well as the washroom. But Luke was long gone.

"Who do you think built this?" William asked her, following her thoughts. "It must have cost a lot to get this much wood."

It was then that Angelica realized that the entire addition had been made out of wood, and not sod like the original house, which made sense once she thought about it. They had been gone a little over six months, and in winter at that. The ground would have been too frozen to be able to cut sod, yet William was right. Milled lumber was not cheap or easy to get in the winter, especially out here.

"I don't know," she answered, sitting down on the edge of the bed. "But someone has certainly done a lot of work around here."

Her words came out lighthearted, but inside, she was worried. How would she reimburse someone for all the improvements that they had made? Provided that she could talk them out of any claim that they thought that they had on the property?

Closing her eyes, Angelica took a deep breath and mentally took a step back. It was a technique that her father had taught her years ago. There was no sense worrying about things that hadn't happened yet. Once she knew who she was dealing with, well, that would be the time to decide what to do. Meanwhile, they were all hungry and tired. It had been a long day. A good hot meal would do them wonders, never mind some much-needed sleep.

Opening her eyes again, she smiled and stood. "I'm ready for some food. How about we see what's in the kitchen that we can just heat up, and tomorrow we'll figure out what needs to be done."

Taking Carol Anne's hand, she led them back to the kitchen and began to get supper together, all the while wondering what the next few days would hold.

●●●

Luke noticed the tracks right away, even though the sun had set and there was just enough light to navigate by. There had been a wagon, three horses, and a cow, by his reckoning. Bringing the gelding to a stop, he sat just out of sight of the ranch house and contemplated his next move. They were back a little earlier than he had expected. He had thought of this moment a thousand times over the last six months and had practiced what he would say, but now that they were here, his mind was blank. Would Angelica like the changes that he had made, or would she be angry at what he had done?

The gelding pranced from side to side. It could smell the other horses and was impatient to get to them. Wolf paced back and forth a few yards ahead, watching with those gold eyes. Indecision ran through Luke's head.

His plan had been easy to envision, but now that Angelica was back, the doubts and reality crowded back into his head.

Leaving Landon's six months ago had been one of the hardest things that he'd ever done in his life, but it was something that he felt that he had had to do. It was torture having Angelica and the kids around and not knowing if he was going to be able to stay or if he could keep the old demons down. It was then he realized that he had to make a choice. It wouldn't be fair to Angelica to only give her half of himself. It would be a hell of a lot kinder to stay away and let her hate him now than to remain and watch her slowly realize that he had betrayed her. So, he had made the decision to leave.

At first, he had no plans. All he wanted was to put some distance and perspective between himself and Landon's. Without realizing it, he arrived at Angelica's ranch. It was as if an invisible rope had pulled him there. She was everywhere he looked. Closing his eyes, he could feel her presence, smell her scent, and sometimes he swore he could hear her laugh. Every memory about her haunted him. Looking around at the place, he noticed all the things that had needed repair or replacing, and a plan formed in his mind. Working days, and sometimes late into the night, he'd set about fixing things for her. There was one last project that he had been working on, and he had hoped to finish it tomorrow and be gone before they got back, but now it seemed as if time had run out. They had returned.

It was decision time.

● ● ●

Angelica was feeding the chickens and checking for eggs early the next morning. The chickens were happy with their new coop and nesting boxes. As soon as she had opened the door, they had piled out, squawking and flapping their wings. Soon they were scratching in the overgrown grass, content to just be chickens. The journey hadn't bothered them much.

The two ranch hands were up and turning the horses out into the pasture, with the cow following placidly, lured by the lush green grass. The children had been stirring as she had risen and got the fire going in the cook stove. It was a beautiful crisp spring morning, and Angelica closed her eyes and breathed deeply. It felt so good to be home, to be in control of herself again. While she was grateful to Landon and Mary for taking them in, she had felt lost being among so many people. Once Luke had left, well, it was like her world had dimmed. All she could think about was getting herself and the children back to her ranch so that she could be alone. Which made no sense, but that was what she had felt.

Back inside the house, she once again wondered where the person who had been here was. The boys had slept in the loft, but she and Carol Anne had slept on blankets in the sitting room. Somehow it didn't feel right to use the addition until she had found out who had built it and why.

"Good morning," she greeted William and Matthew as she entered the kitchen. They were washing up at the sink. "Where's Carol Anne?'

Grabbing a towel, William dried his face. "Still getting dressed."

Angelica figured that she had time to cook some eggs before she had to check on the girl. She pulled down her cast iron skillet, then dumped in a large spoonful of lard and set it on the stove. It was comforting making breakfast in her own kitchen after months helping Old Kate in Landon's. Old Kate hadn't wanted help in the beginning, saying that they were guests, but Angelica had been adamant that if they were going to eat there, then they would all help out with the chores.

Cracking the eggs into the skillet, Angelica silently planned out the day. She'd have William and Matthew prune the trees in the orchard. Carol Anne could sweep and tidy the house while she marked out the garden. William would have to help her plow it tomorrow. Mary, bless her, had sent them with some plants already started in eggshells that contained soil. That would save them several weeks in growing time. The sooner that they got things in the ground, the sooner they could harvest. Now that there were three more mouths to feed, Angelica worried that they would need much more than she could keep up with.

As Angelica flipped the eggs, Carol Anne appeared in the doorway, fully dressed. Her hair was mussed and her face puffy from sleep. Without preamble, she went to the kitchen sink and washed her hands and face. Angelica bit back a smile. It usually took a little while for the young girl to wake up, which was a blessing for the rest of them, as once Carol Anne was awake, she chattered nonstop for the rest of the day.

Setting the plate of eggs and biscuits that Old Kate had sent with them in front of the children, she poured herself a cup of coffee before sitting down at the table with them.

"I'll be working on the garden this morning," she informed them between bites. "I want you boys to prune and fertilize the fruit trees. There are a lot of things that should have been done over the winter, so we're behind schedule. Sometime this week, I'll need to drive into town with the cider and cheese that I made in the fall. We can do without the cider, but we'll have to ration the rest until the cow delivers and starts producing some milk and the garden is ready."

She had checked the cellar last night. Everything down there had been untouched.

Carol Anne looked up from her plate. "Won't the cow's baby need all the milk?" she asked, her brows drawn together.

Angelica smiled. "The calf will need some of the milk, but we can use some too."

Relief replaced the worried look.

They spent the rest of the meal discussing small details and plans. It had been a relaxing morning so far, a day full of promise. Maybe that should have forewarned her.

•••

Wearing an old calico dress of her mother's, Angelica proceeded to the back of the house to where the garden was. It had been dark when they had arrived, and she hadn't come out this way till now. Passing the wood pile, she noticed that it had been stacked and that there was enough wood to last for quite some time. Whoever had been here had certainly been very busy, and it looked as if they were planning on staying for a while. Mulling over the possibilities of her mysterious house guest, Angelica wasn't paying much attention to her surroundings as she turned the corner of the addition. She was almost at the garden when she noticed that it had been plowed, with plants already breaking the surface. Walking to the edge, she looked down at the neat, weeded rows. Just about every square inch of soil had been worked and planted. Her heart sank. Now what was she to do? The amount of work that had been put into the farm meant that someone intended to stay, and she was going to have a fight on her hands. So where were they?

A horse whinnied behind her as if answering her unspoken question. Startled, Angelica turned to find Luke standing next to his horse. Inexplicably, her first thought was that she was wearing the ugliest dress that she owned and that her hair must look a mess.

"I…I didn't hear you ride up," she stammered, embarrassed.

Her mind categorized every detail of his appearance. His blond hair was shaggy and needed barbering, as did the beard that covered his face. His clothes were worn yet clean, but his boots had seen better days. He looked like he had been living in exile since leaving Landon's. His appearance resembled that of a mountain man, and it should have frightened her. Except that his eyes soothed her, which was crazy, considering that he had broken her heart.

Why was he here? She had told him that she would wait a year for him. Was he here to stay? Tamping down the quick burst of hope, lest she got her heart broken all over again, she placed a pleasant smile on her face. "It's good to see you, Luke." That was an understatement. He looked damn good, even better than the last time she had seen him. "The children will be excited you're here."

There was a slight narrowing of his eyes, and a muscle twitched in his cheek, but other than that, he didn't move or show how he was feeling. Gone was the easy alliance that they had shared. His appearance and silence made him a stranger to her, and she could have wept at the loss. Everything that she could have wished for was right here, the children, her home, and Luke, yet this wasn't the Luke that she had dreamed about.

Not knowing what to do, Angelica glanced toward the house, hoping to see one of the children and knowing it was an act of cowardice. Luke saw the move, and it broke the spell that had surrounded him. He gave a gusty sigh and ran his hand through his hair in an act of frustration that angered her. What did he have to be frustrated about?

"What are you doing here?" she snapped. "And so help me, if you tell me it's just to make sure that we're okay because you feel a responsibility for us, I swear I might just take a shovel to the side of your head!"

If she hadn't been so serious, she might have laughed at the look on his face. As it was, she wanted to cry. That was exactly why he was here, she realized as her heart sank.

Running her hands down the sides of her skirt, she looked back over the garden. "Well, you can see that we are just fine. The boys should be in the orchard, and Carol Anne is in the house. I'm sure that they'll be happy to see you before you leave."

She had said the words without thinking. All she wanted to do was to go back into her house and get away from him. In fact, she took a few steps toward the house but stopped at the anger in his voice.

"What is it that you expected from me, Angelica? I've never lied about who I am or who I'm not. You want someone that doesn't exist. I'm not some knight in shining armor that will always be there to save the day. War changed me, and it scared the hell out of me." He ran his hands nervously through his hair again, making it stand up. "I didn't ask for you to fall in love with me, and I didn't make any promises."

Angelica was indignant. "I bared my soul to you, and you just left without as much as a goodbye."

Luke took a step towards her and stopped. "When I left Landon's, I thought I would never see you or this ranch again." The words were being pulled out of him, she could tell, each full of emotion, full of anguish. "But something drew me here, because this is where I could be close to you. At first, I thought that if I could just stay here a few days, then I could get you out of my mind. But you wouldn't stop haunting me. I couldn't think, couldn't breathe, wondering if you were okay or if you had found someone to share your life with." He paused and took a shaky breath. "Somehow you had worked your way under my skin, and I couldn't get you out. So I figured that if I could just make sure that everything was fixed and done for you, then I could stop worrying about you. I just didn't figure on needing to stay—or wanting to."

Her breath caught in her throat at his words and a thrill ran through her body. What was he saying? Had he had the epiphany that she had prayed for? Did that change anything?

She took a step forward, scared to hope. "Are you saying that you care for me, or that I make you ill?"

He let out a short laugh. "Both, I guess."

His words caught up with her then. Luke had done all the work on the ranch. There were no squatters or a family with children that she would have to evict. The relief was overwhelming, as was the knowledge that his actions showed just how much he cared, even if he wasn't ready to admit it.

"What does that mean?"

So much depended on his answer.

He looked her squarely in the eyes. There was a message in that gaze, but she was afraid to read it. She needed him to say it out loud, to spell it out for her, so there would be no doubt as to his meaning.

"What is it that you want from me Luke?" She whispered the words, unable to look away.

It seemed like a lifetime had passed, but in actuality he never hesitated before saying, "You. I want you. I can't promise that there won't be times that I'll have my doubts, and I don't think I'll ever get over the past, but I'm tired of running. I've tried to forget you, but I can't. Every time I try to leave, I find myself wanting to turn around and come home to you." Taking a step forward, he cupped her face and ran a thumb over her cheek. "I know that you deserve a lot better than me, but…"

Tears spilled from her eyes. She wanted to throw her arms around his neck, but there was something she needed to hear first. Even though she knew the answer, she needed him to say it out loud. "Why? Why do you want to stay?"

He knew what she was asking. She could see it in his face. Leaning down, so that he could look directly into her eyes, he smiled.

"Because I fell in love with you the minute that I saw you, and I can't imagine my life without you in it."

Letting out a sob, she stepped into his embrace.

•••

Landon looked out the study window when he heard the sound of hoofbeats. Recognizing one of his men that he had sent with Angelica and the kids, he stepped out onto the front porch to wait for his arrival.

Old Kate was in the kitchen with Mary when she heard Landon let out a yell. The two women looked at each other with concern, but before Mary could get up from her chair, Landon was standing in the doorway.

"What are you making a fuss about?" Old Kate asked, shaking a spoon at him.

Landon looked like a man that was ready to burst. "One of the boys just came from Angelica's place."

Mary's hand flew to her chest in alarm. "Angelica and the children are all right, aren't they?" she asked, eyes wide with fear.

Landon waved away her question. "They're all fine. In fact, they should all be here this coming weekend. Seems that there's gonna be a wedding."

Old Kate's face burst into a rare smile. "Luke and Miss Angelica?"

At Landon's nod, she turned back to stirring her soup. Seemed that her praying had finally paid off. Yes sir, everything was just as it should be.

THE END

9 798986 648019